TH_
MAGPIE'S
SISTER

For Nelson,
Forever a good boy.

THE MAGPIE'S SISTER

KERRI TURNER

PUBLISHING

echo
PUBLISHING

An imprint of Bonnier Books UK
4th Floor, Victoria House, Bloomsbury Square
London WC1B 4DA
www.echopublishing.com.au
www.bonnierbooks.co.uk

This book takes place in Australia, and the characters cross land that belongs to the Dharug, Gundungurra, Wiradjuri, Muthi Muthi, Wergaia and Kaurna people. We, Kerri Turner and Echo Publishing, acknowledge that Aboriginal and Torres Strait Islander peoples are the Traditional Custodians of Country on which this story unfolds, and the first storytellers of these lands as well as those throughout Australia. We recognise their continuing connection to land, waters and culture. We pay our respects to their Elders past, present and emerging.

First published 2023

Printed and bound in Australia by Griffin Press

The paper this book is printed on is certified against the Forest Stewardship Council® Standards. Griffin Press holds chain of custody certification SCS-COC-001185. FSC® promotes environmentally responsible, socially beneficial and economically viable management of the world's forests.

Edited by Elizabeth Cowell
Page design and typesetting by Shaun Jury
Cover design by Christabella Designs
Cover images: Tightrope walker, still from the film, 'Circus World', 1964/Granger; Eucalyptus leaves and gumnuts, by Tegan T/Shutterstock; Theatre red curtain and neon lamp, by iamlukyeee/Shutterstock

A catalogue entry for this book is available from the National Library of Australia

ISBN: 9781760687878 (paperback)
ISBN: 9781760687885 (ebook)

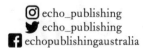
echo_publishing
echo_publishing
echopublishingaustralia

About the Author

Kerri Turner is an Australian author of historical fiction. Her books and short stories focus on female roles throughout history that have been largely overlooked or forgotten, and often include elements of the performing arts. Her first book, *The Last Days of the Romanov Dancers*, was released in 2019, followed by *The Daughter of Victory Lights* in 2020. Her short stories have appeared in several national and international publications, and she has been a speaker for such diverse events as International Women's Day and the Heroine's Festival. With a Diploma of Publishing and an Associate Degree (Dance), she splits her time between writing, and teaching ballet and tap dancing to seniors.

To be natural is such a very difficult pose to keep up.
OSCAR WILDE

Chapter One
Parramatta, New South Wales, 1911

It was the easiest thing in the world to take someone else's identity for her own. What was harder was trying to prevent all her lies from catching up with her.

Looking back, Maggie supposed it all began with the death of the elephants. The Braun Brothers' Royal Circus—which had no brothers, nor anything royal about it—was in Parramatta for its annual winter camp. The circus never performed during the cold months. No circus did. If audiences had been willing to sit on hard benches and shiver through a show, the ringmasters and managers would have said to hell with the difficulties and gone through with it. But in July and August, patrons preferred solid buildings to tents whose joins let in sharp slaps of cold air.

Maggie didn't like these winter months. The days were kept pleasantly busy with breaking in new acts, training the horses, repainting the carts, and sewing new costumes, or repairing split seams, frayed hems and lost spangles on old ones. The ringmaster and manager of the Braun Brothers' Royal Circus, Rafferty Braun—a falsified showman's name if Maggie had ever heard one—maintained a watchful eye over them all, pushing, berating and encouraging so that, come showtime next spring, they'd be able to compete with Hyland's, Wirth's, FitzGerald Brothers and all the best circuses.

If she found herself at a loose end, Maggie volunteered to walk the children the short distance to the few months' official schooling they'd have that year. She was always surprised their parents allowed her this task, and kept a mindful distance so as not to frighten the little ones. Even so, she could hear their grumbles and complaints about having to sit still in a classroom for so long. Most would never receive their Sufficiency Certificate. Unlike Maggie, most would never miss it, or question what else life might have brought them if they'd had that bit of paper. For these children were born to the circus, and it was said that once you'd experienced circus life, the sawdust from the ring got in your veins and you were never rid of it.

Maggie was distracted enough during these daylight hours; yet the winter nights eased themselves in earlier and earlier, and when all went quiet and dark, she would lie on her back and stare at the unfamiliar blank slate of a real ceiling above her, unsettled. Without the endless evening tasks of the performing season— the after-show rituals of taking off and sponging costumes, brushing down the animals and putting them away, wiping skin free of make-up and combing snarls out of slicked-back hair—the thoughts she held at bay for most of the year suddenly deafened her. She didn't want to hear them; she forced her lips to move, a repetitious reminder that she was lucky.

'Be grateful. You know how much worse matters could be.'

The less prosperous circuses disbanded for winter, and their performers could never be sure there'd be a position waiting for them come spring. But the Braun Brothers' Royal Circus had elephants, which made all the difference.

And then Ida died.

They should have seen it coming. The elephant had been lacking her usual vivacity. Her movements were heavy, not just with her own weight, but with a weariness that spoke of a spirit ready to give up. Why hadn't they taken notice of it? Perhaps it was because they were readying for their spring move back to the Haymarket in nearby Sydney. Whatever the reason, when Ida lay on her side on the hard-packed earth during a last, easy rehearsal, those who watched—idly leaning against a paddock fence that would have been useless against Ida and Hercules' bulk if they'd tried to escape—still didn't understand what they were witnessing. Her wrinkled grey skin heaved, gentle eyes streaming as they blinked once, twice, and then no more. Shock rippled through the circus folk. A silence followed, unusual for them. One onlooker climbed over the fence, then paused, uncertain. He was joined by a few others. Those who hadn't seen the elephant's final breath caught the air of something having gone wrong, and neared the enclosure, seeking to understand where the laughter and noise had gone. When they saw, they too climbed inside, gathering some near distance from Ida. Even Maggie drew close, shoulder-to-shoulder with performers and crew. No one registered her presence; all eyes were on the still elephant, and the bull who paced back and forth near her body, not letting them come closer.

It was unlike Hercules to be so aggressive. When anyone tried to step forward—even the most trusted performers, whom he usually allowed to straddle his neck as he lumbered around the ring—he raised his front feet in the air and waved his trunk in a wild motion that was unmistakably a warning. The crowd stepped back, and he resumed his stance, turning to face Ida. He stretched his trunk until the tip of it caressed her side gently, then did the same to her feet; it was as though he knew what had happened but still couldn't resist trying to wake her.

Maggie tried to blink her tears away. Hercules had always been protective of Ida. Looking at him now, she wondered if finding one special someone and then losing them might be worse than being alone. She sniffed, then pulled out a crumpled linen handkerchief and wiped her nose, breathing in the animal scent left on the fabric from her own hands, then shoved it back up the cuff of her sleeve. She wasn't the only one who felt the bull elephant's pain; all around her, tears tracked down the dusty cheeks of circus folk who'd only hours before been caught in the hustle and excitement of packing up.

Rafferty took a step toward Hercules. 'Come now,' he said. 'I know you're suffering. I know you're going to miss her. But we can't just let her lie here.' He spoke in a low, reassuring tone, not at all the commanding one he usually used as their trainer. Maggie stepped away from the crowd, circling behind to get a better view.

Hercules reared up again. This time, Rafferty didn't move back; he took a tentative step forward instead, his arms raised in an 'easy, there' motion. Hercules fell back to his feet. Maggie breathed in sharply; the others were making appreciative noises, seeming to believe Rafferty had won this battle, but she knew otherwise. She could see the elephant's eyes from where she stood. No other animal had eyes as human as an elephant's; she could read the sadness, the despair in them. She wasn't surprised when he lifted his trunk and struck out.

It wasn't much of a blow, just a gentle push to keep Rafferty away. But even a gentle push from an elephant has a deal of force behind it, and the ringmaster went sprawling. Hercules turned back to Ida.

For hours Rafferty tried to get Hercules to move. He sent most of the circus folk back to their work—there wasn't much else they could do—but Maggie was drawn to the stand-off again and again, each time experiencing a stab in the left side of her chest when she saw Hercules keeping guard over Ida's still form.

Four years ago, the Braun Brothers' Royal Circus had been the Braun Brothers' Travelling Circus. They'd travelled the south and east coasts of Australia, sometimes making just enough money to keep them going until the next town. But when the American circus that owned Hercules and Ida went bust, having—like so many international circuses before them—underestimated the difficulty and expense of bringing their endeavour to Australian shores, Rafferty had declared they were looking at a once-in-a-lifetime opportunity to expand their small menagerie of horses, a couple of donkeys and one young Jack Russell. They'd all heard tales that elephants and other exotic animals such as tigers and lions were common in overseas circuses, but that was not the case here. Elephants were rare—so rare they were the kind of attraction that would allow a circus to station itself in a single city for an entire season, attracting crowds for three evening performances a week, plus a matinee on Saturdays. The ringmaster attended the auction, having begged and borrowed from every connection he had, even his own employees. While other owners or managers were unable to resist bidding on monkeys, fresh new carts and the horses to go with them, or sturdy trapeze equipment, Rafferty Braun stood silent and still. And when everyone else had diluted their savings, he became the lucky owner of not just one, but both elephants—for the American ringmaster had refused, even in his dire circumstances, to allow the elephants to be separated. They were a couple and needed to remain that way.

So the Braun Brothers' Travelling Circus became the Braun Brothers' Royal Circus, reflecting their new grandeur, and they'd performed to near-sellout audiences ever since. The Haymarket—which had been home to all the best circuses at one point or another—became their permanent home for nine months of every year, and Rafferty was able to pay his debtors back in full in eighteen months. Every winter was spent in the hired pavilion in the Parramatta township, and every spring saw them make the half-day's journey to return to the Haymarket in Sydney, with thrilling new acts to excite the city crowds. Ida and Hercules mounted pedestals, waltzed around the circus ring, paraded with men and women in sparkling costumes riding on their backs. For four years, the elephant couple had turned the Braun Brothers' circus's fortune around.

Now Hercules guarded the body of his lost Ida, keeping all human company away. Rafferty thought perhaps it was some kind of elephant ritual and that all the bull needed was a bit of time. He instructed them to leave Hercules alone, delaying their departure for another night. But the next day Hercules still refused to let anyone come near. Blowflies were landing on Ida's face and sides, and on the untouched apples and lettuce the ringmaster had scattered nearby for Hercules.

'One more night,' Rafferty said. He sounded confident, but it was his showman's voice. Maggie had known him long enough to be able to tell the difference.

One more night made no change. A smell was beginning to come from Ida, and no one had seen Hercules eat or sleep.

Once again most of the performers and crew gathered just inside the paddock fence. 'We can't let him go on like this,' muttered Itsuo, an acrobat and foot juggler. 'He'll fret himself to death. It's cruel just to watch and let it happen.'

'Take the children to Sydney,' Rafferty answered, his voice loud enough to carry even to those few pretending to get on with their work, as though their attention weren't solely fixed on the two elephants. 'I don't want any of the young ones seeing this.'

'Seeing what?' asked the band leader's boy.

Rafferty didn't answer. 'If you have children, go now. The rest of you can stay and help me,' he said. 'Those who are leaving should begin setting up when you get there. I want everything ready by nightfall. The rest of us will join you either late tonight, or tomorrow.' He turned sharply and stalked off toward the cabin that had served as his accommodation for the last three months.

Noise lifted around them, a buzzing of curious voices asking questions no one had the answers to. Maggie, as always, stayed apart from it. She watched as mothers and fathers forced their children's feet into shoes they didn't want to wear, as the ring horses were rugged and tethered to the wagons, and the spare workhorses let free to trot alongside or behind them. She watched as Judge, the Jack Russell, leapt onto the back of one of the donkeys, his tongue lolling out the side of his mouth in the only expression of joy on all the assorted faces. She watched as even the grooms, who had learned to care for the elephants alongside their horses and donkeys, turned away from Ida and Hercules.

Slowly, the wagon wheels turned, and the circus disappeared down the road, leaving behind a few crew and even fewer performers. Itsuo remained, standing to the left of Maggie, while on her right Greta the sword dancer chewed an already ragged thumbnail.

Rafferty finally reappeared. He was holding an old Snider rifle he occasionally brought out to ward off would-be thieves. Maggie's eyes followed him as he walked toward Hercules; she heard the gasps of those who registered what he was about to do. Everything inside her felt as though it had gone impossibly still; Maggie's heart was no longer beating, her blood not tracking its way through her veins, her breath not gently whispering against her lips. Rafferty stopped in front of Hercules, who turned a wary eye on him.

Rafferty raised the gun a little; not high enough to shoot, but not pointing at the ground as it had been. He hesitated, then lowered it again.

'I can't do it while he's looking at me,' he said. In all her years by Rafferty's side, Maggie had never once heard him sound so uncertain.

'You shouldn't be doing it at all,' said Greta. Maggie had always admired her bravery—only someone who didn't fear pain could do handstands on the points of swords—but her voice trembled now in a way that her hands never did.

'What do you suggest then?' Rafferty was so quiet that had the breeze turned in another direction, they wouldn't have heard him. 'Do I leave Hercules here to starve himself while Ida rots at his feet? What kind of an end is that for him? For anyone?'

No one said anything. Maggie knew they all wanted to argue,

to say that Hercules just needed a little more time. But it was hopeless; the bull was loyal to Ida even in her death and would never leave her. They couldn't abandon him to a long-drawn-out, miserable death of his own. Nor could they leave Ida there, without dignity, spreading who-knew-what manner of diseases.

'Audiences in Sydney are expecting two elephants,' Maggie said quietly. She noticed Greta glance at her, then look away. No one ever wanted to keep their eyes on her for long. 'One elephant, we might get away with. But none ... We'll be just like every other circus then.' She was saying the words no one else was game to, the words they all knew were true. The elephants had been their drawcard. Without them, they wouldn't last more than a few weeks in Sydney. They would all lose their jobs.

'One problem at a time.' Unlike the others, Rafferty hadn't turned his gaze from Maggie. He never did. His eyes bored into hers, trying to tell her something she couldn't understand. Maggie supposed he was instructing her to shut up. 'Now, who's going to help me?'

There was silence, then Maggie said, 'I will.' She hadn't planned to, but her feet were already moving her forward. She didn't look at anyone's reactions; her eyes were on Hercules and Rafferty, who seemed to be getting bigger as she neared them.

'Are you sure?' Rafferty asked.

At this, a spark of irritation took some of Maggie's numbness. Why were people always doubting her? But she knew why. She set her jaw and nodded her assent. The ringmaster didn't ask again. Instead, he said, 'Get him to look at you, and stay looking at you.'

'Righto.' Maggie stepped closer to Hercules, so she was nearer to him even than Rafferty. She took her handkerchief out from her sleeve once again, gave it a shake or two, then fluttered it in the air as high as she could reach. When she'd caught the bull's attention, she waved her free arm toward Rafferty.

'I suggest those of you not helping us turn away or leave right now,' Rafferty said. Most scattered, some stopping halfway and turning back, as though they couldn't decide if it was more respectful to leave or stay.

After one quick glance back at them, Maggie returned her attention to Hercules. She refused to look to where Rafferty stood nearby. She imagined him pointing his gun, high and steady this time.

Hercules lifted his trunk. Was he going to push her away? Maggie almost hoped he would. She wanted him to fight back, to prove that he wouldn't just waste away here in mourning, so they wouldn't have to do this. She didn't want mercy to be so ugly.

But the elephant, with those so-human eyes looking straight into her own, simply curled the tip of his trunk around Maggie's raised wrist, running it up her forearm. The sensation was a shock; no one ever touched Maggie.

She looked in those eyes, her own swimming with tears, and mouthed, 'I'm sorry.' She was sure she saw understanding. Was it real, or only what she wanted to see? She held his gaze; held it as his trunk released her arm; held it as he took one step back from her and closer to Ida; held it until she heard the bang and squeezed her eyelids shut.

Chapter Two

Maggie stood behind the flapping curtain, obscured from the audience, the familiar raw scent of sweat and animal dung tickling her nostrils. She could also make out the waft of buttered popcorn, and when she stepped through the curtain and her slippers crushed the sawdust covering the floor of the ring—half-pulped already by the feet that had come before her—she'd be able to smell that too. But then it would all become lost in the spell of performance, when she ceased being Maggie and became the Lagoon Creature.

The band's blast—was it her imagination, or were they louder than usual tonight, trying to make up for the missing pachyderms with sheer enthusiasm?—was beginning to drop to a lower register. At first, the tone sounded mellow, almost as though they were attempting to lull the audience. But then the beat of a drum rolled, undeniably ominous. That was Maggie's cue. She straightened her costume, nothing more than ragged, uneven squares of brown, green and grey, sewn together to resemble seaweed. There were no sequins or spangles for her. They'd be a waste.

Behind her, she could hear the hushed swearing of the workingmen, who knew they'd be fined if the ringmaster heard them. She lowered her head, jutting her chin forward, then scrunched her shoulders high and a little behind her neck. She moved through the curtain and forward into the ring, dragging one leg behind her, giving the impression it was numb. She hated this moment most of all. When, despite her best efforts to escape into a character that had been made for her, she was still Maggie.

There it was: that audible ripple of fear, a sharp intake of breath that united the audience every single night.

Maggie believed the gasps weren't for the costume or strange, uneven movements. They were gasping at her face. Her true face.

For Maggie did not paint her features, as the others did. She didn't even know if the hibiscus petals they crushed to stain their lips and cheeks would work on her skin. It might just draw more attention to the soft, pink lumps that covered most of her face. Either way, no amount of stain could distract from how her jaw swelled on one side, joining a large fold of neck in one even cascade, nor the protruding right brow that made one eye appear recessed.

Maggie had not even been able to form full sentences yet when this condition of hers began to make itself known. It had started mildly enough, with coffee-coloured patches appearing suddenly on her face, and freckles scattering the skin of her armpits. Her father had thought it a darling little aberration, blowing raspberries in her armpits and telling her that his scratchy stubble had left the marks there. But then the first tumour appeared. They couldn't have known then that the fleshy, pea-sized lump on her cheekbone had anything to do with the unusual patches and freckles. Just as they couldn't have known how much Maggie's life was about to change.

Maggie wasn't sure how her father had paid for the doctor's visit. Stolen something and sold it off, probably. Her mother certainly wouldn't have had anything to do with it.

The doctor, efficient and brusque but with a kindly manner, hadn't known what to make of Maggie's new lump. He hadn't even uttered the word 'tumour' that first visit. But he was a curious man and asked questions of others and read widely until he had a name for what he thought it likely to be. Von Recklinghausen's disease. A diagnosis that didn't come with relief, for there was no cure or treatment. In fact, Maggie and her father were assured it would worsen as she grew older, only finally stagnating sometime in the third decade of her life.

The doctor was correct. Maggie had watched as the face she'd once known—plain, but at least similar to everyone else's—had changed beyond recognition. And then she'd stopped looking.

Maggie steeled herself now against the audience's noise. The dummies, non-speaking clowns who nonetheless ably conveyed horror, went into hiding, ducking behind barrels or other performers. One even dived beneath the undercarriage of a horse. *Traitors*, Maggie thought. She'd always considered herself and her role in the circus as being most like the clowns.

Maggie half-limped, half-crawled around the edge of the ring. A gas-powered spotlight waited in the centre for her, but she would change direction only at the very last moment. She took her time, keeping close to the audience. Rafferty wanted them to see her face and know this was no trick.

But she had her own reasons for getting so close.

She scanned the tiered rows, eyes skipping past women in white hats with curls spilling from beneath their brims; past men in smart jackets and tightly buttoned waistcoats; past children whose wide eyes might make her lose her resolve. Waiting until she found what she was looking for. It happened in every show, and tonight was no different. Maggie's eyes connected with those of a man in a flat-topped hat with a dark band around it. His gaze didn't dart away and she leered at him, stepping closer, nearly breaching the barrier between performer and audience. Those who were game to meet her nightly challenge always had the long-distance look of someone searching for something. She could see it in this man's eyes now as they moved the tiniest bit side to side: the search for a hint of a soul inside Maggie. That's how much they believed her to truly be a monster.

Maggie screwed up her posture even more; the man didn't believe he'd find what he was looking for. They never did. So she met his expectation, and instead of giving him something human, she radiated hate. It was part of the act, a part not for the audience, but for herself. If Maggie hated them hard enough, she could almost fool herself into believing she didn't long to be one of them, pointing and hiding frightened giggles behind their raised hands as they marvelled at the freak.

The audience was restless that night—it had been months since they were last treated to an evening at the circus and they were simultaneously drunk on the excitement and impatient to see the elephants, who were always the stars of the show. But they quietened now, watching Maggie's act. There was never silence in a circus—even if the band stopped playing, there would still be the cracking of a tooth on an un-popped corn kernel, the low clearing of a ticklish throat, the shuffle of hooves from impatient horses backstage—but Maggie's act was the closest it came.

She made her way into the spotlight, where every year Rafferty had her jeer at the audience and threaten one of the more admired performers. This season it was Greta, who performed her sword dance with Maggie hissing and swiping at her, until the sword dancer finally lunged forward to thrust her weapon through Maggie's side, defeating her. A parry timed with precision; the sharp blade slid between Maggie's arm and ribcage making it look as though she'd been stuck through. The moment, although quick and well-practised, left Maggie a little breathless, as always. She knew the blade was real and could slip between her ribs without much difficulty. But the key to any circus act was to trust the person you performed with. Hesitation—even the tiniest flinch— could be deadly. Maggie never knew if Greta was as nervous as she, for they didn't speak beyond what was necessary, but the sword dancer's gaze was unblinking as she made the final thrust.

She didn't look her in the eye, but that, Maggie told herself, was because she was watching where the sword was going.

Vanquished, Maggie fell to the sawdust, careful not to land on the sword's blade. The audience erupted in cheers. Their feet were a triumphant rumble of thunder on the stands, only increasing in volume when Smith, the strong man—whose costume was filled with balled-up scrap fabric to make him look even more muscular —shoved his hands beneath Maggie's back and lifted her above his head to show off her limp form, still staked with the sword.

Maggie's arm was beginning to ache with the strain of keeping the weapon pinned to her side, but she barely noticed it. Her attention was on Smith's palms, warm on her back, even through the fabric of her costume, and she was reminded of Hercules's strong yet gentle trunk meeting her skin. She usually kept her eyes closed in the final death throes of her performance, not wanting to disrupt—or witness—the audience's celebration of her demise. But she cracked her eyelids open a fraction, for tears had gathered and needed an escape. She allowed them to trickle slowly down her cheeks, safe in the knowledge they were too small to be noticed by anyone.

Smith carried her toward the edge of the ring. Maggie could feel the audience's attention shift. They were no longer looking at the Lagoon Creature; she'd been conquered. Itsuo, who came cartwheeling into the ring, caused awed gasps, and with that sound she knew she was forgotten.

Smith pushed through the canvas curtain between the ring and backstage, then put her down with a jolt. Maggie didn't think he meant to hurt her; it was just that he'd never considered she might feel anything. She was nothing more than a sack of potatoes to be carried around.

Maggie dusted off the pale handprints Smith had left on her costume—his hands were covered in fake, a rosin powder mostly used by the equestrians in their bareback riding acts—then she moved to the curtain and pulled it back a fraction. She rarely

watched the show after her act was done, except for the finale—
which she alone wasn't part of, for it would have ruined the illusion
of her death—for the audience's response to the finale told her
whether the show had been a success or not, so she never missed it.
After her act, she usually changed out of her costume right away,
stepping with relief back into her worn and faded blouse and skirt,
cut unfashionably high, just above the ankle, to make it easier to
move around and help out wherever help was needed. Sometimes
that meant brushing the horses down and bedding them, a job the
grooms never thanked her for even though they would be fined if
the task wasn't promptly attended to. But then, they didn't thank
the children whose chore it was to assist them in this job, either.
On other nights, she'd be needed to quickly stitch back together a
torn seam, or talk over a problem in the show with Rafferty, who
seemed to like using her as a sounding-board. Probably because
she never tried to find ways of promoting herself as a solution, as
most other performers did.

But tonight she was uneasy, and stayed put. Rafferty had not
let the audience know there would be no elephants. There'd
been no time; disposing of Ida and Hercules's remains had taken
them to their very first performance. Their posters still depicted
the two grey beasts standing proudly either side of the circus's
name. Maggie couldn't help but fear the audience might feel
short-changed.

Greta emerged from the ring, and Maggie held out the sword
that had dealt her death-blow. Greta took it without a word. She
was moving fast, stripping off layers of her costume to don a new
one. Sensing her tension—Greta had enough time to make the
quick change, but the first performance always felt like a gathering
of every doubt and uncertainty possible—Maggie silently picked
up the short, spangle-covered skirt that was waiting, held it out
so Greta could step into it, then bent over to do up the buttons
on the back, a task made difficult due to Greta moving as she
sheathed her swords. With a whistle through her teeth, Greta

summoned Judge. He danced at her feet, then paused, his energy tightly controlled, proud chest jutting forward. Maggie held the curtain back, and Judge shot into the ring, Greta following him with a bright smile and a wave. She hadn't said a single word the whole time; Maggie wasn't even sure the sword dancer had noticed who it was that was helping her.

Maggie let the curtain fall, leaving just enough of a gap to see Judge pose as a living statue. It made the audience laugh, and their amusement grew as he turned somersaults in the air at Greta's command, his little brown and white body tumbling over and over, tail wagging after each successful landing. Maggie stepped aside again, making way for two donkeys with kerchiefs tied around their necks to amble out into the ring. Judge sprang onto the back of the first donkey, then they trotted in circles around the barrier while he leapt back and forth between them. Maggie thought she could hear the audience getting restless. The act was going on too long, and when the donkeys climbed up onto the high edge of the ring for one final parade, their applause had the hollow sound of politeness.

It was time for the finale. Rafferty had carefully choreographed it for sheer spectacle: the funambulist posing overhead on her tightrope, clowns cavorting beneath her, the horses circling the ring, the feathers protruding from their headpieces bobbing. The riders standing on the horses' backs held their arms up high as Rafferty, on his podium at the centre of it all, cracked his whip.

Maggie could tell a good show by the way the audience began clapping or cheering before the final flourishes had even been completed. Tonight, there was nothing but quiet.

After several seconds, one or two indistinct shouts emerged from the crowd. Then, very clearly, one man's voice called, 'Oy, what do you think you're doing? Where's the elephants?' His words seemed to bounce around the canvas. There were sounds of agreement from those nearest him. Heads further afield turned to see who had voiced what they'd all been thinking, and some men got to their feet.

'We paid for elephants!' another shouted. Maggie saw a young boy in the front row burst into tears.

'Mama, I want to see the elephants. You said we would!' he shrieked, enjoying being part of the noise. His mother pulled him to her bosom with one hand, the wide brim of her hat dancing with indignation.

The band struck up once more, an attempt to drown out the audience's upset. They shouldn't have. The crowd only shouted louder still, standing and raising their fists. Some women ushered their children out, afraid the crowd would turn violent.

'Give us our money back!' The words turned into a chant. Fistfuls of popcorn went flying. Maggie stepped back, taking the curtain with her so it stood open, hoping someone in the ring would see it and know it was time to leave.

A few did, mostly those with animals who were becoming unnerved, their senses picking up that this was not the usual noise at the end of a performance. Maggie saw the flaring nostrils of the horses as they went by, the raised fur on Judge's neck.

And then the band stopped. It wasn't the neat, sudden silence of most nights, but a dwindling of instruments, one by one, as though no one was really sure of their place in the music and they were slowly giving up. Maggie peered around the curtain and saw Rafferty waving his hands at the band, shushing them; their white-helmeted heads turned to one another, a small, jostling sea of confusion. She clenched her hands so tight her nails dug into the calluses—earned from years of handling circus equipment—on her palms.

What was Rafferty doing?

He raised his voice. Maggie made out a faint sound, but it was nothing more than a mosquito hum beneath a storm. Finally, enough people elbowed their neighbours quiet so that he could be heard.

'I know you love and appreciate our elephants as much as we do, and for that we've always been grateful. It is therefore with utmost sadness that I have to announce the recent passing of both Ida and Hercules.'

A roar went through the crowd. Was it disappointment? Shock? The thrill of knowing that their anger could continue unabated? Maggie didn't know. She licked lips that had gone dry, the taste of sweat and sawdust on them.

'You swindler!' shouted a man who'd taken his hat off and was waving it furiously in the air. Others jeered. Maggie could see the whites of Rafferty's eyes as he glanced back at the band, his hands flapping so fast they were almost a blur.

And with a burst, the band began playing 'God Save the King'.

The audience's shouts were cut off in a strangled noise as they groped for the appropriate words. She could see fury settling over their features; they knew they'd been bested by the ringmaster, at least until the end of the song. Even the angriest among them would not disrupt the national anthem.

By the time the final note died away, it was as though someone had extinguished the lit fuse. Many screwed up their popcorn bags and threw them at the ring in disgust as they left. They would not be telling their friends and families about the joy of the circus. The spectacles they'd seen that night, all the marvels they'd ooh'ed and aah'ed over, that the performers had sweated over, injured themselves practising, worked at until their muscles ached and their bodies could do the impossible, would be forgotten. All they'd remember was that there'd been no elephants.

Maggie watched the performers' faces as they filed through the curtain. Did they understand what this meant? Some appeared to. Others just looked tired. A few, the silliest of the lot, tried to laugh about it and make jokes.

Finally, out came Rafferty. His face was pale underneath the rosy paint on his cheeks. He took off his black top hat, exposing the strands of hair that sweat had slicked across his scalp. Maggie could see that his fingers trembled against the hat brim. Performers went up to him, crowding around, piling one question on top of another.

'How are we going to replace Ida and Hercules?'

'Should we leave all the animal acts until the finale? Would that make a difference?'

'What do we do if it happens again tomorrow?'

'Not right now,' Rafferty sighed, holding one hand up. His palm was red from swinging his whip so ferociously. 'You all have jobs to do. Come on, no slacking off just because we had a bad night. Tomorrow's a new day.'

They all moved away quickly. Only Maggie, with no official after-show duties, remained behind. She watched as Rafferty balanced his hat back on his head and ran his hands over his face. She was still, waiting; she knew that he knew she was there.

'We'll have to go,' he said finally, dropping his hands to meet her gaze. There was a bleak look in his tobacco-coloured eyes, disappointment and perhaps the tiniest touch of fear. That should've frightened Maggie too. For Rafferty was a blustery kind of person, always seeing the next opportunity to be taken advantage of, the next fortune to be made. He reminded her a little of her father in that way—only Rafferty had much more success with his endeavours and kept them strictly legal.

But instead of being frightened, Maggie's backbone straightened. The thing had already happened; she wasn't going to waste time being bothered over something that couldn't be changed. That was a lesson she'd learned long ago, living with a face like hers.

'I know,' she said, the simple words flat and devoid of any emotion. She was reminding Rafferty that he couldn't show his fear or break down. There were too many people relying on him. Hearing this silent message, Rafferty also straightened a little. 'How long have we got?' Maggie asked.

'We'll have to make it quick. There's nothing much for us here now. Our bridge is ruined. Tonight's show proved that.' Maggie nodded—the bridge was the circus's outward image, and theirs had always been immaculate until then. 'We should go within the week, if we can manage it.'

The next few days would be busy. There were supplies to purchase, a tracker to be retained. Their horsemanship and tumbling licences would need to be renewed and extended for as long as possible, so they could keep performing. Accounts with their local Sydney suppliers must be paid up and closed. Not to mention packing everything they'd only just brought to the Haymarket.

The Braun Brothers' Royal Circus was about to become a travelling circus once more.

Chapter Three

It was Maggie whom Rafferty sent out to gather the information he needed before he could make any decisions. Not the best choice, in her opinion. Someone who didn't look the way she did would have more luck inserting themselves into the stream of show-business gossip. But then anyone else might hoard whatever information they gathered in hopes of using it to join another circus whose future was not suddenly uncertain. Maggie was the only one Rafferty could rely on never to do such a thing. She knew no other circus would want her.

Besides, she wouldn't be missed for the long hours she crept about Sydney's streets, which could not have been said for anyone else. In the Braun Brothers' Royal Circus, Maggie straddled a strange line between circus hand and performer, not really belonging to either circle. She ate every meal alone, curled up against the side of a wagon; in the dressing tent she slipped quickly into her costume in a dark corner, eyes resolutely cast to the ground so she didn't have to see the other performers flinching or shrinking from her. Maggie suspected they had the notion that if they got too close for too long, their own skin might erupt in soft, pink tumours too.

She told herself she didn't care. That after so many years she preferred her own company to that of any other. And perhaps it was even true. But still a tiny voice whispered, *Oh, to be invited to join their easy camaraderie.* She would say no to any invitation, of course she would; she wasn't one for putting herself where she wasn't wanted. But just to be asked, to be recognised as a human soul who might, once in a while, need a little company, would be something. She wasn't greedy; she didn't require love or friendship or any kind of deep connection. Just a rubbing off of the sharp edges of loneliness would suffice.

But they didn't ask. They didn't even imagine, surrounded as they all were by so many people at all hours of the day and night, that one in their midst could be so alone. Especially not the Lagoon Creature. And after so many years, Maggie's loneliness had become a sort of presence in itself, the only thing she could rely on always to be there.

It took a couple of days, but Maggie was soon able to form a basic sketch of all the circuses, big-name or otherwise, that would arrive in Sydney and its surrounds over the coming nine months.

'Colleano's All-Star Circus is trekking down from the north, hitting all the towns along the coast,' she told Rafferty, ticking the names off her fingertips like they were marked there. 'There's talk that Hogan and Duckworth's Circus, which usually stays in Queensland, might cross the border and come down this way. But they've always stuck to smaller outback places, or so I'm told. And Wirth's Circus'll cover the south coast for their run, coming up from Melbourne.'

'We wouldn't do Melbourne anyway. It might be a showman's goldmine, but the audiences have high standards.'

Maggie nodded. She didn't need to be told that they had Buckley's chance of meeting those standards now they didn't have the elephants.

'There's whispers that FitzGerald Brothers might hit Sydney at some point, but given they're lucrative enough for rail transport it's hard to get confirmation on that one. Trains are faster even than gossip, and most towns or cities don't know they're coming until the big top goes up. You know they'll likely do the east coast, though. It's the most popular route, by wagon or rail. And that's it, far as I can tell.'

Rafferty did not look pleased. Maggie knew it wasn't that he didn't appreciate the effort she'd gone to. It was that all the best runs were already taken.

'We'll have to go inland,' Maggie said. Rafferty's eyes darted to hers, sharp, and she hastened to make it sound like she wasn't giving him orders. 'Seems like it'll be our best bet. No one else is heading that way. We could cross into Victoria, maybe even South Australia.'

'Could be a tough run. Lot of tiny towns. Some with long distances between them.'

'We can earn a motza in small towns. They don't get many entertainments, so everyone'll come out for the show. You remember how it is.' That was how they'd made their money for years before they'd acquired Ida and Hercules. It was a hard life, though, and she knew it was this which gave Rafferty pause.

'It's a bloody long way to Adelaide,' he said. Maggie's stomach dropped a fraction, the way it did when Smith dropped her to the ground too suddenly. She'd been the one to suggest South Australia, knowing it might mean Adelaide, the biggest city in the state. But now she hesitated. Her father was in Adelaide.

She pressed her lips together. Rafferty would think her mad as a cut snake if she suggested a direction in one breath and changed it in the next. Still, some of her reluctance slipped out.

'It'd take us, what? Two to three months if we walked there without stopping for a single performance, and had good weather all the way?' she asked.

'Plenty of time to put on lots of shows and still get us there before the winter break. I suppose Adelaide's as good a place as any to kick off next year's travels. Don't you think?'

And there it was. A slight crinkling at the edge of Rafferty's eyes, a smothered twitch of his mouth. A whisper of excitement. It was the sawdust in his veins, luring him to wherever an audience was.

'Maggie girl, pack your bags. It looks like the Braun Brothers' Royal Circus is heading to Adelaide.'

Chapter Four

When Maggie was a child, the circus had spent two years touring Queensland. It was there that she'd first seen a green tree ants' nest. The way leaves were pulled together, overlapped and held in place with a silky-white substance had made it look like some kind of fairy pillow, and she had been unable to resist stretching her fingers out and prodding it. The ants had gone berserk; if they'd appeared busy before, now they were frantic, racing across the leaves, crawling over her fingers and down her sleeves so fast she'd had to rip the clothes right off her back, howling as they bit her. The other circus folk had laughed, familiar with the frenzy the little creatures could cause; only Rafferty had come to help, calmly brushing the stubborn insects off. Later, in an effort to cheer her up, he told her how you could pluck the ants' bottoms off and eat them.

Maggie felt as though she were in the middle of that ants' nest now.

Circus folk swarmed. The acetylene lighting system had already been dismantled and packed away, and now the big top was coming down, a manoeuvre that would be honed to a fine art over the coming months as they repeated it over again in every new town. The gear men, with cigarettes clamped between their lips, yanked up the stakes, letting the ropes dangle; soon the king poles would be carefully toppled. Each performer oversaw the packing of their costumes into trunks and the loading of their equipment onto the wagons. The members of the band Rafferty had been so proud of were packing up their instruments and saying their final goodbyes. Until the intervention of the German band leader Herr Von der Mehden a few years back, Australian circus bands had been a target of public derision. Now they could play with any of the best, and a sizeable group had declared they would stay in the city to find new, better employment—if they'd wanted to live as travellers, they would have joined a wandering band or light opera company. Rafferty was trying to pretend he didn't feel this blow; he stood with his hands in his pockets, back to the traitorous musicians, talking to Nev, the Aboriginal man he'd hired to be their tracker. Nev would find them running water to camp by, show them the safest paths, supplement their meals with his knowledge of bush tucker, and ensure they didn't get lost.

Maggie couldn't quite guess the tracker's age, but around his eyes he had the deep grooves of someone who had spent many years squinting against the sun. It was a sign of a man who lived most his life outdoors, and that alone inspired confidence.

Rafferty, underneath his insouciant appearance—he broke off his conversation every now and then to throw a crude joke at the circus hands and make them laugh—was keeping a watchful eye over all. He was intent on no one feeling the moment for what it really was: a failure. Better they think of the road ahead as an opportunity than a gamble he was taking with their livelihoods.

Maggie scanned the people she knew so well, noticing the signs of strain despite Rafferty's best efforts. Greta's wiry muscles were tense as she sidestepped a fresh scattering of horse manure. Itsuo, who was loading a case and his foot-juggling pins into the baggage wagon, had such an atypically disgruntled expression as he paused to wipe the sweat from his brow that he could have been the twin he masqueraded as when he switched acts mid-show. Smith, whose English skin had never adjusted to the harsh Australian sun, wore a florid glow of sunburn, the deep red only increased by his efforts to lift the edge of a wagon and free someone's bedding that was caught beneath the wheel.

And then there was Charlotte. Not wearing the sweat and strain of physical hard work, as the others did, but calmly speaking to a man Maggie didn't recognise.

Pronounced the German way, shar-lotta, the tightrope walker's name was as decorative and interesting as her face. She was everything that Maggie was not, her skin pale and smooth as a layer of cream on top of fresh milk. She wore her glorious mass of curling red hair parted in the centre and combed back into big, misty puffs on either side of her face, finished with a ribbon tied in a bow at the front, the whole lot topped with a conical toque hat. The freckles across her cheeks seemed to dance every time she laughed. She was a fizzing, bubbly glass of champagne, whereas Maggie was flat beer.

In this moment she was also an inky-black smear on the colourful landscape. The high, boned collar of her silk dress brushed her jaw as she ducked her head flirtatiously, an excess of cotton net lace and large, decorative buttons showing how expensive the dress must be. A braided black rope was worn as a sash around her waist, making it appear she had been lassoed by the man she was talking to. He wore a suit that stretched too tightly across his middle, and he turned the brim of a felt bowler in slow circles in his hands while he spoke. The Chantilly lace and velvet flowers adorning Charlotte's hat tilted sideways in a coquettish dip as she reached up and gave the man's arm a squeeze. His face coloured until it resembled Smith's, and he puffed his chest even wider.

Maggie snorted. Could the man not see the artifice in Charlotte's actions? If she truly cared for him, she would have had him visit when she could get a signed pass from Rafferty to allow him into the main tent, which was where every visitor truly longed to go. Instead he was there as all the delights were being torn down.

Perhaps Maggie could see Charlotte's falseness because she knew her manner so well. For a time, Charlotte had also grown up living with the circus. Charlotte, like the other children, had been frightened of Maggie's slowly changing face, and whenever Maggie came near she buried her own perfect features in the legs of the nearest adult and cried. During the winter months, she went to classes at a local school, whereas Maggie stayed within the confines of the circus, the only child continuing to take lessons from the circus folk—sometimes even from Rafferty himself. They hadn't spoken much throughout those years, but Maggie had observed her, as she observed all of them, taking in all the details of the kind of near-perfect life that would never be hers. Then, one day when Charlotte must have been around seven or eight, she had disappeared. Maggie didn't know where to, only that she'd returned years later, a grown woman. She was so striking then that Rafferty had immediately wanted to put her under a spotlight, and she'd remained with the circus ever since.

As Maggie watched now, Charlotte made her goodbyes, the man donning and doffing his hat before walking away with a self-satisfied grin. Charlotte's shoulders moved in what could only be a relieved sigh. She studied the man as he left, then shook herself and began stalking aimlessly around the grounds.

'All right, gents, who's up for a bit of fun before we head off down the dreary, dusty roads?' she called. A few of the workers glanced at each other, exchanging nudges. But they weren't going to respond; circus hands didn't mix with the performers unless it was on matters of work.

'Come on, surely someone else wants to say hooroo to Sydney in style?' she goaded, her voice taking on a low, sing-song quality. No one answered. Maggie gazed about, curious. Charlotte was a boom girl, a star of the circus; she should never be short of company.

'You're not going to make me go out on my own, are you?' Charlotte's tone turned to a whine. Maggie couldn't help her grin; how unusual for the tightrope star to have to beg.

Yet it was still with that hint of *Schadenfreude*—a word she had learned from Charlotte herself when, half-tipsy after an excellent show, she'd treated the entire circus to a recitation of her favourite German words and phrases, many of which got her fined for profanity when she explained their meaning in English—that she found herself saying, 'I'll go with you.'

Charlotte's own face showed its one-sided dimple as she turned to see who her volunteer was; the smile dropped when her eyes met Maggie's, her pert nose scrunching up in confusion.

'Was that you?' she asked, as if she couldn't quite believe Maggie's gall. Maggie couldn't believe it either. She shrugged one shoulder. She knew she should leave, hide behind a cart until they all stopped laughing at her, but her boots stayed rooted to the spot. Why shouldn't she go out? She had lived in and loved the city just as much as Charlotte or any of the other performers. She had just as much right to say goodbye to it.

'Really?' Charlotte asked.

'Look, the rest of us are busy, love,' said Gilbert, one of the flunkies, heaving a wad of acrobatic pads into the back of a wagon to emphasise his point. 'It's either her, or no one. Rattle your dags and make your choice, or rack off.'

Charlotte studied Maggie, her eyes running all the way down to her button-up calfskin boots, then back up to her hair, styled less fashionably than Charlotte's in one big mass atop her head. Maggie had tried imitating Charlotte's style once, but worried it only brought more attention to her face. For the same reason, she kept her hair free of ribbons and other adornments.

Charlotte's close scrutiny made Maggie acutely aware of the differences between them. It wasn't just their faces. The tightrope walker was nearly a head taller than her, with a figure that was full and womanly. Maggie's could best be described as childlike.

Despite her efforts not to, she hunched her shoulders, shrinking into herself.

'As long as you're up for a bit of fun,' Charlotte said, drawing the words out. 'You are, aren't you?'

Maggie nearly said, 'Always', knowing it was the answer Charlotte herself would give if the roles were reversed. But she couldn't form the lie. Instead she said, 'That's what I volunteered for, isn't it?'

Charlotte's lips twitched. She seemed satisfied, for she said, 'Let's go, then,' and turned to walk away.

'Just a moment—I need to get my hat.'

Maggie could practically feel Charlotte tapping her toes in impatience as she ran to get the wide-brimmed straw hat she favoured due to its black net veil, which partially obscured her face. She was glad veils had come back into fashion; it was one small thing that made her day-to-day life easier. Jamming the hat on her head and roughly pushing in a tarnished hatpin, Maggie snatched up her large, flat, square leather bag and checked that its contents—a comb, fountain pen, spare ink and nibs, a selection of books, and the packet containing the money she'd saved—were all in place. Charlotte didn't say anything when Maggie came running back; she simply turned and walked out of the busy circus grounds, sure of being followed.

Chapter Five

They passed the rhythmic brickwork and arched openings of the recently built Sydney City Markets. Maggie could see that Charlotte was darting sideways looks at her. She ducked her head. Anyone coming her way would have to step around her, for she was not going to look up.

'We're catching a tram to Tamarama.' It took Maggie a moment to understand what Charlotte was saying; she'd been bracing herself for some kind of pointed question, perhaps even a remonstrance. She squinted her eyes against the dust of the construction at the No. 3 Fruit Market as they rounded the corner.

'Why Tamarama?' There were plenty of other attractions to enjoy right where they were. Maggie was not one for the beach, even at Manly, where sea-bathing was legal during daylight hours.

'Because of Wonderland City.' Charlotte spoke in a voice of barely suppressed excitement. A horse-drawn taxi with signs on the side advertising Lamb's Linoleum Cream came perilously close, its wheels near as tall as Charlotte, and without thinking Maggie put her hand out to grab the other woman's arm. Her fingers stopped before they could make contact, just brushing the silk sleeve of Charlotte's dress. But Charlotte hadn't even noticed. She was glaring above them at the crisscrossing tramlines, muttering about whether it was left or right she was supposed to turn to find the tram stop. Maggie carefully hid her hand behind her skirts. Her lips parted, and she was about to ask, 'And why Wonderland City?' when she thought better of it. Did it matter why? Maggie had agreed to go wherever it was that Charlotte wanted to spend her last hours in Sydney. She was not going to turn coward now, whatever the funambulist had in mind.

***

Maggie and Charlotte came to a stop as if by prior agreement. A cool sea breeze stirred the netting of Maggie's hat, caressing her cheeks. She breathed in deeply. There was no odour of animal dung, closely packed sweaty bodies or city grime here. Instead there was the enticing scent of toffees, musk sticks and peppermints wafting from beyond the gates of Wonderland City.

Maggie glanced to her right. A trio of men, two pale and one dark-skinned, were tap dancing, pennies nailed to the soles of their shoes to make the dull, scratchy sound on the sand-strewn pavement. A battered bowler hat sat upside-down before them, to collect coins thrown their way. The small crowd that had gathered were not paying attention though; instead, their heads were craned back, watching the Airem Scarem, a dirigible that crossed from one shoreline cliff to another on an electric wire. Maggie hoped Charlotte wouldn't want her to get on that thing for a ride. The tightrope walker obviously had no fear of heights, but Maggie wasn't sure she felt the same.

'The park's supposed to be closing down,' Charlotte said. Her fingers fiddled with one of the satin-covered buttons that made a decorative 'V' down the front of her dress. Maggie glanced down at her own unadorned cream-coloured shirtwaist, worn beneath a neat yet aged wool suit jacket.

'I've never been before,' she added, 'and I didn't want to run the risk of it no longer being here when we get back. Because who knows when that will be.'

Her words made Maggie's jaw tense. It was as busy around them as the Haymarket had been: excited children pulled their parents by the hand to hurry them inside, and Maggie could hear the unmistakable shouts of joy from those already enjoying the amusements. If crowds of this size weren't enough to sustain an amusement, what chance did the circus have?

'Come on, let's stop wasting time,' Charlotte said, her hands dropping from the button and flexing open and closed by her sides. 'What should we do first? The double-decker merry-go-round? Watch some boxing? I hear there's a switchback railway, but it's apparently right at the back, so we might want to leave that till last. Work our way toward it.'

Maggie pulled at the black mesh netting of her veil as they entered the amusement park. No one was paying her any attention, though; everyone was too busy darting from attraction to attraction, ducking in and out of tents or fighting for a good place in line.

'Let's find the American Shooting Gallery,' Charlotte said. Her weight was poised on her toes, as though she were preparing to step out onto her rope. 'I've always fancied I'd be a good shot.'

Maggie turned out to be better at hitting the targets than Charlotte was, which annoyed the tightrope walker, who swiftly suggested they walk over the artificial lake to see what the Alpine Slide was all about. This was followed by a visit to the waxworks, where Charlotte mimicked the stiff poses of the figures to such perfection that a man, after bumping into her, tried to inspect her for any damage to the wax, sending her into fits of laughter— and Maggie too, much to her surprise. They bypassed the movie house—Charlotte reasoned they could see a film any time, although Maggie knew it was unlikely, once they were on the road again— and Maggie flatly refused to go into the Haunted House, saying there was nothing in there that could be scarier than her. Charlotte gave her a funny look at that, and Maggie silently berated herself. If her face made people uncomfortable, openly talking about that fact, even in jest like now, only made it worse. She changed the subject by suggesting they put on a pair of rollerskates and try a few circles of the rink. Here, Charlotte outshone Maggie. It was hardly surprising; she did after all make her living from her impeccable balance. As Maggie felt her feet skid in two different directions beneath her, Charlotte skated up to her and grasped her firmly by the elbows. There was strength in those hands, pulling her up and away from a tumble. Maggie's fingers instinctively curled into the fine, slippery fabric of Charlotte's sleeves. She let her sliding feet find purchase beneath her before letting go.

'Stop thinking about your feet,' Charlotte said, still gripping Maggie. 'Think about the top of your head. Pull upwards through it. You can't fall upwards.'

Charlotte's eyes flicked up from Maggie's feet, widened when they met her gaze, and she snatched her hands away. Things were back as they should be.

Maggie turned from her, propelling herself forward on the unnatural wheels, trying to pull up through the top of her head, whatever that meant.

After a ha'penny ice cream and a visit to the seals, Charlotte's endless supply of energy finally began to dissipate. She suggested they head to the Japanese tearooms for a bite, managing to make the suggestion sound like a foregone conclusion. Maggie, whose stomach had not been satiated by the ice cream, didn't argue.

***

'I'm full up to dolly's wax.' Maggie leaned back, her hands resting on her midsection. Charlotte, insisting the meal was her shout, had ordered all manner of savoury bites and delicate sweets, so Maggie had indulged herself. She would have loved to try squeezing in one more of the treats on display on the electroplate stands, but her tightly boned corset wouldn't allow it.

'Wish we could get a proper drink,' Charlotte muttered. Her sunny demeanour had changed while they ate; she'd chewed and swallowed so methodically that Maggie doubted she'd actually tasted a thing. Maggie's lips were still sweet with the lemonade and ginger beer they'd downed, and she couldn't imagine what else Charlotte could possibly want.

They were seated on the tearoom's wide verandah, in wicker chairs padded with tassel-trimmed cushions. The faint sea breeze soothed skin flushed with excitement and overindulgence, and made the ferns dotted around them dance. Charlotte appeared distracted and not in the mood to talk further, so Maggie pulled a small book out of her bag. She sat it on her lap but didn't open it, running her finger down the words on the spine, seeing them through the diamond pattern of her veil. *Mother Maud* by Mrs Arthur. She wasn't particularly fond of this book. Maud was too perfect in her self-sacrifice and her learning of perfectly timed lessons. Yet Maggie couldn't stop herself being drawn to the book's pages again and again. It was the family in it, the way they always came together, even if they'd thrown nasty words at each other. It irritated her, made her feel sure the book was a lie, but it was written so simply that the author must have believed it to be true. One of them was wrong, and Maggie wasn't sure which one she wanted it to be.

She sighed and glanced over at Charlotte.

The tightrope walker had two bright spots on her cheeks. Had the sun got to her? Her toque had no protective brim. Maggie was about to ask, but Charlotte interrupted her, pointing to two women herding six boys in Little Lord Fauntleroy collars ahead of them.

'Watch this lot,' she said, her voice soft. Maggie did as she was told. Every time the women managed to corral the boys into a chattering swarm, one would break off to look at something that caught his attention. Maggie's lips twitched. Even the highly disciplined children of the circus would have descended into jabbering, easily distracted burdens when surrounded by so many temptations. They'd be especially inclined to misbehave if they'd been forced into such detestable collars.

'Just think,' Charlotte said, sinking as far down into her chair as the boning of her corset would let her. 'When they finally get that lot home, those women will still have tea to cook and a house to clean.'

'And?' Maggie, who would never have a house filled with children to feed, felt the familiar pang of jealousy.

'Think how tired they'll be. It's not like the circus, where everyone pitches in and the work is spread around. They have to do it all.'

Maggie didn't answer. She was thinking of that old, familiar wish: that maybe someone, someday, would give her what she most wanted. She wasn't too old yet, wouldn't be for some years still. She could almost feel the movement of a child in her arms, snuggling into her chest, where her heart beat for love of them. It was swiftly followed by the stern tamping down of that beautiful, teasing feeling. She knew better.

'We're lucky really, aren't we, Maggie? That we don't have to live that way. Even if we once thought it was all we wanted ...'

Maggie started at hearing her name in Charlotte's mouth. Then she turned over the other woman's words, so similar to the winter refrain she'd made herself repeat night after night. The difference was that Charlotte wasn't trying to convince herself. Only someone with that beautiful face, and the unconscious ease of life that went with it, could truly believe this life lucky in comparison to other women's. It was easy for her—she hadn't been abandoned by her father to a circus, to make her way in the world as a show-business freak.

And yet, Maggie realised, she had never learned why Charlotte lived with the circus as a child, only to disappear then reappear years later. It struck her as odd: at the circus, gossip usually flew from tongue to tongue faster than any trapeze artist could fly through the air. She looked sidelong at her. It was tempting to ask, but Charlotte's sullen countenance did not invite deep conversation. Instead, Maggie said, 'Should we get going?'

'Not yet. We have to wait for Fairy City.'

'I thought this place was called Wonderland City?'

'It is. But you'll see.'

Charlotte made them wait as the sheer swathes of cloud-dotted blue sky above darkened to a deep indigo matching that of the waves below. It was only early in the spring, and Maggie tried to pull the cuffs of her shirtwaist down over her hands that were going cold; the linen didn't have much stretch. She leaned back, letting her eyelids fall, and took a deep breath. This was the end of one life; tomorrow, she would be a traveller again.

'Fairy City,' Charlotte murmured, making Maggie start. She opened her eyes, blinking several times to clear the dust motes floating before her. But they weren't dust motes; all around her thousands of tiny coloured lights were sparkling, just like the sequins and spangles on a costume. Maggie's fingers flew to her mouth.

Charlotte grinned. 'Couldn't go before we saw it. Worth the wait, don't you think?'

Chapter Six

They left Wonderland City, now Fairy City. Maggie sat next to Charlotte in the closed section of the electric tram, her face turned to the window so that others on board wouldn't stare at her. A man standing in a wagon kept pace with the tram; beyond him, brick and stone building facades flashed by. She could see the occasional white streak of a lady's dress among the darker throng of men's suits, a splash of emerald green or royal blue from little girls' hats, and hear the shouts of those on foot who hurried to jump off the tracks and out of the way.

Charlotte rose and nudged Maggie to follow her off the tram. Maggie accompanied her wordlessly. A quick glance both ways to make sure she wasn't in danger from incoming wagons or trams, then she skirted a man pushing a wide broom to meet Charlotte under the shop awnings. They were on George Street, just passing J.D. Williams' cinema and amusement complex. The looming buildings took on a foreboding look, the occasional electric bulb casting shadows in the recessed windows and a breeze making the laundry thrown over the railings flap. A man closing up his horse-drawn pie-cart tried to tempt them with a cut price on his now-cold goods. Charlotte didn't even notice. She raced ahead, the now-dirty hem of her dress dancing as her feet kicked it this way and that. She seemed revived, but if she had a specific location in mind, she didn't share it with Maggie.

'Here we are,' she finally said, pointing at a building only distinguishable from the others before them by the width of the doors leading inside.

'A stable?' Maggie asked. Had Charlotte lost her wits?

'Where men park their horses, wives and Aboriginal workers while they go in there.' Charlotte's pointing hand swivelled to across the road, where Maggie could just make out the faint sign of a hotel. 'You know they won't let us ladies in, but there's still plenty of fun to be had, if you just ask the right people.'

Charlotte pushed her way inside the stable. They found a cluster of wagons and horses—some tethered to the wagons, some loose in stalls—just as she had predicted. A handful of women sat sewing by the light of a candle stub; two more stood against the walls, muttering to one another. Charlotte ignored them all, hovering near the entrance with her back turned. The next man that came inside, she hurried toward and began speaking urgently. Maggie, who shrank back several steps, couldn't hear what she said; she saw the man's shoulders stiffen. Charlotte just leaned in closer, and soon he was laughing, shaking his head in a way that somehow didn't look to Maggie like a 'no'. He disappeared outside, and Charlotte held a finger up to Maggie, instructing her to wait.

Around ten minutes later, the man returned, his arms crossed over his torso in a closed-off, secretive manner, his hands hidden beneath his jacket.

'Ta da!' he said, whipping out two glasses of beer, one with the foamy top slopping over the rim. Charlotte gave a deep, happy sigh and took the glass that hadn't spilled. She closed her eyes as her lips met the drink and downed half of it without pausing for breath. The moan that followed was nearly enough to make Maggie blush.

'That butcher's yours,' Charlotte said, wiping her mouth. She licked her hand, savouring the drops that had ended up there.

Maggie smiled. She hadn't heard anyone use the word 'butcher' for a glass since the circus had left South Australia.

'No thanks. Never really warmed to the taste of beer.' Maggie half-expected Charlotte to put the acid on—she'd seen that was the usual way, no one ever wanting to drink alone—but Charlotte simply said, 'More for me, then.'

Charlotte repeated this performance every time a new man came into the stable, only avoiding the ones who came with wives. Some of the men evidently knew her, and greeted her with shared jokes Maggie couldn't understand. Maggie could, however, see why it was hard for them to resist Charlotte. The more she drank, the more her hips swayed and her smile widened, displaying the crossed front teeth that increased her impish charm. Her gestures became bigger, yet somehow more intimate and inviting. After a while, even Maggie found herself wanting to join in. She drank two lukewarm lagers in quick succession, cringing and pulling a face at the bitter, yeasty taste so that Charlotte laughed. It felt good to make someone laugh like that—not cruelly, but because they found her funny. Maggie accepted a third beer, peering at Charlotte over the foamy top as Charlotte saluted her with her own empty glass.

'It's better out here with you lot,' said the man who'd just delivered them a smuggled, half-empty bottle of port. 'They're rowdy in there but no fun. It's all just noise and hot air. Now you, you're a lass who knows how to enjoy yourself.'

'Am I ever.' Charlotte flung her arm around Maggie. 'Just ask Maggie here how much fun I am. I gave her the best day ever today. Didn't I, Mags?'

Maggie's mind was tripping over being called 'Mags'. Her father was the only person to ever call her anything other than Maggie. It was pleasant, though, and she smiled as she forced her fuzzy thoughts to the rest of what Charlotte had said. The tightrope walker was right. It had been the most fun she remembered having in ... well, perhaps ever.

'Yes, you did, Charlotte.'

Charlotte swung around so they were almost nose to nose. 'I like the way you say my name. The proper way. Don't ever call me Charlie, will you? The warbs do that. Not to my face, but when they know I can hear.'

'Warbs' was a word some people used for the circus hands. It was not a friendly term.

'They're a pack of prawns,' Maggie said dismissively.

'That's what I think!' Charlotte said, as if it were the most extraordinary coincidence in the world.

The man, disgruntled at no longer having Charlotte's attention, began to dance around the limited space, using the bottle of port as a partner. The horses shifted nervous feet, tails swatting the man when he got too close.

'Oy, Mags,' he called. 'Catch!' He flung the nearly-empty bottle at Maggie as he swung past, then snatched Charlotte up and danced on, pulling her in close—closer than necessary, Maggie thought. He should be ashamed; he was old enough to be her father.

The thought made Maggie wonder what her own father would do if he were to come through that stable door. He would likely bring them a drink, but whether he'd have paid for it was another question.

'Maggie!' Charlotte shrieked. The bottle slipped from Maggie's hands, landing with a crack on the hay-strewn ground. She took a step forward; had the man's hands strayed? Would the two of them together be strong enough to fight him off?

But Charlotte was laughing, one hand holding the man's hat and waving it wildly in the air. The man himself was on his knees. Maggie went to them cautiously.

'Would you look at this,' Charlotte cried. She was drumming her fingers on the man's bald pate, making him twitch and laugh. Tattooed on his scalp was a large, curving butterfly in black ink.

'That's not real, is it?' Maggie asked. Living in the circus she'd seen a lot of strange things, but never a man with a butterfly drawn on his head.

'As real as these horses,' the man said. 'As real as you and me.'

Charlotte licked the pad of her thumb, then vigorously rubbed it across one of the butterfly's wings.

'Charlotte!' Maggie gasped, her eyes tearing with amusement at the absurd sight of this man on his knees, one of the circus's star performers furiously rubbing his head with a spit-dampened thumb to check it wouldn't budge.

'Maggie, we should get one,' Charlotte said. She turned to her with an eager expression, one red lock tumbling out from underneath her hat. Maggie reached down and flicked at the tattoo with her index finger.

'I have too much hair for that. We both do.'

Charlotte turned back to the man. 'Where'd you get it done?'

'Fella called Fred Harris did it. He hangs around Sussex Street, says he's going to have a shop there one day.'

'We could walk there, Mags!'

'It's near midnight.'

'So? He could be hanging around, hoping for customers.'

'You can't be serious?'

'Why not? Come on, it'd be the perfect way to say goodbye to Sydney. And you know tattoos are becoming very fashionable.'

'Are they?' Even though many in the circus had tattoos— even a few of the women—she couldn't imagine most regular people she passed in the streets bearing permanent ink on their skin. Then again, she would never have known this man had a butterfly tattooed on his head if Charlotte hadn't exposed it. Who knew what others were hiding behind their long sleeves or hats or dresses?

'Please?' Charlotte wheedled. She clasped her hands in front of her and batted her eyelashes, the very picture of childlike innocence.

Maggie made an exasperated noise. 'All right, fine. As long as this fella walks us there to keep us safe.' She thought about it briefly, then added, 'And keeps his hands to himself.'

What could it hurt? They weren't likely to find this tattoo man anyway.

Chapter Seven

'Not many ladies get tattooed, you know.' Fred Harris was eyeing them sceptically. Maggie could hardly blame him. Charlotte was at that moment swinging her arms in wide circles, singing a tuneless song she'd made up on the way, while Maggie herself had broken out in a visible cold sweat. She swallowed, looking at the man's hands. They looked steady, but would they still be steady when he was wielding a needle?

She wasn't about to be outdone in courage by Charlotte, though. She had more grit, more determination, than the tightrope walker would ever need to muster in her charmed life. And even though her palms had gone slick when Fred Harris opened a box to show them his machine, Maggie rather liked the idea of making her skin different by her own choice, rather than by nature's whim.

'You're not refusing, are you?' she asked. Maggie could feel his eyes on the exposed part of her neck. 'It won't be anywhere that has ... these,' she said hastily, gesturing to the tumours.

'In that case, as long as you've got the money, I can do it.'

'I've plenty of money,' Charlotte said, breaking from her wandering melody. Maggie hoped this meant she would be paying for both of them. Maggie was good with her money, saving it for a future whose shape she couldn't see and thus needed to protect herself against—and in the back of her mind, she still had some vague idea of a family that she was saving for, so she didn't relish the thought of spending a chunk of her savings on something so frivolous.

'Righto, I'll go first then,' she said to stop the fretful thoughts. She'd never been impulsive before—never had the chance to be, really—and she didn't want to back away from her one opportunity. Fred Harris led them into a room behind the shop. Maggie wondered if this was the building he wanted to buy; she was about to ask him when he said, 'What'll it be, then?'

'Pardon?'

'There's a lot I can do, but keep in mind the ink is black. Birds, butterflies and flowers are the most popular choices because they've got nice lines.'

As soon as he said it, Maggie knew what she wanted.

'A magpie.'

Her father had always called her Mag-Pie. He meant it in the manner of 'Sweetie-Pie', as a term of endearment, with an emphasis on the first syllable. Maggie's feelings toward the nickname were complex. She could only ever think of the birds with their razor-sharp beaks, so studiously avoided by people who hated the whir of their wings or the sing-song call that signalled they were nearby and ready to swoop. It made a more fitting nickname than her father had ever intended.

'Right you are.' If it was an odd request, he didn't show it. He began setting his equipment up with assured movements as he asked, 'Where do you want it?'

'Oh. On my arm, I suppose.' It would be easy to hide it under her sleeve. She shrugged her suit jacket off, handing it to Charlotte. She unbuttoned the cuffs of her shirtwaist and slowly rolled the sleeves back, exposing the skin of her inner arm, as soft and unblemished as a newborn's.

'Oh! You don't have them there,' Charlotte blurted. She was

staring at Maggie's skin as though she'd never seen such a thing before. A small crease formed between her brows; her eyes flicked to Maggie's and her cheeks coloured, but she pushed up her chin stubbornly. 'The bumps,' she said, as if Maggie didn't know exactly what she was talking about.

'No.' What else was there to say? The tumours had tracked down her neck; three scattering on the right side of her chest, and another handful on her upper arms, but that was all. She'd reached an age where the rest of her skin, according to her doctor, would likely remain clear. Maggie had wasted many hours wishing it was the other way around; that the tumours were concentrated where they could be hidden beneath cotton sleeves and collars, leaving only a few blemishes on her face.

'Does it hurt?'

Maggie glanced at her arm, stretched out and looking strangely vulnerable against the dark wood of the table as Fred Harris cleaned her skin.

'He hasn't started yet.'

'Not that. I mean ...' Charlotte gestured to her own faultless face.

Maggie was startled. No one had ever thought to ask her that before. Her lips began to pout, ready to be annoyed, but then something inside her let go. It was a relief, in a way, to have someone ask her so directly about her condition. It was the scurrying glances, the whispers behind raised hands, the disgust when they thought she was out of earshot, that truly bothered her.

'No, they don't hurt. Not physically, anyway.' Maggie hadn't intended to say the second part. She wondered if Charlotte understood what she meant.

'Will you die from them?' Charlotte wasn't dancing anymore. She'd taken her toque off and was clutching it in her hands, Maggie's jacket having fallen to the floor unnoticed. Her wispy mounds of hair framed the expression of concern on her delicate features, and Maggie experienced a strange sensation in her chest.

If she hadn't known better, she might have thought the tattooist had started inking her there.

'The doctors don't think so,' she said softly. It was almost as though she were reassuring Charlotte.

'I'm ready to start now,' Fred Harris said. His face was a mask of blank professionalism. Maggie gave him a nod. The electric machine started up, a strange buzzing sound making the room vibrate with energy. Three sets of eyes followed the needle's point as it moved toward Maggie's soft, exposed skin.

'Wait!' Maggie cried. The point had just touched her, nothing more than a mosquito bite of pain.

The tattooist pulled back sharply, his eyes going to hers, his hand wavering in midair.

'Changed your mind?'

'Not about getting it.' Maggie was no longer nervous. She wanted this tattoo, wanted her magpie to carry about with her always. 'But I want it here instead.' She patted her chest, above her heart. 'Can you do that?'

'Certainly. But you've got a black dot on your arm already that'll never go away.'

Maggie looked down at the little freckle of ink.

'Doesn't matter.'

Charlotte helped her unbutton her shirtwaist, marvelling at Maggie's daring in removing her clothing in front of a strange man.

'At least let me hold your jacket across to protect your modesty, Mags.'

'He can hardly tattoo my chest without seeing me in some state of undress.' Even as she pointed this out, Maggie couldn't help feeling gratitude to the tightrope walker for her show of consideration. Charlotte stepped aside, and Maggie pulled down the short, frilled sleeve of her chemise, exposing flesh no one else had ever seen, not since she was a child. The tattooist's eyes flicked to the few tumours visible beneath her right collarbone, but he didn't flinch.

It was faster than Maggie expected. It hurt, but that too was different from what she'd thought it would be. The pain felt like a test, a trial to be overcome, and she took a strange kind of pleasure in withstanding it.

Then her magpie was done, and she was standing up so Charlotte could take the seat. She examined her new bird with fingers that hovered just above the tender skin. It was with a warm glow that she slipped her arms back into her shirtwaist sleeves.

'My turn,' Charlotte chirruped, her feet pattering the floor like the tap dancers they'd seen earlier. Fred Harris narrowed his eyes at her.

'You been on the turps?'

'Not at all. Well, all right, I had one glass of wine after tea, but that's hardly drinking now, is it?'

She lied with such steady, unblinking confidence that Maggie almost believed her. The tattooist studied her for a minute, then gave a nod.

'What'll it be for you?'

'I like Maggie's magpie. I'll have one of those too.'

'No!'

Maggie's voice was so loud they all jumped. Charlotte pouted, hurt drawing her eyebrows together, and Maggie's heart raced; she didn't want to upset her, not now, not after this day and night so full of fun and something akin to intimacy. But the magpie was hers. It didn't feel right to share it.

'I mean ...' She cast around, looking for the right thing to say to fix the moment. 'You should get a bird, so we match. But it should be a different bird. Something beautiful, like you.'

Charlotte's face softened. 'What then? A peacock?'

'Too ostentatious. What about a rainbow lorikeet?'

'Not going to look so nice without its colour, is it?'

'I suppose not. How about ... a lyrebird?' Lyrebirds were not only beautiful; they were natural-born performers who couldn't help commanding attention and admiration.

Charlotte drew in a pleased breath. 'A lyrebird,' she said slowly, nodding. She turned to the tattooist. 'Can you do that? With the long, curled tail feathers?'

'Want me to sketch it out on paper for you first?' He hadn't made Maggie the same offer, but she didn't care. She cupped her hand over her tattoo, gently throbbing beneath the linen of her shirtwaist.

'You'll have a lyrebird, and I'll have my magpie,' Maggie said, her voice a satisfied whisper. 'That way we're the same, but different.'

Chapter Eight

Maggie woke later than intended. She hadn't heard the dawn shifting about of boots and hooves as the animals were fed, which was usually enough to rouse her. She supposed she had last night's beers to thank for that, and for the dry, sour state of her mouth. She sat up, sunlight forcing its way between her eyelashes and making her squint, and ran her fingers through her loose hair. Her heart pinged like a fingernail flicked against the string of an instrument. Today was the day they were officially a travelling circus again.

She made herself sit and unpick the bigger of the knots her fingers had caught on, allowing her heavy eyelids to lighten and the slight swimming of her head to fade. She dressed quickly, careful not to touch the raw skin where her newly drawn magpie was. As she pinned her hair on top of her head, she thought about last night and grinned.

Charlotte, for all her enthusiasm and bravado, had not handled her tattoo nearly as well as Maggie. She'd pulled up her skirt, undone the nickelled brass fastenings and rubber buttons of her stocking supporters and exposed the flesh of her bare thigh. When Fred Harris began his work, Charlotte's smiling lips had compressed into a tight line. The tattooist kept asking if she was all right, and she nodded again and again, but by the time her lyrebird was done she had tears streaming down her face. She was laughing, though, ridiculing herself for being so weak compared to Maggie. Then they'd stumbled back home, Charlotte with one arm around Maggie's waist, like a character from one of Maggie's schoolgirl books, her free hand holding her heavy skirts away from her leg so they wouldn't brush the freshly needled skin. She'd tucked her stocking supporters into her corset to keep them out of the way, and complained the whole way about her left stocking being pooled around her ankle.

Maggie's hand hovered over the place where her tattoo was covered by her blouse—a travel-suitable brown, so dark it was almost black, matching her skirt. Her lips danced in a way they hadn't in a long time. The world felt new today. Her stomach gave an indelicate rumble, and she decided to go straight to the cook, Rosemary, for her breakfast. She was married to Adlai, an equestrian who clothed himself in a wig, stockings and short dress to make the other half of the 'Steeplechase Sisters'. Audiences hadn't noticed the sisters changed every few years, nor that one performed as a male clown in an earlier act.

Rosemary had her hands full with her husband and a brood of children, but her meals were always on time. She'd already have made breakfast for the circus hands, but the performers ate later, so there'd still be plenty of food. Maggie passed the open-topped baggage wagon, already harnessed to the workhorses, and skirted around a covered wagon whose sides had been freshly painted with the circus's name in bright colours. Beneath the odour of paint, the scent of brewing tea and johnny-cakes was just reaching her nose and making making her suck in her cheeks with hunger, when she saw movement which she instantly recognised as not belonging to the circus.

It was the suit that made him stand out—so neatly pressed, readying the wearer for a day that clearly did not involve physical labour. Then she recognised him: it was the man she'd seen talking to Charlotte yesterday, wearing the same felt bowler he'd twirled in his hands as they spoke. His eyes skipped over the quiet activity around him, searching. Maggie remembered Charlotte's barely disguised desire to get away from this man. She turned toward him.

'Looking for someone?' The man gasped as his eyes landed on her face. He took a step back, one hand going to his chest.

'Oh. Um, yes. I know it's appallingly early, but I wasn't sure when you'd all be leaving, and I didn't want to miss the opportunity to give her ...' He flapped an envelope in the air. Tilting her head, Maggie read Charlotte's name on the envelope. She couldn't help but pity this man for his hopeless, and obviously unrequited, love for the tightrope walker.

'I'm afraid you've already missed her,' she lied. At his crestfallen expression, compassion weakened her resolve. 'I can take the letter for you, though. I'll be catching up to her at our next stop. I'd tell you where that is, but we won't know until we're on the road. It depends on where we find grass for the horses, you see.'

The man's ribcage swelled, as though hope were filling him up. Maggie had an absurd image of him taking off and floating away, a human version of the Airem Scarem at Wonderland City. She had to press her lips together to stop herself giggling.

'Would you?' he asked. 'Only she was so kind to me, and is so lovely, and I felt we... well, we understood each other. I came to say goodbye to her yesterday—I've watched the show every year, you know, and must have seen her nearly a hundred times by now—sad business about the elephants. I don't know why I didn't think of it before, but last night I realised it needn't be goodbye—we could write to one another. I suppose that might be difficult, if you never know where you're going to stop ...' He trailed off, briefly uncertain. 'But you said you'd know once you're on the road. She could send me a letter from each town, letting me know where you'll stop next, and I can send letters to her at the post office there. Don't you think she'd like that?' His eyes were slightly averted to the left of Maggie throughout this babble. It made Maggie tired, and less inclined to suffer his sincere devotion to Charlotte.

'Oh, I'm sure she'd be just overwhelmed,' she said. Maggie took the letter from him, having to renew her promise that it would be delivered to Charlotte three more times before the man finally left. She stuffed the envelope in the waistband of her skirt—what she wouldn't give for pockets like the men had—then finally set out to have her breakfast and help the circus finish readying for their eight o'clock departure.

Satiated with eggs and toast, Maggie was just checking the reins of a workhorse harnessed to a covered wagon when she heard a familiar laugh. She turned to see Charlotte, her puffs of hair looking decidedly lopsided, but her smile ready as she accepted a steaming pannikin of tea from Rosemary. There was a small crowd around her, made up of those who hadn't volunteered to go out with her the previous day, now wanting to find out what she'd got up to. Maggie patted the horse's neck, its mane coarse beneath her fingers, then wiped her palms down her skirt. She walked toward the group, unsteady fingers pulling the envelope from her waistband, her heart performing a nervous skitter at so many being there to hear her speak. She reminded herself it was Charlotte she was there to talk to. The rest of them didn't matter.

'Wonderland City,' Charlotte was saying, her lips puckering as she blew on her tea to cool it. Maggie thought she might have tinted them even though they weren't performing. 'It was a riot. You should be sorry you missed it.'

'What we really want to know is what happened with *her*,' said Itsuo. His faint accent had a quality like rustling paper, softer than Smith's rolling burr or the yawning vowels and half-dropped consonants of those who grew up in Australia. Maggie knew instantly he was talking about her, and she faltered.

'Who?' Charlotte asked.

'You know ...' Greta wheedled. Judge was sitting on her lap, and her hand stroked the short fur of his back in time with her words. 'The Lagoon Creature.'

Charlotte choked on her tea, slopping some of it over her fingers. It reminded Maggie of the way the beer had spilled the night before, how Charlotte had licked the foam from her fingers.

'The Lagoon Creature?' Charlotte said in an incredulous voice. 'What are you talking about? I would never.'

'But you did!' said Itsuo. 'We all saw. She so rarely speaks to any of us, and we want to know—'

'Liar!' Charlotte's lips were curving up, as if she'd just heard a joke she found only slightly amusing.

Annie, a contortionist, crossed her arms, frowning. 'The pair of you walked out of the circus grounds together,' she said.

'Then she must have followed me. I'd hardly have just linked arms with her and—'

Itsuo nudged Charlotte, interrupting her. He'd just seen Maggie standing there, listening. As Charlotte turned to look at her, Maggie half-expected to see guilt within her eyes, or at least haughty defiance. But there was nothing, just the blank stare of a stranger. Maggie's chest rose and fell so rapidly she felt as if her magpie were about to take flight. It hurt—the skin burning from the damage of the needle, and something else more difficult to put into words.

'Good morning, Maggie,' Itsuo said politely. 'Letter for one of us?'

They were all going to pretend they didn't know Maggie had overheard them. She looked at her hand, stretched before her with the envelope in it. Her fingers closed hard, crumpling it.

'No. For me. Letter from my father.' The words had to be pushed through gritted teeth. Maggie turned, the heel of her boot creating a divot in the ground as though one of the tent pegs had been planted there. She stalked off, balling the hand that still held the envelope into a fist against her chest, increasing the pain of her tattoo by pressing on it. She heard someone behind her say, 'I didn't know she had a father.'

Of course they didn't know. No one had ever asked. And no one would ever think to. Because monsters didn't have fathers. And that's all she'd ever be to them. A monster. A freak. The Lagoon Creature.

Chapter Nine

Charlotte watched the Lagoon Creature—Maggie—stalk off. She had the unmistakable feeling she'd done something wrong, but she wasn't quite sure what. Of course it had been unkind to talk about her within earshot, but Maggie had such a quiet footfall it was impossible to know she was near. She seemed to scurry about the circus, everywhere and nowhere at once.

Charlotte turned back to the others, but she could no longer make sense of the words that were being tossed around like Itsuo's juggling pins. She looked down at the muddy-coloured water in her pannikin; it tasted of nothing. She needed to add some spice to it, to bring herself back to life. Without waiting for a pause in the conversation, she excused herself and went to the baggage wagon to find her pouch-shaped dorothy bag. Checking no one was watching, she pulled out a flask made half of sterling silver, half of glass covered in crocodile skin. She flipped the hinged top back, tipped a good slug of low-quality rum into her tea, then stuffed the flask back in the bag. Instead of putting it back in the wagon, she slipped her wrist through the bag's short drawstring. Best to keep it close when they were on the road.

Charlotte leaned back against the side of the wagon and took a sip of her tea. She closed her eyes as she let out a long breath. Much better. Her left hand fell against her thigh, and she winced.

What on earth had happened the day before?

She had woken that morning with a burning pain on the front of her leg. At first she thought she must have scraped up against the corner of a wagon. But when she'd lifted her skirts to inspect the damage, she'd instead seen a black, curling image of a lyrebird and sworn softly in confusion. She had no memory of getting it. *Why a lyrebird?* she wondered. It wasn't the strangest thing Charlotte had ever woken up to discover she'd done, but it was the most permanent.

She sighed, upending the pannikin so that she caught the very last dregs on her tongue. She knew she had been to Wonderland City. She could see in her mind's eye the colourful lights when it turned to Fairy City, feel the thrill of air rushing past her face on some of the rides. Everything else was a bit of a blur. But she'd been alone. Of that, she was certain. For there was only one person who had ever been game to get up to the kind of mischief she enjoyed. One person she wanted to spend her hours with. One person she both fiercely loved and fiercely hated, in equal measure.

So why did the other performers insist she had gone out with Maggie? They'd known each other as children, of course, but they had barely spoken a few dozen sentences to each other back then. They hardly spoke now—there was no reason to—and they certainly hadn't spoken yesterday.

It seemed strange now, but she'd been jealous of Maggie when they were small. Charlotte was something of an anomaly. Not because she was a stray—giving illegitimate children to a circus was common enough practice—but because her parents sent generous sums to Rafferty for her upkeep, including the best dresses and any little trinket her heart desired. Thanks to this generosity, Charlotte had always known she had parents somewhere out there, if not where or who they were. Maggie had joined the circus under very different circumstances. She'd been old enough to have memories of a time before it, and was granted a long goodbye—not to mention several visits over the years—from a man whose face always became wet with tears at his departure. Charlotte was never able to pout or wheedle her way into the one thing she really wanted above all else: to be with the mysterious family who still provided for her, the way Maggie got to be with her father.

After seven years with the circus, she'd finally got her wish: her parents, married now and with a baby daughter who hadn't needed to be hidden away, used an intermediary to bring Charlotte home. But by then it was too late. Charlotte found she didn't fit into the strange new life she'd always longed for. She missed the excitement and variety of the circus, the smell of sawdust and the feel of the narrow boards beneath her bare feet as she tested her impeccable balance, driving herself on to greater and greater feats. She missed sitting on the grass while learning her lessons during the spring and summer months. She'd never enjoyed going to a regular school in winter, and the confines of her new classroom was equally stifling, the separation of girls from boys unfamiliar. She often found herself in trouble for things that she didn't know were wrong in the first place.

But it was pretending to be adopted to cover her sudden appearance in the family that most curdled her insides. Adoption was common enough, and she understood the need for the lie—an illegitimate child was a terrible thing in those days, and in her parents' circles—but it made Charlotte feel the outsider. It were as though Alma, Jakob and Elisabeth were one unit that she was only tangentially attached to, not really a part of. Every room in the house she now lived in taunted her with the knowledge that her toddling little sister, Elisabeth, grabbed at things with confident hands because she was growing up knowing no other walls or roof or floors. Resentment became a stony flint sending off sparks inside her. Unable to express her hurt, she chose instead to pinch Elisabeth's soft flesh when no one was looking and refused to obey the rules that made no sense to her. Perhaps she was testing her mother and father, pushing and pushing to see how much it would take before they sent her back to the circus, where she belonged.

And then Will came into her life—a neighbour boy who seemed to share in her impulse to shake the world from its hinges, but in a way that made him laugh instead of rage. He smoothed Charlotte's hard edges, turned her desire to push back and poke at people into an urge to take part in pranks at their expense instead.

Will had saved her.

And then he'd ruined her.

Charlotte sighed. What time was it? The commissariat wagon, guided by the new tracker Nev, would be setting off soon—it was always the first to depart, with the cook also on board so she had time to prepare dinner or tea before the rest caught up. She headed off to find Rosemary, to return the pannikin. Soon it would be all hustle and bustle as each of the ten or so wagons left one after the other, two-hundred-yard gaps between them so they wouldn't choke on the dust thrown up by the wagon in front. Best get ready, Charlotte thought, if she wanted a seat on her preferred wagon.

Perhaps by the time it set out, she might remember some of the night before.

Chapter Ten

Maggie took her sandwich with a quiet thanks and wandered away from the others. They'd travelled near four hours before stopping for midday dinner. There were still enough buildings and shops around them for Rafferty and the higher-ranking performers to buy themselves a hot meal, while the rest made do with egg-and-lettuce sandwiches assembled by Rosemary. Once they'd left Sydney and hit the bush, Rosemary would cook proper dinners, but for now she didn't want the trouble of lighting a fire.

Maggie leaned on the rump of one of the donkeys as she ate. His long, pointed ears twitched and his tail flicked, keeping the blowflies at bay, and she was grateful for his efforts. Glancing sideways to ensure no one was watching, she pulled her old copy of *Seven Little Australians* out of her leather bag, then slipped the sealed envelope meant for Charlotte from where it had been hidden between the pages.

Each footfall of the horses' hooves on the road had felt like a ringing accusation: *how could you have dared believe she wanted you as a friend? What kind of world do you think you're living in? Don't you know better by now?*

Maggie had accepted each question, knowing the truth of them, hardening herself with a barrage of internal words that were crueller than any other person could throw at her.

She heard a small, soft noise and lowered both book and envelope to see Judge sitting at her feet, the very tip of his tail moving, his eyes intent on her sandwich.

'Oh, so that's how to get some company around here, is it?' she asked. She'd noticed Nev laughing with two gear men as they ate; new to the circus, and he already had more friends than she. Finishing off most of her sandwich, she threw the last crust to Judge, who caught it midair and swallowed without chewing. Not bothering to wipe the crumbs from her fingers, she tore open the envelope.

Maggie was glad she hadn't read it while eating, for she might have choked on her sandwich. It was full of the kind of sentiment that would make most sensible bellies turn. There was something so pitiable in seeing this man shower compliments on a woman who didn't care for him at all—who didn't care for anyone except herself. Maggie had done him a service by not delivering the letter. Charlotte probably wouldn't have replied anyway, throwing it on top of a pile of similar letters that she simply accepted as her due. Maggie seethed at the thought. The man might be tiresome, but he was harmless, his garrulous tendencies coming from unbridled enthusiasm and admiration. If it were her letter, she would respond. She would take as much care and time as the man had. It was only fair. If it were her letter...

Maggie looked down at the paper in her hand, neatly lined with curling ink. It was her letter. She hadn't delivered it to Charlotte, and Charlotte's eyes hadn't taken in the message. But Maggie's had.

What if she *were* to respond to it?

Maggie shook her head, telling herself she was being ridiculous. She opened her book, meaning to put the letter back between its pages, then paused. She'd spent so much of her life escaping into the written word of authors like Ethel Turner. Could she possibly create a believable story with written words herself? This man wanted the glittering, glamorous tightrope walker to respond to him. But he would never see which hand it was that wielded the pen …

Maggie peered over the donkey's back. The circus hands and performers were enjoying their hour-long break before they went on the road again. Her eyes darted from face to face, looking for red hair and pretty, freckled features. She couldn't see Charlotte anywhere. Perhaps she was catching some extra sleep after their late night. The night Charlotte denied sharing.

Maggie plunged her hand into her bag, pulled out her fountain pen and tugged off its cap, then tore out one of the blank end pages from her book. She put the nib to the paper—thankful it was one of the new kind that didn't blot if you paused too long—then scribbled, *Dear Mr O'Lehry*. She hesitated, thinking. How would Charlotte respond, if she were the person this man wanted her to be? The person Maggie herself had believed her to be only the day before?

I thank you for your kind letter, sir, and gratefully accept your invitation of correspondence. How pleasurable it will be to have someone to share the sights encountered on the long journey ahead. It has been quite some time since I travelled with the circus, but I recollect how the days can seem endless, and the uncertainty— well, perhaps frightening isn't the right word, but it is something akin to that. Knowing I'll have letters from you awaiting me at each new town will make any difficulties easier to bear.

So please, Mr O'Lehry, tell me everything about yourself, to ease my weary and bored hours. Remind me of everything we've already spoken of, and tell me things that are new. Speak to me of what is happening in Sydney, for I will miss it. And in return, I will share with you tales of the country and life in a travelling circus.

> *Until the next time,*
> *Your grateful friend,*
> *Charlotte Voigt*

Maggie perused the words she had written. Was it too much? Had touches of herself seeped in, despite her best efforts?

She supposed it didn't matter. Mr O'Lehry would be so thrilled to receive a letter from his beloved that he wouldn't pause to question its tone, nor why she'd asked him to remind her of their previous conversations. Maggie thought this last a clever bit of trickery; it would prevent her from making any mistakes or contradicting something Charlotte might have said earlier.

She waited for the ink to dry, then folded the letter in half. She glanced at the sun, so high above them, then at the circus hands. They were beginning to pack up, preparing to set off again. She'd need to be quick.

She looked around until she found the ringmaster and hurried over to him. 'Rafferty, do you have an envelope?' she asked, almost breathless with the thrill of the deception she was carrying out.

'Let me see if I can find one for you.'

Rafferty rummaged through the baggage wagon while Maggie tried not to let her impatience show. He pulled an envelope out of a leather case and held it out for her. When her fingertips closed on it, he didn't let go.

'Everything fine with you, Maggie girl?' His eyes were shaded by the straw boater he wore, but Maggie could see the crease between his brows nevertheless. She let her face go blank. That was one good thing about the way she looked: it acted like a mask that was difficult for most people to read. Rafferty was the best at it, but even he could be fooled.

'Of course. I just realised I hadn't written to my father about leaving Sydney. I suppose he deserves to know. Particularly as we're headed in his direction.'

Rafferty's face relaxed. 'I'm glad of it.'

'Actually, you wouldn't have any writing paper to spare, would you? I might start writing to him regularly. See if I can't patch things up a bit.'

Seeing the pleasure on Rafferty's face made her feel guilty, but she had to lie to give herself cover should Mr O'Lehry respond and she was seen both writing and receiving letters.

'Get your letter off quick, before we set out again,' Rafferty said, 'and I'll bring you the paper and more envelopes tonight when we set up camp.'

'Thank you.' Maggie didn't stay to let her guilt compound; she raced off to find the nearest postbox.

And then it was done.

All she had to do now was wait to see if this man would believe the lie. If he would allow her the chance to become Charlotte.

Chapter Eleven

As the gaps between buildings became wider and wider, and the few macadamised roads disappeared behind them, Maggie had a sense of the world opening up around her. They weren't exactly beyond the black stump yet, but with Nev's calls to keep an eye out for feral pigs, which were apparently rare but not unheard of in this area, it was beginning to feel close to it. Either side of the rough dirt road, long tufts of grass bent away, pushed back by wheels and by the horses, donkeys and camels who had traversed it over the years. Speckles of yellow so pale it was almost white, like churned butter, gave a dusting of colour every now and then. Beyond, a tangle of scrubby trees—some spindly, some full-leafed, some showing a flash of bright red at the tips of their leaves—piled one on top of another, looking as if they were crowding to see the sky first.

Maggie had found herself a perch on the back of a jinker. The low-wheeled cart was made for haulage, not passengers, and she was sitting uncomfortably on the back edge, her head bobbing with the uneven motion. She watched the steady billowing of the cloud of dust they created behind them. Sometimes it cleared enough for her to make out the horses pulling the next wagon, but not often.

A niggling, scratching sensation between her shoulder blades made her squirm. The letter she'd posted in Sydney had been reproaching her across the miles they had travelled since then. To distract herself, Maggie pressed her fingertips against her healing tattoo, the pain a kind of punishment that was smaller than she deserved. For the truth was, even though she knew what she'd done was wrong, she wouldn't change her actions even if she could. The tingle of anticipation as she thought ahead to the letters she might find at each new post office, waiting for her—or at least a version of her, hidden behind Charlotte's name—was too intoxicating. The only thing that gave her slight pause was the dawning realisation that this aberration of bad behaviour meant she'd suddenly taken after her father. Maggie had admonished him again and again for indulging his own whims instead of doing what was right. And now here she was, doing the same thing.

Maggie sighed and pressed her tattoo harder.

As they continued on, the trees around them became jacketed in black bark. Maggie wondered if fire had ravaged this place, bringing both destruction and regeneration. It was something they'd have to be wary of, but not today. Above, the grey smear of sky appeared to be hanging so low she could almost touch it. They'd be in Bowral soon, and Rafferty was already fretting about arriving without prior billing. He'd hurriedly printed new posters in Sydney, but there'd been no time for the newly hired advance agent to get ahead of them yet. They called it 'bouncing the town', turning up without having drummed up any publicity first, and it was something any good circus tried to avoid. Rain would only make matters worse, for it would keep people inside come showtime.

Maggie had reminded Rafferty that, while undesirable, if they were going to bounce any town, Bowral was the place for it. Bowral was where men who'd made their fortunes in Sydney established their second homes—homes filled with people who had access to Sydney's menageries, carnivals, vaudeville and marionette shows, phrenologists, visiting ballets, movie houses and beaches. They wouldn't be drawn by the promise of music, animals and acrobats anyway. It was only further out, where there were no big cities nearby to offer such a variety of amusements, that people would come in droves, sometimes from a day or more away, to see the circus.

For this reason, Rafferty didn't bother with a parade when they reached Bowral. The first drops of rain were beginning to fall, and Maggie jumped off the edge of the still-moving jinker. The wide-brimmed straw hat she'd worn to keep the sun off her face gave her some protection from the drizzle, and she headed toward the wagon which carried pieces of the big top. They would be erecting it for the higher-ranking performers and Rafferty to sleep in. The tiered seating and lights weren't going up; Rafferty told them to set up the tents as quickly as they could and leave everything else for the following day.

With deft hands, Maggie helped the gear men tie the ropes to the pegs hammered into the softening ground, checking that they were taut and not likely to come undone. The rain was somehow getting beneath the brim of her hat, and Maggie wiped her forehead on the sleeve of her jacket. She wasn't sure if she made it drier or more damp. Wet dirt—not quite mud yet—stuck to her boots; give it much longer and her skirt would be weighed down by it.

The tent erect, she grabbed half a packet of Arnott's biscuits from the small tent Rosemary shared with Adlai and their children. Some of the circus folk might venture into the town's shops to find hot sausages with gravy and bread for their tea, but Maggie wouldn't be one of them. She searched out the baggage wagon, then bent over and quickly ran her hands over the hem of her skirt, checking for the prickly little bindi-eyes that had a propensity to catch there. None found, she undid the side buttons on the ankles of her tan and beige calfskin boots, pulled them off and kicked them underneath the wagon. Then she undid the single oversize button of her jacket, took it off and pushed it between the spokes of the large wagon wheel.

Making sure no one was watching—they were all too busy ducking for cover of their own—Maggie untucked her shirtwaist and undid as many buttons as it took to reach inside and loosen the fastenings of her corset. When she felt the boning give and her ribs spread apart, she snatched the rolled-up wool blanket she'd stashed down the side of the baggage wagon and gave it the quickest of shakes. With one hand, she pulled out her hatpin and tossed her hat carelessly on top of the jumble of cases and trunks in the wagon. Crouching, she slipped off her shirtwaist, snatched her jacket from the wheel spokes, then got down on her hands and knees and crawled under the wagon, pushing the blanket before her.

It took some contorting to get the blanket underneath her, then some more to roll over onto her back. She had to shimmy out of her skirt, which was easy enough, as was undoing and removing her stocking supporters beneath her chemise—she had the crossover kind, with suspender tabs that went from the outside of her knees to the bottom of her corset, a modern extravagance no one would ever suspect of her. It had given Maggie quite the thrill to order them. As she brought her knees to her chest to roll down her stockings—damp from standing a minute without her boots on—she wondered what Mr O'Lehry would think if she told him about the supporters. The very thought made her laugh aloud.

Bundling her jacket up, Maggie propped it behind her head for a makeshift pillow. Her shirtwaist she draped across her now-bare feet to keep them warm. Then, finally, she relaxed, letting the tension of the day leave her muscles. It was a comfortable set-up she had. The damp couldn't penetrate the blanket, she was kept dry by the wagon above her, and the now-steady drip of the rain outside her little shelter brought the earth to life with a rich scent that made Maggie feel as though she'd only just discovered fresh air for the first time. She breathed it in, listening to the throaty warbling of frogs excited by the downpour.

Maggie had stopped sleeping in the big top when she was twelve, the night she'd overheard someone—to this day, she still didn't know who—expressing disgust at the way her neck was beginning to form one solid shape with her jaw. She had taken her meagre belongings and moved outside. Rafferty had tried to coax her back in but was never successful. The children of the grooms and circus hands curled up next to the foals to keep themselves warm while they slept outside, but Maggie didn't join them. She had learned her lesson. She wasn't going to stay where she wasn't wanted.

Some of the crew, like the tent boss, had small one- or two-man tents of their own. Not Maggie. The undersides of wagons had become a familiar and comfortable ceiling for her to gaze at—and when the weather was good, the stars made a breathtaking canopy above. Many nights she had reached out and tried to grab them as she rolled over, wanting to cloak herself in them, as though they were a comforting blanket stitched together on a navy background just for her. In those moments, she'd understood the scale of the world around her, and considered running away to live somewhere open and free. But she knew she never could. She didn't know the land the way trackers did, didn't know how to read it and live off it. She would eventually find herself wandering back to a town or a city for supplies and shelter, and then what?

She lay staring at the dirt and flecks of grass spattered across the underneath of the baggage wagon. There was a spider near her head, but it was only a daddy-long-legs and wouldn't come near so long as she didn't bother it. She decided she'd give the underside of the wagon a clean in the morning. It would only get dirty again once they left Bowral and journeyed on, but what did that matter? She could take pride in making things nice, even if no one else saw them. Just like her undergarments.

Maggie shifted onto her side, curling one arm beneath her

bundled jacket. Perhaps she could tell Mr O'Lehry about the wagon's clean undercarriage. Could she do it without revealing her real identity, though? It would be tricky. Women like Charlotte didn't do menial labour. But as her eyelids drooped and her breathing slowed, Maggie thought she might try to find a way. Nights under a wagon could be lonely, but not if you had a friend to share the details with.

Chapter Twelve

Charlotte stood in the porch—the main entrance of the big top—watching as a hatless and stocking-footed Maggie, bent double, half-undressed herself in the rain, then crawled beneath the baggage wagon. Charlotte's stomach was paining her. Was it exhaustion from the day's travels, or something else? Something akin to guilt?

Perhaps. For three days now, as they'd travelled from Sydney to Bowral, she'd felt the other woman's eyes on her every time they stopped for dinner or to make camp. Mostly she tried to ignore it, but every now and then she turned to catch Maggie in the act of staring at her. A second later, she'd be looking up at the sky, or down at a book, or busying herself with some task. It unsettled Charlotte, made her wonder if she was imagining things.

She shook herself, then slid out from the porch into the darkness, moving quietly around the tent's perimeter. The big top glowed a gentle, blue-tinged white; night had fallen quickly, hastened by the rain. Any other time, the men would have put out a table and chairs, sitting in clusters to drink from glass bottles of beer bought from the town publican and kept in a tin tub at their feet, and Charlotte would have tried her luck in stealing one or two. The men found it a real laugh whenever a woman wanted to join in their drinking—or they had, right up until they realised she could outdrink any of them, and they no longer wanted to share. But the rain had sent them all reaching for shelter and an early sleep.

All except Charlotte.

She knew her hair would be a bedraggled mess, and her clothes would be damp for the next few days, but Charlotte didn't want to take an umbrella with her. She didn't want to attract any attention. Keeping her weight on the balls of her toes so that the heels of her boots wouldn't make any noise, she silently moved out of and away from the circus.

She breathed deeply when the tent and wagons were far enough behind her to be out of sight. She bent down to hike up her skirt and pull out the flask she'd secreted in her stocking holder. She'd had to wear only one stocking—the tattoo was still smarting too much to wear both holders. She squinted at the dim outline of the lyrebird, shaking her head at the peeling skin before dropping her skirt and straightening back up. What had she been thinking?

Snippets of that lost day and night had been coming back to her. Charlotte was having a hard time admitting it to herself, but she thought the others might be right, that she hadn't been alone. She could remember a presence—a woman, she thought—whose elbows she'd held when they'd rollerskated at Wonderland City.

Could it have been Maggie?

No one else had owned up to it. Still, Charlotte couldn't shake the idea that they were playing some elaborate joke on her.

She thumbed open the cap of her flask. She'd have to make sure she found somewhere to top up her supplies in the next few days. Who knew how many of the towns they passed through would be big enough for her to buy liquor without being questioned.

She tilted the flask back, swallowing one mouthful, then letting the second sit on her tongue for a long moment as rain spattered her face. The guilt she was experiencing made her uncomfortable.

It made her think of her sister. She had to remind herself Elisabeth was the one who had the most to feel guilty about.

Charlotte drummed her fingertips lightly on the brown crocodile skin of her flask, staring about her aimlessly. Bowral was a place of rich greenery, turning everything around her to shades of inky navy under the faint sliver of moon that was nearly eclipsed by the rain. Large trees were dotted with half-unfurled leaves and tiny buds on their otherwise naked branches, signalling that spring was still only awakening. Those bare branches made Charlotte realise she was cold. She'd been so eager to escape to her flask that she'd forgotten to put on the machine-knitted coat she liked for warmth. She wasn't ready to turn back, though. Her thoughts were caught up in memories of her sister, and if she went to sleep with those in her mind she'd have nightmares. She needed to drink some more first.

There'd once been a time when Charlotte had thought she and Elisabeth might become friends. At the tender age of six, her little sister had shown a defiance Charlotte couldn't help but admire. Charlotte and Will had determined, for their latest piece of mischief, to sneak onto the construction site of Adelaide's Happy Valley Reservoir. They'd heard about the works that had been going on for a few years, and often joked how fun it might be to find a way in and get an up-close view of the strange equipment that threw so much dust into the air it had forced the local school to relocate. At some stage it had stopped being a joke and became an actual plan.

Elisabeth tried to tag along, as she so often did. And as they often did, Charlotte and Will refused her company. Will reasoned with her that she should be content with the lesser adventures they let her join—fishing, eavesdropping on unaware adults, pinching passionfruit from the neighbour's vines. This adventure was a much bigger undertaking, the reservoir being a long distance from their home, and she was just too little to take part. They didn't know that Elisabeth had only pretended to go back to her room to play with her peg dolls. They didn't hear her small footsteps following in their wake; not until they were boarding the horse tram to Mitcham.

'What about the little one? Got a ticket for her?' the conductor asked them. That was when they'd turned to see Elisabeth, pulling a face and complaining that her feet were tired from the walk. Charlotte regarded her with appraising eyes. Perhaps they did have something in common after all.

Charlotte and Will quickly pooled their saved pocket money, trying to figure out if there was enough to cover tram tickets for all three of them. They couldn't just send Elisabeth back home on her own; she was too young, and would surely get lost.

'Rattle your dags, you lot,' the conductor said, blowing out his moustache. 'You're holding us all up.'

Everyone on board was staring, eyes wide and unabashedly curious, and Charlotte became flustered. She tried to count the money, Will doing the same thing at the same time, and coins went spilling from her hands. The conductor lifted his eyes heavenward.

'Right, that's it. I didn't come down in the last shower. If you ratbags think you're going to get a free ride, you've got another think coming.'

'No, sir,' Will started to say, but the conductor grabbed him by the ear, making him squeal. Not a single argument was listened to as he forced him off the tram. Charlotte followed, pulling the now-crying Elisabeth by her sticky hand.

Elisabeth's tears continued all the way home. When Charlotte yelled at her that it was Will who'd been hurt, not her, she only cried harder. She stopped when the familiarity of their neighbourhood surrounded them again, but the damage was done. Her eyes were red, her nose swollen and her cheeks splotchy with tear stains. When their parents demanded to know the cause, the whole story came tumbling out of her mouth. Charlotte found herself in trouble for Elisabeth's actions as well as her own. Alma said that, as the older of the two, it was her responsibility to know better. Jakob, her father, yelled that she could've got them both killed. He used his belt to make sure the message sank in.

Charlotte's brief admiration for Elisabeth's rebellion came to an end with her bottom smarting and tears soaking her pillow. Will later told her that not every adventure could be a triumph, but to Charlotte it was more than just a failed adventure. It was another reminder that it was Elisabeth whom her parents cherished. That Charlotte was a mistake that could never be made quite right.

It would be some years before Elisabeth succeeded in inserting herself into Charlotte and Will's fun again, but when she did, the damage would prove impossible to undo.

Chapter Thirteen

Thankfully, the rain eased enough for the crowds to come out the next day. Those who had seen the circus in Sydney grumbled audibly about the lack of elephants, which put the performers on edge. But others, particularly the children, who knew from the way their mothers had dressed them in their smart white dresses or short trouser suits that this was a special occasion, were more receptive. Rafferty disguised his jitters well, but they were there to see for those who knew to look for the signs. The way he tugged on the points of his waistcoat, and the size of the knot in his double-sided tie—small, as though it had been pulled tight more than once—told Maggie everything she needed to know. For herself, she played her part without any enthusiasm. She'd bribed the wood-and-water joey with a penny to go to the post office, but there'd been no letter for her. It was too soon, of course, but that didn't stop her feeling disappointed, and her usual Lagoon Creature leers had a twist of bitter disappointment to them.

The applause at the end of the show wasn't the kind they'd been used to with Ida and Hercules as their stars, but it was solid. When Maggie saw Rafferty rubbing his sleeve across his forehead, she knew it was relief that made him do it, not post-show sweat. He caught her eye, and the sullen weight that had been bunching her shoulders dissipated. His expression was one of such unfettered triumph, as though this small and semi-enthusiastic Bowral crowd was all the indication he needed to know they'd be a success on the road.

'Good enough for at least a couple more shows here, wouldn't you say?' Rafferty asked, coming up to her after the audience dissipated. Maggie was slouched on the bench seat of the baggage wagon, guarding it. She wasn't ready to sleep yet, the nervous energy of performance still zinging through her veins, but she didn't want one of the circus hands to pinch the wagon for his own use. She had a book in her lap, *Galahad Jones*, a tragicomic play by A.H. Adams, which the glow of the campfire illuminated just enough for her to read if she squinted.

Rafferty heaved the wicker suitcase he was carrying by a leather handle into the wagon, then climbed up to sit next to her. Maggie closed her book, watching a lost balloon drift along the ground, pushed by the breeze that had stirred as soon as the rain let up. She could see it had distracted Rafferty; he was probably thinking that he'd need to check the stock against the sales, to see if it had been lost by a loose-fingered child, or if the balloon salesman had been lax and let one escape.

'The night's takings were decent,' he finally said, as the balloon came to a bumping halt against the big top. His hand rested on the battered wicker suitcase. Maggie was the only other person in the circus who knew what that suitcase contained. If she were to open it, the first thing she'd find was a jumble of soiled women's undergarments. They weren't truly dirty, only made to look so, to disguise the precious thing beneath their folds of fabric. The thing which made the suitcase so heavy. The thing which Rafferty said was best hidden in plain sight, disguised as just another object the circus had to haul around, because then no one would ever think to look at it twice. An iron cashbox with brass handles, a brass lock and the British coat of arms on the lid. It had to be nearly a hundred years old, but Rafferty refused to update it, saying the creator of the lock, Joseph Bramah, had boasted his locks to be unpickable and tamper-proof. Rafferty said Bramah hadn't been proved wrong yet, so why change it? The brass key that fit the lock was on a long piece of calfskin cord that hung around Rafferty's neck.

'You ready and able to take up your old role again?'

'Just watching it? Or doing the figures too?'

'Both, if you'll have the job. The account book's in the case. It'll mean a little something extra in your pocket, of course. When we can afford it. You'll be able to decide when that is.'

Maggie nodded, considering. From childhood, she had shown an aptitude for figures. When the other children had played at one plus one equalling a window, she'd realised it made two. She liked knowing that with numbers, right was right and wrong was wrong, and no one could argue. Rafferty had seen that and taken her aside from the general lessons the other children participated in to tutor her privately, eventually introducing her to the circus's finances. She'd learned exactly how much everyone was paid at the beginning of each week, the sum increasing for those who excelled in more than one act, the first week of earnings held back against the fulfilment of their contracts. She'd watched him keep his meticulous account books—always an E.S. Wigg & Son one—detailing the circus's earnings and expenses for a full year. She was sure he made deliberate mistakes every now and then, wanting to see if she would catch them. She always did. And then one day he'd given her responsibility for them. He was still the one to unlock and lock the cashbox, but it was Maggie's head that did the calculations, her hand that inked the figures. He only ran his eye over them. When she'd proved herself reliable, Rafferty gave her the wicker suitcase, so that both figures and cash sat with Maggie.

When they'd set up in Sydney, Rafferty had shifted everything to a bank, and the staff there took care of matters. Maggie had been surprised by how much she missed the methodical adding and subtracting that seemed to set a slow, steady rhythm with her heartbeat. She missed the responsibility that came with it, too. It had made her feel like a someone. Like she was important.

Maggie shifted her book to one hand, resting the other next to Rafferty's on the wicker case, her fingers just short of touching his. His hand turned palm up, and she caught a glimpse of the calluses that lined his palms after years of gripping reins and bridles, tightly tethering ropes, lashing lights to king poles. They were a mark of Rafferty's past, and the man he was. They mirrored Maggie's own hands.

Rafferty didn't look at the case, and Maggie followed suit, keeping up the pretence that it was just another piece of luggage.

'What do you say, Maggie girl?'

'Happy as Larry to take care of it for you, boss.'

'That's a girl. Keep it quiet from the others, remember.'

'I always do.'

'And Maggie?'

'Yes?'

'I want you to be the one to fix up the butcher and baker at every town from now on.'

Maggie groaned. Obviously the accounts had to be settled before they left, but it was not a job she wanted.

'You know I dislike having to talk to the townspeople.' Maggie gestured at her face, not needing to say any more. His hand moved, closing the small gap between them.

'I know, Maggie girl. But someone has to do it, and you're the only one I trust not to get fleeced, or to pinch some coin off the top to get yourself a treat. You can wear your veil.'

It hardly made the prospect more appealing, but Maggie didn't want to let him down. She stifled a sigh before responding.

'You can count on me, Rafferty.'

'That's one thing that's always been true,' Rafferty said.

***

As they left the deep greens and sprawling homesteads of Bowral behind them, the countryside began to change. There was more space between the trees, as though they wanted room to breathe; several were tall and spindly, their grey branches so fine they looked like cobwebs, while short bushes were sprinkled with white blossoms, like snow-dusted mounds in this spring landscape. The grass either side of the dirt track was short, exposing dull patches of tightly compacted earth, but the occasional bright burst of an orange-yellow flower broke through the swathes of grey and sage green. Above, the sky was a canopy that seemed to stretch on forever.

Maggie was driving the baggage wagon. Apart from Nev, who always drove the commissariat wagon, they all took turns driving. There was a sense of pride in guiding the horse-drawn vehicles over the rough terrain, and it was rare for anyone to try to shirk their turn. Maggie liked driving; it allowed her to pretend that the reason no one spoke to her was that they were letting her concentrate.

Annie, the contortionist, was curled up in a tight ball at the other end of the bench seat, fast asleep. A little tuft from the profusion of brilliant red bottlebrush flowers Maggie had suddenly found herself driving through rested on Annie's upper lip, twitching with every exhalation. Between them sat two children, giggling as they watched it. They only took up the space of one adult. Maggie's palm tingled, wanting to feel the smallness of one of their hands in her own. She switched the reins to one hand and yanked out her hatpin with the other. The breeze caressing her face was cool, and she was going to enjoy the feel of the sun on her face before it became uncomfortably strong and she had to hide from it.

She threw her hat back on top of the piled-up baggage, then let the rhythmic motion and Annie's slight snoring lull her into a relaxed, almost trance-like state. As the children tried to spot echidnas—an impossible task, given the reclusive nature of the creatures and the fast pace of the wagon—she imagined being Mrs Allars from Lilian Turner's *Young Love*, the book she'd just finished the previous night. The character, despite dying on the second page of the book, still got to experience the glory of motherhood to two boys, one natural-born and one taken in. The fancy was broken by Rafferty shouting at the musicians to strike up a tune as they neared Moss Vale. She hurried to grab her discarded hat and jam it back on her head, pulling the veil down low.

The townspeople stopped what they were doing when the circus entered their streets, emerging from picket-fenced homesteads and places of business to watch the colourful and noisy spectacle. Many of them had likely travelled to nearby Bowral to see the show, which was why Rafferty had decided not to stop here. Maggie lifted the brim of her hat to see children waving energetically. Itsuo sprang from the still-moving wagon in front, feet barely meeting the ground before he turned three cartwheels followed by a flip-flap. He reached heights the other acrobats weren't quite able to achieve. Maggie had overheard him once telling Greta he must have a natural aptitude, for he hadn't begun learning until he was fifteen. His parents were frustrated by always finding him swinging from the branches of trees or attempting to vault over the pets of neighbours—it was difficult enough adapting to a new country without having an eccentric son. When he'd run away with a visiting circus, they'd coaxed him back home with promises that he could begin training. Maggie wondered if they'd known then that they would permanently lose him to the big top within two years.

Townspeople were pointing to Itsuo now, their astonished cries loud enough to be heard over the small band. Two other acrobats had joined him, and were flinging themselves into the air too, but they didn't command the same attention as the Japanese man. It was only when two women began to do flip-flaps, not minding how their skirts caught at their legs or their jackets restricted their arms, that the townspeople shifted their stares.

Eventually, those who cavorted raced to catch back up to the wagons and jump aboard. That too was part of the show, for Rafferty would never have left them behind.

Moss Vale was a small place—although larger than many they'd be seeing on this journey—and they passed through it quickly. Then nature was stretching out around them again, yawning expanses of fields under a washed-out sky. The scenery had changed again: here and there clusters of trees huddled like schoolchildren whispering about the passing circus. Some were thick and bulbous, while others reminded Maggie of Christmas trees.

When they stopped for their midday dinner, a steady symphony of cicadas kept them company. Maggie supposed it would be some time before they heard them again—if she remembered correctly, cicadas tended to swarm closer to the coastline. Even the children seemed to sense there was something significant about this moment and didn't raise their voices as they usually would or run about in excitement. Was it awe at finally being out here, truly on the road, leaving all that was familiar—even the sounds—behind them? Or was it simply the early morning catching up with them?

They spent two nights on the road. On the third day, when the wind picked up and whipped the horses' tails in all directions, causing everyone to lower their heads and try to hide their watering eyes beneath the brims of their hats, they came to a halt about half a mile outside of Goulburn.

'Tucker first, then you know what to do,' Rafferty called, clapping his hands as though obliterating a pesky mosquito. The very thought made Maggie shudder; as the weeks passed and summer came to meet them, that would be another thing they'd have to contend with.

They ate their meal, a slow buzz of anticipation building among them. The advance agent should have arrived in Goulburn days ago, which meant the town would be plastered with bills announcing them. Tonight's audience should be a good one.

Whatever water was left in their waterbags was poured down the sides of the wagons, washing the dirt from the red and gold lettering of the circus's name. It was important to look their best on first sighting. The gear men hooked small wooden stepladders onto the backs of the tallest wagons and climbed up to retouch the painted clown faces. Maggie checked the harness hames, but they didn't need to be repainted just yet, so she started to groom one of the finest horses, brushing away the sweat marks on its coat. Only the most impressive horses would be paraded in; the others would join them later, when there were no townspeople paying attention.

When she was done, Maggie put the brush away, then found a small tin, pried the lid off and used a rag to oil the horse's reins and collar until they gleamed in the afternoon sun. Nearby, the few musicians Rafferty had managed to retain were polishing their instruments, warming up their lips and releasing spit valves. The clowns practised jokes they would call to one another. Itsuo and Annie both stretched out their muscles, ridding their bodies of the creaks and cracks that came with the first movement after sitting for so long. They all worked as one, readying themselves to whet the appetites of spectators as they passed by and create enough of a frenzy that the local children would be granted a half-day holiday from school.

Maggie and Nev volunteered to stay behind and look after the workhorses. Maggie found a stump to sit on, her hand already reaching for a book, when she realised Nev was looking at her. He sat cross-legged on the ground, his back against a tree, hat in his lap.

'I don't think I know your name ...' he said. Maggie was surprised. Not that he didn't know her name, but that he was talking to her. Even so, there was a wariness in his eyes, and Maggie wondered if it was because she was white, or because she was the Lagoon Creature.

'Maggie,' she said uncertainly, slipping the book back into her bag. 'And your name's Nev?' She already knew this, of course, but didn't want to sound reproachful. She didn't need more people in the circus taking a set against her.

'It is now.' Nev must have seen the emerging question on Maggie's face, for he explained, 'White fellas gave me a baptism when they took me from my mum and dad. I've been Nev ever since.'

'You were taken from your parents?'

'Stolen.' There was a world of pain in that single word. Maggie knew nothing she could say in response would be right, or appropriate. For while she knew how it felt to be separated from one's parents, she'd never had the added agony of knowing that those she loved most were also suffering. Her father had given her away willingly, by choice.

Maggie wanted to ask him what his birth name was, but wasn't sure if it would be rude. Every time she'd found herself on the cusp of asking her father not to call her Mag-Pie, she'd shied away, for names—even nicknames—seemed to hold so much weight. Carefully, she ventured, 'I can call you by another name, if you would like.'

Nev closed his eyes, dappled shadows moving across his upturned cheeks. 'Nev is fine. It's easy.' He paused long enough that Maggie was just about to pick up her book once more, then said, 'Hear that song? That's a magpie. Marriyang, we call it in my language.'

The sound was a beautiful, warbling tune, a simplified version of something the circus band might play.

'I didn't know they could sound so musical,' Maggie said.

'One of the best songbirds there is. You know the babies are born blind and featherless?'

'Truly?'

Nev made a sound of assent. 'Most white fellas think magpies are mean, but they only swoop when they've got those young ones to protect.'

By the time a circus hand was sent to tell them the parade had ended and the public had dispersed back to their regular lives with murmurs of excitement about that night's show on their lips, the light was fading.

Maggie and Nev herded the workhorses into the grounds Rafferty had chosen, tethering them and passing their care to the grooms before heading to the campfire behind the big top—hidden so that the human needs of food and rest wouldn't disrupt the audience's perception of the performers as otherworldly beings. Maggie was just reaching for a tin plate of roasted pigeon and carrots when the wood-and-water joey came uncertainly up to her. His eyes were round, and he held his hand out in a way that told Maggie he would dart away as soon as he let go of what he'd brought her. She didn't care. For what was in his hand was an envelope.

'Off with you, then,' she said, snatching it out of his little fist. Maggie didn't leave the comfort of the campfire before tearing it open with trembling fingers. There was no one near her anyway.

She unfolded the letter, her eyes going straight to the bottom of the page. It was from him. She wanted to read it right away, to see if he had believed that she was Charlotte. But the performers were already sidling into the dressing tent to paint their faces, nimble fingers doing up fastenings on costumes and sliding pins into hair. The gear men had disappeared under the wide canopy of the big top to make their final lighting checks. Soon the smell of popcorn would waft on the night air, and the loud calls of the jerry—one of the circus folk, pretending to be a customer buying multiple tickets from the spruiker, to stir the crowd into a purse-loosening eagerness—would begin.

Now wasn't the time to read the letter. It was the time for her to erase Maggie and bring forward the Lagoon Creature.

Maggie went through her performance that night without giving it much thought. So impatient was she to devour the letter's contents that she almost forgot to meet an audience member's eyes and challenge them with her own. At the last moment she remembered, and caught the gaze of a woman with a withered face and a hat that had seen better years. Maggie was fretting about the possibility the letter might declare that Mr O'Lehry knew her to be an impostor, but the steady, unwavering way the woman gazed back at her so distracted her for a moment that she couldn't help it. One side of Maggie's mouth quirked up. The woman's eyebrows rose; she wasn't quite sure of what she'd seen—was it possible for a Lagoon Creature to smile at someone?—but Maggie had already turned her back on her and was weaving and ducking the whizzing blade of Greta's sword.

As soon as Smith had dumped her out of sight of the audience, Maggie raced to change back into her plain day dress and wool coat. Greta could find someone else to help her into her next costume. Snatching up an old piece of fabric that looked as though it could belong to a costume, she made her way to a well-lit corner of the backstage area that she often used when making quick repairs to costumes mid-show. She bunched the fabric around the letter and hunched herself over, so she'd appear to any prying eyes as if she were intent on sewing. And then, finally, she read.

My dear Miss Voigt,
I cannot begin to describe the pleasure your letter brought me. I knew you would find this correspondence agreeable, but one can't help worrying, can one? I should have put my trust and faith in your good nature and our remarkable connection.

Maggie tipped her head back, the corners of her mouth stretching toward her ears. Above her, the tent's canvas ceiling disappeared in a wavy blur as her eyes danced with the laughter she didn't dare let out, lest she draw unwanted attention.

She'd done it. The man believed she was Charlotte.

It took several lifetime-long seconds before she had composed herself enough to continue reading. The letter was full of Mr

O'Lehry's admiration for Charlotte—followed by minute details of his rather ordinary life.

Although the profuse compliments weren't really meant for her, Maggie felt the warm glow of them. They made every little mundane detail he shared seem interesting. No, she hadn't heard of the fish and chip shop where he'd bought a penn'orth of chips and received less than he was due. Yes, she was fascinated to know about the latest trend in toe-shapes for men's shoes at Grace Bros. In her head, Maggie was already crafting her response to him, seamlessly melding herself and Charlotte together under Charlotte's name.

Behind her she could hear the closing act: the blare of the trumpets, the drumming of the horses' hooves as they raced around the ring and the awed gasps of the audience as they saw the entire cast, except for Maggie, in a last colourful display. For the first time in Maggie couldn't remember how long, she didn't get up to hold the curtain back and peek at the world she was half-in, half-out of. For the first time, she was content to be alone with all that she had.

Chapter Fourteen

'Keep the bloody spotlight still,' Charlotte muttered. She could feel it wavering at her back as her hands wrapped around one of the low rungs before her. Yass was their third town since leaving Sydney; surely they should've figured it out by now. What were the bloody warbs doing? It was bad enough that she couldn't tell the audience to hold their breath—although many of them would, soon enough—and stop their children fidgeting. She stretched her fingers, dusted with fake, out a few times before letting them curl around the ladder rung again, the feel so familiar. She took a long breath, then lifted one foot and put it on the bottom rung.

There was the drum roll. Not the full-throated, body-piercing vibration that it would become once she was standing at the top and spreading her arms in a flourish. But a low purr, like the thrumming of fingers on a solid surface, letting the audience know that something exciting was about to happen.

Charlotte climbed up the narrow ladder, its rope sides giving a little, so that it swayed slightly beneath her. She didn't mind; it helped prepare her for what lay ahead, making her aware of her body, of how her balance shifted with her weight. She moved neither fast nor slow, allowing the audience's eyes to follow her in her sparkling green and purple costume—like a peacock, Charlotte thought. Now why hadn't she got a peacock as a tattoo? She chased away the thought. Now was the time to pay attention to what she was doing, not turn over half-remembered moments in her mind. As she climbed higher and higher, she let her eyelids droop, so she could only see the ladder through the blur of her eyelashes. When she did this, she sometimes felt she was soaring up to the big top's ceiling; that any minute now wings would sprout from beneath her shoulder blades, and she would fly up and up, until she tore through the tent and out into the night sky beyond.

Her hands reached the platform. She clambered up, holding her pose with a blinding smile the audience would see even from way down below. The band's cymbals crashed. A good five seconds' pause, then she turned toward the tightrope she'd made her name on, rubbing her hands together as the audience applauded. Some funambulists used long poles to help them balance—or create more of a show—but she never did. Charlotte prided herself on her skill—and there were tricks that could not be performed if she held a pole.

She stepped to the edge of the platform and lifted one slipper-clad foot. The ribbons crossed her ankles like a ballerina's shoe, and she pointed her foot as though she were indeed about to dance. The audience quietened. Charlotte could hear one man cough, a wet, distracting sound, and she frowned. Didn't he know how difficult this was?

The soft sole of her slipper met the rope, and Charlotte shifted her weight forward, bringing her left foot in front of her right. She took another long breath, then calmly inched her way further out onto the rope and away from the safety of the platform. She could feel the solid line of the rope beneath her soles, almost cutting into them, and the air on either side of it. Her arms she held out to the sides, moving them higher or lower, or to this angle or that, when she felt her weight shift too far in one direction. They were minute movements, too small for the audience even to notice, and this was what made her so good.

She was in the middle of the rope now, exactly halfway between the two king poles, nine yards up in the air with nothing but sawdust below. Charlotte loved this moment. This sense of complete mastery, knowing, all the while, how easy it would be to fall. She began to walk backward. The audience gasped, as they did every night.

But this was only the beginning.

When her heels met the platform, she turned and scooped up a hood she'd left lying there. She slipped it over her head, and then, suddenly blind, she walked forward again. One confident foot after another, all the way to the opposite platform, where she ripped the hood off and waved to the frantically applauding audience.

She made her way back to the centre of the rope. This time she swept her arms in graceful, albeit careful, arcs, as if she were dancing, then paused. Again, the drum roll started, softer now, because of how far above the band she was. She tried to tune it out, to concentrate on the rope before her. Most nights the sound faded away, but tonight she could still hear it, a tinny buzzing in her ear, like a mosquito. She shook her head, and her balance shifted. She was fast enough to correct it, but the audience let out a moan. Rafferty wouldn't mind—near-misses only caused further excitement—although he would want to know what had happened. Charlotte would tell him she'd done it deliberately, to thrill the audience. She held her arms out to her sides, her weight shared equally between both feet. She bent her knees in as deep a plié as she could manage, then pushed off, somersaulting backward. A quick whirl of colours around her, then the rope was back in her sights, her feet meeting it once more, losing it for two little steps as her balance wavered, then anchoring themselves as she straightened up, in control once more. Applause broke out, louder than any up to that point. But Charlotte ignored it, concentrating on her next movement.

This was the highlight of her act. She had mastered the most difficult feat in tightrope walking: the forward somersault. When she did a backward somersault, she was facing downward as her feet hit the rope; she could see what she was doing. With the forward somersault, she was facing upward as she landed; she couldn't see her feet, or the rope, just the ceiling of the tent; she had to rely purely on the feel of it to land without pitching over.

Not many could do it, but it was Charlotte's specialty.

But tonight there was still that buzzing in her ears. Charlotte took a few extra steps forward, trying to leave it behind her. Her eyes were on the rope, and she felt for the first time as though she was noticing how thin it was. She licked her lips. God, her mouth was dry. She needed a drink. She thought of her flask, hidden in the folds of her daytime clothes. It was another balancing act, swallowing just enough to calm her nerves but not enough to dull her reflexes—but she had always been good at balancing.

Only it seemed she'd got it wrong tonight.

She licked her lips again, tried to prepare herself for the forward somersault, but it wouldn't come. Her eyes fell downward, to the bright red and black smudge that was Rafferty, standing among the white helmets of the band. What was he doing there? Was he telling them to start playing? Was he going to send the next act on? He must know something had gone wrong. Usually by now Charlotte was at the other end of the rope, bowing to the audience, drinking in their applause.

Charlotte would not be cut off mid-act. Whatever was happening, she was a professional. She shifted her feet, did another backward somersault, then hastened to the end of the rope. The smile plastered to her face lasted only as long as the spotlight on her.

***

Maggie watched Charlotte speed down the ladder. The funambulist was moving faster than she ever had before. Around her, Maggie could hear the buzz of gossip. The other performers were asking the same thing Maggie now asked herself.

What had happened?

They all knew each other's acts inside out and upside down. When the time had come for Charlotte's famed forward somersault, she'd simply frozen. It had felt an eternity, watching the small purple-and-green figure up there, staring into space before her. Rafferty had run for the band, preparing to cue the next act, then Charlotte had done a second backward somersault and raced for the end of her rope.

She was headed for the backstage area now, her face still and expressionless, hair and costume incongruously brilliant. Maggie pushed past the whispers, reaching the tent flap a moment before Charlotte did and holding it back for her.

'Thanks,' Charlotte murmured, although her eyes looked beyond Maggie.

'Are you all right?' Maggie asked. Charlotte's hand went to her red hair, trying to tuck in strands that were not loose, pulling at the green ribbon which had been tied in a bow at the front. Her cheeks were flushed from the crushed petals, her lips matching but slightly smudged around the edges, as though she'd been in a hurry to do it.

'Yes. I–I'm fine.' Her distracted gaze shifted to where the show was carrying on without either of them. One shoulder went up, the muscle beneath her costume bunched with tension. Maggie thought she should leave her alone, but it didn't feel right. She cast around for something to say.

'Can I do anything? Get you anything?' She had no idea what could possibly help, but Charlotte's eyes left the circus ring and met Maggie's with such intensity Maggie took a step back.

'I know you heard us that day,' she said.

'I–I don't understand.'

'When we were talking about Wonderland City. I didn't remember, when I said what I said. I thought I was telling the truth.'

Was it Maggie's imagination, or did Charlotte's hand hover above her thigh, where her lyrebird tattoo was concealed by her thick stockings?

'I remember now,' Charlotte whispered through those smudged lips. 'And I'm sorry.'

And then she was taking long strides away. Not leaving Maggie time to ask if she was sorry for forgetting, or sorry for having spent the time with her.

***

Charlotte could barely get the silver collar of her flask to her lips without spilling. Her mind was racing, a jumble of colour and noise, as if she had fallen off the rope and was tumbling down, shocked faces spinning through her vision. But the drink was the safety net that would catch her.

She swallowed several times before slowing and dabbing her mouth with still-trembling fingertips. The steady warmth seeped through her limbs. She thought of Maggie, the Lagoon Creature. How could she have forgotten that day so completely?

She rubbed one eye with the heel of her hand, grinding it in until spots danced in front of her closed lid. Then she took another, slower mouthful of rum.

God, it was good.

Charlotte remembered the first time she had ever tasted a drop of alcohol. It was a bottle of rum, pilfered by Will from his father. They'd climbed the branches of an English elm—one of the last times Charlotte had climbed a tree, having been forced into corsets not long after, which made it too difficult—and sat so close that their legs pressed against each other, Charlotte's toes knocking Will's every time she swung her feet. They'd drunk straight from the bottle, Will offering it to her first, saying that he was a gentleman. Charlotte had laughed, responding that no one would know it, and he'd elbowed her in the ribs. His hand had landed in her lap afterward, and she'd let it stay there as she brought the bottle to her lips.

She tried her best not to cough, but the taste was so strong that she couldn't help it. It was Will's turn to laugh then. He didn't cough with his first mouthful, and Charlotte accused him of trying it without her at an earlier date. He insisted he would never do such a thing—he was just made for the drink, being a boy.

Charlotte snorted now, bringing her flask to her lips once again. That pommygrant strong man was watching her, and she jutted her chin out at him. Hadn't he seen how she choked up there on the rope? Anyone would need a drink in her situation.

She glared as she drank slowly, and eventually he turned away. She smirked. Will was wrong about girls not being made to drink.

When they'd got through enough of the bottle that both of them fancied they were on a carousel with the way their heads spun, Will had leaned in and kissed her. A stolen kiss to go with the stolen drink. Charlotte's balance had not budged with every sip of the bottle, but it reeled then; she'd had to grab onto Will to keep herself steady. But she was only steady on the outside. She would never be steady on the inside again.

She sighed.

The taste of liquor would always be the taste of Will's lips on hers.

That's what made it so hard to resist.

Chapter Fifteen

Another town behind them, another dirt road disappearing beneath the churning wheels of the wagons. The landscape was dotted with silver-leafed gums losing their bark in long, bronze strips, the yellowing grasses of the paddocks curved over from day after day of being buffeted by wind. They'd passed fields of the most vivid purple Maggie had ever seen, and now the rolling hills in the distance were topped with a carpet of the same purple, gradually fading into a cheery green. It had been a good drive. They'd had another sprinkle of rain, not enough to slow or bog the wheels, although it did make the donkeys, who hated the wet, reluctant. At least it lessened the ever-present threat of bushfires. Maggie slapped at a mosquito that had landed on her ear and wondered how long their luck could last.

She was on one of the earliest wagons today, only the commissariat wagon ahead, laden with its bags of provisions and hay bales to supplement the horse and donkey feed. Gilbert the flunky sat behind her, and Bastian, a French gear man who'd flinched at her presence when she'd climbed up next to him, drove them in silence. Maggie ignored him right back, watching the sway of the horses' rumps before her, the flicks of their tails as they kept adventurous bushflies away.

When they caught up with the commissariat wagon, Maggie knew something was wrong. It had stopped, but not for dinner; Nev's left hand was in the air to warn them to keep back, his other tightly controlling the reins of the horses that were shuffling skittishly. Maggie leaned to the side and saw what was creating the commotion: an eastern brown snake was in the path before the commissariat wagon. It would be disastrous if the snake got under the horses' hooves. Its bite could be fatal.

Rosemary, seated in the back of the wagon, clutched Victor, one of her fidgeting children, in her lap. Maggie held her breath, afraid the child's noise would rile the snake. But after several minutes of catching the sun on its scales, the reptile slithered away from them, a fast flash as it disappeared into some grasses. Nev's palm still cautioned them to stay back. He made them wait long enough that the next two wagons caught up.

'Give us a couple hundred yards again,' he called over his shoulder, setting off with a wave. Bastian waved back, holding the horses steady. While they waited for the asked-for two hundred yards to stretch between them, Maggie watched Victor's attempts to climb out of his mother's lap. The increasingly sharp way Rosemary pulled him back to safety gave her a restless feeling, like some nervy, fractious animal had curled up inside her chest. Perhaps she should write to Mr O'Lehry about her dream of having children. After all, Charlotte would surely have them one day: a whole tribe of healthy, ruddy-haired sprites who would learn to balance and do flip-flaps just like their mother.

The wagon picked up its steady pace again, and Maggie chewed at her lower lip, pondering how she'd word this dream to Mr O'Lehry. Soon, she tasted blood. She dabbed at the split skin with the cuff of her coat.

The distant cloud of dust from the commissariat wagon

disappeared, signalling that it had rolled to a stop. Either they'd come across another snake or Nev had found the running water they needed to make their dinner camp. When they came close, Maggie saw a wide stretch of water, sunlight refracting off its surface in a manner that made her want to turn it into a costume for one of the performers. Nev, noticing the way Maggie stared even as she shielded her eyes, said, 'The Murrumbidgee. It means big water. One of the longest rivers you'll find in all of Australia.'

Victor, who'd clambered down from the commissariat wagon and was frantically freeing his feet from their shoes, started running around making loud whoops, not noticing the enormous goanna that went scuttling into the scrub to escape all the noise.

'Would've been good eating if we'd caught it,' Nev said.

Rosemary made an exasperated sound, then shouted after her son, 'Watch out for bindi-eyes!' She turned to Maggie's wagon. 'Gilbert, pitch the dinner tent, will you?'

Maggie climbed down after Bastian, giving the lead horse a grateful pat on the rump for his hard work, trying not to breathe too deeply the musty smell of his sweat. Bastian was already untethering him for his hour's feed and rest.

'I'll see you back on the road,' Maggie murmured in the animal's twitching ear. It was the first time she'd used her voice all day.

Gilbert was having difficulties hammering one of the tent stakes into the unyielding ground. Rosemary stood over him.

'You're doing it wrong, don't you know a peg won't go in at that angle? After all these years ...' She tutted. Gilbert's face deepened to a scarlet tone that told Maggie he wanted to snap back but didn't dare, for fear Rosemary would make him go without his dinner. The campfire hadn't yet been lit, so Maggie turned from the scene to attend to it.

Once Rosemary was satisfied that the tent was up, she unearthed a large tin bowl and began to knead together flour, salt and water for a damper that would be cooked in the ashes of the fire and eaten with the last of the rosella jam they'd brought with them from Sydney.

'Gilbert, Nev, would one of you get me some water, please?'

'I'll do it,' Maggie volunteered. 'Like Victor, I'm keen to kick my shoes off for a bit.' Unbuttoning her boots, she slipped them off, tucked her canvas waterbag under one arm, then grabbed a billy in each hand. She headed down to the edge of the river and waded into the shallows to fill the billies and waterbag. Back at the campsite, she suspended both billies above the fire, careful not to disturb the pots in which the rabbits Nev had collected from the traps that morning were already simmering with carrots, onions and dried bay leaves. The scent was tantalising, and Maggie licked her lips, then flinched as her tongue ran over the split. She turned back to the wagon she'd arrived in, hooked her waterbag onto its side, then stretched her arms above her head. It was good to be on her feet after so many hours of sitting. The grass seemed to prickle and move beneath her soles, and she wiggled her toes, enjoying the sensation for a brief moment before pulling her boots back on. With snakes around, it wouldn't do to be barefoot for long—a sentiment she heard echoed by Rosemary, whose shouts were ignored by Victor.

When the billies were releasing enough steam to tell her the water was boiling, Maggie returned to the campfire and used a thick piece of flannel bundled around her hands to pluck them free. She scooped in some tea leaves taken from a tin; they turned the water into tigers-eye patterns. There was a sound behind her, and she looked up to see the next wagon arriving. It was an elaborate affair, its sides cut into wave-like shapes, and had three rows of bench seats, meaning it could fit eight adults, more if they squeezed in. Itsuo vaulted over the side instead of waiting behind those who were slow to descend, his nose twitching at the scent of Rosemary's rabbit stew. Victor, still barefoot, went speeding up to him and grabbed his hand.

'You wouldn't believe how good my cartwheels have got—I

land on my feet every time now,' the boy crowed. 'I've been waiting all day to show you! Come watch.' He tugged at Itsuo's hand, but the acrobat held him back for a moment.

'Only if you put your shoes on first,' he said, his voice loud enough to carry to Rosemary. 'If you're going to be an acrobat, you need to protect your feet.' Victor ran to collect the discarded shoes, and Rosemary mouthed a silent 'thank you' in Itsuo's direction.

On the wagon, Annie and Charlotte were pretending to toast one another with the empty pannikins they'd pulled out, while Smith grumbled at them to get a move on. Maggie hurried to wrap her right hand in the flannel again, then swung one billy in big overarm circles to settle the tea leaves to the bottom. She did the same with the second billy; the water had now turned a satisfyingly dark and even brown. She poured some tea into her own pannikin, and then left, knowing the others wouldn't want her around while they served themselves.

After digging in her leather bag to retrieve some goods, Maggie moved to a spot where she had a view of the grassy banks gently sloping down to meet the slow-moving amber river water. Nev, Bastian and Gilbert were already throwing in fishing lines, hoping to catch something fresh for that night's supper. Maggie sipped her tea, savouring the earthy flavour, not minding the sting of it on her split lip. Kneeling on the grass, she dug a little divot to place her pannikin in. Then she took out the book she was reading—*Fair Ines*, by the same author who'd written *Seven Little Australians*—and put it down next to her tea. Carefully, she spread a sheet of the paper Rafferty had given her on top of the book cover. Not the best surface to write a letter on, but it would do. She curled her legs to the side, letting the pointed toes of her boots peek out from beneath the damp hem of her dress, and hunched over to indicate to any watchers that she didn't want to be approached. Not that anyone would have dared, anyway.

Which was why it startled her when she heard someone close by say, 'Maggie.'

Maggie's hand paused, and she looked up, not bothering to hide her irritation. She'd barely begun her letter to Mr O'Lehry.

Charlotte stood before her, her fingers wrapped around her own steaming pannikin. Her cheeks coloured slightly at Maggie's unimpressed expression.

'Did you say my name?' Maggie asked.

'Yes.' Charlotte bent down, placing her pannikin in the dirt like Maggie's, then used one hand to brace herself as she sat. Her close-fitting skirt made it difficult, despite the ten-inch slit in it.

Maggie scrabbled to hide the letter beneath her own skirt, moving so quickly that she tore the edge of the paper and stained her thumb with the still-wet ink.

Had Charlotte seen?

Maggie reminded herself that she hadn't signed the other woman's name yet. And what were the chances she would remember the name of the man who had bothered her in Sydney? She had so many admirers ...

Charlotte didn't seem to be paying attention anyway. Her head was lolling back slightly so that the feather on her impractical white toque hat bobbed and swayed. She was gazing out over the river, one hand shading her eyes, the other absent-mindedly pulling at her side. Probably the boning of her corset was digging into her.

'I can't do it anymore,' she said. 'The forward somersault.'

Maggie looked down, rubbing at the ink stain on her thumb. In the three performances since that night in Yass, Charlotte hadn't even tried the forward somersault. She'd just left it out of her act completely. Maggie felt no urge to offer sympathy, but she also knew that what was good for each act was good for the circus. She'd seen it reflected in the account books time and time again; in their most impressive months, when the cast was full and the acts unlike any that patrons could see elsewhere, they turned the most profit. She braced herself; she knew what she had to do.

'It was an off night. That's all. I'm sure if you gave it another burl, you'd be able to do it again.' Rafferty must have said similar to Charlotte by now. Why, then, was she here annoying Maggie with her doleful sighs?

'That's what Rafferty said,' Charlotte confirmed. 'But it's not right. Something... Something's happened.' Maggie heard her voice catch, and despite her best resolution she couldn't help the trickle of sympathy that ran through her. 'I don't know, maybe it's age or something. Whatever the cause, I've talked to Rafferty, and he agreed with me—but only if you agree to it too—I mean ... Maggie, I want to put together a new act. With you.'

Maggie's mouth fell open. No sound came out. She frowned, then looked behind her. Was someone there, ready to laugh at this senseless joke? But only the horses were present, their long necks bobbing up and down as they methodically chewed grass. Maggie turned back to Charlotte, who was watching her intently.

'I'm sorry, I don't understand. Why would you want me? No one ...' No one ever wanted Maggie. 'Everyone knows I'm not a tightrope walker.'

'You wouldn't need to be.' Charlotte shuffled closer, her blue eyes alight. Was that right? Was someone really moving to be closer to Maggie?

'You see, instead of being the villain, I thought you could be a helpless creature.' She was talking in that fast way which made her freckles dance across her face. 'A creature that's been displaced from its home and can't get back because of the dangers in the way. I don't know what those dangers would be—Greta with her swords, maybe, or perhaps a dummy could put their clowning skills to a more threatening-looking use. And then I come along and rescue you by carrying you across the rope, above them all. Out of reach.'

'You ... you want me on the tightrope with you?'

'On my back. That'd be the best way, I think. I can adjust my balance and still see the rope before me. It shouldn't be too hard. Not once we've practised it and I get used to the feel of your weight added to mine. And imagine how it would look—it'd be simply thrilling for the audience.'

Maggie narrowed her eyes. 'Why me?'

That slowed Charlotte's excitement. She scrunched her nose, like she hadn't considered the question before. 'Well ... because you're the Lagoon Creature.'

A hot flash of frustration shot through Maggie. 'Yes? And who says this trick needs a Lagoon Creature? Why can't Annie do it, or one of the others? Someone with sequins that'll sparkle just as much as yours.'

As she said those words, Maggie realised why Charlotte had chosen her. She didn't want to share the spotlight with someone who glittered just as brightly. No solo performer did. It would dull their own shine. With Maggie there was no danger of that.

'I suppose ...' Charlotte said slowly. Maggie wondered if she was trying to think up an excuse other than the obvious: that standing next to Maggie, she'd look even more beautiful and impressive. 'You're such a slight build, though, perfect for carrying. The strongman says you barely weigh a thing. And anyway, wouldn't you like to not be the villain for once?'

No one had ever thought to ask her that before. Maggie's fire dissipated. She didn't understand what was happening. This was the same Charlotte who had denied even spending a day with her, and now she was seeking her out, asking her to *perform* with her. She was glad her hat shielded her face—she didn't know how to feel, where to look, what to do.

'Rafferty agreed to the concept of this new act?'

'He said it was your choice. If you want to do it, he'll help Greta and Smith come up with new acts—if they aren't part of ours, that is—and adjust the show to make it work.'

Maggie cursed the ringmaster under her breath for making her take sole responsibility for this decision. How could he expect her to know what she wanted when she'd only ever done what she'd been told?

'I need time to think about it.'

'Of course.' Charlotte stood up, brushing bits of grass and dirt off the cambric of her navy skirt. 'No rush. I can make do with my act as it is, for now. Only it really would be better with you. The backward somersault isn't enough on its own. Bringing you in would make the act something special again.'

She glanced down, the feather in her hat casting an odd, spiky shadow across one eye and cheek. Maggie could smell freshly cooked damper mingling with the savoury scent of rabbit meat on the air, and her stomach gave an inappropriately timed rumble. Either Charlotte didn't hear it, or she was clever enough at schooling her face not to show any amusement.

'I'll leave you to your letter writing,' she said.

Chapter Sixteen

'Now climb on my back.'

Maggie looked at Charlotte, standing before her in pale pink attire that would be scandalous in any other setting. It was an old costume, the sequins and spangles removed to be reused elsewhere. She was wearing stockings, but her bloomers, stitched in gathered scallops so they looked like theatre curtains, only went to the tops of her legs, and the loose-fitting blouse she'd tucked into them had short, puffed sleeves that left her arms exposed. Maggie had seen her dressed this way hundreds, if not thousands, of times, but being so close, about to have so much of their skin touching, made her hesitate.

'Haven't you got a practice outfit?' Charlotte had asked when Maggie came to meet her that midmorning. It was a Sunday, the closest thing the circus had to a day of rest. They'd only travelled a short distance before setting up the tent and would stay put for the rest of the day. The acrobatic pads had been rolled out for the children to practise and train on until noon, and Charlotte had pinched some to begin Maggie's training for the new act.

'Never really needed one,' Maggie responded sullenly. She'd learned posturing, balancing, dancing and gymnastics as a child, but when the others went on to learn the more awe-inspiring skills of stilt-walking, slackrope, tightrope, broadsword combat and riding, Maggie had turned away in favour of her books and mathematics. She knew she'd never be a boom girl, so why bother? Since then an ordinary day dress had been plenty serviceable for her needs.

Maggie crossed her arms. Her shoulders were unbearably tight. She didn't even know why she'd agreed to be in Charlotte's act, except that Charlotte's words had struck a chord—she was tired of always being the villain. But a little voice inside questioned if what she really wanted was to observe Charlotte up close, so she could finesse her written impersonation of her.

Either way, they were here now, a rope laid out in a straight line on the ground before them, with acrobatic pads arranged on either side. 'Just to get the idea of it,' Charlotte had said.

'Come on, climb on my back,' Charlotte said again now, turning away from Maggie.

'Climb on your back ... how?'

'Like a piggyback,' Charlotte said, as if it was the most obvious thing in the world. Maggie looked down at her black skirt. It wasn't as fitted as the ones Charlotte wore, and she kept it hemmed off the ground so she could move freely, but it was hardly made for clambering on top of someone. She sighed, then shrugged out of her jacket and flung it aside. She rolled her shoulders back a couple of times. It was the strangest thing, the way her insides tumbled and jittered. It wasn't as though this was the first time she'd ever learned a new act. It happened every season, when she was given a new enemy to fight and new defensive skills to learn.

Maggie came close to Charlotte, still waiting with her back turned. Ever so gently, she snaked her arms around Charlotte's shoulders, crossing them in front of her chest. She kept her touch as light as possible, but then Charlotte leaned forward, causing Maggie to tilt with her until her feet left the ground, her chest pressing against Charlotte's back as the tightrope walker took her weight.

Maggie tried to bring her legs up, but the toes of her boots got caught in her hem. She floundered for a second, struggling to free herself, then exhaled loudly and slid off Charlotte's back, stepping away.

'What's the matter?' Charlotte asked, turning to her impatiently. Beyond them, somewhere in the trees, a magpie called, the same tune Nev had pointed out to her. Maggie's eyes tried to find it, but the bird stayed in hiding.

'I can't do it like this.' Maggie sat down, quickly undoing the row of buttons along the ankles of her boots and tugging them off. Standing again, she grabbed the hem of her skirt, pulled it up and tucked it into her waistband. Her thighs were still covered, but her knees were exposed; she could feel the breeze caressing her stocking-clad calves. If they were in public, she could be arrested for such a display. She caught a flicker of movement out of the corner of her eye and turned to see Smith, the strongman, observing them. Maggie scowled at him. She didn't want to be watched. No doubt he was curious, for if their act was a success, his own act would need to change. But Maggie didn't care. Thankfully her glowering seemed to get her thoughts across, for he turned away and disappeared inside the big top. Probably to gossip with the others about what he'd seen. There was never any privacy in a circus.

'All right, let's give this another burl,' Charlotte said, readying herself once more. This time, with her skirt out of the way, Maggie managed to clamber onto Charlotte's back and wrap her legs around her waist. Charlotte hooked her hands underneath Maggie's thighs, keeping her in place.

'Are you right back there?' she asked.

'Right as rain. The rest's up to you now.'

Charlotte hitched Maggie a little higher, then stepped onto the rope, slowly tracing its path. Maggie was conscious of the way her magpie tattoo was pressed against Charlotte's shoulder blade, and wondered if the other woman could feel her heart hammering beneath it. She dropped her head, the loose hairs at the nape of Charlotte's neck tickling her face.

Charlotte reached the end of the rope and turned around. 'I'm going to let go of your legs now. I need to keep my arms out to the side to help my balance. Do you think you can hold your legs up yourself?'

'Righto.' Maggie interlocked her ankles, and Charlotte's hands dropped away.

As Charlotte walked across the rope a few times, Maggie's thigh muscles began to tremble with the effort of keeping her legs in place. Finally, Charlotte said, 'That's enough for now.' Maggie slipped from her back and took a couple of steps away, rubbing her palms up and down her quivering thighs.

'Did you hurt yourself?' Charlotte asked.

Maggie shook her head. 'Only a bit weak. I'll get better with practice.' Now that they'd begun, she wanted to prove that she could do this.

'It'll be much more difficult on the real rope,' Charlotte warned.

Maggie only just managed to stop herself from snapping, 'Obviously.' Instead, she said, 'Do you think you can do it?'

Charlotte looked at the rope lying on the ground, her head dancing from side to side as she considered. 'I don't know. Maybe. It's very different, having another person's weight strapped to my back, even someone as slight as you. But we'll set the rope up nice and low to start with, see how it goes.'

'Sounds fair.'

Charlotte turned back to Maggie and scrutinised her in a way that was hard to read.

'What?'

'It's just ... It felt like you were hiding your face. In my neck.'

Maggie's cheeks bloomed with warmth. 'Well, can you blame me?

'What do you mean?'

Maggie gave a small, animal-like grunt. Why did Charlotte have to make her spell out what was so patent?

'You think an audience wants to look at this face in the spotlight? It's all right when I'm the evil Lagoon Creature, and they get to boo and jeer me. But you want to sell sympathy with this new storyline. Trust me. It's better if they only see your beauty.'

Charlotte had the good grace not to deny that she was beautiful. She lowered her gaze and nudged the edge of one acrobatic mat with her slippered toe.

'It must be hard,' she said in a soft voice.

Maggie ducked her head, avoiding an answer.

'Beauty's an odd thing, isn't it?' Charlotte continued. 'It can make life so much easier—yet if you have too much of it, no one ever sees you. Just your lovely, shiny coating. Or they hate you and try to take what you have. Sometimes they even succeed.'

Charlotte's words pierced Maggie like an accusation. Is that what she'd been doing, writing to Mr O'Lehry under Charlotte's name? Hating her and trying to take what she had?

But then Charlotte smiled again, a bright performer's smile that would never show its brittleness from the distance of a rope strung between two king poles. She spread her arms—the way she did whenever she was regaining her balance—and began enthusiastically talking over her plans. They would graduate from practising on the ground to a low-slung rope, raising it a little higher every day, until eventually they reached the dizzy heights that would be their welcome every night, should their act succeed.

As Maggie watched her, nodding in all the right places, she couldn't help but think that perhaps Charlotte didn't really want anyone to see who she was beneath all that beauty anyway.

Chapter Seventeen

'What's *that*?'

Charlotte stared at the scraps of brown and green material hanging from Maggie's body. She'd seen the Lagoon Creature's costume plenty of times before, but not in broad daylight. Had it always been so ugly?

'You said I should find something else to practise in.' Maggie's voice had an edge.

Charlotte paid no attention. Now was the time for work, not dancing around hurt feelings. 'I said you should wear one of my practice outfits—why are you in costume?'

Maggie looked down at the sparse grass that tomorrow would be covered over with fresh sawdust scattered by the ring waiters. Was it Charlotte's imagination, or was Maggie blushing beneath her pink bumps? She didn't want to frighten her off; not now, when they were about to climb up the ladder for Maggie's first experience on the rope.

'I suppose my clothes would be too big for you anyway,' she said in a conciliatory tone. 'This is at least made to fit you. It'll do until we get your new costume sorted.'

Maggie's head snapped up sharply.

'New costume?'

'Of course.'

'But I'm still the Lagoon Creature. Why would my costume need to be any different?'

Charlotte huffed. Was Maggie being deliberately dense?

'As you yourself have said, we need to make you more sympathetic, so the audience will side with you.'

'You mean you need to make me more wretched.'

Charlotte was about ready to stamp her foot. They were wasting precious time. It wouldn't be too long before Rosemary was calling them for dinner; then blankets would be unrolled, and they'd be chased out of the tent by those ready to turn in for an early night after their full day's travel.

'No, I mean exactly what I said. Your costume can be similar to this one, but it needs fewer ... flappy bits about it.' She snatched at one of the scraps, holding it out to the side. Maggie's hand rose, as though she wanted to smack her fingers away but had stopped herself in time.

Charlotte let the fabric go. 'When we're on the rope I can't have the extra movement of so much fabric,' she explained. 'The costume will need to be shorter, and closer to your body, as well as prettier.'

Maggie's fingers dug into the mound of hair piled on top of her head. Charlotte was getting better at reading Maggie's face, and her current look was one of distaste mingled with a slight hint of horror. She seemed ready to pull her hair out by the roots.

'I need to talk to Rafferty about this,' Maggie said, and she stalked off. Charlotte followed her out of the tent, calling her name, but Maggie was moving too fast, and she gave up. There was no point. She'd just have to wait until Rafferty talked sense into her—if he could, that was.

Charlotte closed her eyes for a second. A dull ache was beginning behind them. Was this act ever going to work? Or was she doomed to perform a now incomplete solo act forever? She'd thought the new act a grand plan when she'd come up with it. Maggie was so petite, and thanks to her childhood training she moved with a natural grace, even if she didn't know it. But getting her up on that rope might turn out to be impossible. Charlotte's upper lip broke out in a fine layer of sweat, and she swiped at it furiously.

She needed a drink.

She opened her eyes, and her vision swam for a second. She put her hand out to steady herself. It took a moment before she could see what direction she was facing, and when she did it was to discover that not fifteen yards away were the younger children of the circus, practising their posturing. She herself still did those very same poses on top of her platform once she'd climbed her ladder. She'd been working on adapting them to include Maggie, clinging to her side like the helpless creature she was portraying.

Rafferty had been instructing the children, but only Judge, sprawled in the shade thrown by one of the donkeys, was watching them now. Maggie stood before the ringmaster, a small yet immoveable rock, feet wide apart, hands on hips. Rafferty's hands moved through the air, as if Maggie were an orchestra he was conducting. Charlotte was sure he was explaining the practicalities of the situation, using the same arguments she had. Rafferty wouldn't let anything get in the way of the new act being the best it could be. Which meant wearing the right costume.

She tried to hide any hint of amusement as she walked over to the children.

'Want to play a game while you wait?' she asked, thinking to buy Rafferty the time he needed to settle the argument with Maggie. The children jumped up and down, cheering, and she wondered where they got their boundless energy from.

'What about Green Gravel, Green Gravel?' a little girl asked. She reminded Charlotte of Elisabeth at that age.

She shook her head. 'No, I don't like that one. Who else has a suggestion?'

'Chasey!' said a boy barely taller than Charlotte's knee.

'No, you need to stay here—Mr Braun will be back soon.' She could see she was beginning to lose their interest, and said, 'How about Consequences?' It would keep them still and in the one spot for Rafferty's eventual return.

The children didn't know the game, so Charlotte quickly went through the rules, explaining how they would each take turns writing a boy and then a girl's name down on a piece of paper, followed by a place they met, what they said and what the consequences were. In the end it would come together to make a funny story.

Charlotte had always found the game a riot as a child. Her lips were curving upward at the memory of it—until a different, unwanted memory barged its way in, making the late-afternoon sun lose its warmth.

She and Will had shared many kisses by then, enough that Charlotte had stopped counting them, no longer thinking they were something she needed to tally and hoard, for she knew there would always be more. She'd been too old for the game—at least sixteen, perhaps a little older—but they'd played to indulge the neighbourhood children. It made her feel grown-up and magnanimous, and she liked the way Will looked at her when she was kind—he had long since revealed an inclination to help or protect those he saw as vulnerable, and when Charlotte was kind it was as though he simply couldn't wait to burrow his fingers into her hair and press his lips to hers.

The children chose Will and Elisabeth's names at the beginning of the game, and the consequence of the cobbled-together story was that they ended up married. The littlies fell about, clutching their sides at the absurd notion of getting married, while Elisabeth's face went scarlet. Only Charlotte, who'd read the finished story aloud, didn't laugh. She stood up, letting the scribbled-over paper fall into the dirt.

Will came to her side. 'It doesn't mean anything,' he said. He bent over and picked up the piece of paper. The children's attention had diverted elsewhere, bored now the game was over, so none of them noticed or minded as he slowly, deliberately ripped the paper into pieces. 'It's just a silly little game. That's what makes it so funny, don't you see?'

Charlotte was torn between dragging him behind the house and making him kiss her more fiercely than ever before, or flouncing off to her bedroom to cry hot, angry, irrational tears. In the end she'd reached for his hand and whispered, 'Let's go steal a drink. Just the two of us.' It had become their secret ritual, along with the kisses.

Charlotte shook herself. The children—not the neighbourhood children of her memory, but the circus children, in their practice gear and bare feet—were staring at her, waiting. She clapped her hands together, a sound so sharp and unexpected that she made herself jump.

'Right. We'll need some paper.' It occurred to her now that this had not been the most practical game to choose. But there was no going back after she'd roused their excitement. 'I'll go get some. You lot stay here. While you're waiting, sort out what order you want to take turns in.'

She set off for the baggage wagon. She knew Maggie kept pen and paper, for she'd seen her writing letters to her father. Surely she wouldn't mind her borrowing some to play a game with the children. She'd just reached the wagon and was trying to remember which bag or case was Maggie's, when Maggie appeared at her side.

'What are you doing?'

'Lord, you startled me!' Charlotte pressed her hand to the base of her throat, then laughed. Maggie frowned, and Charlotte hesitated. Was she really that upset about the costume?

'I was fossicking for some paper, to play Consequences with the children,' Charlotte said. 'Do you remember that game? I thought it would be fun while they waited.'

'They're back to practising with Rafferty.'

Charlotte swallowed. Why was it that she so often felt in the wrong around Maggie?

'Oh. I guess no time for Consequences, then. Never mind, they were more keen on chasey anyway. Are ... are you all right?'

'Fine. We haven't got much daylight left, though, so we'd better get cracking if we want to try the act out before everyone settles for the night.' She snatched the bag Charlotte had been about to reach for, holding it close to her side as she marched back to the big top.

Charlotte was poised to follow, but paused, calling out, 'I–I just felt the stitching on the lace of my slipper break. Hold on while I run and get another pair.'

'I can get—' Maggie started to say, but Charlotte had already sidled away.

Charlotte could feel Maggie watching her from the porch. She wanted to turn and shout at her to mind her own business. She stopped when she reached an equipment wagon and plunged a hand in to pull out one of the slippers she'd hidden beneath a coiled rope—it always paid to have a ready-made excuse—then waved it above her head. Maggie finally disappeared back inside. Charlotte didn't hesitate; she would be expected back in less than a minute, so she needed to move fast.

She reached back into the wagon and retrieved the flask she'd pulled from the slipper before showing it to Maggie. Charlotte emptied it—it threatened to repeat on her, she had to swallow so fast, but she forced it down anyway—then wiped her lips and bent over to untie the still firmly attached laces of the slippers she was wearing.

Chapter Eighteen

M aggie stood backstage, butterflies disturbing the familiar heaviness that sat inside her. The sensation amplified her fears of all that could go wrong.

It was too soon. Maggie had said it until her voice all but disappeared. They'd only been across the high rope a handful of times. Granted, each time had been a success, Charlotte's balance perfect and sure-footed, but that was not nearly enough to make Maggie comfortable, let alone confident.

But Rafferty insisted the timing would never be better. And despite her protestations, Maggie understood his reasoning. Wagga Wagga was the biggest town they'd be seeing in a long time. Charlotte had insisted that she was ready, and Maggie, knowing the hit the circus's books had already taken, capitulated.

She shuffled closer to the tent flap; beyond, Itsuo was making the audience squeal at his dummy falls and gasp at his flip-flaps. Soon he would be jumping through a tunnel made of wire and lit candles without extinguishing a single flame.

And then it would be their turn.

Maggie's costume shimmered in the dim light. She looked down and ran her hands across it with a feather-light touch. She didn't want to knock a spangle free, for hours of work had gone into it. It was still an assortment of scraps sewn together, but it was shorter and more fitted now, the loose ends tucked in, to create something akin to what Charlotte and the equestrians wore. Dotted here and there, the blue and green sequins were meant to mimic drops of water still clinging to her, the occasional brass spangle resembling light glinting off the water. She was the Lagoon Creature, but not as any audience had known it.

She exhaled, a long, shuddering breath, then turned to peer out again at Itsuo, who was finishing his act to raucous applause. The children in the audience particularly loved him. Who knew how many eggs they would waste trying to copy his specialty somersault—a full revolution in the air that saw him snatch two eggs from suspended cups mid-turn. Over the years Rafferty had received plenty of complaints from exasperated mothers whose plans for breakfast had been ruined.

Would the children love her, too? They never had before, and she didn't think they would now. She didn't believe the audience capable of loving the Lagoon Creature, no matter how sympathetic Charlotte tried to make her—but perhaps they might learn not to be afraid of her?

A pain in her chest was so sharp Maggie thought her magpie might be tunnelling into it, and her breath came in short gasps. Then Charlotte was next to her, saying words that she couldn't hear through the muffled ringing in her ears, pushing her into the ring, and it was too late to back out. She stood there for a moment, in full view of the audience, stunned; the band were playing a low, melodic sort of song, not at all the threatening music they used to play for her. There was the familiar ripple that went through the audience as they caught their first sight of her. It broke the spell that had come over Maggie, and she hunched over, remembering she was there to play a part.

Rafferty had worked with Maggie to perfect a new way of moving. Instead of raising one shoulder and dragging a leg behind her, she sank into herself, so she'd look meek and uncertain, and made her uneven eyes as wide as possible. Maggie hated it; she preferred being defiant, staring right back at the mugs and daring them to despise her.

But this version of the Lagoon Creature wasn't like that. She minced her way forward, then waltzed in a slow, dreamy circle, peering this way and that, her hand above her eyes, until she pointed to her lagoon—long strips of green fabric, waved by the dummies who held the ends—on the other side of the ring. The music picked up for a moment, and Maggie's steps became light with joy as she cartwheeled in the direction of the lagoon; then it dropped again as Greta stepped out of the shadows, wielding her swords.

Maggie's dance stopped, and she cowered as Greta juggled two swords, lunging ever closer. When she finished her act, balancing on her hands on the very tips of her blades, she tilted her head up and gave Maggie a glare so fierce that Maggie didn't have to act taken aback.

She dodged to the left of Greta, trying to take advantage of a gap, but Annie the contortionist stepped forward, taking Greta's spotlight and blocking the way. Like Maggie, she was so tiny she looked almost still a schoolgirl. She twisted herself into knots Maggie couldn't have tied with a rope, let alone her own body. She stood on her hands, her body bending so far back that her extended legs rested on the top of her head, toes pointing at Maggie like an accusatory finger. She bared her teeth. The red sequins on her costume had a menacing edge, the slashes of colour a warning, making Maggie think of a redback spider, or the small, sandy-coloured octopus she'd once seen at Manly Beach, whose tentacles had become ringed in bright blue stripes when some children poked at it with a stick. Elegant, but deadly.

Maggie had no way to get to her lagoon. She looked around helplessly, when a shrill whistle sounded and a sudden spotlight shone on one of the king pole platforms. Charlotte had climbed up there in the dark, unnoticed by the audience, and now stood high above them all in a triumphant pose. Charlotte gave the awed murmurs time to die down, then beckoned to Maggie, exaggerating the gesture so that its message was unmistakable: she wanted the creature to climb up and join her.

There was a low rumble of anticipation as the audience wondered if the frightened Lagoon Creature would venture so high to meet the beautiful tightrope walker.

Maggie felt as if she'd left her stomach back on the sawdust-strewn ground as she went higher and higher on the ladder. She didn't stop to wave, as Charlotte might have done, nor could she control her pace. All she could think about was getting to the top, and what would happen then.

As her hands met the platform, Charlotte reached down to help her up. Maggie cowered once more, and Charlotte stroked her head as if she were some sort of animal. They paused in this position, and the audience dutifully clapped. It was impossible to tell if there was any real enthusiasm in the applause. Then Charlotte was walking out onto the rope, showing them all that she could do. Maggie stood as close to the edge of the platform as she dared—which wasn't too close, for her head was already spinning from the great height—while Charlotte walked forward, backward, jumped, put a hood on to cross the rope blind, and did her backward somersault. After each trick she paused and beckoned to Maggie once more, her hands slowly moving through the air in a 'come here' motion, trying to coax her out onto the rope. Maggie shook her head, too afraid to step out no matter how safe the tightrope walker made it seem.

Eventually, Charlotte directed an oversized shrug at the audience, and raced back along the rope toward Maggie. She stepped onto the platform, and with a brief flash of a smile, turned her back to Maggie. Maggie swallowed. Charlotte stood impossibly still, waiting; every taut muscle of her back spoke of concentration, which gave Maggie some reassurance. Maggie inched close to her, draped her arms around her shoulders, then lifted her legs—stronger now, thanks to their practice sessions— and entwined them around Charlotte's waist. Charlotte put her hands underneath Maggie's knees for a moment, shifting her weight until she was in the exact position she needed. Then she crept forward to the very edge of the platform and pointed one foot so her slippered toes met the rope. Far beneath them, Greta was dancing with her swords and Annie was repeating her contortions. The silence was nearly complete, as it had always been for Maggie's entrances; she knew it was the silence of a held breath.

'Are you ready?' Charlotte whispered, her voice only just reaching Maggie's ears. Maggie wanted to say no, but she couldn't speak. Her heart was thundering. She pressed the right side of her face against the back of Charlotte's neck, so that she was as close to her as it was possible to be while still allowing the audience to see her frightened expression—an expression which did not require any acting. Charlotte took this agreed-upon pose as an answer, and unfurled her arms like wings. Maggie's locked-together ankles tightened with extra tension. Charlotte took three slow steps out onto the rope, then stopped. Maggie could feel the minute shifting of her weight beneath her and closed her eyes. She was no more used to this weightless feeling now than she'd been at their first rehearsal. She knew she had to trust Charlotte, but all she could think of was the distance down to the ring below.

Charlotte kept moving, placing one foot in front of the other, swaying a little with each step to regain her balance. The walk across seemed to take an eternity, but was also over in the blink of an eye. Charlotte was on the platform on the far end, shrugging Maggie off, posturing triumphantly while the audience erupted. Maggie trembled, frozen to the spot, until Charlotte's eyes cut toward her with a pointed look. She quickly scrambled to the ladder. She was supposed to climb down as fast as she could, to bring the act to its end, but her hands and knees were so unsteady that she missed one rung and slipped down half a yard. This only seemed to encourage the audience, who cheered louder when she caught herself. Wanting it all to be over, she threw caution to the wind and jumped while there were still four rungs below her. Her feet hit the sawdust, causing little clouds to puff around her slippers, then she was running to her lagoon. She dived between the strips of dancing fabric and waved in gratitude to Charlotte, still high above on her rope. As Charlotte waved back, the music reached a crescendo, then crashed into a quiet lull.

The lights dimmed, and it was over.

Maggie's arm fell, but her fingers fluttered, not quite able to let go of that final wave yet. She bent double, resting her palms on her cotton wool knees, and took a deep breath. Her forehead was coated in sweat, and a droplet ran down her nose, clinging to the very tip of it. There was no time to dawdle, though—she had to make way for the next act. As she ducked through the shadows toward the backstage area, she saw Smith holding the flap open for her, as she'd done for so many others. She tried to thank him, but no sound came from her dry lips.

'Maggie girl!' Rafferty cried, coming up to her in a swirl of red and black. He grabbed her shoulders and shook them so excitedly her teeth nearly rattled. 'Can you hear that applause? And that slide down the ladder, followed by the jump—inspired! Make sure you keep that in tomorrow night.'

He gave her an effusive kiss on the cheek—a movement that startled Maggie as much by its intimacy as by the way the brim of his hat knocked her in the eye—then he was gone. Without his strong grip on her shoulders, she could no longer stand. Her knees buckled, and she hit the ground. She sat there, digging her fingers into the sparse grass and dirt. She didn't care if she stained her sparkling new costume; she needed to be close to the earth.

Someone emerged from the ring behind her. It was Charlotte. She circled in front of her, hands clasped as if in prayer, eyes questioning.

'Well? What did you think?'

Maggie opened her mouth. No words came out. Instead, she started to laugh, with a force she could not explain or control. She doubled over, a stitch forming in her side. Her eyes watered, and through the filmy fog of amusement she saw that Charlotte's feet were beginning to move impatiently. She forced herself to gulp, bringing the laughter to a hiccupping stop.

Finally, she looked up at the tightrope walker.

'So that's what it feels like to be Charlotte Voigt,' she said.

Chapter Nineteen

W agga Wagga was a triumph. It became their longest
stay in a town or city to date, and by the time they left
Maggie could finish the act without collapsing to her knees
afterward. She still hadn't braved opening her eyes during it,
but Rafferty said that didn't matter. No one could tell from the
audience anyway.

It was strange, no longer having the audience cheer her demise.
Maggie wasn't sure she liked their new pity any better. She could
see it in the eyes of the ladies who wore their best hats and long
necklaces and clutched their children close to their sides. They
still viewed her as a creature, but instead of sparking revulsion,
she drew from them a melancholy sympathy that allowed them to
leave the tent glorying in their sensitivity to her suffering.

Maggie sat in the baggage wagon once more as the circus left
Wagga Wagga, reluctant to let the suitcase—now considerably
heavier—out of her sight. The motion of the wagon churned her
insides. She looked at the vast yellow stretches of waist-high grass
either side of her, dotted with only the occasional tree; ahead, the
landscape shimmered in the heat, which only made the queasy
sensation worse. Under her breath, she began to recite Banjo

Paterson's 'Rio Grande's Last Race', in an attempt to distract herself. When she paused to twist the tight knots from her neck, Bastian, who was driving the wagon, said, 'Well, don't stop there. How does it end?'

Maggie blushed; she hadn't realised he could hear her.

They halted for their midday dinner near Currawarna, a small rural community. The grass was dry and scant, and Rafferty told the grooms to slip the horses and donkeys into the paddock of a nearby farm so they could eat. A few head of cattle, huddled in the shade of a solitary tree, eyed them warily but didn't move. The tent hadn't gone up, in case the farmer came across them stealing feed for their livestock and they had to leave quickly. For the same reason, Rosemary was heating up camp pies for their dinner. The gelatinous tinned meat was no one's favourite, but its drawcard was speed of preparation, not taste.

A flock of sulfur-crested cockatoos had taken flight at their arrival, soaring in wide arcs before settling in the grasses again. They bobbed their heads now, their yellow plumes dancing like the feathers that wealthy women in the city pinned to their turbans. Their clever, beady black eyes turned to Maggie, and their chattering gave way to gravelly, high-pitched screeches. Maggie sensed they knew she'd stuffed her pockets full of peanuts she'd pinched from the commissariat wagon to snack on later. At the very least they were waiting for her to share the final bite of the leftover johnny-cake Rosemary had brought out to accompany the camp pie. She turned one shoulder to block it from their view. Cockatoos were smart and wouldn't be afraid to steal the wheat-cake right out of her fingers. It might be a little dry and stale, but that didn't mean she wanted to share it.

Maggie swallowed the last mouthful, all the while dreaming of the fat, red saveloys she'd bought for a penny each in Wagga Wagga. She'd given three to Victor—the boy had an insatiable appetite that made him easy to bribe—in exchange for a visit to the local post office. Sure enough, there'd been a letter for her, and their lengthy stay meant that Maggie was able to write her longest reply yet. She had so much more to write about now: she told Mr O'Lehry how it felt to be high up on the tightrope, the dizzying thrill of it, the sound of applause like waves breaking over giant rocks. Her new proximity to Charlotte made the subterfuge easier, too, just as she'd suspected it might.

She was sensible of an intense pleasure as she composed her letter. It was only as she signed it, her pen looping as she began the curling 'C' of Charlotte's name, that she hesitated, shame at her lies blossoming. But the life she was offering Mr O'Lehry in her letters was more Charlotte's than her own, she told herself. So the deception wasn't so great, was it?

Maggie tried not to consider the question too deeply. She was fairly certain she wouldn't like the answer. She wondered instead if Mr O'Lehry had already sent his next missive to Narrandera, the town they were headed to now.

The sun was warm on the backs of her hands, turning them a faint shade of pink. Maggie brushed the crumbs from her fingers, then took a swig of water from her canvas waterbag. It had been strung from the side of the wagon while they travelled, so that the rush of air that passed over it performed a clever trick, cooling the water, until you'd have thought it had been sat inside a sawdust and ice refrigerator.

'What's that?' Rosemary's son shouted. His voice was so loud that the entire circus turned to look in the direction he was pointing, and a handful of cockatoos took off again, screeching and squawking.

A group of twenty or so men, women and children had appeared on the horizon. Some were on foot, some on horseback. As they came closer, Maggie could see they were led by an Aboriginal woman, holding the hand of a young boy who looked strikingly like her. The circus folk gathered close to one another, readying themselves, in case one of these strangers was a boundary rider come to throw them off the property—unlikely, with so many for company, but it always paid to be cautious. When the group came within cooee, the little boy broke free of his mother and raced forward; before he got very far, the woman caught up with him and took his shoulder in a firm grip, pulling him back against her body. Victor, who'd also begun to run forward, faltered. The two groups were still, looking at one another. After a few seconds, Nev stepped forward.

'They're all right,' he said, addressing himself to the woman. He tilted his head back to take in the circus folk. She held his gaze for a moment, then let go of her son. The boy and Victor raced forward again to meet each other, then veered off with the easy chatter that comes so naturally to children.

'We heard another circus had stopped nearby,' the woman said by way of greeting. 'Wanted to see if it was true. Say hello, trade stories.' A ripple of interest ran through the crowd.

Rafferty walked up to stand next to Nev. 'Another circus?' he asked.

Maggie bit down on her thumbnail. Had she missed something when she'd gone digging for information back in Sydney?

The woman nodded, casting a glance over to where her son and Victor were now demonstrating cartwheels to one another. She showed signs of grey around the hairline, and wore a high-collared white blouse decorated with tucks, with a wombat-brown cambric skirt and matching double-breasted coat. Rafferty, who was in his travel outfit of blue shirt, ready-made moleskin trousers, straw boater and red cotton handkerchief serving as a necktie, looked worn and dusty next to her.

He stuck out a hand. 'Rafferty Braun. This here is the Braun Brothers' Royal Circus.'

'Gladys. Ringmistress of McLeod's All-Star Circus. We're camped on the other side of Currawarna.' They shook hands.

A female circus manager? Maggie knew they existed, even if she'd never met one before. But to meet a circus manager who was both a woman *and* Aboriginal? That was really something.

'I didn't think there were any other circuses travelling this way,' Rafferty said. His eyes cut sideways to Maggie. She swallowed, the johnny-cake not sitting well.

'Which way?' Gladys asked.

'We've come from Sydney. Heading to Narrandera next, eventually making our way to Adelaide.'

'Different paths, then. We've come up from Melbourne, just passed through Cummeragunja way. We're heading north now, probably toward the coast—depends on the weather.'

Maggie let out a sigh of relief. Gladys's dark brown eyes flickered to her, and her eyebrows twitched. Maggie pulled the brim of her straw hat lower, as always trying to hide what had already been seen.

The two circuses mingled, the hum of chatter different to their usual dinner breaks. It wasn't just the excitement of seeing fresh faces—it was talking to people who weren't there to be entertained, who understood the ways of the circus.

Maggie sat earwigging as Gladys and Nev settled by the campfire, sipping pannikins of billy tea.

'Come up through Cummeragunja Station, did you say?' Nev asked.

'Yep. The Yorta Yorta have it bad there. Government's taken back the land they were granted.'

Nev grunted. 'They your people, the Yorta Yorta?'

Sensing the talk was about to get more personal, Maggie quietly shifted away.

She found a pine tree far enough from the group that she would have some solitude, and rested her back against it; after half a day in the wagon, she wasn't keen to sit again right away. She had a copy of *Some Everyday Folk and Dawn* by Miles Franklin in her hand, borrowed from Rafferty, but she was distracted from opening it by a tiny bird that landed right by her on a protruding knot of the pine's trunk. It had a black head and wings, a little pointed black beak with a white tuft above it, and a proud, protruding breast of the brightest fuchsia pink Maggie had ever seen on a creature. It flitted to the ground, hopping about and pecking here and there. Maggie wished she had a little johnny-cake left so she could sprinkle some crumbs, for it wasn't so demanding as the cockatoos had been. Ever so slowly, she slid down into a crouch, her skirt pooling around her boots.

'Hello, little fella,' Maggie said in a low voice.

'He's a long way from home.' It was Gladys, standing with her hands relaxed at her sides, also watching the tiny bird. 'He's a pink robin. Never seen one this far inland before. Must've got lost.'

They watched the bird in silence, Gladys eventually dropping to her haunches too. She plucked a long, wide piece of grass from the ground, folded it in half and licked her lips. Bringing the grass to her mouth, she blew gently; the buzzing noise it made was the softest, most playful music Maggie had ever heard.

'That's lovely,' she said when Gladys stopped playing her tune. She let go of her book so she could tug at her hat, making sure it was still in place. It wasn't the veiled one, for they hadn't expected to see any strangers, but if she kept the brim low enough, it might cast some shadow on her face. 'Were you a musician for your circus before you became the ringmistress?'

'No, I worked with the horses.' Gladys sat back, settling her skirt around her. 'Nev and I were working out our kinship,' she said, 'but my boy wanted to show him some tricks. Left them to it, because I wanted to talk to you.'

Maggie tensed; no matter how she tried to separate or distance herself, people's curiosity would always follow her. 'Did you now?'

'Yes. What's your name?'

'Maggie.'

'Are you here because you want to be, Maggie?'

It took Maggie a moment before she understood. 'Oh! Why, yes. I mean to say, I didn't exactly choose the circus life for myself, but they aren't keeping me here, putting me on display against my will. I'm treated well.'

'If that ever changes, you come find me. There'd be a place for you at McLeod's.'

'Thank you.' Maggie had never had an offer outside of the Braun Brothers' Royal Circus before. She wondered what it would be like to have a female boss. 'You own and run this All-Star circus, all by yourself?'

'I do. It's hard yakka. But it's better than working on a station or as a domestic. And if I keep moving, there's less chance they'll take my boy away from me.'

Something sharp moved inside Maggie. She thought again of what Nev had said, about being stolen from his mother. Maggie didn't have many memories of her own mother, just that she had always been distant. That distance later became physical, leaving her with only a father who gave her away when life became complicated. She couldn't imagine being fortunate enough to be born to a mother like Gladys, who wanted to stay close and did everything in her power to ensure that happened, only to be ripped apart like Nev had been.

'You said you worked with the horses before becoming ring-mistress?' Maggie asked, her fingertips absent-mindedly trailing in the dirt. The pink robin took two little hops closer to her, and Maggie forced herself to be still so she wouldn't frighten it off.

'Bareback rider,' Gladys said. 'Just like the famous Billy Jones.' Billy Jones, known in childhood as 'Little Nugget', had risen from bareback rider and rope-walker to become the famed Aboriginal ringmaster of the FitzGerald Brothers' Circus. His death a few years back had been reported in every newspaper in the country— even overseas, or so they'd heard.

'When I read about him taking over the FitzGerald circus, I decided I wanted my own circus too. Took a long, long time, and we've only ever stayed small. But that's how I prefer it. Don't want to draw too much attention. Not all white fellas take kindly to seeing a black woman make her own money or boss other white fellas.'

Maggie knew it was true, but it made her feel uncomfortable to hear it.

'They don't like it when we hang about town too long, either,' Gladys added. 'Worried about white men having black babies.' She looked as though she might say more but was interrupted by a shout that had a showman's ring to it.

'Ladies and gents, ladies and gents—boy, is it your lucky day!'

Maggie turned; a man with sunburned pink skin and rather worn shoes was flourishing and posturing before the campfire. He had on a round-collared shirt, a tie which proved to be double-sided when he bounced around and it flew in all directions, and a straw boater with a red ribbon tied around it. He was quite the magsman, commanding the attention of the entire group.

'One of yours?' she asked Gladys.

The ringmistress's face was grim. 'No. He did try to join us once, but I wouldn't have him because the fella's a pinch artist. Caused me a lot of trouble after that. Your lot best be careful.'

Maggie's lips pursed. Pinch artists stole the acts of other performers and tried to pass them off as their own. She noticed that Rafferty was tilting his head to one side, as if giving the man serious consideration.

'I'd better go tell my ringmaster. Thanks for the warning.' With a departing nod, Maggie made her way back toward the campfire.

'You've never seen a rider as good as me, that I can assure you of,' the pinch artist was saying. His voice had a melodic, almost hypnotic quality, and his accent was broad; he came from the country, not the city. 'My special act is the Peasant's Frolic. I begin seated in the audience, then come into the ring, as if I've been on the turps, yelling that I want to take a few turns on horseback. Your fine ringmaster here has a bit of a barney with me; then, sensing I won't go away, lets me have a try. I mount the rosin-back and perform the most death-defying stunts imaginable, leaving the audience breathless, feeling terrified for this poor drunk fella.

Only at the end do I tear my clothes off and a reveal a brilliant costume. The audience realises I was part of the circus all along and erupts into cheers.'

The act was a bobby-dazzler. Maggie saw Rafferty's eyebrows rise a quarter of an inch in appraisal, and she hurried toward him. Putting one hand on his arm, she whispered, 'He's a pinch artist. That bonza act doesn't belong to him.'

Rafferty's demeanour changed instantly. It was nothing more than a flicker before his showman's smile was in place, but Maggie didn't miss the disgust that twisted his features. He gave Maggie's shoulder an appreciative squeeze, then strode forward, taking off his boater and flinging it aside. He came to a stop next to the pinch artist, who was discussing favoured poses plastiques with Adlai.

'A fine act, a fine act,' Rafferty boomed, far louder than anyone needed him to speak. The circus folk swapped confused looks. Maggie noticed Gladys gathering her crew to her with a short, sharp gesture.

'All the hallmarks of a classic,' Rafferty said. 'Audience deception, showmanship, a surprise at the end.'

The pinch artist was the only one who didn't register the unnatural tone of Rafferty's voice. He gave a slow grin that exposed more gum than tooth. 'The act, and I, could be yours for the right price.'

Rafferty stroked his chin. 'Yes, a classic act indeed. I suppose that's why you stole it?'

A ripple of noise went through the watchers. The man's smile dropped. Beyond him, Maggie saw Gladys give her a subtle wave goodbye, and nodded farewell in return.

'Who says I stole it?' the man asked. His voice had lost its baritone effect, and was now sulky. There was a hard, almost threatening edge to his whine, though.

'Is it true?' Rafferty challenged. The man tucked his hands into his armpits, his chin jutting out.

'It's not like any act can really belong to one person.'

'And yet you were trying to sell it to us as though it belonged to you. Get out of here. We don't have time for pinch artists.'

The man's arms dropped and he took a step toward Rafferty, so they were nearly nose to nose. The ringmaster held his ground.

'Go ahead and try it,' Rafferty said, in a pleasant, conversational tone. 'You think you can take all of us on?' Part of Maggie wanted to run and hide beneath the sanctuary of the baggage wagon; another part of her wanted to dash forward and push Rafferty out of the way of the man's fists, which were tense and trembling with energy at his sides. She noticed for the first time Rafferty's thinning hair, his spreading midsection; he wasn't as vital as he used to be. Smith stood up, cracked his knuckles; Itsuo was only a step behind him, smaller but wiry with tensed muscle, his weight on the balls of his toes. She stayed rooted to the spot.

The man's upper lip lifted—whether in a sneer or an attempted smile, Maggie couldn't be sure. 'No need for all that,' he said. 'It's your loss. There's plenty of other circuses know a good thing when they see it.' He tilted the edge of his boater back: a salute that would have been believably civil, if not for the angry red flush climbing up his neck. 'You'll be sorry,' he said, 'speaking to a decent man as if he's a charlatan.'

Rafferty chuckled. 'I can assure you we won't.' He slid his hands into his trouser pockets.

The man sauntered away, as if it didn't bother him at all to lose face in front of so many—but Maggie saw the dark look he threw over his shoulder.

'Don't even think about coming back,' Rafferty called after him. 'I've got a Snider rifle, and I'm a pretty good shot with it. Even brought down an elephant once.'

When the man disappeared over the horizon, Maggie released the breath she'd been holding and went up to the ringmaster.

'Let's get packing,' Rafferty said, not aiming the words at anyone specific. He used his toes to kick the brim of his discarded boater, making it flip up into the air, where he caught it with one hand and jammed it on his head. 'Damn pinch artist's wasted most of our dinner break. It's time to get on the road again.' Maggie tucked unsteady fingers into Rafferty's elbow.

'You'd better hope we never cross paths with him again,' she said. Her voice had a whispery quality to it that belied how frightened she'd been for a second. She'd really thought the man was going to hit Rafferty. 'Did you see the way he looked at you? The man wants to kill you for humiliating him like that.'

'He'd have to get to me first,' Rafferty said.

Chapter Twenty

They were in Carrathool, a bustling town Rafferty had chosen because its railway and the nearby river port ensured it had a steady supply of people coming in and out. Their first night was the kind of success he'd hoped for, selling so many tickets that some people had to sit in the aisles. The clowns, who had become adept at changing their jokes and antics to suit the local areas, proved particularly popular, and judging by the mess of popcorn, deflated balloons and waxed toffee papers left behind, the concession stand had also been a hit.

'Almost finished,' Maggie said on their second night there, sliding a needle through Charlotte's slipper. The stitching on one lace had broken again, and Maggie had offered to sew it back on while Charlotte prepared for the performance. Charlotte was jittery, her hands flitting from one task to another without ever quite completing anything. Maggie thought she could smell rum on her breath, which made her nervous, but there was still more than an hour to go before their act. Plenty of time for any drink to wear off.

Maggie tied off the thread, breaking it with her teeth. 'There you are, good as new. You really need to learn to sew better. I saw those big, looping stitches of yours—it's no wonder they keep breaking. Have you always been so untidy?' Maggie handed the slipper to Charlotte, who put her foot into it and then forgot to tie the laces, rubbing at her cheeks with the heel of one hand, muttering that she'd coloured them too brightly. Maggie looked down at her own feet, flexing her toes. She wore the same thick, pale stockings that Charlotte did, but without slippers. The stockings gave her toes a webbed look, which Rafferty said worked perfectly for her character. It meant that the soles of her stockings got stained quickly, but Rafferty said that didn't matter either, for who expected Lagoon Creatures to have clean feet? Still, the next time they halted for dinner on the road, she would use whatever body of water they stopped by to give her costume a scrub against the washboard. If she had time after replying to Mr O'Lehry's latest letter.

His notes were increasing in warmth and length. He'd enjoyed Maggie's half-truths about the glittering purple-and-green costume, and the difficulty of carrying the Lagoon Creature across the rope. With each letter, she became more tangled in her lies, until she wasn't sure she could get free of them. Not that she was going to try.

'Is it short for Margaret?' Charlotte asked. She was tying a purple ribbon around her hair, doing it up in a bow and then undoing and redoing it.

Maggie hadn't been listening. 'What?'

'Maggie. Is it short for Margaret?'

'Give me that.' Maggie pushed aside Charlotte's fumbling fingers; they tried to reach the ribbon one more time, but Maggie didn't let them. She began making careful loops. Charlotte tilted her head down so she could reach better; her warm breath skimmed over Maggie's chest.

'I don't know. I suppose so, only my dad never called me anything but Maggie or ... or a nickname. My mother left when I was so young I hardly remember anything about her, let alone what she called me.'

'She left you?'

Maggie finished the bow and stepped away to peruse it. 'Perfect. Don't go fiddling with it anymore, or you'll wreck it. Now stay still.' She crouched low, taking up Charlotte's slipper ribbons and carefully crossing them around her ankles, not so tight they'd cut into her skin, but not so loose they'd risk coming down. Charlotte rested one palm on her shoulder, a touch that was as natural to the tightrope walker as it was unnatural to Maggie.

'Is it really any surprise my mother left?' Maggie asked. 'Who'd want a child like me?'

'But you're *her* child. Mothers are supposed to stay with their children, no matter what.' Charlotte sounded so petulant Maggie couldn't help laughing. She finished the laces, spitting on the knots to help keep them in place, and stood up.

'Wouldn't it be a fine world if all mothers thought the way you do?' If Maggie had a daughter with a face like her own, she'd have kept her even closer to protect her from the injustices the world would bring her way. Just as Gladys did with her boy. But she'd long ago given up questioning why her mother hadn't felt the same way. 'What about your parents?' she asked.

Charlotte shrugged and turned away. She began stretching out her calf muscles, letting her knees sink in deep bends to warm up her thighs and joints. 'They had me out of wedlock, and they were afraid of being judged, so they sent me to the circus. They brought me home when they were married. They'd had another baby by then, a legitimate child. I had to pretend I was adopted.'

'Why'd you come back to the circus, then?' Maggie couldn't imagine leaving behind any kind of family that wanted her. She wouldn't care if it meant pretending to be adopted. Better that than having to pretend you didn't care that you'd been abandoned.

'Because my sister stole the life I was meant to have.' The words were said with such ferocity that Maggie went still. Charlotte was swinging one leg back and forth, arms out to the side, as she practised her perfect balance. Maggie had the sense she was wishing that leg would collide with someone—possibly the sister she'd mentioned. She ventured her next words carefully.

'How does someone steal a life? And why didn't you steal it back?'

Charlotte turned to face her. In the dim gaslight of the dressing tent, her painted face suddenly looked harsh. She stared at Maggie for a second, eyes unblinking, her jaw tense. Finally, she spoke in a voice hardly recognisable.

'Who says I didn't try?'

***

Charlotte had been so sure she and Will would be married. That's why she'd been patient, letting the years slip behind her as all the other girls in the neighbourhood took that longed-for walk down the aisle and started families—sometimes in the reverse order. She tried to fill her days, practising her balance when no one was looking; she'd kept it up all the years away from the circus. But with Will always busy with his studies—he was preparing to become a barrister—the days stretched out before her, longer and longer, until the creeping poison of resentment began to settle in, a snake slowly making its way around her body and claiming her insides for its own. The feeling panicked her. Will had always been the one to keep it at bay, and nothing else seemed to work. Nothing, she found, except drinking. Rum stilled the snake and stopped her ugly thoughts from making their way out of her mouth, where they would turn everyone even further from her.

When Charlotte did see him, she teased Will about becoming so staid and grown-up. The smile he gave in return was always rather flat. She assumed it was because he disliked the truth in her words. Or perhaps he was just tired, his studies taking so much of his time.

And then her sister, at the age of only seventeen, had announced her engagement.

To Will.

Later, Elisabeth tearfully tried to explain that she and Will had wanted to tell Charlotte in private—as though they were the always-linked pair, and she the outsider. Charlotte hadn't cared to listen to her excuse that their parents had ruined the considerate plan. The pain of that moment—Alma and Jakob holding champagne glasses aloft as they announced the engagement to all those attending their dinner party—ensured she'd never listen to anything Elisabeth said again. Charlotte had thought her fingers would shatter the coupe she gripped. Elisabeth's eyes sought her out in the crowd, panicked, but it was Will whose gaze Charlotte met as the room tilted around her, Will whose lips mouthed something that looked like 'I'm sorry.'

Charlotte had stared in dazed confusion as her father presented Will with a monogrammed sterling silver and crocodile skin flask. An extravagant gift meant to welcome him to the family. She threw back the contents of her glass in one go, not even spluttering, then grabbed the nearest bottle by the neck. The hem of her good white dress danced about her feet as she ran through the back door into the garden. She gulped from the bottle, not noticing what it contained. Will, who had followed her, was saying her name.

'You lied to me,' she snarled, turning to face him. 'I believed you, and you lied to me!'

He looked troubled. 'I never lied.'

'Oh? Then what were all those kisses?'

'They were the stuff of childhood, Charlotte.' It was a shot to the heart. Charlotte groped around for a handkerchief to wipe her running nose, then took another swig from the bottle. She tried to calm her racing mind; Will and Elisabeth weren't married yet, only engaged. There was still time to fix this.

'I thought you were at your studies, all this time,' she said. She thought of that bottle of rum they'd shared with their first kiss, and the pain was nearly enough to double her over. But she kept her eyes on his. She didn't miss how his gaze flicked downward for a second. Didn't miss the sound of the sigh that escaped him.

'For god's sake, Charlotte, could you put that bottle down for just a second? Let me explain? I *was* studying. I was working to create a future. For Elisabeth and me.'

'That was *my* future,' Charlotte shouted. Will glanced back toward the house, where all her parents' guests were celebrating.

'Would you quiet down? You're going to embarrass yourself.'

The tears stopped cold on Charlotte's cheeks. She looked at Will as she would look at a stranger. She didn't know this man in his smart suit who cared about what others thought. What had Elisabeth done to him? And how had Charlotte not seen it happening?

Among all the busy wedding preparations over the next year, Charlotte found the flask her father had given Will and hid it in her room. She said nothing as first Will, then Jakob, wondered out loud where it could have got to.

A baby followed so shortly after the wedding that Charlotte knew Will and Elisabeth hadn't been able to wait until they were married to become intimate.

That was when she'd returned to the circus.

Chapter Twenty-One

The Braun Brothers' Royal Circus traced the bank of the Murrumbidgee River from Carrathool to Hay. The land became more arid as they went, the bushflies more of a nuisance. A single night camped on the road provided them with a decent meal of yabbies fished from the water, but it left many complaining about the mosquito bites that dotted the backs of their hands and necks. Some even found their cheeks decorated with the little red marks, which made Maggie want to laugh. Let them have a taste of what it was like for once.

They arrived in Hay with fortuitous timing. The town—widely considered the hub of the surrounding district—was hosting an agricultural show. The state government had put on special show trains with subsidised fares, and their parade entrance was slowed by milling crowds, as big as you'd see in any city. Maggie was certain that the next day she'd have a sizeable entry to add to the account book.

Rafferty gave the performers permission to spend the afternoon exploring the town or visiting the agricultural show, as long as they returned in plenty of time for that night's show. The gear men and grooms would have their turn tomorrow; now they were needed to set the tent and equipment up, and tend to the animals.

Maggie considered asking Charlotte if she wanted to go to the agricultural show with her. She couldn't tell if the idea made her uncomfortable, or had her fizzing in hopeful anticipation that the other woman might just say yes. She didn't get the chance to put the question forward, though; Rafferty had barely finished speaking before Charlotte left the circus grounds, declaring loudly that she was going to the nearest hotel to try her trick of getting men to bring drinks out to her. Maggie saw Smith, Itsuo and Adlai eyeing one another; she guessed that they, too, were wanting a cool glass of beer at whichever hotel the advance agent had set an account up at. But they didn't join Charlotte, waiting until her dancing feet had taken her out of sight before making a move themselves.

Maggie put on her hat with the veil, then picked up her copy of *Such Is Life* by Joseph Furphy. It was an unusual book in which the main character, Tom Collins, travelled various bullock trails that were never given their real names. But Maggie had heard it whispered that one of the locations was Hay, and she carried the book in her hand now hoping to recognise something from its pages.

It didn't take long for her to realise it was an impossible task. There was too much happening around her, and she didn't want to read and walk at the same time lest she miss something or cause an accident. She pocketed the book and turned toward Hay Bridge, with its swinging middle section that allowed steamers to pass through. Most of the crowd were headed in a single direction, and the pull was irresistible. She allowed herself to be swept up in the tide and carried on to the showgrounds.

A familiar mix of scents soon met her nose. Fried potato and dough, animal sweat and dung, humans in close confines. Maggie entered the showground and was immediately shoulder-to-shoulder with men and women of all ages and sizes. Ordinarily, such proximity would make her nervous, but no one paid her any mind, not even when they barged into her and waved a barely-there apology. There were so many people, so many exciting things to look at, that Maggie had become invisible behind her veil.

She grinned, slipping her hand into her leather bag and feeling around for the little bundle of wages that she'd accumulated. Despite not being a big spender, she was enjoying the sense of possibility that a wad of money at an agricultural show brought. She let her feet move aimlessly, the motion of the well-dressed crowd bringing her near the open-air ring. It was much bigger than that of the circus. Within, men who'd thrown their jackets off were displaying their prowess at chopping wood. Maggie watched for a second, then moved on.

She passed the refreshment booths without stopping, noticing as she went by that Rafferty's advance agent had done a good job of plastering advertising bills on nearly every surface. They each depicted Charlotte in the middle of her rope. The Lagoon Creature, of course, did not feature in the image with her.

The stockyards, in which captive horses displayed their driving, trotting and hurdling, and the various dogs and fowl waiting to be put on similar display, did not entice Maggie. She passed them all, then slowed at a stall selling cheap jewellery, until she noticed that the showman running the nearby hoopla stand was about to direct his shouted enticements toward her. She hurried on, veering toward the pavilions. One would be half-filled with tables of jams, cakes and dairy goods, with the other half devoted to needlework and crafts. The next pavilion would be packed with gardening equipment, flowers and plants of every colour and type, and locally grown fruits and vegetables, from prunes and rhubarb to French beans and beetroot. It would be a riot of noise and colours and smells, the competition between the crowds to get the best view as fierce as the competition between the entries.

The earth was becoming sludgy underneath the tread of so many feet, and Maggie saw more than one woman worrying about the ruined hem of her dress. She was grateful yet again for the practicality of her unfashionable ankle-length skirts. Distracted for a moment by the thought, she was knocked to the side; receiving no apology this time, she turned to see who the culprit was. Three boys were zigzagging around the legs of the adults, each with a fist closed around what was likely a penny they'd been given to use as they wished. They, unlike she, clearly knew where they wanted to spend their money. With a quick glance around to check that no one thought she was odd for following, Maggie trailed after them.

As they approached two rows of canvas tents facing one another to form a narrow alley, the noise, already an excited bustle, became a roar. It was hard to decipher the different calls of the cheapjacks who stood on wooden platforms, drumming up interest in the special attractions hidden inside those tents. Maggie walked as though she were in a trance; to the right, a showman playing the bagpipes was doing his best to drown out his nearest neighbour, who was going red in the face with the strain of keeping his voice up. Maggie had heard it said that showmen had leather lungs, but this one was clearly struggling. She tilted her head back to read the enormous painted banners hanging above the tents. The man who could barely be heard was apparently promoting a group of dancing ducks. Amusing, but she wouldn't go inside yet. Not until she'd seen what else this sideshow alley had to offer.

In the explosion of colour and noise, she'd forgotten the children for a moment, but as she came level with a tent advertising a snake charmer, Maggie spotted them again. They were lifting the corner of the tent, trying to scramble underneath. A hand shot from the crowd and hauled one of the boys back by the seat of his pants. He hollered and kicked, and received a swift smack around the ears for his efforts. Maggie took an unconscious step forward, heart lurching in defence of the boy, but he was already off to try his luck at sneaking in to see the world's smallest horse instead.

No one in this makeshift alley was looking where they were going, and Maggie had to dodge this way and that to avoid getting trampled. The sound of the bagpipes—which reminded her of the braying of the circus donkeys—faded a little, and was replaced by the steady beating of a drum. Its player was bellowing about 'Mrs General Mite', and Maggie's breath caught. She'd heard of this woman before; she was said to be the smallest woman on earth. Was it true, she wondered, or a showman's trick? Perhaps a short woman walking convincingly on her knees. Maggie wanted to find out, on the slim chance that this woman—like her—was a true oddity. She hesitated, though; the line was long, and she was in no hurry. It could wait.

She kept moving, hurrying past the boxing tent with banners spruiking a special match, black versus white, which seemed to have piqued the interest of the men who crowded up to the ticket seller. A second tent, featuring women boxers, was drawing just as much attention.

At the far end of the alley was a merry-go-round, its swings full of squealing children with kicking feet, their heads thrown back to catch the breeze. Maggie turned and slowly made her way back. She couldn't keep a steady pace, nor a straight line. She paused near the sign advertising a six-legged jumbuck—a fine swimmer, apparently—and skirted around the machine that tested a person's strength. The American tattooed lady sounded interesting, and Maggie was a little curious about the peep and cinematograph shows, although she'd never have admitted it, let alone be seen going into one. Not that women were allowed anyway. It was a poster for aerialists that really caught her attention, though; she pondered if their act was worth an invitation to join the Braun Brothers' circus, and hurried toward their tent. But before she reached it, another banner snagged her eye.

'Marley the Ghost Child,' the banner announced in bright blue letters against a lighter blue background. Crammed next to the words was an illustration of a waif-like girl, her head tilted to one side to rest on the 'd' of the word 'child'. Maggie frowned; on the board outside the Ghost Child's tent, the showman was blasting a cornet, stopping every now and then to collect money from eager patrons.

'A genuine ghost right here, ladies and gents, like nothing else you'll ever see in your life,' he called. 'The poor lass's mother read Charles Dickens' *A Christmas Carol* when she was expecting and was so frightened by the notion of being visited by ghosts that the wee bairn came out as one.' He shook his head sorrowfully. 'I managed to capture her, and named her after Jacob Marley, that very first ghost to visit Mr Dickens' Scrooge.'

Maggie had read *A Christmas Carol*. It wasn't frightening. Not unless you found your own deeds catching up with you to be a frightening prospect. Which, on second thought, many people probably would.

She wondered how much truth was in the rest of his words. Was there really a child sitting in that tent, waiting to be gawked at? Or was it just another trick?

She had to know. Aware she was likely being foolish, she made her way to the showman and paid her entry fee, keeping her head down so there was no chance he'd see beneath her veil. She didn't want to be found out as another freak.

'Make sure you touch her,' the man said as he tucked Maggie's money away.

'Excuse me?'

'Rub her arm or her cheek, to prove to yourself it's not a trick. You'll see there's no pale paint to come off.'

Maggie's heart beat a peculiar staccato. She didn't like this. She wanted to turn around, to run away to the safety of the circus. But she made herself enter the tent.

The light was dim inside, and it took a moment for her eyes to adjust. While she waited, she breathed in the scent of the sawdust scattered on the ground. Everything was so similar to the circus— the tents, the sweets and popcorn being sold, the almost tangible sense of excitement—yet it was also so different. The crowds here weren't lining up to take their seats, but were huddling together in a tight bunch that extended to the very edges of the tent. They were all looking in the same direction. The tent blocked a great deal of the outside noise, and Maggie could hear the awe and curiosity around her.

'Go on, touch her,' one woman murmured to her husband. 'Like the man said. See if she's real.'

Maggie threaded through the people, careful not to tread on any toes or draw attention to herself, until she met the two-yard gap that separated the crowd from the ghost—a gap that seemed to be created by the patrons' own fear, for there was no rope or barrier to keep them back.

It was indeed a child. That much was impossible to doubt. She was a delicately built girl of around nine or so, clad in the sort of frilly white dress that the daughters of fine families in Sydney wore to Sunday church. She was perched on a chair, oversized to make her look even smaller in comparison. A spotlight—the only light inside the tent—shone down on her. Her skin was so white it was almost translucent, and she had long, silvery-white hair kept back by a white ribbon tied in a bow on top of her head. Her eyes, which were violet, were framed by lashes and eyebrows just as light as her hair. As Maggie took her in—from the limp bow down to the small bare feet trailing patterns in the sawdust—her heart constricted. She supposed ghosts didn't need to wear shoes, but children should.

The girl looked down as a fully grown man approached her and seized her wrist, then rubbed vigorously at her skin with his thumb.

'Nothing,' he breathed in awe, holding his hand up to show the crowd.

'Does she feel like a ghost?' a woman in a turban asked, stepping forward, her hand outstretched and hesitant.

'Her skin feels odd—cold, like?'

Maggie wanted to be sick. He was lying, but the crowd would believe what they wanted to. She needed to get out of there; she needed to leave this tent that could have been her own home, her own life, with the slightest change of fortune. She turned and, not caring whose toes she trod on, raced out. She didn't stop when she reached the crowds of Sideshow Alley; there was still no air, and she needed to get somewhere she could lift her veil and breathe.

For the rest of her life, Maggie would never remember the race back to the circus grounds. Only the panic, and the relief washing over her once familiar faces were back in sight. Without pausing, she discarded her hat and crawled beneath the baggage wagon, her chest aching as her heart finally, ever so slowly, returned to its normal beat.

And then, guilt skulked in. Every time she closed her eyes, she saw that little girl again, surrounded by people yet so alone. And she, who should have understood, who should have seen the hurting human beneath the showman's display, had run off.

Maggie rolled onto her side, bringing her knees up to her midsection and hugging them. Distance gave her clarity, and she knew her panic for what it was now: cowardice. The Ghost Child's life would never be Maggie's life; her father's decision to give her to the circus, for all the complex feelings she had toward it, had ensured that.

'Put your selfish fears aside,' Maggie snarled to herself. 'You're grown. That Marley girl isn't.'

She stuck her head out from under the wagon; it was too late to go back now, for the light was starting to change, and soon they'd be getting ready for the night's performance. She must have stayed in her panic longer than she'd thought.

'Tomorrow,' she whispered, making it a promise. She would slip away and find the Ghost Child again. And if Rafferty missed her, she would remind him how many years' service she'd given to the circus. They could do without her for once.

Chapter Twenty-Two

Maggie tiptoed forward, moving carefully and unobtrusively until she was standing near the little girl. She had waited, patient, inside the tent until the crowd thinned, their curiosity satiated after two women and a child had run their mitts over the Ghost Child's arms. Those that remained slowly lost their quiet reverence; the mystique of the girl was dissipating, and an argument over whether this counted as a haunting broke out.

Sensing her moment had arrived, Maggie quietly called out, 'Hello, Marley.'

The little girl's head jerked up and Maggie raised one hand in greeting. The girl frowned, but she didn't look away.

What now? Maggie had experienced a sleepless night, wracked with guilt that she hadn't taken the opportunity to speak to the girl. But now she was here, ready to make things right, she didn't know what to say. Thinking there was nothing else for it, she opened her mouth and let whatever words were there fall out.

'I'm sorry. About all this. About us.'

The child still frowned, but it was a different frown now. She tilted her head to one side, causing her silvery hair to fall in a wave.

'I try to make *them* the show,' the girl said in a soft, shy voice, gesturing at the talkative crowd around her. Maggie had to step closer to hear over their din; it took her into the gap between the remaining crowd and Marley, but if anyone cared they didn't show it. Either they were too busy arguing, or they thought she was going to touch Marley to test her ghostliness for herself.

'I pretend I'm the audience, the one looking at them,' the girl said. 'I try to guess who might be kind, what it would be like to live with them. Only ...' She glanced down at her lap, pulling at some of the lace. Maggie could see now that the dress was aged and a little too short for her. She wanted to snort; what kind of ghost outgrew its clothes? 'My eyes aren't very good from a distance,' the girl continued. 'So it's hard.'

One man had stepped level with Maggie; not wanting him to paw at the girl, Maggie moved in front of him, practically shouldering him out of the way. He made a sound of protest, but when Maggie kept her back resolutely turned to him, he declared there was better to see elsewhere anyway. She turned slightly to watch him exit the tent; the rest of the crowd went with him. Knowing it would only be a matter of minutes before new patrons came in, Maggie knelt down in front of Marley, and asked, 'Can you see me if I'm this close?'

Her little chest sank back; she was probably afraid of being touched again. She bit her lower lip and nodded. Maggie took the edge of her net veil in quivering fingers.

'I want to show you something.'

She glanced from side to side, but the tent was still empty apart from the two of them.

Carefully, Maggie raised her veil. As if by instinct, Marley leaned forward. Her lips parted in surprise, and then her face lit up.

'Oh! You're different too!'

Something lodged in Maggie's throat. She had to cough several times to dislodge it.

'Yes, I'm different too.'

'Do they also put you on display?'

Maggie's instinct was to say yes, but she hesitated. She wasn't on display, not the way this poor girl was. A tent for a cage, and crowds she could never get any distance from, exhibited alongside the six-legged sheep and tiny horses and dancing ducks, as if she were no more human than they.

'No,' she said. 'I perform in a circus.'

Marley drew in a long breath, as though she'd never heard anything so impressive. Maggie grinned at her.

'My name's Maggie. It's a pleasure to make your acquaintance. Is Marley your real name?'

The girl shook her head.

'I don't like the name Marley. I've read the book. Marley was a man. Jacob Marley. A bad man too. I'm not bad. And—' She stopped herself, her face suddenly fearful.

'And you're not a ghost.'

In response, tears welled. Maggie longed to reach out a hand but didn't dare. This girl had to put up with hands on her all day long.

The girl beckoned Maggie closer, wanting to say something that she was afraid would be overheard, even though no one was near. Maggie shuffled forward, still on her knees, careless of how the sawdust dirtied her skirt.

'I don't know why I look like this. Why I don't look like everyone else.'

Maggie thought she might tear up too. She'd asked herself the same question so many times as a child.

'But I'm really not a ghost,' the girl said. 'My eyes aren't even violet. They're regular old blue. The spotlight makes them look this colour.' The words were the faintest whisper, a shared secret.

'What's your real name?'

'I don't know.' She nodded at the entrance of the tent, where the showman shouted his made-up stories about her and took money from those who would never see her as anything but the mystical Ghost Child. '*He* only ever calls me Marley, or *girl*.'

'Is he your father?'

'No. I don't have a father. Or a mother.'

Maggie knew this couldn't be true; the child's parents, like Maggie's mother, must not have been able to face living with a daughter so different from what they'd expected. The thought made Maggie clench her jaw. She was careful not to let any of her anger slip where the child could see it, though. She didn't want to frighten her.

'Would you like another name?'

The girl's lips twitched, a brief flitter of a smile crossing them. But then two children burst through the tent's entrance. They let a sliver of light in, and before they'd even had the chance to let their eyes adjust, they were poking at Marley's face with rough, sticky fingers, the elder one lifting great clumps of the girl's silver hair and letting it fall back down in shimmering waves, calling out to her father in excitement. Maggie thought she might break apart, watching Marley sit there and take such manhandling with quiet resignation. It wasn't right.

She stood, waiting until the children tired of their entertainment. When they finally ran away, it was to the rumble of a fresh crowd making their way inside the tent. Maggie hurried to speak again before anyone could reach the two of them.

'How about Robin for a name?' she said. The girl was running her fingers through her hair, trying to untangle the knots they'd made in it.

'Robin?'

'A few weeks ago I saw a pink robin,' Maggie said. 'It looked different to most other robins, but it was all the more special and lovely because of it.' She'd found the robin somewhere it didn't really belong, too, but she kept that part to herself.

'Robin,' the girl said again. She closed her eyes, pale lashes nearly disappearing against her cheeks. She swayed a little from side to side, chanting the name. Those who had entered the tent and gathered at just over a yard's distance pointed in a frightened way. Finally, she went still again and opened her eyes to look at Maggie. She smiled, exposing the kind of crooked teeth that told Maggie they'd only recently grown in new.

'I like it. Thank you.'

'You're welcome.' Maggie glanced at the impatient crowd, shifting ever so slightly closer. One woman muttered that she was spoiling their view. 'I have to go. I don't want to get this crowd stirred up, and I'm needed back at the circus soon anyway. But I'll come back to visit you again.'

'All right.' The hollow way Robin said it told Maggie she didn't believe her.

'I promise. Tomorrow, I'll be here. How about I bring you a book? You must be quite a good reader to have got through *A Christmas Carol* at your age. Do you like to read?'

'Not *A Christmas Carol*.'

'Of course. I'll bring you something else. Something that's not about ghosts. Would you enjoy that, Robin?'

At the name, the girl showed Maggie her biggest smile yet. Maggie could see the leap of faith she was choosing to take.

'Yes, please,' she said. And then the woman who'd complained about Maggie was standing next to her, shouldering her out of the way just as Maggie had done to the man before, hand already stretching forward. As her fingertips met Robin's cheek, the little girl barely even flinched. She still looked at Maggie, who saluted her as she hitched her bag onto her shoulder and stepped away.

'See you tomorrow, Maggie.'

'See you tomorrow, Robin.'

***

That night, as she stood backstage waiting for the cue that would turn her from Maggie into the Lagoon Creature, Maggie made a decision. She didn't know how, but she was going to rescue

Robin. She was going to take her away from that life of exhibition and unwanted pawing. She was going to take her under her wing, and do what no one had done for Maggie as a child: give her the life she deserved.

Chapter Twenty-Three

'Here you are.' Maggie rummaged around in her leather bag and pulled out her worn copy of *Seven Little Australians*. Robin's surprise that she had actually kept her promise to return was so affecting, she needed the distraction of the book to stop herself from misting up. 'This is one of my favourites. My father gave it to me the last time I saw him.' He'd probably stolen it, but Robin didn't need to know that. Maggie pulled out her fountain pen and carefully inscribed *For Robin* on the title page, saying the words out loud as she wrote them. Then she held it out to the girl. 'Books can make you feel surrounded by friends when you're lonely.'

Robin hesitated for a second. Then she took the book, her fingers tracing the cover and spine. Maggie hoped that the man who ran the tent wouldn't take it away from her; if he did, she would make sure to buy her another copy when she'd taken her away from this awful place.

'Thank you,' Robin said quietly. 'For the book, and for keeping your promise.'

'I always do. And you're welcome.' They shared a look of companionship, and Maggie knew this moment was as rare for the little girl as it was for her. Outside the light would be starting to dip; she'd only been able to escape the needs of the circus in the late afternoon. It meant the Sideshow Alley crowd had lessened while patrons went in search of an early tea, which was good. But it also meant Maggie wasn't able to stay for long.

'I'm sorry I have to leave again so soon today. Tomorrow I'll do better.' She didn't tell Robin that tomorrow she also planned not to walk out of that tent alone. She'd already pinched a dress from one of Rosemary's brood, plus one of Adlai's dark wigs and some of the petals Charlotte used to stain her lips and cheeks. A quick bribe to one of the local children who were always hanging about Sideshow Alley would mean the showman would see her enter the tent with a child. Once inside, she'd wait until a quiet moment; the bribed child would be sent to slip out from underneath a corner of the tent, just as she'd seen the trio of young boys attempt on her first visit there—no one would care to watch for a child sneaking out instead of in. A quick change of clothing, the wig donned and colour added to the pale cheeks and lips, then Maggie and Robin would exit side by side. She might even carry the girl, the way Charlotte carried Maggie in their act. A daring trick, right underneath the showman's nose, but Maggie knew people only ever saw what they were presented with. A veiled woman and her black-haired child would draw no interest from the man.

They would have to be quick to leave the alley and the agricultural fair, though—the very next patron inside the tent would send up the alarm that there was no Ghost Child to be seen. Maggie wasn't concerned; she had a lifetime's experience in avoiding notice and being lightfooted; she would get them back to the circus before the showman had even finished searching Sideshow Alley. There, Robin would be easy to hide until they moved out of town. And if Rafferty started asking questions— well, he'd just have to live with her decision, the way she had always lived with his.

Maggie was putting faith in Robin being quick to understand

and follow instructions. It was a risk, but telling her the plan in advance seemed a greater risk. What if she accidentally let something slip to her guardian?

All Maggie would allow herself to say was, 'Tomorrow is going to be a better day, Robin. I promise you.'

The girl's arms curled around the book, holding it close to her heart.

'All right, Maggie. I already can't wait.'

Chapter Twenty-Four

Maggie trudged back to the circus, barely aware of her surroundings, her mind on Robin back in that tent, so utterly helpless because she was a child, and a girl, and a 'freak'. Maggie hated that word—she always had. Rafferty had expressly forbidden anyone at the circus to call her a freak, so the only time she ever heard it was from the occasional audience member.

Back in the dressing tent, Maggie glanced around; there was the usual buzz of motion and chatter, but Charlotte wasn't there yet. She changed into her costume with mechanical movements, her fingers automatically pulling up her stockings and closing her fastenings. It was only as everyone was putting the final touches to their costumes that Maggie began to worry about Charlotte's whereabouts. When the man who was both ticket seller and spruiker began shouting his enticements loudly enough to penetrate the tent, she started to panic; and when Itsuo had finished dressing in his costume of light-coloured trousers tucked into knee-high boots, and headed outside to do some warm-up flip-flaps, she followed him and began circling the wagons.

She checked beneath them in case Charlotte had fallen asleep under one, even though she never slept outside. She even poked her head into the big top, where the mugs were beginning to argue over seats and spill their popcorn. Charlotte was not there.

Heading back to the dressing tent, Maggie spotted Smith. Without stopping to think, she marched right up to him and said, 'Have you seen Charlotte?'

His expression was startled. He didn't say anything in return, only frowned a second later. With an impatient kick at the ground, Maggie asked her question again.

'No,' Smith said. 'Isn't she usually with you before a show?'

Maggie resisted the urge to retort that if Charlotte were with her, she wouldn't be asking after her.

Then she saw Greta, sliding her swords from their sheaths to check their blades, Judge loitering at her feet.

'Greta!' she called. Had she ever said the sword dancer's name before? Had she even addressed her directly? Maggie shrugged the thought away. 'I'm looking for Charlotte. Have you seen her?'

At least Greta was quick to reply. 'No.' Her eyes traversed the tent, just as Maggie's had already done. 'Is she missing?'

'Maybe—I haven't seen her since she went out looking for a drink.'

Greta's eyes widened. 'We can't do our act without her.'

'I know—that's why I'm trying to find her.'

'Where have you looked?'

'Everywhere within the circus grounds.'

Greta sank her teeth into her lower lip. 'We need Rafferty,' she said.

Judge, sensing something, started whining.

The two women took off, side by side, Judge at their heels. They found Rafferty backstage, shining the gold buttons on his jacket with the cuff of his sleeve. Already, the band were playing 'Tarador', a composition by Herr Von der Mehden that Rafferty liked to open the show with.

'Rafferty, we can't find Charlotte,' Maggie said. 'I've looked everywhere for her.'

Rafferty closed his eyes for a second. In that moment, Maggie saw him again as she'd seen him when the pinch artist was making threats. How long had he worn those creases either side of his mouth? She exchanged a glance with Greta.

'It's too late to keep looking for her, isn't it?' Greta asked uncertainly. 'The show's about to start.'

'What'll we do? Our act hinges on her,' Maggie said.

'I know, I know.' Rafferty looked upward, his lips moving in silent calculation. 'We'll have to do the old version of the show. The one we started the season with. Think you can manage that?'

Maggie's mouth set in a straight line. It was months since she'd been jeered—since her death was the high point of the act.

But they were performers, and that meant adapting to changes at the last minute.

'Let Annie and Smith know,' Rafferty ordered. 'Then gather everyone to me for a run-down of the new running order. And ladies, let's remember: those people out there have paid the same as any other mug in any other town. It's up to us to make sure they don't know tonight's show was different.'

***

Maggie felt the audience's horrified gaze on her as she crept out into the ring. The old, exaggerated movements were uncomfortably familiar, as was the stitched-together costume, which looked more like rags than ever. She didn't seek out an audience member to stare in the eye, though, as she used to. She couldn't bear to.

She reminded herself that at least she didn't have to endure their touch, as Robin did.

As she limped toward the spotlight, she realised she might have to perform this old act for the duration of their stay in Hay. Rafferty wouldn't want word getting around town that one single audience had seen a worse show. He would either stick to this show— spreading the sympathetic lie that the tightrope walker had been injured after their first few performances—or alternate between the two different versions. The thought of enduring repeated scorn made Maggie angry with Charlotte, and she scowled as she came face to face with Greta and her swords.

For the next few minutes, she had to concentrate, so Greta's final thrust wouldn't hurt her. Maggie thought the sword dancer was making her jabs less forceful than they'd been in the past, and she was grateful for the consideration.

They went through the motions, Maggie spitting and snarling before finally miming her death. Then she was in Smith's arms, being lifted high above his head. The audience cheered, and just as she'd done in those long-ago Sydney performances, Maggie closed her eyes, as if that could shield her from the sound.

Chapter Twenty-Five

W hen Smith put her down out of sight of the audience, Maggie scanned the backstage area, chewing the nail of her thumb. Still no sign of Charlotte. She asked around again, not caring that each face she met wore a startled expression at her approach, but she was only met with shaking heads. This disappearance was unlike Charlotte—even when the forward somersault had deserted her, she still showed up every night and put on the best act she could. Something must have happened. Was she right at this moment somewhere where she needed help? Was she thinking that her colleagues would notice her absence and send someone out to look for her?

After changing back into her regular clothes, Maggie picked up a ring harness left carelessly on the ground and put it away, but her mind was only half on the task, her eyes constantly flitting up at any noise, in the hope that it was Charlotte.

And then, just as the cast were filing backstage, letting in the sounds of the audience making their way out of the big top, Charlotte arrived.

She half-stumbled into the tent, looking like she was about to faint. Maggie raced up to her, but Rafferty, his face shining with sweat from his final curtain call, reached her first. He threw an arm around Charlotte's waist, supporting her; she looked at him in a manner that said she didn't really see him. Her eyes danced for a bit, then found Maggie's, her face crumpling as she stretched her arms toward her. Maggie caught her hands, their fingers intertwining. An overwhelming odour of smoke clung to Charlotte's clothes, her skin, her hair: a rich, intense scent that made Maggie pull back in fear. Charlotte began to cry.

'What is it?' Maggie asked. 'What happened?'

Charlotte didn't answer. Rafferty shouted for the wood-and-water joey to bring her something to drink. Maggie tried to straighten Charlotte up enough to look at her face. There was a dark smudge on her jaw, like a bruise. Maggie ran a thumb along it, leaving a trail. It was soot.

'It was an accident,' Charlotte hiccupped. 'I didn't mean for it to happen. I don't even really know how it did. One minute it was all laughs and dancing and drink, and the next, everything w–w–was ... alight.'

The joey brought a canvas waterbag, and Rafferty pulled the cork and held it to Charlotte's lips.

'Are you hurt?' he asked. Charlotte shook her head. 'Was anyone else hurt?'

'No. Everyone got out in time.'

'Got out of what?' Maggie asked.

A crowd had gathered around them, the performers' painted faces either rapt or fearful. The children who were old enough to still be awake hovered in the background, puzzled by this sudden break from their post-show routine.

'The hotel,' Charlotte said. 'I waited outside for some men to bring me a drink, and when a couple of young fellas agreed, they seemed rough around the edges but otherwise harmless enough. We had a good time for a bit—only, they got bored when the turps really took hold. That's when they decided it would be funny to try and smuggle me inside.' Charlotte's tears slowed. Her eyes and nose were red.

'Charlotte, don't tell me you agreed to this fool plan?' Rafferty shook his head. 'You could've ended up in the watch-house.'

Charlotte sniffed. Maggie pulled out her handkerchief and handed it wordlessly to her.

'I know,' Charlotte said. 'I just—I didn't want the fun to end. One of them gave me his coat, and another his hat. We thought if I kept my head down, no one would even notice me—or if they did, they'd think I was a man.'

'Only a complete dingbat would fall for that,' Maggie said. Charlotte gave the smallest of shrugs.

'I think it did work, for a little bit. At least ...' She scrunched her eyes up. 'It's so hard to remember. It all happened so fast. I had a drink, or maybe two. And then some man came over to us, shouting to the rafters.'

Rafferty groaned. No one else dared to interrupt.

'He was irate about a woman being where no woman belonged. The fellas that were with me jumped up real quick, and exchanged words. They got nose to nose with the man, and they were all swearing like you wouldn't believe. And then—then one of my fellas took a swing. I panicked—I didn't want to cause a fistfight. So I threw off the coat and hat, yelling to lay off because it was my fault, and I would leave if they would all just shut up. Maybe I made it worse, because all hell broke loose then. A couple of punches turned into a brawl. There was glass breaking, men beating each other with chairs. And then ... a fire.'

Maggie could barely breathe. 'How?' she asked.

'I don't know!' Charlotte twisted the handkerchief in her fingers. 'Someone threw a match down without thinking? Or–or maybe it was deliberate? All I know is it went up so suddenly ...'

'What's left of the place?' Rafferty asked. Charlotte grimaced. 'The hotel,' he pushed. 'How badly was it damaged?'

Charlotte dipped her head, so all they could see was the limp bow tied in her hair, turned the off-white colour of a brolga from smoke and ash.

'It's still standing.' The words floated up to them. 'I stayed until the fire brigade put it out. I know we had a show, but it seemed only right, when I ...'

'When you were the one to cause the fire,' Rafferty said softly.

Charlotte flinched, but now that she'd begun telling them what had happened, she didn't seem able to stop. 'I didn't get to see inside afterward. The fire brigade were keeping everyone back, in case the roof fell in. There were black stains on the outside walls, but I think they were from the smoke and soot more than the flames ...'

'When you took the coat and hat off, did many people get a good look at you?' Rafferty's words were clipped.

Charlotte licked her lips nervously. 'Maybe. Hard to tell, given the brawl, but some men did stand to the side to watch for a bit before choosing a side.'

A ripple of sound went through the crowd.

Rafferty pressed his fingers to his eyelids. He took a long, steadying breath, then turned away from Charlotte to face the rest of the group.

'It'll be all over town by morning that some Jane from the circus burned down the local hotel. Start packing. Be quick and quiet about it. Leave the tents until last, so nothing can be seen by passers-by. Where's Nev?'

'Here, boss.' Nev stepped forward, fingers plucking at the buttons on his waistcoat. It was the first sign of nerves Maggie had ever seen from him.

'Can you lead us in the dark?' Rafferty asked.

Maggie heard more than one person gasp. Nev's affirmative response could barely be heard over the increasing mutters.

'Good. We'll have to do a night flitter.'

Chapter Twenty-Six

A shocked silence followed this pronouncement.
Maggie was the first to speak, surprising them all.

'Rafferty, we can't.'

He sighed. 'I know we won't find crowds like this again soon. But they're not going to come now. Not after this.'

'You know it's not just that.' Maggie paused. In all her time with the Braun Brothers' Royal Circus, they had never done a night flitter, and the thought of it filled her with shame. 'We can't just sneak away like thieves in the night and then parade into the next town with our heads held high. Gossip spreads faster than fire in country towns—the news will be all around the district in no time.'

'The next few weeks will be tough, no doubt about it,' Rafferty said. 'But there's nothing we can do about that.'

'Couldn't we stay and try to make amends?' she asked. 'Maybe put on a benefit show, to raise funds for a rebuild, or the district hospital or something, to win back their good will?'

But Rafferty shook his head. 'They'll think we're trying to buy them off, and we'll look worse for doing it under the guise of charity.'

Maggie tried to protest again, but he cut her off. 'We can't stay, and that's that.' His voice was gentle but stern. 'We'll be lucky if they don't try to set our tents alight. There's no time for goodbyes, let alone making amends. We need to get on the road.'

No time for goodbyes. The words hit Maggie like a blow.

She'd promised Robin she'd come back tomorrow.

She'd promised herself she would rescue her.

And now she couldn't.

She couldn't even make a quick trip to the agricultural fair to explain to Robin why she wouldn't be able to visit anymore; at this time of night the grounds would be closed and the gates locked. Tomorrow, the little girl would be waiting, expecting Maggie to show up; it would be one more disappointment in a lifetime full of them.

Tears stung her eyes, and she swiped at them angrily. She looked one way then another, hoping to find some magic answer; Charlotte reached for her hand, a gesture of concern that enraged Maggie, who snatched it away as if her fingers had met with a hot coal.

'Do you know what you've done?' she snapped. She'd never spoken with such venom before, not even to her father. 'How could you be so reckless?'

'I didn't mean for this to happen,' Charlotte said. 'You know I didn't. I would never—'

'Wouldn't you? Because as far as I can see, you do exactly what you want with no thought for others, and always have. *Your* day out, *your* drinking, *your* act. Do you ever think about anyone but yourself? Or does your selfishness run so deep that there's no room for thoughts of others in that pretty, empty head?'

Charlotte looked as though she'd been struck.

'That's enough now, Maggie girl,' Rafferty said. 'All of you, go, and pack your things. I want to be on the road within the hour.'

*

Maggie paced the circus grounds. It had just gone midnight, and most of the packing was done. Maggie had barely helped; instead she'd tossed around idea after idea, trying to decide what to do about Robin. At one point she'd even pulled out her paper and pen and begun to write a letter. But who could she get to deliver it? There was no one she knew, and the townspeople wouldn't want to help her after Charlotte's stunt.

Bloody Charlotte.

It was a hot night, the hottest they'd had yet, and the heat got beneath her skin and invaded her senses, fuelling her anger and frustration. She scrubbed at her forehead with her sleeve.

Maggie came to a standstill in the spot the spruiker usually stood in as he spun stories of the wonders loitering crowds could expect to see inside the big top. His wooden stand was not there now, nor were the carts for popcorn and balloons. A passer-by wouldn't think this unusual; they'd assume everyone had gone to bed for the night. Only the big top remained, the dirt around it pockmarked by horse and donkey hooves and heeled boots, to hint at the excitements to come the following day. But Maggie could sense the universally-held breath of the circus folk; by the time the townspeople rose the next morning, glittering memories and the divots from the tent pegs would be the only traces of the circus left behind.

Maggie had to talk to Rafferty. She didn't care how busy he was, or how distressed by the turn their night had taken.

She found him near the entrance to the grounds, his back to the circus, as though he were about to abandon it.

'Rafferty, I need to speak with you.' His eyes shot sideways, regarding her for a moment.

'Come with me, then.'

'Where are we going?'

'There's something I need to see.'

Maggie fell into step beside him. As he led her out of the circus grounds, she noticed his shoes barely made a sound on the dirt roads; he was walking softly, and she mimicked him. Footsteps at midnight might draw unwanted attention.

Rafferty wove his way through the town, only stopping when they came to a corner made by two dirt roads meeting at the southern end of the town's centre.

Opposite them, beyond the dirt road, was a hotel. It had only one storey, but the broad verandah, with its cast-iron posts and lacy trimming, and the ornate writing of the hotel's name on one wall just below the roof, gave it an atmosphere of grandeur. Half of the name was obscured by smudges as dark as the night around them, and the stripes on the curved tin awning only just showed beneath the stains of ash and smoke. The glass in two of the rectangular panelled windows had shattered. In the meagre moonlight Maggie could see that the front right corner of the roof was missing, presumably collapsed in.

Rafferty took a couple of uncertain steps forward, then stopped, leaning against one of the tall, spindly trees that lined the dirt road before the hotel.

'Lucky the building is mostly brick. Damage could've been much worse otherwise,' he muttered, as if he were trying to convince himself.

Maggie nodded. The odour of smoke still hovered in the air, so that every breath was acrid on her tongue. She wondered how long it would take for the smell to dissipate. Or would it forever linger in the walls, no amount of fresh paint enough to take away the memory of the circus woman who'd started a brawl?

'Do you want to go in?' she asked softly. There was something awful about looking at the burned building. Maggie tried to tell herself it was just bricks and iron, but she knew that wasn't right. It was someone's livelihood, and probably their home, too. It was a place where many people might have died, if they hadn't controlled the blaze so quickly. She wasn't sure she wanted to see inside, but she'd go with Rafferty if he wanted her to.

'No,' he said. 'They've put ropes across the door anyway.'

Maggie squinted in the dark; the entrance was angled toward the corner, proudly facing the intersection of the streets. Rafferty was right.

'Do you mind if I just stay here for a bit?' Rafferty asked. Without waiting for an answer, he let his knees slowly fold so that he slid down the trunk of the tree. 'A night flitter, Maggie girl. Never thought I'd see the day.'

Maggie hitched up her skirt and sat down next to him. 'There's nothing else you can do now, you know,' she said. 'We don't have enough in the coffers to pay for that kind of damage. They're bound to have insurance, anyway.'

'I know. Still doesn't make it right.'

Maggie bent her knees up before her, resting her forearms on them. A mosquito was hovering by her ear, and she bobbed her head away from it. She didn't want to disrupt the night air by slapping it.

'There's something I need to ask you,' she said, then stopped, not sure how to go on. 'I've been to the agricultural show every day since our arrival,' she said slowly. 'Visiting Sideshow Alley. I found a little girl in one of the tents there. Robin.' Maggie wanted to catch the name, cup it in protective hands and hold it close to her heart. 'That's not her real name. But it is now. I gave it to her, you see.' In a breathless rush, Maggie told Rafferty all about Robin, her unusual pale looks, how she was at the mercy of a heartless showman, how audiences pawed at her all day long. Finally, she finished with, 'And I promised her I'd be back again. Tomorrow.'

Rafferty's head fell back against the bark of the tree. Maggie looked at him, taking in the changes in his familiar face: the deeper shadows beneath his eyes, the lines fanning out from their corners. He looked weary, but there was something else in his expression Maggie couldn't quite define. Was it just the stress of the night flitter? Or was it something more? She shuffled a little closer to him.

'Are you all right?'

'Yes, Maggie girl. It's just that everything seems harder since Ida and Hercules died. Every decision weighs more heavily.'

Sorrow crept through Maggie. She could see it now, the way the ringmaster grieved the elephants. She'd been so caught up in her letters to Mr O'Lehry and her new act with Charlotte that she hadn't noticed before. She wondered: did he dream of them at night? Did his finger again and again feel that final squeeze of the trigger that ended Hercules' life? She touched him gently, just a flutter of her two smallest fingers on his sleeve.

'You had to do it,' she reminded him. 'Hercules wasn't going to budge.'

'I know. Being the ringmaster means making painful decisions for the good of the circus, even when you don't want to. Which is why I have to say no to your request, Maggie.'

Maggie was startled. 'But you don't even know what I'm going to ask for.'

'I think I do. You want to stay back when we leave.'

'Not for long,' Maggie rushed to clarify. 'Only for half a day or so. Enough time for the agricultural show to open so I can get to Robin. To say goodbye to her, or to—'

Rafferty was already shaking his head, not giving Maggie time to broach the subject of a potential rescue. She huffed in frustration and dug her fingers into the ground, so that dirt jammed underneath her nails.

'I'd catch up with you all before we reached the next town. The act needn't be affected,' she said.

'Maggie, I know you can ride, but you're not experienced enough to catch us up that quickly. And even if it were safe to leave a wagon and horses behind so you could follow, you wouldn't have Nev to show you the way. You could easily get lost.'

'You could leave some kind of markers for me to follow.' Maggie heard her voice growing in volume, and forced herself to drop it again in case any sleeping townspeople were woken by it. 'It would only be a few shows without me, at the very most.'

'I don't want to put on any number of shows without you. Regardless, I'm not leaving you here on your own. If the circus is in danger, you are even more so.'

'Me? I didn't do anything.'

'You know that, and I know that. But we also know that men are always eager to blame people different to themselves for all the wrongs in the world. And Maggie, my girl, who is more noticeably different than you?'

'I don't care,' she said, jutting her chin out. 'I'll take the risk.'

'No, you won't. I'm your boss, and I do care. I forbid you to stay behind.'

Maggie had to take a few breaths before she could speak with any sense of calm. 'I've been your Lagoon Creature without complaint, Rafferty.' She'd known from her young adulthood that she'd have to be a performer; she didn't have the physical strength for a circus hand, nor the confidence and command needed for an animal trainer. With Rosemary already employed as cook, there'd been no other role left for her. But she hadn't dedicated herself enough to training to have any special skills outside of the general clowning, flip-flaps, balancing and posturing that all who grew up in the circus knew how to do—all she'd had was her face. 'It turns out that all this time I could've been a sympathetic character. Only for all your care, you still couldn't see my face as anything other than fearsome, could you?'

Rafferty rubbed a hand over his eyes. 'I tried to do what was best for you, Maggie. I know I failed. I've never been able to separate myself from the showman, the ringmaster who only ever sees the potential for shock and surprise. Every audience we have seen, and every audience we might see, lives in my head, and my loyalty has been to their entertainment. I should have done better by you. I'm sorry. Even so, I do hope I have been something more to you than just a boss who constantly fell short. I have watched you grow, taught you all that I know, trusted you to take over the most delicate and important parts of the business. I cannot—I *will* not—let my Maggie girl be hurt. I'm getting old, and I just don't know how much more pain I can bear witness to—'

Maggie wanted to cry. She'd never heard Rafferty admit to any vulnerability before, never seen him shrouded in doubt and fear. She wanted to be angry with him still, wanted to fight for Robin, but she didn't have it in her after all that he'd confessed to. She wondered when life had got so complicated.

'My name's not Rafferty, you know,' Rafferty said abruptly. There was that showman's voice, creeping in and pushing away the moment of exposed weakness. For a second Maggie thought of not playing his game; but she knew how it felt when a moment of raw honesty clouded over with fear or regret, so that it became something you needed to quickly put behind yourself.

So she said, 'I guessed as much. Rafferty fits too perfectly. And I long ago assumed you don't have any brothers, since I've never seen one in my many years with the Braun Brothers' Royal Circus.'

That got a brief smile out of Rafferty. 'No, I don't have any brothers. No family at all, as a matter of fact. I'm not even a Braun. Just Jack Bryennios, an orphan nobody with dreams as big as his surname.'

'Why Braun Brothers' then?'

'Bryennios was too hard for most people to wrap their minds and tongues around. Australians don't take well to more than two syllables, no matter how many generations the name's been here. And a circus needs a name that's as easy to remember as it is showy, or you've lost before you've even begun. Brothers was because I fancied having a large family.'

They went quiet again, the only sounds around them the chirruping of insects in the night. Maggie pondered the complicated nature of names, the pleasure and pain they could carry. Jack and Robin and Mag-Pie. She bit her thumbnail, tearing a crescent moon from it.

'You really won't let me stay?' she eventually asked.

'I'm sorry. I'm not doing it to hurt you. It's for the best.' Rafferty gave Maggie's knee a squeeze, then stood up, holding his hand out to help her to her feet. When she rose, he kept his grip firm around hers for a moment. 'I'm going to have Smith watch over you all night, Maggie. If you try to sneak off or hide, he'll stop you and bring you back, even if he has to carry you.'

So that was it, then. Maggie was denied any chance of keeping her promise to Robin.

Chapter Twenty-Seven

It wasn't her fault.

That's what Charlotte told herself as she trudged toward Rosemary. The big top was coming down, the final part of the circus's packing for their hasty departure. The commissariat wagon would be setting out any second now, and she wanted to be on it.

'Can I ride with you and Nev?'

Charlotte didn't have to ask permission—Rafferty's rules were that they could join any wagon, so long as there was adequate room—but she thought after the night's events it might be best. Rosemary, who'd been settling a sleepy Victor in next to Nev, turned, her expression fierce.

'You think I want you where you can influence my boy?' she snapped. She hauled herself up into the wagon. 'Find someone else who'll put up with you, for tonight it's not me. Don't you go hassling Adlai, either—he's got the rest of our brood with him.' With a sharp gesture at Nev, the wagon jerked forward. Charlotte was grateful for the darkness, as it hid her burning cheeks.

Turning, she caught sight of Itsuo, who'd paused in the process of throwing his case into the baggage wagon. He was staring at her, and she half-raised her hand in greeting, but he turned away, flinging his bag and sprinting away before he had the chance to check it had landed. Greta, seated in the driver's position of the baggage wagon with Judge asleep on her lap and Bastian next to her, smothered a laugh in the crook of her elbow.

The indignation smarted. Swivelling around, Charlotte scanned the emptying grounds; spotting the empty jinker waiting near the gear men—who had just finished toppling the king poles—she scurried over and crept aboard. She sat, head low, staring at her lap until everything had been put away and she was joined by a flunky who didn't say a word to her. The final wagons of the Braun Brothers' Royal Circus began to move out of Hay.

It's not my fault, she thought again, silently repeating the words in time with the turning wheels of the jinker. Her head was throbbing, and the sound of the wheels, and the gentle, scratchy clopping of the horses' hooves on the dirt roads, seemed so loud in the quiet night. What if it woke the townspeople and sent them outside to witness the circus sneaking away like thieves?

Charlotte missed the usual noisy shouts of goodbye, and the children waving and waving until the wagons passed from view. Without them, there was nothing to distract her from the uncomfortable sensation in the pit of her stomach. She kept her gaze on her folded hands, barely visible in the dark. She'd washed herself down with a wet rag and changed into fresh clothing, but she could still smell the smoke on her. Was it just the memory, and the intense heat of panic that went with it? Or had the smoke somehow seeped through her skin, into her blood and bones, becoming part of her?

The flunky driving the jinker—Gilbert, she thought his name was—was silent on the narrow bench seat next to her. It was a pointed silence; the shoulder nearest her was raised slightly, as if to block her out or create a wall between them.

Charlotte wrapped her arms around herself and hunched low. How had it all happened? She had asked herself that question so many times in the blur of the last couple of hours. She knew she'd been rash and a little foolish, but that didn't mean the men in the hotel had to start a fire, did it? And who knew if the fire was even a result of the brawl? She decided to point this out when Rafferty issued the inevitable fine for her bad behaviour. Maybe the fire would've happened anyway. Maybe a stove had been left on, or there was some other innocent explanation ...

She wanted to say this out loud, so loud that everyone could hear. Particularly Maggie, who had sat stone-faced next to Smith in one of the equipment wagons, refusing to acknowledge Charlotte when she'd tried to speak to her.

An involuntary shudder ran over Charlotte. There was only one other time in her life when she'd felt this low, this blamed.

The back of her throat was raw from inhaling so much smoke, and she wished she could pull out her flask and have a sip to soothe it. It might stop her head from aching too. Perhaps if she turned away from Gilbert, he wouldn't see ...

She shifted, her eyes meeting the dark shapes of the town's buildings passing by. Silent, squatting giants, rebuking her, just like Rafferty, and Maggie, and everyone else around her.

She slid her flask out from under her jacket and heard the slight scrape of silver on silver as she pried the hinged lid back. She brought her lips to the collar and took a quick swig.

Beside her, Gilbert gave an unmistakable tut of disgust.

Chapter Twenty-Eight

Maggie was no stranger to shame—she lived with it, had grown used to it, like a cut that never quite healed—but this mute, furtive retreat was something else entirely, and her anguish when she thought of Robin made it almost unbearable.

Smith drove the wagon. Every time he glanced at her, his brows lowered, as if to discourage thoughts of escape. Itsuo, on her other side, had his arms folded tightly across his chest and was staring resolutely ahead.

Thank goodness the moon was nearing fullness, giving them enough light to navigate the rough dirt roads. They'd have to travel right through the night—far enough that anyone who came after them couldn't catch up and would have to give away the chase. Perhaps no one would bother, Maggie thought. Perhaps the town would be glad to see the back of them, after they'd wreaked such havoc. But she found herself wishing someone *would* come after them. Not to cause any trouble, of course; she wouldn't want to see anyone hurt, or the circus to suffer in any way. But if someone from Hay caught up with them, she might be able to explain that she'd had no part in the fiasco, then find a ride back with them. Or at the very least give them a letter to deliver to Robin.

As they broke past the edge of the town, a voice inside screamed at Maggie to jump off, run back and find Robin. If she weren't certain Smith would come after her, she'd have tried. She was sure she could outrun him, given his bulk, but she'd need a decent head start, which was impossible with him so close. For all she knew, Itsuo was also under instructions to grab her if she tried to jump over him and make a run for it.

All Maggie could do was turn and watch the town disappearing behind her. She imagined Robin waking up in the morning; saw her taking her place on the stool under the lavender-tinted spotlight and watching, alight with expectation, as the crowds came through the tent's entrance. She was looking for a face different to the others, a face as different as her own. Maggie flinched, clutching one hand to her chest. Beneath that hand, beneath the fabric of her dress, beneath the magpie inked on her skin, she felt something crack. And there was nothing she could do to mend it.

***

It rained at the break of dawn, which suited the general mood of the circus. The children were fractious and bored, tired from the late night and from being confined to the wagons without a single break to stretch their legs. Even the horses hung their heads, their manes dripping into their eyes as the downpour forced them to move slower. There would be no dry ground for Maggie to sleep on that night, no matter where they brought the wagons to a stop. She would simply have to hope the damp wouldn't seep right through her blanket; she didn't want to lie shivering on wet bedding all night and wake up with a chill.

On the second day, the rain still hadn't slowed, and at midmorning they encountered a section of the track which was underwater. Nev told them there was nothing for it but to go straight across: if they tried to go around, they'd find deeper water in one direction and thick scrub in the other. To lighten the load for the horses, they all hopped off the wagons and waded waist-deep through the swirling, muddy waters, carrying the children on their hips and emerging with loose grass and debris all over their sodden, clinging clothes. It took nearly an hour for the grooms to coax the donkeys across; during this time Rosemary handed out jam sandwiches as an early dinner, saying they'd have to wait until tea for something hot. It did nothing to improve the mood.

That evening it was difficult to get a fire going. With Nev's help, Rosemary eventually had a decent blaze; she brewed hot tea, which Nev spiked with dried lemon myrtle leaves he'd crushed between his palms, telling them it would help ward off any colds. Maggie kept her fingers crossed that he was right. The last thing they needed was fever rampaging through the circus.

The rain finally stopped on the third day. For the children, who succumbed to joy as quickly as they did to tears and tantrums, it was cause for celebration. They immediately ran wild upon waking to the clear sky, splashing in puddles and coating themselves in mud. As the eight o'clock departure neared, shouts of resistance echoed as mothers tried to corral the stubborn tykes back into the wagons. Their exuberance was the first thing that had made Maggie smile since they'd left Hay.

But the musty smell of damp fabric; the way the wood had softened on some of the wagons, signalling potential for future rot; the impossibility of feeling completely dry until the sun had had enough time to reach their under things, kept the mood of the adults suppressed.

***

Late on the seventh day, they finally reached the outskirts of the next town. Balranald had a decent enough population. And, more importantly to Maggie, it had a post office. She was anxious to let Mr O'Lehry know their itinerary had changed—though she would not, of course, tell him the real reason for their sudden and unexpected departure from Hay. She wondered if there had been a letter from him waiting for her at the Hay post office, never to be collected. The thought pained her; his letters offered the few moments of joy she was guaranteed. They might be fawning, and filled with frivolities, but escaping into the easy nature of his life soothed the difficulties of her own.

Rafferty made them stay one more night outside the town. The wagon wheels were clogged with dried mud, the horses' bridles dull, and the clown faces on the backs of the wagons nothing more than pairs of unsettling eyes peering through caked-on dirt. They needed a good scrub and some fresh paint before appearing in town. Maggie was glad of the reprieve. She hadn't spoken to Charlotte since she'd shouted at her, and she wasn't looking forward to their next performance. Wrapping her arms around the tightrope walker and clinging to her back seemed too intimate for two who were not on speaking terms.

Because of their sudden flight, they'd caught up to the advance agent before he reached Balranald, so they were once again bouncing the town. Rafferty was talking to the agent now, issuing instructions to continue on to the next town, to try to get ahead of them again. Maggie was sure the man would have liked a rest and some use of the town's amenities—the bank, post office, not to mention any establishment that could offer hot, ready-made food served with a cold drink—but he just nodded and asked who would contract the meat and flour supplies, and horse and donkey chaff, here in Balranald. She was almost sure she heard Rafferty begin to say her name in response, but he changed it at the last moment to Rosemary. Was it because he knew Maggie was still angry with him for not allowing her to stay back? Or was it that, after events, he couldn't take the risk of unsettling the townspeople with her presence?

The performers gathered in a rough semicircle around the campfire to eat their tea. The circus hands were a scattered constellation further from the fire, but still near enough to serve themselves seconds if there were any leftovers. The shame of the night flitter seemed to have washed off a little with the caked dirt. Maggie heard the occasional muttered joke, and was glad of it. The sounds of camaraderie, of jovial arguments and men and women outdoing one another in the fight for attention, was the sound of home; without them, it was like being lost in a place that should have been familiar.

Maggie collected a bowl of curried mutton and took a seat on a fallen log with the others who hadn't been swift enough to grab one of the collapsible chairs. Her eyes ran over the group, their faces flickering under the firelight. They wore the signs of travel: eyes tired by squinting at the road ahead; skin browned deeper by constant sun; and clothes in dire need of the scrubbing board, their armpits stained and their hems and cuffs thick with dust. They twisted and turned while they ate, unconsciously trying to loosen kinks gathered from hours in the wagons.

Charlotte was sitting alone, at some distance from the others, the firelight only just reaching the tips of the boots that poked from beneath her dress. The evening was warm, but she had wrapped her arms around herself, a solitary hug. The bow around her hair had come loose, so that the ends of the ribbon pointed limply toward her forehead. Charlotte clearly hadn't noticed, and no one was likely to tell her, for Maggie wasn't the only one who had refused to speak to her since they'd left Hay. As if she felt her gaze on her, Charlotte glanced up; their eyes met, and Maggie quickly looked away.

Maggie shifted uncomfortably on the tree trunk. As someone who'd always been on the periphery of the group, it wasn't easy to watch another subjected to the same treatment, no matter how much she'd brought it on herself.

***

When she woke the next morning, Maggie could've sworn she'd had no sleep at all. Her lids were drooping and her limbs were heavy with their own weight. She hoped she wasn't getting sick after all the rain-soaked days on the road.

By midmorning they were ready to go. Maggie was prepared to stay back with the workhorses again, but Rafferty wanted her by his side and left Nev and Gilbert behind instead. When she saw the way his gloved hands kept curling into fists and then unfurling, she decided not to ask why, and instead climbed up next to him in the wagon that would lead the parade, and pulled her veil into place.

The land to either side of them stretched out to the horizon, dry and yellow. The bark of the occasional eucalyptus looked shredded, clinging to the trunks in chequerboard pieces; the leaves pointed listlessly to the earth. Clearly the rain that had slowed them for so many days had not reached this place. They soon began to pass a lonely building here and there, squat and firm in the middle of the dirt and trees. The band were in the wagon right behind Maggie and Rafferty's, and they struck up 'Waltzing Matilda'. Maggie's toes tapped along to it, her lips silently mouthing the lyrics. She readied herself to raise a hand and wave at the crowds who would soon be drawn by the music.

But no one came rushing out to meet them. The farmers would be busy tending to their land and animals, of course, but they should have spotted at least a face or two peering curiously from a window—a farmer's wife, or a child too young to help work the land—yet there were none.

As the spaces between the buildings lessened, and farmland gave way to houses and gardens, the expected faces finally began to appear—but it soon became clear that something was wrong.

Not one of those faces was lit up in excitement. There was no loud calling to others to come see the circus, no rushing out to meet them and return their waves. Maggie saw one child run to her door only to be roughly pulled back. She exchanged a glance with Rafferty, standing majestically beside her, one hand holding the reins, the other waving grandly in the air above his head. She dropped her own half-raised hand.

As they made their way into the main street, the band switched songs to 'The Bare Belled Ewe', and the performers leapt from their wagons, whooping and cheering, to do their flip-flaps and cartwheels. But that, too, wasn't enough to entice the townspeople out. Even Judge, who had been racing around the feet of the horses, slowed and cocked his head in confusion.

'Where is everyone?' Maggie said, puzzled.

Rafferty sat back down with a thud. His showman's smile had disappeared. 'They're doing a freeze on us,' he said. 'But how did word get here so fast?'

'You think this about what happened back in Hay?'

'What else could it be?'

Maggie perceived a couple up ahead of them, walking their way, and nudged Rafferty. He sat a little higher. When the couple saw the circus, they hesitated. As the wagon drew near, Rafferty turned toward them and lifted his bowler in salute.

'Good morning to the gentleman and his fine lady! Do we ever have a bobby-dazzler of a show to impress you with tonight. Have you heard of—'

But before he could say any more, the man slid his arm protectively around his companion's shoulder and turned them both so they had their backs to the circus. Rafferty carried on with his spiel, but it had a tight, strangled sound to it.

The same thing happened when they passed some workmen installing a telephone line in the town. The ringmaster's greeting and the spruiker's shouts were steadfastly ignored, while the performers' attempts to impress were met with stony faces.

Finally, Rafferty went quiet, his hands gripping the reins so tightly that his knuckles went a jaundiced colour.

Despite the frosty reception, they went ahead and set up for the night's show, hoping that the townspeople would come around when they saw the white peaks of the tent and the buzz of activity around it. They needed an audience after seven whole days on the road. Gilbert and Nev brought the workhorses in, Nev glancing nervously from side to side as if he could sense the closed-off reception the circus had received and was expecting trouble.

Maggie had been planning on saying something to Charlotte before their act—what, exactly, she wasn't sure—but decided it could wait. Watching the others change into their costumes, their movements hesitant as they warmed up for a show they weren't sure there would be an audience for, made her bilious. She looked down at her brown skirt, her sturdy buttoned boots, the blouse that was becoming shabby from so much travelling. She would not remove them until she knew there was a reason to put her Lagoon Creature costume on.

She left the dressing tent and entered the big top instead.

The ring was lit, the rows of tiered seating waiting for people to fill them up. Maggie wandered through those rows, the sound of her boots loud in the empty space. She sat down. There was something so wistful about an empty, waiting tent. It should be full of children fighting over popcorn or crying because someone in a large hat had sat in front of them and blocked their view; men propping little girls up on their laps so they could see better; women pointing up at the tightrope, wondering when and what it would be used for. She wanted the small band to take its place, Rafferty to come bursting out in his red jacket with his booming voice, the horses to prance around the ring so that the faux feathers of their headdresses, made of combed-out cotton wool, bobbed and weaved. A ring wasn't supposed to be silent and still.

When the ticket seller came into the tent, looking for Rafferty to tell him that only a pair of tickets had been sold, sorrow swelled within Maggie.

Chapter Twenty-Nine

With Balranald doing a freeze on them, they had to pack up and move on the very next day. Rafferty refunded the couple who had gone against town wishes and bought tickets, and it was, once again, a subdued circus that made its way out of town and onto the road. When a kookaburra called, it was hard to not think the distinctive laugh was directed at them.

Maggie rode between Smith and Itsuo again, on Rafferty's orders. He was still worried she might steal a chance to go running back to Robin, though they'd travelled so far from Hay that the notion was ludicrous. She was surprised to realise she'd become used to the bulky, silent presence of Smith on her right, and Itsuo sitting in quiet contemplation on her left. Her once intense awareness of the nearness of them, her careful concentration on making sure her sleeves never brushed theirs, relaxed into something that was not quite easy company, but at least close enough to solitude that Maggie could lose herself in silently reciting half-remembered poems. She even found herself dozing every now and then.

After two more days on the road, Nev told them they were approaching Wakool Crossing. Rafferty hesitated, then instructed him to lead them around the village. He couldn't be sure that news of the fire hadn't made it there. Best to get as much distance between themselves and Hay as possible, he said. They circled around, coming within cooee of an open-air school where girls and boys in hats sat at roughly assembled desks beneath the scant shade of loosely-scattered trees. They all looked up from their lesson, and one or two even ventured a wave.

'Don't take it as a sign of warmth,' Rafferty called from his wagon. 'Schoolchildren will welcome any distraction from their studies.'

The sun was growing stronger with every passing day. Maggie kept her wide-brimmed hat on at all times, afraid of getting burned. Her wrists and ankles itched with the red bites of mosquitos, and her lips were so dry that licking them only worsened the sting. Sometimes her nostrils twitched, and she was anxious, thinking she smelled smoke. They were trying to outrun the fire in Hay, and perhaps would manage it yet, but a summer bushfire was a disaster of a different magnitude, devouring the landscape faster than any living creature could ever hope to run from. A bushfire in these conditions could be the end of them.

Their days had a sombre regularity to them. There was the rhythmic turning of the wagon wheels, the clopping of horseshoes on dirt roads, the occasional rolling puff of air from beneath a horse's lip, or the wheezing bray of a donkey. A child might wail, hungry and bored, or a driver cluck a noise of encouragement if the horses lagged.

It was nearing two weeks since Maggie had last spoken to Charlotte. She began to wonder if they would ever break their silence. Did she even want to? Maggie wasn't sure. But despite her anger, the thought of dismantling their act and going back to a kind of side-by-side existence where they never acknowledged one another made her toss and turn at night, unable to get comfortable.

Even whiling away the travelling hours by writing to Mr O'Lehry no longer soothed her the way it once had. It was as though the world was a wagon with one wheel come off; everything recognisable was tilted just off its axis and made wrong.

Maggie sat in the wagon, her eyelids drooping under the weight of all that had happened. She could feel herself sinking sideways, Smith's shoulder taking some of her weight, but she couldn't make herself snap back upright as she would have a few days ago. Not until Itsuo grabbed her by the arm and shook her.

'Look!' he said.

For a moment she was confused, wondering what she'd done wrong, till she saw that he was pointing back at the dust cloud they'd stirred up in their wake.

There, emerging from the cloud of dirt, was an unmistakable silhouette. The rust-red kangaroo bounded closer to them, zigzagging between saltbush shrubs, until it was alongside their wagon. Maggie held her breath, watching the powerful creature keep easy pace with them. Every now and then it outstripped the wagon and would pause, waiting for them to catch up, before pushing off with its hind legs and thick tail to lope along the dusty dirt paths again. It was as though the kangaroo were playing with them. Maggie had seen it happen before, when she was a child, but she'd forgotten how the sight of it could bring home to her the expanse of the country they were travelling, and the joy of suddenly remembering you belonged to a world greater than the thoughts in your own head and the trials of your daily life.

Itsuo flashed a smile at Maggie, and she couldn't help returning it.

Nev brought them to a stop outside of Tooleybuc, a town on the banks of the Murray River. After Smith climbed from their wagon, he held out a hand to Maggie to help her down. For a second she just stared at it, not knowing what it was for. He'd never done that before.

The kangaroo seemed to have broken the tension within the circus, for there was once again easy laughter as they set up camp and discussed who had seen the creature. Those who'd missed out lamented the fact, and the children hopped about pretending to be joeys while their parents argued over how big the animal had been—anything from three to six feet.

After Rosemary bullied Gilbert into helping her collect the meat and flour from the supplier in town, she told them all that Tooleybuc had a large sheep station, some budding fruit crops and a hotel overlooking the river. Rafferty looked sharply at Charlotte.

'You stay away from that hotel. That's an order.' Charlotte's cheeks coloured, but she said nothing.

Rafferty still would not let them perform that night. He seemed set on crossing the border into Victoria, as if he sensed they'd be safe there from the ugly rumours chasing them. The next morning they'd take the Tooleybuc punt across the Murray into the neighbouring state. Maggie could hardly believe they'd come so far.

Just as Rosemary was building the fire to boil the corned beef on, a group of men, women and children of all ages showed up. Some were in wagons of their own, but most were on foot. Tension rippled through the camp; no one had forgotten the hostile reception they'd had in Balranald. Nor had they forgotten the last time unexpected strangers had shown up, when the pinch artist had threatened Rafferty and nearly caused a fight. They drew together, ready to defend themselves.

But there was no need. The visitors turned out to be Tooleybuc townspeople who had heard of the circus from the shopkeepers serving Rosemary and Gilbert, and they wanted to see a show.

A grin spread like a crack in the earth across Rafferty's face. He clapped his hands together and rubbed them briskly. They hadn't put any of the tents up—with the night so fine and the weather so warm, they'd all agreed to sleep under the stars—but for such a small audience, that didn't matter.

They invited the locals to join them for a meal of salty corned beef, the juices mopped up with rough hunks of damper. Despite their impatience to put on a show—it felt so long since they'd last had the opportunity—they went through the usual motions of cleaning up any traces of their tea, not wanting to attract opportunistic dingoes with the smell of it. Then the local men helped the circus hands find fallen tree trunks and stumps. They dragged them so they lay end to end in a circle, creating a rough ring. Rosemary filled some empty tins with animal fat and old socks, then scattered them between the logs. Maggie would not be part of the show—with no tent, there were no king poles for the tightrope to stretch between—so she took a twig, lit the end of it in the cooking fire, then walked from tin to tin, lighting the socks to create lamps.

She didn't notice that Charlotte was doing the same until they met at the final tin. They both paused, looking at one another, then Charlotte wordlessly gestured for her to go ahead. Maggie crouched down, careful to tuck her long skirt back so it wouldn't be near the flame, then held her twig to the sock. While she waited for it to catch, she watched Charlotte's boots shuffling uncertainly before her.

'Are you sorry not to be performing tonight?' Maggie asked. Her voice was low, nearly drowned out by the chatter of the townspeople, who were taking seats on the logs while the circus performers changed into suitable shoes. She looked up; the lamp flickered orange light over Charlotte's features, which were twisted into an expression one might use if they had a toothache. Her lips opened, hovered there for a second, then quirked into a fast flash of an unhappy smile.

'Of all the things I'm sorry for, that is probably one of the least.' Her voice was bitter as lemon rinds. Maggie stood up, then cleared a little patch of dirt with the heel of her boot. She dropped the burning twig, stamped out the small flame and then leaned down to pick it up, intending to throw it on the cooking fire just to be safe.

'I know it wasn't deliberate,' Maggie said while her face was averted. It was hard to admit. 'Still, you need to understand how much hurt you caused.'

'Oh, I understand. Everyone ignoring me has made it very clear.' There was a whisper of tears in her voice now. The wall inside Maggie started to crumble. For a second, she tried to resist, tried to hold it in place. But it was too much effort. She didn't want to be angry anymore.

'Come on,' she sighed. 'Let's chuck these twigs on the fire, then we may as well find a log to sit on.'

They sat under an inky sky so thick with stars it would be impossible to count them if anyone tried. The log was rough beneath their backsides, their faces half-disguised by the dancing light of the makeshift lamps. The children were sprawled in the dirt, ready for the show. The band sat among the logs too, instruments in their laps, their heads bare of the white helmets they wore for regular performances.

It was the first time Maggie had seen the acts from the audience's point of view, instead of from behind a curtain or off to one side during rehearsals. Some performers had put on their full costumes, others a mix of costume and regular clothing. It didn't matter. She was able to appreciate it all in a new way, marvelling at the dexterity with which Greta wielded her swords, the knots Annie could tie herself in, the extraordinary heights Itsuo achieved in his jumps. Judge made the small audience laugh, jumping through hoops and riding on the backs of the two donkeys. When his act was done, he delighted the children by running over and joining them, barking whenever they clapped, which only encouraged them. The Steeplechase Sisters were next, riding their horses around the ring, the thud of their hooves reverberating through the ground. The horses came thrillingly close, but Maggie knew how carefully their riders controlled them. She could see the muscles rippling in their haunches as they moved, smell their animal sweat as they made circle after circle of the ring while their riders stood on their backs and somersaulted mid-ride. It was no wonder no one ever noticed that one of the sisters was a man.

When Rafferty came in at the end, posturing triumphantly, the audience shot to their feet. Maggie stood up with them, clapping so hard that her palms stung. It was the smallest standing ovation they'd ever received, yet its sheer joy and enthusiasm made Maggie's knees weak. They'd done this: the circus, even without all the trimmings, had brought these people to a state of hollering and whooping joy.

Those performers who didn't have animals to tend to stepped into the audience, their faces coated with sweat and their chests still moving with fast-paced breath. The children cuddled Judge, making the Jack Russell so happy that he rolled over on his back and cycled his paws in the air. As the townspeople eventually began to dwindle away, Maggie felt more at peace than she had in a long time. It was only the whispered memory of Robin's voice, the thought of how much she might have enjoyed this moment, that was able to spoil it.

The horses were rubbed down, the lamps extinguished, headgear and slippers taken off and put away. Quiet descended over them once more, but it wasn't the heavy quiet of previous days. It was relaxed, satisfied—content, even.

Maggie fetched her blanket from the baggage cart and rolled it out in the middle of the ring. She removed her boots, loosened her corset and took her jacket off to bundle up as a pillow. Stretching out on her back, she folded her arms behind her head and stared up at the speckled sky. Her breathing began to slow, but before she could fall asleep, a silhouette appeared above her.

'Mind if I stretch out next to you?'

It was Charlotte, in a knee-length white cotton nightgown not at all suitable for sleeping outside. She sounded uncertain. Maggie hesitated, then reached out and patted the ground next to her. Charlotte unfurled a velvet-lined blanket, leaving just enough of a gap that if they rolled onto their sides there would still be breathing room between their noses. Then she lay down beside

Maggie, and stared up at the stars too. Around them, the sounds of the circus were settling into a comfortable hush. There was the occasional snore, the sound of bodies turning over in their sleep, a soft voice murmuring a goodnight prayer, one final bray from a restless donkey.

'I really am sorry, you know,' Charlotte whispered.

'I know.'

Maggie thought of telling Charlotte about Robin, to explain why she'd been so angry with her. But it didn't feel right, not yet. Instead, she held out her hand; it was a gesture she'd never made before, her open palm an invitation, and she was frightened it wouldn't be accepted. But a moment later, she felt Charlotte's warm hand curl around hers. She let her fingers close.

'You know, the next time we put the tent up, you should sleep inside,' Charlotte said.

Was it Maggie's imagination, or had her voice faltered, regret already seeping in before the offer was finished being made?

'You've got Buckley's chance of that happening,' Maggie said.

***

It took them all day to cross the Murray River, bringing the wagons over one by one.

The punt's launching point was directly in front of the hotel, and it was lost on no one that Rafferty made Charlotte go over in the first crossing. He evidently didn't trust her around such temptation. Maggie stayed with the baggage wagon, fourth in line, keeping a hand on the wicker suitcase with the money in it.

When she reached the other side, she paused amid the hubbub of disembarkation and took a long breath. They were in Victoria. In leaving New South Wales behind, she hoped they would also leave behind the bad luck that had plagued them so recently.

The punt was moving slowly back to the side of the river where the rest of the wagons, horses, donkeys and people still waited their turn to cross. Maggie climbed into the baggage wagon and drove it out of the way, parking it close to the others that were already waiting, their horses fidgeting and nickering. She threw the reins onto the seat, then climbed down to inspect the wagon. She thought she saw a crack in one of the wheels, and felt the beginning of a headache; a broken wheel could set them back hours. Crouching down to examine it, she was relieved to find there was no crack; it was just some dried grass tangled around the spoke. She was pulling at it carefully, trying to unwind it, when voices came close.

'It's cruel, you know, what you're doing.' It was Greta, sullen and accusing. Maggie's attention pricked.

'What am I doing?' Charlotte's voice answered. She sounded weary, perhaps a touch defensive. Maggie started to stand; despite her mixed feelings toward Charlotte, they couldn't all stay angry at her forever.

'What you're doing to Maggie.' Greta's voice had gone shrill now, indignant, as though she were the one being criticised.

Maggie froze, her back bent in an uncomfortable, half-upright position.

'I heard you last night, telling her to join us in the tent,' Greta continued. 'Let her live her life the way she likes to.'

'You're both lucky and a fool if you think anyone likes to be so alone,' Charlotte retorted. Maggie heard the scrape of her boots fading away as she stalked off. Greta huffed, turned a little on the spot, then slowly followed in the tightrope walker's footsteps.

Letting herself sink back down into a crouch, Maggie rested one hand on the wagon wheel. Unseen, she smiled to herself.

Chapter Thirty

They had arrived in Ouyen. Over by the baggage wagon, Maggie was in a whispered conversation with a small boy, who ran off with his fist tightly closed around what must surely be either money or a sweet. Charlotte had noticed Maggie often did this on arriving at a new town; she would corner someone small, put something in their hand, and off the boy or girl would skip. Charlotte wondered what errand it was that needed doing over and over again. Probably something for Rafferty, who seemed to trust Maggie with things the rest of them didn't even know about.

They were friends again—at least, Charlotte hoped they were. And while she would never admit it, she was in some way glad that Maggie hadn't taken her up on her offer to sleep inside the tent. The moment the words had left her lips she'd wanted to pull them back. Thank goodness Maggie had been lying on her back, staring at the stars, so she couldn't see the relief cross Charlotte's face when she refused. She might have misinterpreted it if she had.

For it wasn't Maggie's company she wanted to avoid—it was her sharp eyes. It was already hard to hide the bottles of beer she stole from the warbs when they weren't looking, the bribes she offered them to refill her flask when the circus passed a wine shanty between towns—and how often it needed refilling. It was bad enough that Rafferty was constantly keeping watch over her. Ever since the fire in Hay, she'd felt his eyes, the gaze of a man who no longer trusted her. Sometimes she wanted to shout at him that his ceaseless vigilance only made her want to drink more.

No, she didn't need Maggie watching her too.

Charlotte looked around her. Ouyen was only a few years old, the streets spanning out from a railway station that had stretches of cleared land around it, with stubborn eucalypts clinging to the landscape in thick clusters. The locals' wide shoulders, callused hands and browned arms and faces told her that this was a place where people worked hard. She hoped that meant the circus would be a welcome respite. She didn't know if she could cope with a repeat of Balranald.

Thankfully, Charlotte's fears were unfounded. Luck seemed to have turned their way since the impromptu performance outside Tooleybuc. The crowds were generous with both their money and their applause, and this, combined with a successful return to her act with Maggie, made the first evening in Ouyen the highlight of the entire journey for Charlotte so far. Rafferty put on an extra show after the two he'd planned and advertised, meaning they had to leave on a Sunday instead of their anticipated Saturday. Not wanting to upset the townspeople by working on a day of rest, they moved out as quietly as possible in the earliest hours of the morning—this time with Charlotte seated next to Maggie—and travelled only a short distance before setting up camp for the rest of the day. The acrobatic pads were unrolled and the children, under Itsuo's instruction, worked on their cartwheels and posturing until dinner.

Shows at Underbool, Boinka and Murrayville followed, and the bright, dry weather meant they made good time as they travelled from town to town. Rafferty had them perform makeshift shows, similar to their Tooleybuc one, first at a shearing shed and then a railway construction camp. Charlotte and Maggie, of course, could not perform without the big top and its king poles—Charlotte missed the dizzying height and the applause directed at her, but Maggie said she was glad of the respite.

On Christmas Eve, another Sunday, they crossed into South Australia, the children singing 'All Things Bright and Beautiful' in a disjointed mishmash of voices and half-remembered words. Rafferty and Nev brought them to a stop half a day out of Pinnaroo: the festive day would be their own to celebrate, with no shows or practice or schooling.

Christmas morning was begun with bowls of Granose; Rosemary refused to supply anything more exciting than the box of flaked wheat biscuits, saying she needed to get on with the cooking early. The advance agent had joined them in the middle of the night, bringing with him a whole lamb carcass bought from the open-front butcher in town. The beast was speared and hoisted on a spit above the campfire. They were to have it with damper, mushy peas and potatoes cooked in their skins in the coals of the fire. By midmorning the air was already taking on a mouth-watering gamy scent, deepened with every drop of fat that sizzled when it met the flames.

Rafferty distracted the children from questioning Rosemary about when the food would be ready by bringing out a giant sack and yelling that Santa Claus had managed to find them, even on the road. When they all rushed him at once, Maggie stepped into the fray and persuaded them to line up, the littlest ones first, excitement creasing their faces and making their toes dance. When it came their turn, each child dipped an eager hand into the sack to pull out a gift: a skipping rope, a painting book, several spinning tops, a small bag of marbles, a football, and skeins of wool for crocheting dolls' clothes. Tears only appeared once, and were settled when an older child swapped her packet of chalk for the offending buttons and beads that had been the cause of the upset.

The adults sat back and let the children run around with their presents, playing and arguing and showing off, until Rafferty finally corralled them into a game of leapfrog. Charlotte used the ringmaster's distraction to her advantage and took two mouthfuls from her flask.

After the game of leapfrog was finished, Rosemary brought out the preserved fruits, biscuits, penny boxes of chocolates and peppermints that the children had learned to expect every year. They were never able to find them before the festive day, even though it was a tradition for the older ones to hunt for them in the middle of the night. They were always grateful for Rosemary's secrecy in the end—it made the moment of their arrival all the more thrilling. There were no mince pies, and no hot plum pudding; Rosemary insisted that campfires were no way to cook puddings and pastries.

Finally, Rosemary served up the dinner that had been tantalising them all morning with its savoury fragrance. Charlotte ate with a hearty appetite, her fingers soon glossy with the juices of the lamb. Rosemary's cooking, always satisfying, somehow took on even more flavour when pre-empted with a little liquor.

Stuffed full, the children who didn't immediately fall asleep were entertained with a game of football refereed by Nev. It was time for the adults to exchange gifts. Charlotte went to find the book she'd been hiding, wrapped between the folds of her costume, and ran a hand over its embossed cover, feeling uncertain. She didn't know if Maggie would like it. She saw her reading so often, but what if she already had this one? Or what if she refused it? She'd accepted Charlotte's apology, but there was often a tightness around her eyes that made Charlotte wonder if she was still angry. Sometimes words seemed to dance on Maggie's lips, as if there was something she wanted to share. Charlotte waited, but the words never came.

Holding the book close to her chest, she made her way back to the group and looked around for Maggie, knowing she would be off to the side somewhere—not exactly alone, but not one of them either. To her surprise, she saw her standing with Smith, whose huge bulk made her seem tinier than ever. His shoulders were hunched close to his thick neck, his cheeks bright with colour. Maggie's head was ducked in that familiar way, as though she could stop people looking at her face if she angled it just right. But her hand was reaching out, accepting the book Smith was giving her. Charlotte swore softly. What kind of friend was she if Smith, who barely spoke two words to anyone, let alone Maggie, had known to get the same thing?

There was nothing for it now, though. She could hardly run into town and bang on a shop door until someone opened it so she could find something else. Charlotte would simply have to give Maggie the book, and hope that her lack of thoughtfulness didn't once again widen the distance between them.

***

Maggie looked down at the book in her hand, speechless.

'It's not so much a Christmas gift,' Smith said. His eyes were directed at the toes of Maggie's boots, and she had to resist the urge to look down and see if she had donkey dung stuck to them. 'Just something I've had for a long time. I never look at it, and while we were in the wagon I noticed you seem to read a lot. Better it go to someone who might crack the pages open every once in a while.'

He shrugged. Maggie didn't think she'd ever heard him speak at such length before. Certainly not to her.

'Thank you,' she ventured, not sure what else there was to say. But Smith was already turning and shuffling back to the festivities. It was only a second or two before he was replaced by Charlotte, who was also clutching a book.

'Merry Christmas,' she said, holding her arms out straight. Maggie couldn't hide her surprise.

'For me?'

'Yes.'

'Oh.' Her heart sank. It had never occurred to her that Charlotte would want to exchange gifts. Maggie didn't have one for her. In previous years, she had only ever swapped gifts with Rafferty, silly little trinkets or practical items they knew the other was in need of. This year she had made him a double-sided tie, stripes on one side and gingham on the other, and received a handkerchief box in return.

Maggie's hand was reluctant in taking the book from Charlotte. She turned it over. It was *Seven Little Australians*, the same book Maggie had given Robin.

Her throat constricted. What must Robin's Christmas look like? Would there be any gift for her? Or would the showman have found a way to put her on display, even on this special day? Maggie's fingers tightened around the book's spine, the fine lines on her knuckles suddenly showing red against the pale skin.

'I know Smith already gave you a book,' Charlotte said in a rush. 'I'm sorry, I should've got something more thoughtful.'

Maggie cleared her throat so she could speak. 'No, no, it's fine. They're ... Well, they're very different. Smith's is English, something I've never read before.' She looked down at Smith's gift, still in her other hand. '*New Grub Street*, it's called, by a Mr George Gissing. Yours is by Ethel Turner, a woman whose work I've long admired. I used to have a copy of this one, but I ... I lost it.'

Charlotte looked crestfallen. 'You've already read it, then?'

'Yes, but it's a treasured favourite. One I'm glad to own again. So thank you.'

'You're welcome. Well ... Merry Christmas.' Charlotte gave a lopsided shrug.

'Wait there just a second,' Maggie said, tucking both books under one arm, and running to the baggage wagon. She could hear Charlotte protesting behind her—she knew Maggie was off to get her a gift—but she ignored her. She hadn't bought Charlotte anything, but there was something she could give her. Something that really belonged to her anyway.

It had come with Mr O'Lehry's last letter. Some scented toilet powder, and a rich emerald ribbon that he knew would look striking against Charlotte's red hair. It would never have contrasted with Maggie's mousy locks so well, she thought, as she pulled it out from its hiding place and let its slippery coils pool through her fingers. There was a moment of regret looking at it; Maggie reminded herself it had never been meant for her.

'Merry Christmas,' she said, returning to Charlotte and holding the gifts out. Charlotte made the appropriate noises of appreciation, and Maggie thought Mr O'Lehry had done well. It made her uncomfortable to receive the praise that belonged to him, though, and she insisted on tying the ribbon around Charlotte's hair—like a river of green running through rust-red country—to stave off further expressions of gratitude. Soon Rafferty was calling them over to join in the three-legged races. Once that was over, it would be time for food again—somehow finding room in their very full stomachs to fit more in—and then a rendition of 'Silent Night' over pannikins of hot billy tea, before finally falling asleep under the stars.

It was only late that night, as Maggie lay on her back, that she was able to think some more of Robin. She wished she knew where she was now, and how she was faring. She wished she'd been able to send her a present.

'No space of regret can make amends for one life's opportunity misused,' she whispered. Marley's words to Ebenezer Scrooge in *A Christmas Carol*.

Maggie pressed her fingertips to the corners of her eyes, stilling the dampness there.

***

On Boxing Day the circus moved into Pinnaroo for a handful of performances, and then they were on to Lameroo, where crowds from nearby Parilla, Parrakie and Geranium proved they were willing to travel to bring in the new year in the company of a circus. Rafferty handed out free balloons to the children and invited the locals to stay inside the big top after the show. The new year found its way to them in a cacophony of drink, music and dance, yet Maggie caught an expression flit over Rafferty's face, something wistful and still. It was only there for a second before he noticed her watching him and saluted, his showman's smile firmly back in place. She wondered if he was thinking about Hercules and Ida. In the earliest moments of a new year, it was hard not to think about those you'd left behind. For Maggie this year it was Robin, as well as her father, who was foremost in her mind.

Chapter Thirty-One

Charlotte was up on the rope, where she belonged. There was the warmth of Maggie nearby, but not on her back yet. The taste of rum on her tongue. The solid feel of the platform beneath her slipper-clad feet. The prickles of light that the weave of the hood she wore let in. It was all so familiar.

But something was different tonight in Cowirra. It was a popular township, about ten years old, on the east bank of the Murray River, and the audience was sizeable. Everything until that moment had run smoothly. But as Charlotte's feet moved her forward, leaving Maggie behind her on the platform, her breath was loud in her ears. She gave her head a shake of irritation, frowning as her toes found the rope. At least wearing the hood meant she didn't have to smile for the audience. She was free to let her lips quaver, free to try to squint the sweat out of her eyes.

Sweat damped her stockings, too, at the backs of her knees and inside her slippers. She was sure she'd never felt so warm before. She took two tentative steps forward, and again her breath roared in her ears. Ragged, panting. Distracting. She had to keep moving. Her feet lifted, whether obeying her silent order or simply from habit, she could not be sure. For a second, her head spun; beyond the noise in her ears, she heard the audience gasp. They must have seen her wobble. Charlotte tried to take another step forward, tried to straighten her shoulders and exude confidence. But all of a sudden she couldn't remember where she was. The big top, on the rope between the king poles; that much she knew. But how far out had she come? Was she in the middle, or still near her starting platform? Which direction had she been going? Forward or back?

Charlotte's breaths were coming shorter, sharper. She moved her slick feet in her slippers, just the slightest tensing and releasing of the muscles to remind herself that the rope was still beneath her feet. The hood was suffocating, her skin moist with her own hot breath; with a cry, she lurched forward, doubling over, her hands wrapping around the tightrope so that she was stretched along it like a cat on all fours. She could feel it cutting into her palms, knew she was gripping it tightly enough not to fall. But tears ran down her cheeks all the same; she tasted their salt on her lips, heard the little choked, snuffling noises she wasn't aware she was making. Every inch of her was taut yet trembling, frozen to that rope.

'Charlotte!'

The bellowed word made its way through the fog surrounding her. She shifted her head, the tiniest fraction.

'Maggie?' she called. Her voice was that of a lost child.

'Charlotte, it's all right.' The words had a worn quality, as if Maggie had repeated them many times before Charlotte finally heard. 'Just take the hood off.'

Charlotte's head shake was barely more than a tremor. She couldn't take her hands off the rope.

'You can do it, Charlotte,' Maggie insisted. 'Take the hood off, and come back to me.'

If the audience was making any sound, Charlotte could not hear them. It was only Maggie's voice that existed, a lifeline she could use to pull herself back. Charlotte let her head droop as far as it would go, then very carefully forced each finger on her right hand to unfurl and stretch toward the hood. She tugged at it; it came free, the sudden force of the spotlight making her gasp and reach for the rope again. The faded linen hood spiralled as it fell down, down, to land in the sawdust, sending up a little rippling cloud. Charlotte wondered how much bigger a cloud she would make if she fell.

'Maggie?' she cried out again, her voice high with panic.

'I'm right here. I'm right behind you. I can't come to you, you know that, so you're going to have to come to me.'

Charlotte squeezed her eyes closed. Her chest was so tight, soon she'd hear the cracking of her ribs as they splintered under the pressure.

'Come to me, Charlotte. Please.'

Unbidden, the image of her lyrebird tattoo came into Charlotte's head. So beautiful with its long, curling tail. Did lyrebirds fly? Charlotte realised she didn't even know. She'd chosen the bird for its beauty, nothing else. But she decided to believe they could fly. She needed to unfurl those wings and make her way back to her magpie.

She did not have the elegance of a bird in flight, though. It was an ungainly, backward crawl, slower than she'd ever been on the rope before, tears dripping off the end of her nose. The band struck up Herr Von der Mehden's 'Bucephaleon'—obviously an order from Rafferty, to distract the audience from the disaster unfolding above—and colours swirled beneath her. Charlotte was frightened he'd turn the spotlight off, leaving her to find her way back in the dark, but he didn't. He must've known she needed it.

Charlotte felt her toes hit the platform; not thinking about it, she pushed back with her arms, sending herself sprawling on her backside on the blessedly solid surface, nearly colliding with Maggie's legs. Maggie tried to move away, to give her more room, but Charlotte wrapped her arms around her knees, keeping her in place.

'It's all right,' Maggie whispered, leaning over so her breath disappeared into Charlotte's hair, decorated with the emerald green ribbon she'd given her. 'I've got you. Everything's fine now.'

***

Maggie didn't know what had happened. One minute the act had been going along as usual—albeit with Charlotte looking a little paler and more grim-faced than most nights as she pulled the hood down over her head—and the next minute she was clinging to the rope like the last shivering autumn leaf holding on to a branch. The moment seemed to stretch on forever, the audience growing nervous and then becoming restless as Maggie called out to Charlotte again and again. She'd begun to think the only way to get her off the rope would be to crawl out there herself, but she didn't know how she could or would.

Getting Charlotte down the ladder was easier. The tears she seemed to have no control over continued unabated down her face, turning her skin blotchy and the tip of her nose swollen, but she obediently moved her hands and feet, following Maggie, who'd gone first to coax her down.

As her feet hit the sawdust, Maggie was conscious that they were leaving the act unfinished. She caught Rafferty's eye. He was standing in the middle of the ring, and beneath his practised smile his expression was grim. He was silently acknowledging what she knew to be true: this time, Charlotte's actions couldn't be overlooked.

Maggie helped Charlotte change out of her costume, gently sponging her down with water warmed over the cooking fire. By the time she was checking Charlotte's boots for spiders, preparing to slip them on her feet, the colour was returning to her cheeks, and her lips pursed into a little rosebud that formed the word 'Sorry'.

'You don't need to apologise.' Maggie held one boot out, waiting for Charlotte's foot to slide inside. As she did up the buttons, she said, 'What happened out there, Charlotte?'

'Yes, what did happen out there?' Rafferty arrived in the dressing tent, red-faced and sweating. He must have run straight from his final bow, for no one else had joined them yet.

Charlotte tried for a charming smile.

'I'm sorry, boss. I think it must've been all the New Year's celebrations. Or something like that.'

'Something like that?' Rafferty appeared to deflate before them. Maggie's heart thumped, like the big drum in the band, heavy punches that told her whatever was coming next, it wouldn't be good.

'I'm sorry, Charlotte,' Rafferty said, 'but you're out of control, and it can't go on. I know you drink—'

Charlotte gasped, and her eyes darted around the dressing tent to see if anyone had entered and might hear. But Rafferty must have instructed everyone to stay away, for it was still just the three of them.

'You hid it well, but nothing escapes a ringmaster. I should've said something long ago. Before this, before the fire, before it went too far. But it's so hard when you've known someone as a child. You don't want to see them face such difficulties.'

'Too far?' Charlotte squeaked.

'I'm sorry, Charlotte. I don't want to do this, but I have to. For the good of the circus and all the livelihoods that depend on it. You're fired.'

Charlotte's mouth dropped open. Her recently regained colour fled once more, so that her freckles stood out in stark contrast to the rest of her complexion.

'Rafferty,' Maggie protested. He didn't listen.

'We can't have you risking the show. First it was the forward somersault, now this—Charlotte, you could've killed yourself. Or Maggie, if she'd tried to do more to help you. I can no longer rely on you, can I?'

He said this as if pleading with Charlotte to prove him wrong. There was still hope, then, Maggie thought.

But Charlotte only licked her lips, then gave a tiny shake of her head.

'You can rely on me, though,' Maggie blurted out.

Both heads swivelled to look at her. It was like being in the spotlight in the ring.

'I can keep an eye on Charlotte, and on her drinking. I can help her get better again. And—and we'll work on the act, put something in place, so that if she ever has a ... has a ...' Maggie didn't know what to call what had happened to Charlotte. 'If she ever can't continue again, there'll be something I can do.'

'Like what?'

'Give me five minutes to think of something,' she snapped.

The ghost of a smile flittered over Rafferty's face. Maggie saw her opportunity and pounced.

'When have I ever let you down, Rafferty?'

'This isn't just about you, Maggie girl.'

'I know. But it's me that's asking. You couldn't give me the only other thing I've ever asked you for. Please give me this.'

Rafferty turned to look at Charlotte, studying her face. Maggie didn't know what he was looking for; all she saw were two people who were tired and empty.

'What do you think, Charlotte?' he asked. 'Can you, with Maggie's help, get your drinking under control and make sure we don't have any situations like this, the somersault or the pub again?'

Charlotte winced at each mention of her failings and misdeeds. Her shoulders were slumped, but Maggie could see the force with which she made herself meet Rafferty's eyes.

'Yes. With Maggie's support, I can.'

'Then I suppose that will have to be good enough for now. But I'm warning you, Charlotte—any more upsets and even Maggie won't be able to save your hide.'

220

Chapter Thirty-Two

'Thank you,' Charlotte said as Rafferty exited the dressing tent. Maggie tried to offer her a sympathetic smile, but the tightrope walker's eyes were cast down into her lap, where her fingers pleated seams in the fabric of her dress. 'Without this circus, I would truly have nothing. I—I don't know what I would've ...'

'Your sister stole the life you'd planned. I couldn't let you lose the life you've made for yourself since.'

Something like a grimace moved across Charlotte's face. Perhaps it was a failed attempt at a smile.

The performers began to trickle back in. Many threw glances Charlotte's way, curiosity written plain across their features. Maggie moved so that she blocked them all from view.

'I think it's best we start fixing this right away, don't you? Let Rafferty see you making good on your promise.' Maggie knew what she had to say next. She kept her voice low. 'Charlotte, I need you to show me where you keep your drink. So I can get rid of it.'

Charlotte looked stricken, but she swallowed and said, 'All right. There's my flask, which I keep on me most of the time.'

Maggie held her hand out.

'It has great value,' Charlotte hurried on. 'Not in terms of money, but it belonged to someone very special to me, and I—' Her voice faltered.

Perhaps she was making excuses, but something inside Maggie thought she recognised the ring of truth in the words.

'It will be safe in my keeping,' she said gently. 'You can see it and hold it anytime you wish. I won't let harm come to it.'

Still, the expression Charlotte handed it over with was one of pain, which only worsened when Maggie flipped the top open and they both watched the stream of rum darken the earth beneath them.

'One done. Show me what else you have,' Maggie said.

Charlotte led her around the circus grounds, showing her one hiding place after another. Inside shoes, roped to the undersides of wagons, one bottle even tucked inside an empty biscuit tin. It started to dawn on Maggie the size of the task she'd volunteered for. She had no way of knowing if Charlotte was keeping some hidey-holes secret still.

She had no idea if it was possible to save Charlotte from herself.

***

The next day, Nev told them it wouldn't be long before they had to cross the Murray River once more. It snaked across the land, twisting and turning so that anyone travelling long distances in this region would be forced to encounter it many times. He led them to Cowirra, saying the town had a hand-operated punt like the one they'd used to cross the river at Tooleybuc.

'We did have a punt, until not too long ago,' the operator said when they arrived. 'It sank the other day.'

Charlotte raised her hands as if to say that this time the event wasn't her fault, but no one acknowledged her.

'Happens every few years,' the punt operator said, scratching

his beard. 'Weather, the forces of the water, poor workmanship.'
He shrugged. 'Always something.'

'Is a new one being built?' Nev asked.

'Supplies arrived for it yesterday. Work's starting today.' Nev looked at Rafferty, questioning.

'The wait'll be too long. A few nights performing in Cowirra would be fine, but any longer and we'll run out of audiences.' Rafferty chewed his bottom lip, considering the expanse of moving water before them. 'Think we could cross it ourselves, Nev?'

The tracker was quiet for a while, turning the question over.

'Not here, but about an hour or so south the waters are tamer and the river narrower. We'd manage it all right—assuming you folks have done a river crossing before.'

'Most of us have. Righto, let's get to it then.'

***

They rose early in the morning. Rafferty insisted on a hearty breakfast, so they ate tinned anchovies on toast and leftover pie made with the meat of some parrots they'd shot the day before. Maggie kept a watchful eye on Charlotte, making sure there was nothing but tea in her pannikin. Then they tidied up the remains of their breakfast in focused quiet.

They had made camp at a spot near the riverbank that was dotted with tall, thick gums whose impossibly broad trunks leaned ever-so-slightly to one side, as though trying to escape some unknown thing. In the morning lull an emu had emerged from the bushland, and now stood knee-deep in the river water, its tasselled feathers quivering as its blue-black head swivelled to watch them. When Rosemary extinguished the fire and the circus hands began to throw the baggage aside none too carefully, the emu took off, its long, powerful legs with the backward-pointing knees propelling it to the shore and away from the sudden noise and fuss. No one besides Maggie paid it any attention.

Turning back to the task at hand, Maggie used a small piece of rope to tie her bag—now bursting at the seams with the addition of her Lagoon Creature costume—and her rolled-up blanket to her body. The sound of hammers pounding at different speeds, of nails reluctantly being released from wood which had been their home for so long, filled the early-morning air. There was something unsettling about seeing the wagons pulled apart. It wasn't just the family of white-tailed spiders that came scuttling out of one of the covered wagons and caused the circus hands to shriek and jump back. They relied so much on the wagons that it was like watching a home be torn down. Maggie was glad she wouldn't be there to see too much of it.

Her stomach was in an upset of anticipation, and her eyes sought out Charlotte, panicked at having lost her for a moment. She found the tightrope walker carefully knotting the laces of her performing slippers around her neck so the shoes sat just below her collarbones. The two of them had been chosen to cross first—Charlotte, to keep her away from any temptations, and Maggie, to watch over her and escort the money—along with Nev and Gilbert.

'Righto, we're ready,' Maggie said to Rafferty once she'd escorted Charlotte down to the water's edge.

'You'll go right behind the case?'

Maggie nodded. The wicker suitcase containing the circus's takings had already been strapped to the back of Nev's horse, the tracker being the strongest rider of the four of them.

'Won't let it out of my sight, in the water or on the road.'

'Give us about four hours before you start floating the things downriver,' Nev instructed, hauling himself into the saddle with ease. 'It'll probably only take us three, but better to be on the safe side in case we have any troubles circling Reedy Creek Swamp. If the going's smooth, we might throw some lines in; there'll be sizeable flathead there Rosemary can cook up for tea. We can check the lines on the way back to meet you lot. I'll turn back as soon as the gear starts washing up, probably meet you halfway, maybe more.'

'Sounds good. Here's the ribbons.'

Rafferty handed over a rainbow fistful of ribbons, donated by the women of the circus. Nev had agreed to tie one to a tree every now and then, to assure those following in the small group's wake that they were headed in the right direction. Maggie noticed that Charlotte's green ribbon remained firmly tied to her head.

There was nothing more to be said. As the men tied bowyangs beneath their knees, pulling the leather straps tight around their trousers, Maggie let Smith boost her onto the back of the workhorse she'd been assigned—a red-maned mare called Bilby, chosen for her biddable nature. Maggie was riding bareback and as free of tack as possible, to make it easier on the horse. The feel of the beast beneath her legs was unusual; Maggie knew how to ride, but she did it infrequently. She took the rope tied to the bridle in her gloved hands—it was too hot for gloves, but she needed a good grip and the suede would help with that—then took her place behind Nev. Charlotte lined up behind Maggie, and Gilbert brought up the rear.

Nev clucked his tongue. The horses moved slowly forward. Despite their anxiousness to get going, the riders allowed the horses to take their time, letting them paw at the water, their hooves turning the shallows into a busy white froth. They needed to become comfortable and familiar with the water, for this wasn't just a flooded road they were crossing. Maggie checked the long rope—usually used to hold the big top in place—coiled loosely at her waist, matching the one Nev had tied to the leather belt holding up his moleskin trousers; it would unravel easily as they rode. The other ends were in the hands of Adlai. Once across, the ropes would be secured on both shores, to be used as guide lines for the subsequent crossings.

Maggie felt the slight hesitation of Bilby beneath her as they moved further into the river. She held her breath as the water met the toes of her calfskin boots. Her long skirt drew the water up, so that by the time her knees were submerged she was already damp to the waist. She shifted the bridle rope to her left hand, not wanting the mare to tangle in it and risk drowning them both, then leaned forward, keeping her body low to the horse's neck as she wound her fingers through her wiry mane. The thick, dark water of the river was swirling around the mare's shoulders now. Maggie could feel the current snatch at her skirts, and the strong muscles of the mare resisting its pull. The pungent odour of wet animal, the deep murk of the river clinging to hide, filled her nostrils. The waters sluiced over her gloved fingers, its muddy brown waters turning clear as it made shallow rivulets down her arms.

The sun was already warming the sky, but Maggie's teeth chattered. How deep would the river go? The horses could swim, but Bilby's grunts and heavy breathing told her how hard she was working. Maggie's own breath was fast and shallow and she wished she'd loosened her corset that morning. A breeze caught at the brim of her hat, testing the grip of her hatpins. She suddenly remembered she was supposed to be watching Nev in front, ensuring he didn't run into trouble with the added weight of the wicker suitcase. She lifted her chin, trying to ascertain from the moving shape before her what was animal, human or case. It was difficult to tell, although all looked to be in one piece. Maggie hoped that behind her, Charlotte was keeping her cool. She didn't want to risk a look over her shoulder to find out, in case the movement unsettled Bilby.

The horse's movement changed; they were deep enough now that she was swimming. Her strong legs would be moving gracefully underwater, yet would be dangerous to any person who slipped from her back. The river made Maggie weightless. She felt herself lift from the mare's back, cupped by the river water, and pressed her knees together to keep her body in place. Her fingers could not wrap any tighter in Bilby's mane.

The strange, weightless swim seemed to go on forever. The

mare had her nose, ears and eyes lifted out of the water, and not much more. Up ahead, a nearly-submerged Nev kept the pace steady, angling on a diagonal to counteract the force of the current. Finally, Bilby's hooves met ground again. She moved faster with the surety of earth beneath her, and the water began to drop around Maggie, her weight sinking back onto the mare's back. They emerged together in a cascade of water. Maggie didn't have time to feel relief; she had to hurry and untangle her skirts from her legs, slide off the horse and hotfoot it away before the mare hit the ground and began rolling about, legs waving in the air. She heard laughter and turned to see Nev, also sodden, watching his horse roll about in the same ungainly manner. They'd known to expect this, and the exhilaration of the animals, as well as the success in their crossing, brought them together, shaking each other's damp palms in satisfaction.

With a quick glance to check on Charlotte—she'd got further behind, but appeared to have her mare under control—Maggie pulled out the brush she'd stashed in her bag and returned to Bilby who, at the sight of her waiting, stood and snorted loudly. Maggie murmured soothing words of gratitude in her ears and ran the brush in wide curves down her flanks—imperative for the horse's health—breathing in her raw, wet smell. She only paused when Charlotte emerged, white-faced, from the river; when she'd jumped down and skirted out of reach of her own rolling beast, Maggie went back to her work.

Once the mare was groomed to satisfaction, Maggie undid the rope around her waist. She moved to the bank where Gilbert was just emerging, and held the rope up high, calling a cooee across the river. Adlai, on the opposite bank, held his arms up in response. She felt a slight tug as he moved to tie his end to the bridle of another waiting horse.

Another cooee, and some echoing barks from Judge, told them the next crossing was ready. This time it was two riderless horses, carefully directed by the lead lines tied to their bridles that Maggie and Nev pulled. Behind the horses, on a raft made from the bottom of the wagon with the sides shaped like waves, were eight wagon wheels. Itsuo and Smith swam at the back corners of the raft, helping the horses with the weight and balance of it, yet far enough from them to be out of range of their kicking feet. Both men had knives ready to cut the lines going from raft to beast should the animals suddenly be at risk. There was a tense moment when the current started pulling them downriver; as Maggie frantically hauled on her lead line, she had terrified visions of the horses getting their hooves caught in some underwater plant, or a sudden cramp taking one of them. Her gaze darted between each moving creature, her mind calculating, seeing every potential for risk, every possible solution.

The horses pushed back against the current, the men following in their wake; when they reached land, Maggie moved quickly with Nev to grab their bridles and release the attached ropes before the horses dropped and rolled. Charlotte and Gilbert waded back into the water, helping Smith and Itsuo drag the raft on shore. The two swimmers leaned their hands on their knees, panting; Maggie was nearly overwhelmed with the urge to go over and clap them both on the back. Instead, she silently cursed the punt for sinking.

Conscious that the sun had already shifted its position in the sky, the six of them pulled out the tools Gilbert had brought with him and hastily assembled a rudimentary wagon from the few pieces that had been swum across. They loaded the excess wheels and hitched two of the horses to the wagon. Then Nev, Maggie, Charlotte and Gilbert climbed aboard. Maggie looked over to where the donkeys were already being prepared for their own swim across. It had been decided that they should swim without carrying anything. Despite being more buoyant than the horses, they were reluctant swimmers, and if water got in their ears or they tipped over, they would drown. Knowing this, and that the children would soon be crossing—such small lives surrounded by such a great expanse of moving water—made her wish she could stay and help. But she had a job to do, and a funambulist to keep an eye on.

The foursome and their wagon of odd equipment set off. They were headed to a spot on the riverbank just south of Caloote. Rafferty and the circus folk were going to float the rest of their gear down the river. It was easier than trying to swim it all across; as the horses grew tired, it would only become more dangerous. Nev had calculated where the river's current would wash the equipment ashore, and it was Maggie, Charlotte and Gilbert's job to collect the flotsam downriver to begin the task of reassembly. An old circus trick, but one they'd not had to rely on for many years.

There was only the driving seat in the wagon—all the other bench seats would be washed downriver—and Maggie and Charlotte let Gilbert and Nev take it. The women clambered into the back instead, where their legs tangled in the spokes of the piled-up wheels as they spread their skirts out and leaned back on their elbows to let the steady sun dry them.

Maggie watched Charlotte out of the corner of her eye. When Charlotte had shown her all those hiding places for her drink, she'd been unsettled by their sheer number and ingenuity. She'd known Charlotte liked a drink, known she could go a little too far with it—hadn't Charlotte completely forgotten that first day out they'd spent together?—but she hadn't realised the lengths she'd been going to every day.

Charlotte's papery-thin lids were closed, twitching against the movement of her eyes. She wore a sickly pallor, and a strip of sweat lined her upper lip. Her hands trembled as they lay flat against the base of the wagon. Had she found a way to drink without Maggie noticing? Or did she look this way because she wasn't drinking at all? Maggie didn't know, and that made her nervous. How could she control Charlotte's drinking if she could never quite be sure if, and when, it was happening? And what happened when they went back to performing? Rafferty had not allowed them to do their act during the two shows in Cowirra, saying Charlotte needed a break and some drink-free days before he could trust her in front of an audience again. Would the pressure of being on the tightrope in front of so many eyes make her turn to liquor once more?

Charlotte's eyelids fluttered open, squinting against the bright sunlight.

'Maggie, can I ask you something? What did you mean when you said to Rafferty that he didn't give you the one thing you've ever asked him for?'

Maggie looked away, pursing her lips. There'd never been a time that felt right for telling Charlotte about Robin. In those early days of anger and resentment, the story would have been a punishment, a reprimand, and Maggie had decided she didn't want to use Robin for that. The little girl was already used for the needs and whims of the adults around her. And now? The circus had known such misery. Maggie didn't want to create any more. But she also knew a gentle reminder that entire worlds were still going on around Charlotte while she was lost in the one of her own making would do the funambulist some good.

'There was a little girl,' Maggie said slowly. 'At the agricultural fair in Hay. She was like me: different. They called her a ghost girl, because she was so pale, with silvery hair and light blue eyes that shone violet in the spotlight. She had no family, and I promised her I would come to see her again and be her friend. Then the hotel caught fire, and we had to do the night flitter ...'

'Oh, Maggie ...' The apology ran through Charlotte's voice, a tense expression of more than words. Maggie couldn't look at her; she was afraid of seeing the culpability, afraid she'd know she'd done the wrong thing in telling her, that Charlotte would go running to whichever bottle she could find. But Charlotte's quivering fingers rested on her forearm, encouraging her to look up.

'Tell me about her,' she said.

Chapter Thirty-Three

That evening they camped again on the banks of the river, reassembling the wagons from the pieces plucked out of the water. Charlotte helped the equestrians check the horses for ticks. Maggie, who had been using a hammer with surprising force given her diminutive build, immediately dropped it and joined her, and Charlotte knew she was being watched closely.

As they worked, they supped on flathead and potatoes cooked in their skins. The children, exhausted from the strangeness of the day, slept early and soundly while the adults carried on late into the night, and when the sun rose the next morning it was difficult for all to lift their heavy heads. But they needed to finish putting the gear back to rights, and then head into Caloote to set up for a couple of nights performing.

Caloote gave them decent crowds and fine weather. Afterwards came a single night camped out under the stars, then one performance in Harrogate, before setting up in Woodside, where the wealth of the old Bird-in-Hand mine had filtered down through the generations. There was some argument over whether to stop at Oakbank or Balhannah next, the two towns being within an hour's ride of one another. Rafferty settled it by reasoning that performing in Balhannah meant going through Oakbank first; if they made enough of a spectacle on their ride through Oakbank, the residents would travel to the bigger town to see them.

All this time, Maggie's eyes were on Charlotte, steady and unwavering. Not so much daring Charlotte to defy her as reproaching her in advance. Charlotte found herself making her every movement slower and bigger, so that Maggie could take in the fact that she wasn't drinking.

At least not where Maggie could see her.

For it was not possible for the other woman to keep an eye on her every minute of the day, even if she tried. Charlotte snatched furtive mouthfuls from a bottle filched from Rosemary's supplies whenever she hiked up her skirts to urinate behind the privacy of a bush. Guilt always followed, but Charlotte reasoned to herself that if she hadn't completely given up drinking, she had at least cut back. And if no one could tell that she was drinking surely that meant she had matters under her control again—Rafferty had even allowed her back on the rope in Woodside, and she'd not wavered once.

Charlotte's insides hardened when Rafferty mentioned the next town they'd be performing in. It was a resistance that only deepened as they made their way into Hahndorf. 'Hahn's village', the word meant in German. She'd rather have skipped the town completely, if the next stop after it weren't Adelaide itself.

Charlotte overheard Nev telling Maggie that the place belonged to the Peramangk people, and had been called 'Burkatilla' until it had been overtaken by German settlers. It was this German heritage Charlotte observed as they paraded down Main Street. Beyond the exuberant protrusion of leaves on the chestnut, cork, elm and plane trees that lined the commerce strip, she glimpsed Fachwerk architecture, adapted here and there to the Australian climate with the addition of bullnose verandahs. Lutheran churches brought back uncomfortable memories of her family, the childhood she'd tried so hard to forget. She could almost taste

Elisabeth's favourite *Kartoffelpuffer* topped with applesauce on her tongue, a tongue which even now curled silently around the syllables of the language Jakob and Alma had ensured she and her sister could speak a little of. Charlotte had avoided uttering any German, aside from the occasional swear word she amused herself with, since she'd run away. Some superstitious sense told her it would be like a beacon calling to her family, telling them where to find her.

***

Maggie could hardly believe it. After months crossing the land, where'd they'd seen soil of every colour, from dark ash to brick red, terracotta to sandy blonde, rich brown to parched, faded grey; after makeshift performances, wind and rain and blistering sunburn; after sunken punts, pesky mosquitoes, and half-burned pubs, they had finally reached their destination.

Adelaide.

The city that had once been her home.

They had Nev to thank. He had seen them through so many difficulties, ensured they never got lost or went short of food. Maggie knew they'd be toasting the tracker at that night's pre-show tea. But before then, they still had to make their parade entrance and set up their tents.

Rafferty wanted to perform in the very heart of the city, so they stayed seated in their wagons, saving their energy for when they were closer to their final destination and the crowds would be at their biggest. Maggie did not volunteer to stay behind with the workhorses, for she needed to be alongside Charlotte, keeping watch over her. As she slid the hatpin through the crown of her straw hat to keep her veil in place, she resented the necessity; on the road, she hadn't had to hide her face so frequently and she had enjoyed the freedom. But Adelaide, with the proximity to her father that it brought, would be overwhelming enough without having the attention of hundreds of people drawn her way.

The trickle of children following the train of wagons turned into a waving crowd, and their excitement was infectious. Despite her apprehension, the triumph of having reached this city—this city that had seemed so far away from Sydney when they'd devised their last-minute run—made Maggie hum with pleasure.

She glanced at Charlotte, sandwiched between herself and Gilbert. Her face had lost its waxy pallor, and her eyes were returning to their former sparkle. Her teeth flashed at Maggie in a grin; then she was crawling over her lap in a cloud of meringue-like voile and heavy perfume, vaulting over the side of the wagon, and beckoning to the astonished Maggie to follow. She was so much the Charlotte of their day out at Wonderland City that Maggie could have sworn no time at all had passed. She stood, holding Gilbert's shoulder to steady herself—something she would never have dared mere months ago—but before she had time to consider the dangers of leaping from a moving wagon, Smith was there, jogging alongside and offering his hand to help her down. Maggie resisted the urge to pull back, sit down and turn away from the strong man; instead, she climbed over the wagon's side, half-falling into his arms. Itsuo was there too, and helped straighten her up; she gave a shy smile of thanks to both.

Small children weaved between the four of them, which Itsuo took as a cue to flip-flap high in the air, making them shriek and laugh. Maggie longed to reach out and touch their tow heads. One little girl, barely big enough to walk on her own, grabbed a fistful of her skirt, her face tilted upward in expectation. She couldn't see underneath Maggie's veil, so no expression of fear crossed those tiny features. On impulse, Maggie stopped and lifted the girl by the armpits, swinging her up and around in the air, so that she squealed with delight, her feet pedalling so fast that she took off as soon as they met dirt again.

Maggie watched her go, the girl trying to catch up with Itsuo to see more of his acrobatics. She balled great bunches of her skirt in her fists, mimicking the way the little one had held it; then she pulled it so high that her stockinged knees were exposed and ran, with sheer abandon and joy, to catch up with the others. Charlotte's arm caught her around the waist as she drew level, and the two swung in a giddy semicircle. Maggie didn't care that sweat was collecting under her arms and beneath her breasts; didn't care that her hair was tumbling down from under her hat, tangling in strips around her neck.

They'd made it to Adelaide. Against all odds, they'd really, truly made it.

***

The big top was erected on 'circus acres', two bare parcels of land on Angas Street. The spot had received its name due to its popularity with travelling circuses. Rafferty declared it a miracle that no other circus had yet laid claim to it. They heard there was one performing at the Yorke Peninsula—perhaps an even better spot, given the summer crowds the seaside attractions drew— which was a little close for the ringmaster's liking, but it was a scratch act, a new company still breaking in its acts. No real competition for the Braun Brothers' Royal Circus. So the campfire was lit, the horses and donkeys put to temporary pastures, and the wagons parked in unobtrusive formation where they wouldn't be seen by the mugs who came to the show that night.

The advance agent had already opened accounts with local suppliers, and Maggie was sent out to get new tumbling and horsemanship licences for Itsuo and the Steeplechase Sisters. When she came back, she took the wicker suitcase and paid Nev what he was owed for getting them there. The tracker would be leaving the next day to see what work he could find in the city. Maggie knew Rafferty was hoping whatever work he found wouldn't take him far, in case circumstances forced them on the road again.

For the first time since they'd left Sydney, the high-ranking performers would not be sleeping inside the tent. Rafferty had booked them rooms at the Prince Alfred Hotel, a gesture that was both tradition when they reached big cities, and a reward for the group of people who'd learned not to expect anything—even the fulfilment of tradition—in their nomadic lifestyle. Maggie watched as Annie, Itsuo, Smith, Greta and the others gathered their personal belongings into bags that were small enough to be carried the few blocks' walk to the hotel.

'You'll need to go with them, you know,' Rafferty said, causing Maggie to jump. She hadn't seen him come up behind her. He had Charlotte with him, her arm tucked in his in a way that told Maggie he'd been the one to put it there.

'He wants you to still keep an eye on me,' Charlotte said. 'To make sure I don't go looking for a drink.'

Maggie had assumed Charlotte would stay on the circus grounds at night. She frowned.

'I told you she wouldn't want to come,' Charlotte grumbled. 'You should let her stay on the grounds. It's not like I could find anywhere that would let me in anyway, being a woman.'

'That didn't stop you in Hay, and I doubt it would stop you again,' Rafferty said.

'I've not caused any trouble since Maggie started watching over me though, have I?'

'No, you haven't. Which is why she'll keep watching over you. Look, Charlotte, I want to be able to trust you again—'

'Have I given you reason not to lately?'

Rafferty sighed. His arm slid from Charlotte's, and he pressed his fingertips to his eyelids. His face beneath his hands wore the weary roadmap of the months they'd travelled.

'You know I can't stay in a hotel,' Maggie interjected. 'I'm not the kind of person who can go into hotels or department stores or restaurants and have a pleasant time of it. It's all stares and whispers behind raised hands. Sometimes even a pointed request to leave, because I'm disturbing other patrons.'

Charlotte recoiled, seemingly repulsed by the things Maggie had said. But it was the truth. There was only so much a veil could hide when in the close confines of city establishments.

Rafferty regarded Maggie for a second, then turned to Charlotte. 'You'll have to stay here in the tent then.'

Charlotte's voice instantly became a whine. 'Oh, no. Please, no. If it's a choice between being minded at the hotel or having to stay here, I choose being watched over. Please, Maggie. You don't know how I long for a canary.'

Despite her misgivings, Maggie's lips twitched. Trust Charlotte to become dreamy over the prospect of a bath in a hot metal tub.

Seeing the beginnings of a smile encouraged Charlotte. 'And a real bed!' she enthused. 'Just imagine sleeping with a proper ceiling above us! And breakfast cooked on a stove instead of a campfire.' She was just about swaying on her toes as she listed the luxuries waiting for them.

And even though Maggie knew no ceiling could be better than the canopy of stars out in the bush, and no bed would make her as comfortable as the solitude she was used to, she also knew she was going to say yes.

Chapter Thirty-Four

The Prince Alfred Hotel was a respectable place, within easy walking distance on King William Street. Maggie stood outside, looking up at the three levels of windows, tall decorative columns, railed rooftop parapet, and the imposing tower of the adjacent Town Hall. She did not belong here.

'Come on, Maggie, you can't stand on the street forever,' Charlotte said. 'I've been inside already, and it's not too intimidating, I promise. We'll be quite cosy together.'

They had a shared room, with two small beds, each pushed tightly against the wall to allow a little space to walk between them. Charlotte had already taken up most of this space with more bags and belongings than Maggie thought it was possible for her to own. How much of that had floated down the Murray River? Maggie's lips twitched as she wondered what the other hotel patrons would have to say if they knew about that particular adventure.

She picked her way carefully over Charlotte's bags, then took a seat on the frilled eiderdown covering her bed. Charlotte had already littered the small shared bedside table with hatpins, ribbons, handkerchiefs, a handful of paper-wrapped milk poles, a pair of stocking supporters and a half-eaten neenish tart. Maggie cleared a square of space for *A Little Bush Maid* by Mary Grant Bruce, leaving the rest of her books in her leather bag, which she dropped to the floor and shoved underneath the bed with her toes. Hidden between the pages of those other books were the letters from Mr O'Lehry. Maggie had agonised over whether to bring them; she'd have preferred to leave them on the circus grounds, but Rafferty had taken the wicker suitcase back—its contents were being delivered to the bank that very day—and she could think of no other spot that would keep them free from prying eyes. Charlotte seemed to have found every single hidey-hole in the circus when she used them to conceal her liquor. Charlotte didn't read, so she figured the books would remain untouched, the letters safely concealed within their pages. Rafferty always said the deception carried out right under someone's nose was the one most overlooked.

It had been some time since she'd last received a letter from Mr O'Lehry; Maggie supposed with the last-minute change in river-crossing location, she might have missed one somewhere along the line. They could correspond more regularly now that she was stationed in a big city. She eyed Charlotte, contentedly sitting on her bed and stretching her stockinged toes out; her boots were discarded on the floor where a maid would later pick them up and polish the months of travel off them as best she could. She looked relaxed yet strangely vulnerable without them. Maggie wondered how she could possibly share a room with her while continuing such duplicity.

The room was close and stuffy, not having been aired out. This, combined with her thoughts, made Maggie uncomfortable. She slipped her jacket off, took out her hatpin, and let her veiled hat fall onto the bed. The hair at the back of her neck was sticking to her skin, and she undid the first three buttons on her shirtwaist, holding it open and flapping it back and forth to try to create a breeze.

'Why, Maggie, you have a tattoo!' Charlotte cried out. She was sitting bolt upright, her eyes wide. 'No, don't cover it up, I want to see. Is it a magpie? How funny that we both have birds!'

'I thought you said you remembered our day out in Sydney?'

'I remember some of it. Not all.' Charlotte flopped back on her elbows with a sigh, her blue eyes studying the white ceiling. 'I would dearly love to, though. Won't you tell me about it, Maggie? Tell me about that day, and how we both ended up with bird tattoos.'

Maggie chuckled. 'That was your doing. After our day at Wonderland City trying out all the attractions—you even got me on skates, although I was woeful at it and required your help to stay upright—we met a man with a butterfly tattooed on his bald head.'

'No!' Charlotte exclaimed. 'You'd think I'd remember that, of all things. Who was he?'

'A stranger. Although you made him a friend quickly enough. The two of you were calling me 'Mags' by the time we left the stable to get tattoos.'

'Stable?'

'It's where we were drinking.'

'You as well?'

'Me as well. Clearly I didn't know better yet.' Maggie stretched her leg across the gap between the beds and nudged Charlotte's leg with her booted toes, to soften the reprimand.

'What a time we had,' Charlotte breathed. 'I wish there weren't so many gaps in my memories of it all. Will you tell me again, Mags? Only this time, start from the beginning and don't leave out any details.'

Over the next two weeks, Maggie found herself repeating the story again and again. Charlotte seemed to find the tale soothing. Almost every night, after they'd performed to the loud, enthusiastic crowds Adelaide was bringing them, she asked Maggie to tell it one more time. She often fell asleep to the now-familiar words, giving Maggie a chance to sneak the latest letter from Mr O'Lehry into her waiting books.

***

On their second Sunday in Adelaide, Maggie woke up early, dressed quietly with Charlotte still snoring softly in the next bed, and slipped out of the room. She hadn't planned on making this short journey today, but when her eyes had fluttered open in the indigo light of the dawning morning, she'd been overcome with a certainty that today was the day.

Others might have questioned whether or not he would be there. Not Maggie. She knew, just as she knew she would recognise him from a hundred yards' distance; the certainty of him being in Adelaide Gaol was just as much a part of him as his grizzled, half-shaven chin, his eyes that crinkled at the edges with his ready smile.

After writing her name in the register, and the name of the prisoner she was there to see, Maggie filled the waiting time by finding someone to speak to about donating books to the gaol library, which she knew from her father's complaints to be poorly stocked. She parted with her copy of *Galahad Jones* and two volumes of poetry by Bernard O'Dowd, as they were her books that were in the best condition after being carried across three states and two river crossings. Donation made, she was instructed to wait with a crowd of a dozen or so other people.

She kept her head high, afraid that if she bowed it, like she wanted to, the warder might think her behaviour shifty and assume she was trying to smuggle something in under her veil. She didn't want to have to take it off in front of this lot.

Finally, they were let out of the waiting room to assemble in the tunnel-like prison entrance, wide enough to have let two wagons through simultaneously but no more. A brass bar had been put across from wall to wall. On the other side of the bar was a cluster of men and women, the prisoners already waving and shouting at their family and friends. The curved shape of the entrance bounced the noise around, so it was a cacophony of voices that the warder had to shout to be heard over.

'No further than this point,' he declared, rubbing his foot along an invisible line a few feet behind the bar. 'Anyone steps closer, and visiting time is over.'

Maggie moved through the crowd, eyes straining to see beyond her veil.

And then she saw him. Standing next to a woman whose ungainly, full blue skirts brushed the legs of his clean but worn trousers. Maggie's breath caught at the sight of him; clean but worn would be the perfect way to describe him in general, she thought. His hair had thinned on the top, greying wisps curling out the sides and around his ears, and the anticipatory smile he wore exposed a missing front tooth. But otherwise he was the father she remembered. If they'd been permitted to get close enough to hug, Maggie was sure he'd smell of tobacco, soap and beer, as he always had.

The first time Maggie called out, her father didn't hear her. She bellowed the word 'Pa,' again, as loud as her lungs would let her; his eyes skipped over her neighbours, landing on her veil with uncertainty. Maggie flicked up the edge of it, so he caught sight of her face. His mouth widened in the silly grin which had always made her laugh as a child. So few people responded with joy when they saw her face. It had only been her father and Robin.

'Is that my Mag-Pie?' Pa shouted. Maggie gritted her teeth. Could she really be anyone else? Pa's feet did a quick soft-shoe shuffle on the ground, and she relaxed, shaking her head in an exasperated manner.

'You came back to Adelaide!' Pa yelled.

'The elephants died,' Maggie shouted back, earning a few curious glances from prisoners and visitors alike. Her father looked perplexed, but she couldn't think of any way to explain what had happened, not without taking up the remainder of the twenty minutes they were given for visiting. It would be another full month before the gaol would allow Maggie to visit again. Who even knew if the circus would still be in Adelaide by then?

'How are you?' Maggie asked. A question that sounded strange, shouted across the entry of a gaol.

'Keeping well, Mag-Pie. There's been no hangings for over a year, and the Salvation Army's been coming round to talk to us every now and again, which is real nice. The gaol's stopped making olive oil, though, after some other places complained about the competition. So I lost me job in the groves.' Maggie couldn't catch what he said next, but she knew what a blow losing that job must have been to him. The olive groves had meant fresh air and a brief respite from the mundane hours behind the same four walls.

'What are you in for this time?' Maggie called. Pa shrugged.

'You know how it is.'

Maggie did. 'Will you be here much longer?'

'Some time yet, my Mag-Pie. Not worth hanging around Adelaide on my account, if that's what you're thinking.'

'I see.' She didn't care to waste any more of their limited time with seeking further explanation of his misdeeds. There was no point; she would only become annoyed, and he defensive and melancholy.

'Pa, I need some advice. How do you get someone to stop drinking for good?' Liquor was one of the few vices that hadn't tempted her father, and Maggie thought he might have some secret for resisting temptation. Those who overheard her question in the jumble of voices laughed, but Pa didn't. Pa had never laughed at her. Instead, he scrunched his face up, rubbing his hand over his head and then down his face.

'I don't rightly know, Mag-Pie love,' he yelled back. 'I don't reckon you can. Not if they don't want to.'

Maggie nodded. It was what she thought too. She hoped they were both wrong, though. She hadn't seen Charlotte take a single drop since she'd started watching over her. Maggie always woke before Charlotte and fell asleep after her, so it would be nearly impossible for her to drink unnoticed. She knew she was taking a risk by leaving Charlotte alone now, but it was Sunday, so the tightrope walker would sleep late. Maggie would probably be back before she'd cracked an eyelid. And right now, she needed to be here, needed to see the man she'd resented for so long.

'I understand now, Pa,' Maggie called, her voice breaking on the words. Pa cocked his head to one side; Maggie wasn't sure if he hadn't heard or was waiting for her to go on. 'The helplessness ... There was this little girl, you see. She was different, a bit like me. They put her on display at an agricultural show, as though she were one of the pigs or the geese or a six-legged sheep. I wanted to do something to help her, but ...'

Pa leaned forward, to catch her words. She forced herself to speak up again. It was difficult shouting such intimate things, with strangers able to listen in and think whatever they would. But Maggie needed to keep going.

'I've always thought you giving me away to the circus was a terrible act. That it forced me to be an outsider forever. I've been angry for so long that you wouldn't just let me try for an ordinary life with you. But I see now what you were trying to do.'

Tears were streaking down Pa's face. His hands twisted into his shirt, as though they needed to hold on to something.

'I couldn't let them parade you around as a freak.' His voice was filled with pain and doubt. Maggie must have been too young to see it before, but she could see it now: he, too, had questioned himself all this time. He too had berated himself for not being a better father, not staying out of gaol, not being able to think of any better life for his daughter than one with a circus.

'I begged that Rafferty fella to take you in and give you a good life. He said circuses don't usually deal in ... in ...' He couldn't make himself say the word 'freak' again, and Maggie was glad of it. 'I told him you were a fast learner, could do all sorts of things if someone showed you how. And I never sold you, like some do. No money ever changed hands. Did I do wrong, my Mag-Pie? Is it a bad life?'

'You did the only thing you could, Pa,' she said. A year ago, even some months ago, she wouldn't have said the same thing. But she'd learned so much since then. 'You did far better than me. I just left her there.' Maggie's words edged on shrill. She wanted to search for absolution she knew she wasn't deserving of, but she caught the warder hovering at the edge of the crowd. Panic made her pulse quicken. There was so much more to say.

'Pa, I need to tell you something else.' As hurriedly as she could, she told him about the letters to Mr O'Lehry, how she'd pretended to be Charlotte. She didn't care now if those around her heard. Most were too busy with their own confessions or expressions of love anyway.

'And now we're sharing a room and I can't shake the feeling that I'm being deceitful to someone who doesn't deserve it.'

'Oh, Mag-Pie,' Pa said. 'It's just some letters. You wrote the first one because you were hurting. Maybe you wanted a little revenge, but you're not exactly a conniving swindler.'

Maggie couldn't help saying, 'And you're an expert in swindling.'

Pa tipped his head back and roared with laughter, showing that another two teeth were missing at the back.

'But I'm no good to Gundy, am I? If I were an expert, I wouldn't keep landing here.'

Before Maggie could respond, the warder yelled out that it was time to say their final goodbyes. Maggie wasn't ready. She wasn't ready to watch her father walk away, back to the cell where he'd crawl inside a hammock and eat every meal by himself. Back to a world in which cleanliness was a priority but bathing could only be done in a slate slab bath in an open courtyard. Where wrongdoings could mean a flogging that would split the flesh from his back.

'Pa,' she said, and she could feel her face cracking. She didn't want to cry, but the tears were not paying attention to her desires. They gathered in her eyes, making her vision as blurred as if she'd dropped a second veil. She dashed at them with her sleeve, wanting to keep him in view for as long as possible. She wanted to say sorry, for all the anger she'd held in her heart, to tell him again that she understood now, to thank him for his muddled attempts at fatherhood.

'Love you, Mag-Pie,' Pa called.

A strangled sob escaped Maggie's mouth. She wasn't the only one crying; to either side of her, people were wailing, their faces twisted in pain. Small children stretched out their arms, trying to reach for a mother or father whose embrace they were forbidden. Maggie understood how they felt. She, too, wanted to feel her father's arms close around her, to shut her eyes and breathe in the familiar scent of him—the one person in the world who had always loved her, had always done his best for her, in his own imperfect way.

'Take care, Pa,' she called across the gap, before being shuffled out of the gaol.

Chapter Thirty-Five

It wasn't long after Maggie's visit to the Adelaide Gaol that Charlotte began agitating for another day out. Maggie wanted to remind her it was her own fault that she didn't remember their day at Wonderland City, but she bit the words back. Charlotte was doing so well; she'd admitted that the desire to drink was sometimes so intense that her fingers itched to jump right off her hands and go crawling to the nearest bottle. But she'd remained faithful to her promise and reached for Maggie's hands instead, finding strength in their grasp. It wouldn't be fair to remind her of the damages of her drinking when she'd been working so hard to redeem herself.

Especially when Maggie hadn't done anything to right her own wrongs. Despite her father's words, her unease at impersonating Charlotte in her letters to Mr O'Lehry was increasing with each day. Maggie had started to think of Charlotte as a friend. Yet she couldn't shake the feeling that you couldn't truly be friends with someone you were lying to—or if not lying to, at least withholding the truth from. If Charlotte found out, maybe she would remember all the things she'd confided in Maggie—all the truths, the life her sister had stolen from her, the inconveniences of beauty—and know that all along Maggie had not been sharing the truth back. She might feel a fool, deceived by the Lagoon Creature, of all people.

Mr O'Lehry's letters to her had abruptly stopped, but that didn't settle her conscience; all it meant was that Mr O'Lehry had tired of her—having transferred his affections to some new and more exciting woman, perhaps.

Maggie couldn't relax, couldn't be completely natural in Charlotte's presence, with such a secret hanging like a low, thunder-filled cloud over her. It grew heavier and more difficult to bear with every night that passed, as she lay awake listening to Charlotte's soft breathing next to her.

But how to tell the truth?

Maggie had never known what it was to have a friend before, let alone to lose one, and the thought of it paralysed her. By the time she gave in to Charlotte's desire for a day out, she still hadn't found the courage to confess what she'd done.

They were going to the Barossa region. Charlotte had got it in her head that she wanted to visit the Whispering Wall. She'd left South Australia while it was still being built, and she wanted to find out what it was she'd missed, if the magic trick it was said to be capable of was really true. The visit, and the return journey, would take them most of the day.

They travelled through valleys so green they made them both squint. The trees in the distance were such a deep, dark colour that the gentle undulations of the land were almost a mirror image of the violet cloud hanging above. After some distance, the valleys gave way to fields of ankle-deep yellow flowers, their heads bobbing and dancing in the breeze. Even after everything they'd seen, Maggie still marvelled at the ever-changing landscape of her country. Australia was unpredictable, a place of extreme contrasts, but with a steady, immovable sameness. Fires might ravage the land, droughts might kill the grass and force animals into hiding, but there would always be stubborn pink gums and pine trees, the song of magpies, the laugh of kookaburras, the squawk of cockatoos. Always animals scurrying from their burrows—wombats sharing theirs in times of bushfires, or so Nev had told Maggie—and koalas, possums and even goannas clinging to tree branches. Always a clash of intense heat, dry desert, humid rainforests, coastal oases, pummelling rain, and wind that could be hot from travelling across the centre of the country, or be the carrier of flurries of snow.

When they reached the bush surrounding the Whispering Wall, it was a different landscape again. Maggie and Charlotte skirted around a termite nest—a firmly packed mound of clay about as high as the lyrebird on Charlotte's thigh—then walked on for several minutes, dry leaves and twigs crunching beneath the soles of their boots, until they came to the reservoir. Maggie drew in a breath of pleasure that echoed Charlotte's. They stood at one end of the wall; it looked like a long concrete path arcing out from their feet. But on one side was a yawning chasm, dropping so far down that they could not see where the wall met the earth again underneath the tangle of scrub. The manmade structure dominated yet somehow complemented the natural landscape.

Charlotte insisted it should be Maggie who walked across the wall to the other side. Maggie didn't argue. She moved slowly along the top of the wall, her eyes flicking from side to side as she tried not to be overcome by vertigo from its lopsided nature. On her left, the dappled waters of the Barossa Reservoir, so close she could've reached down and touched them, seemed to play with the breeze; on her right, the sharp, ninety-four-foot drop-off of the dam's retaining wall, curved like the inside of a seashell. It made her head swim. She looked down, concentrating on her feet, watching the toes of her boots appear from under the travel-worn hem of her skirt, then disappear again, conscious of Charlotte at her back, watching and waiting. She reminded herself that this was not a tightrope. The wall was wide enough for two people to pass one another; however wobbly she felt, there was no balance required to make this crossing.

And then she reached the far side and stepped off the wall, a racket of excited bird calls greeting her. Down a few steps she went, taking herself into a quiet little pocket lower down the wall's drop-off side, knowing Charlotte was doing the same at the other end. She could see her still, a little dot of muslin across a gaping maw. A blur of motion told her Charlotte was waving one arm high in the air; Maggie returned the wave as she took the final steps down. Then she waited, breath held.

'Mags?'

Charlotte's voice was uncertain, yet as clear as if they were standing right next to each other.

Maggie let out an exhalation that was also a laugh.

Charlotte, catching it, began to laugh too. 'Maggie!'

'I can hear you,' Maggie said. The long distance between them made her want to shout, but the crisp clarity of Charlotte's voice told her there was no need.

'I can hear you too!' Charlotte gasped. 'So it's true then.'

Somehow, the strange curve of the wall carried their voices.

'Magic,' Charlotte said, in a voice full of awe.

Maggie stared at the speck of white across the divide. How much easier might it be to confess an unpleasant truth if she didn't have to see Charlotte's face as she did it?

She could feel the admission rising in her. Could feel her father's rejoinder that it was just some silly letters, not such a big deal as she'd made it out to be in her own mind. Her lips were dry from the breeze that caused tiny strands of hair to tickle her face, and she licked them. Her right palm was flat against the sun-warmed stone of the wall, her entire body quivering with the same combination of apprehension and nerves that always took hold of her before she climbed the ladder to the tightrope. This was the moment. She should tell Charlotte the truth now.

Maggie's lips parted. No words came out. Beyond the roar of adrenaline in her ears, Charlotte's voice carried on, ecstatic, but she couldn't make out the words—only the sound of her second's worth of courage being drowned by the fear of losing her one friend.

The moment was gone.

Chapter Thirty-Six

Charlotte didn't appear to notice Maggie's withdrawn mood as they travelled back to the city. Maggie made an effort to nod her veiled head when she knew it was expected of her, and that seemed enough to keep Charlotte happy. Inwardly, she was busy berating herself—whether for the missed opportunity, or for nearly letting the truth slip along the curved wall to Charlotte's waiting ears, she couldn't be sure.

They decided to go to the circus grounds on Angas Street instead of the hotel. Charlotte wanted to tell anyone who would listen about the wall, and Maggie—who knew the circus hands would have bottles of beer on this night off—figured it best to accompany her. The grounds, when they reached them, were quiet, but a round of laughter came from behind the big top. Charlotte was about to run toward the campfire and join the noise when she stopped and pointed at a stout man in a suit that fit him too tightly, who was hovering uncertainly near the spruiker's stand, twenty yards or so from them.

Maggie was going to tell Charlotte to see to him—sure that the unexpected visitor would rather meet with her pretty face—but something about the man made her pause. His back was to them, so he hadn't spotted them yet, but there was something about the way his feet shuffled nervously—as if he were searching for something—and at the same time expecting that his search would be fruitful, that Maggie thought she recognised. Then his hand went to the rim of his bowler hat, and her stomach dropped the way it did when a wagon went over a rut too fast.

It was Mr O'Lehry.

Rapid thoughts tumbled one over the other. What was he doing here? He was supposed to be in Sydney. Why was he here when he had stopped writing to her?

Oh god, had he found out the truth?

'I'll deal with him,' Maggie said, her voice strangled and strange to her own ears.

But Charlotte was already turning away. 'No need,' she called. 'Rafferty's spotted him.'

It was true. Rafferty had emerged from around the edge of the big top, leading one of the horses. He passed the reins to Bastian, who he'd been speaking to, and changed direction to head toward Mr O'Lehry.

Maggie's panic increased. Her eyes darted around the circus grounds frantically, looking for something, anything, to alter the course of events. They skipped over the candy peddler's stand; the pegs keeping the tent firmly anchored to the ground; the entrance to the dressing tent. Then her gaze landed on Judge, sniffing around the wheels of the baggage wagon, looking for the perfect spot to relieve himself. Maggie dashed over to him, calling out to Charlotte that she'd join her at the campfire soon. Thankfully Charlotte's steps were not slowed by curiosity, and she disappeared behind the white canvas.

Maggie reached Judge and crouched down, her skirt billowing up like a parachute around her as she exclaimed in her most excitable, high-pitched voice, 'Judge, Judgey, look who's over there! Why not go say hello to the man?'

Judge began to turn excited circles, his stub of a tail wagging so fast it nearly blurred. Maggie stood and raced toward Mr O'Lehry, and Judge darted after her, a wide smile thrown her way every few steps as he checked he was headed in the right direction. Finally, he saw the man Maggie was gesturing at, saw the permission to unleash his full enthusiasm. He shot forward, outstripping Maggie to greet him, scrabbling at Mr O'Lehry's waistcoat with dirty paws, leaping high enough to lick the man's face. Mr O'Lehry shouted, his hands reflexively reaching out and closing around the little dog, who struggled in his arms. It was a few seconds of chaos, long enough for Maggie to turn to the approaching Rafferty and call out, 'Sorry, he just took off. I couldn't stop him. I'll deal with it.'

Rafferty hesitated, looking from Maggie to the man, who had now dropped Judge and was brushing at his dirtied clothes ineffectually. The ringmaster seemed to consider the matter for a moment, then decided it was too much effort and gestured for Maggie to go ahead.

Maggie let out a small sigh of relief. She reached for the now-bouncing Judge and caught him in midair; his tongue lolled from the side of his mouth as she held him close. She could feel how fast his heart was racing beneath his wiry coat and taut muscle.

'I'm so sorry,' Maggie said. 'He gets a little worked up when we're not performing. Judge, you know better than this disgraceful display of poor manners!' She put Judge on the ground, then shooed him back toward the campfire. She'd bring him a mutton bone tomorrow for his troubles.

'Let me help you clean up,' Maggie said, stepping forward and reaching out to brush the remaining dirt from Mr O'Lehry's suit. He took a stumbling step back, his mouth opening and closing a couple of times, before finally choking out, 'It's ... it's *you*.'

Maggie froze, her arm stretched between them like a tightrope between two king poles. How did he know?

'The–the Lagoon Creature,' he stammered.

With a crash of realisation that took her breath away—was it relief or pain or a mixture of both?—Maggie understood. It wasn't one soul recognising another it had been communing with. In the commotion with Judge, her veil had flown up and was caught on the brim of her hat.

'Yes, I am the Lagoon Creature,' Maggie said. She went to pull her veil back down, but then stopped. What was the point? He already knew what lay beyond it and would only spend the rest of their conversation trying to get another peek anyway. She let her hands fall to her sides. Her voice, when she spoke again, was flat. 'Can I help you with something?'

'I sincerely hope so.' Mr O'Lehry's hand groped for his coat pocket. Unable to find what he was fossicking for, he had to tear his eyes away from her face. When he produced a letter from his pocket, Maggie's fingers danced toward it, but he snatched it out of reach.

'I'm looking for Miss Charlotte Voigt.' He pronounced her name the Australian way: shar-litt, not shar-lotta. In all this time he'd been writing to her, he hadn't even known how to say Charlotte's name correctly.

'May I ask why?'

Both their eyes flicked down to the letter. It was obvious why. But why couldn't he have mailed the letter, as he always had? Why did he have to be here, in Adelaide, threatening everything?

Maggie glanced over her shoulder. If she didn't hurry and make an appearance at the campfire soon, Charlotte might come looking for her. Or she might be tempted by her sudden lack of supervision to reach for a drink.

'I have a letter for her, from her sister,' Mr O'Lehry said.

'Her sister?' Maggie's attention snapped back to the man.

'Yes, it's rather a peculiar story. I ran into a woman so strikingly similar in appearance to Miss Voigt that I thought it was her. This was at the Yorke Peninsula, and we were both there for the same reason. We'd heard talk of a circus and had hoped it was the one

Miss Voigt performs with. For the woman was a Mrs Gunn, Miss Voigt's own sister.'

'You don't say.' Maggie was impatient to hurry him on. 'And what has Mrs Gunn to do with this letter you're hand-delivering to Miss Voigt?'

'Well, I really did believe it to be Miss Voigt, they look so alike, and I knew Miss Voigt was in this area. We're great friends and have been writing for several months now. She always lets me know which city or town she'll be in next. Only I'd decided we'd gone too long without meeting, and took an opportunity to come to Adelaide for business.'

'And the letter?' Maggie prompted again. Would this man ever get to the point? His verbosity was not nearly as frustrating when it was on paper.

'Once I told Mrs Gunn of my friendship with her sister, she confided in me that their mother is ill. She'd written to Sydney, not knowing as I did that Miss Voigt had left. The letter was of course returned. She's been searching for her sister since, visiting every circus that comes to this part of the country in case it should be hers.'

'Then why isn't she here, instead of you?'

'She seemed to believe that an unexpected visit from her might cause Miss Voigt ... some distress. Once I informed her that the Braun Brothers' Royal Circus had settled in her city, she thought a letter delivered by myself might be more welcome, and more likely to be read, coming as it would from a friend. What luck for her that we met.'

'Indeed,' Maggie said. 'But, ah, I'm afraid Miss Voigt is also unwell. Nothing serious,' she hastened to add, realising she'd never be rid of him if he thought Charlotte were on her deathbed. 'Just unwell enough to take to her bed for a while. She's not here right now.'

Mr O'Lehry's face fell. 'Oh, no. Shall I return tomorrow, then?'

Maggie pretended to give his suggestion some thought. 'It's

best she receives her sister's letter sooner rather than later, don't you think? I'll take it and deliver it.'

'Couldn't you tell me where she's staying? I can bring it to her right away.'

'I'm afraid that's not possible. You see, she's terribly contagious. I'm the only one who can see her, for I've caught the illness before and can't get it again.'

Mr O'Lehry stared at her face, his eyes wide. She could see him wondering if her tumours were the result of this mysterious illness. His features went slack with horror at the thought that his beloved Charlotte—whose name he couldn't even pronounce correctly—might be disfigured. Maggie said nothing, staring at him steadily.

'I ... I suppose if you think that's best ...' he said. 'Only it does seem a shame to have come all this way and not see her.'

'Doesn't it?' Maggie said, plucking the letter from his fingers. She gave a half-bow in goodbye that she'd seen Charlotte perform before. His eyes widened, startled. Had he recognised the movement as Charlotte's?

If only you knew, Maggie thought.

Chapter Thirty-Seven

Charlotte's sister Elisabeth wrote in a stilted, formal style. Mr O'Lehry had said she was unsure how she would be received, and the tightly crammed lettering, the short spaces after each full stop, as though she were hurrying to fit more words in before the reader looked away, spoke of that desperation and uncertainty. Maggie's fingers traced the words curiously. Her mother's illness was described in vague terms, and there was no reference to how severe it might be.

She wasn't sure what to do. She knew there'd been a rift between Charlotte and Elisabeth long ago, and that Elisabeth was the one at fault. What if this were a ruse to bring them together again? After all, Maggie knew all too well just how easy it was to lie in a letter.

Maggie wasn't willing to risk Charlotte's sobriety with an upset when there was a chance the story in this letter was false. She would write back to Elisabeth herself, once again donning Charlotte's name, and try to find out more before deciding what her next action would be.

Maggie tried to keep her letter carefully neutral, conveying no warmth, only a curiosity to know more about the situation.

Elisabeth wrote back immediately. Her tone was slightly less formal this time, opening her letter with wishes for her sister's health, and Maggie wondered if her own letter had been too friendly. Then the meaning of Elisabeth's next words sank in, and she stood, her boots moving, her fingers still holding the letter before her as she blindly went to find Charlotte.

Elisabeth feared that their mother, Alma, would die, though it was hard to know how long she had. Some days she seemed almost herself again, then others brought her so low she could not get out of bed. Maggie knew she had made the wrong decision in not telling Charlotte right away. What if the mother were to die before Charlotte could get there to see her? Her stomach turned. She did not question the truth of Elisabeth's story now; surely not even the most dastardly, thieving of sisters would dare make up something so serious.

Only Elisabeth's final words gave her pause.

I know you likely fear coming back to us, Charlotte, but please know we forgive you and have only love in our hearts for you.

Why would Charlotte need forgiveness? Wasn't it her sister who should beg Charlotte's forgiveness?

Maggie shook her head. That didn't matter right now. What mattered was finding Charlotte and delivering the news of her mother.

She circled the tents and wagons, her hands trembling, so that the letter creased and bunched.

What would she say, when Charlotte demanded to know how it was that Maggie had this news? How could she explain why Elisabeth had replied to a letter Charlotte had never sent her?

It appeared the time had come to tell the truth.

That night's performance was over, and the lights went off one by one, making her flinch each time as the grounds grew darker and darker. When she didn't find Charlotte anywhere, Maggie realised she must have gone back to the hotel without her. The thought made her uneasy. She'd become used to always knowing where Charlotte was, always being able to set eyes upon her at a moment's notice.

'Please, don't be drinking,' Maggie whispered. She needed Charlotte to be aware and alert. She thought of the twenty minutes she'd been granted with her father, how she'd felt the time passing almost as if it were a physical sensation, every minute pulling away from her with such force that she could never slow it down or claw it back. She couldn't take any more time away from Charlotte than she already had.

Maggie raced to the Prince Alfred Hotel. She lifted her veil as she went; it was too hard to see in the dark with it down. She heard gasps as she ran, and knew that she must seem more startling than usual, appearing from the darkness and dashing by in a mad rush, panting loudly. She didn't care. She reached the hotel, lowered her head out of habit and ran up the stairs and down the hall to their room.

Opening the door, she saw with a burst of breathless relief that Charlotte was there. Then she saw what Charlotte was doing, and went cold from the tips of her fingers down to the pointed toes of her boots.

Charlotte was sitting on Maggie's bed. In one hand she held the flask Maggie had confiscated from her, its hinged cap open even though it was empty. Maggie's bag, usually hidden beneath the bed, was at Charlotte's feet, where her books were also scattered. In her other hand were Mr O'Lehry's letters.

Chapter Thirty-Eight

Charlotte held the letters up. There were three of them, but their contents told her there'd been more. Two were addressed to her and hinted at a long correspondence; the third, in a different hand, was signed with her name.

'Maggie, what is this?'

'I–I ...' Maggie's eyes were wide, darting around the room.

'Why do you have letters with my name on them? I didn't receive these. And I didn't write this one.'

'I know. I did,' Maggie whispered.

The two women stared at one another. Charlotte had the distinct impression that she was standing on a precipice, and as soon as she stepped off, everything would change. She wanted to back away from it, to close her eyes and pretend that the ground was as steady and even as it always had been. But she knew she was powerless. Whatever it was that she'd started had a will of its own now—she could tell, because Maggie hadn't even mentioned the flask.

Maggie moved into the room and closed the door behind her. She stepped carefully around Charlotte's belongings strewn on the floor, then sank onto the edge of her bed, crossing her feet at the ankles. In her hands she held a piece of paper.

Another letter?

'It was stupid, and wrong, and more than a little sad,' Maggie said. Her eyes were cast down. 'After you forgot about our day at Wonderland City, I was hurt, you see.'

'Wonderland City?' Her own voice sounded distant, Charlotte thought, as if it were coming from miles away. What did that place and time have to do with any of this?

'Yes. A man visited you that day, a Mr O'Lehry. Do you remember?'

'No.'

Maggie's face twisted; it seemed Charlotte's answer had pained her.

'Well, he was a great admirer of yours. He came back the next day, to ask if you'd write to him when we left Sydney. I didn't think you liked him, so I told him you'd already gone on ahead. He had a letter for you, and I said I'd take it to you. I did, sort of—I was walking over to you when I overheard you deny that you'd spent the day with me.' Maggie was talking fast now, as if she'd been holding back words and they'd finally caught up with her. 'I was angry and hurt and so alone, Charlotte. I thought I didn't mind being alone, but after that day with you ... Anyway, I saw an opportunity. I took the letter and I ... well, I wrote back to Mr O'Lehry. Pretending to be you.'

Charlotte still didn't understand. Her brows quirked downward.

'So you've been corresponding with this man, posing as me, since we left Sydney?' All the time they'd been getting to know each other. All the time they'd been working on their act, performing together in front of crowds. The times they'd slept next to one another under the stars.

'I'm sorry, Charlotte. I should never have done it.'

'I don't give a rat's behind about your stupid letters.'

'You ... you don't?'

Charlotte heard the little swell of hope in Maggie's voice, and felt a fresh surge of anger.

She wished she'd never found the bloody things. She'd been retrieving her flask when she came across them by accident. It was a fair guess that Maggie kept the flask in her leather bag under her bed. She'd promised to keep it safe, and Charlotte had seen that this bag held her favourite books and the occasional letter from her father. She'd found her moment when Maggie was held back at the circus grounds; not sure how much of a head start she had, she'd hurried back to the hotel. She knew the flask would be empty, but she thought she could slip it back into her own belongings, fill it later. When she'd pulled it out, a book had spilled from the bag— the copy of *Seven Little Australians* that she'd given Maggie for Christmas. Charlotte had experienced a momentary flash of guilt; as she picked the book up by the spine, three letters fell from its pages.

She could have minded her own business, put the letters back and returned book and bag to go on with life none the wiser. But curiosity got the better of her. What did Maggie say in her letters to her father? Did she mention Charlotte at all? Were the letters full of complaints at being saddled with the task of watching over her, or did she perhaps consider her a friend after all they'd been through together?

Charlotte, never known for resisting temptation, had unfolded the letters. In the first, she read words that were attributed to her, but were not hers. It was dated from three days before; a letter written in breathless excitement about the visit to the Whispering Wall. There was no mention of Maggie at all, but Charlotte could see her in every word. The lively prose, the amusing twist she gave each anecdote, had no relation to Charlotte's own style of writing. If she hadn't been so baffled by what she was seeing, she would have been impressed by her skill.

And then she read the other two letters, written by a man full of pompous self-importance, who believed he'd created a deep friendship with Charlotte. And she realised: all this time she'd been so busy ducking and hiding from Maggie, Maggie was doing the same thing.

Charlotte held one of the letters up now. 'This one here is dated around Christmas time. It mentions the gift of a green ribbon. The one you gave to me.'

'It was always meant to be yours,' Maggie said.

Charlotte stood, the letters falling to the floor. Poison twined around her heart, trickling through her veins, threading its way through her torso, down her legs. How could Maggie so completely miss the point?

'It was meant to be from you. A gift from you, my friend. Not some man I don't even remember, not pilfered from a letter, not a last-minute gesture because you'd forgotten to think of me at all. I wore that ribbon with such pride, Maggie.'

Charlotte's eyes swam with tears.

'I didn't want you to have nothing,' Maggie whispered.

'Nothing would have been better. At least I wouldn't have gone around with that stupid ribbon in my hair like some proud peacock who doesn't know they're making a complete prawn of themselves.'

Charlotte reached up, her fingers finding the end of the bow that sat on top of her head. She pulled on it, feeling the silky coils unwind. One end fell down in front of her eyes, and she hurried to undo the rest of the knot so she could slip it from her head. Then she didn't know what to do with it. Her hand curled into a fist, but one little green end poked beyond her pinky finger. She didn't want Maggie to see how she was pained by even that slight glimpse of the thing, so she left it as it was.

'I'm afraid there's more,' Maggie said.

'More?' Charlotte's voice was incredulous.

'Yes.' Maggie held out a sheet of paper. It shivered in her grasp as Charlotte reached for it.

It was another letter. For a moment, she didn't recognise the handwriting. Her eyes flicked to the bottom of the page, and she saw a name that made her freeze.

'Why do you have a letter from my sister?'

'I wrote to her too.' Maggie seemed to shrink back in fear. Charlotte remembered how good she was at contorting her body so that people saw what Maggie wanted them to see—frightening, threatening Lagoon Creature, or poor being simply trying to get home. Was she playing at being meek and apologetic? Or did she really feel as sorry as she seemed to?

There was no way to tell. Maggie had proved to be as accomplished a liar as Charlotte herself. Her mind swam, and she tightened her grip on the ribbon in her fist.

'Charlotte, I know you're angry, but listen to me: you need to read that letter.' Maggie must have seen some change in Charlotte's face, for she was hurrying to get her words out now. 'Your mother is sick. They don't know how much time she has left.'

'Why don't you write to her and ask?' Charlotte snapped. The tips of her ears were red hot, and she reached for the flask on the bed. Maggie made a sound of protest, but Charlotte glared at her.

'Go to the circus, Maggie. You can sleep there from now on. And you'll be leaving this here with me.' She lifted the flask higher.

'Please don't go getting into any trouble,' Maggie begged. 'Please don't sneak into a hotel or–or something of the like.'

'You don't need to worry about me, Lagoon Creature. I won't risk any trouble over the likes of you.'

Chapter Thirty-Nine

Maggie was prepared to make up some story if Rafferty questioned or criticised her for moving back to the circus grounds and not keeping her promised eye over Charlotte—she had, after all, proved adept at telling lies. She didn't think she could tell him what had really happened, what she'd done.

She spent a sleepless night under the stars. She kept seeing the slow way that green bow had come undone, the moment it disappeared behind the white knuckles that betrayed more distress than Charlotte would ever realise. She'd never dreamt that giving Charlotte the ribbon would hurt her more than anything else she'd done. Could never have realised the weight of friendship—a friendship Maggie had feared to be one-sided—the funambulist had placed on it. And now Charlotte knew the gift had been nothing but a lazy gesture to save face.

The following night, Charlotte came stalking into the dressing tent and began getting ready without saying a word. Arguments were banned in the dressing tent to keep everyone's attention on the show ahead. The person who started one would receive a hefty fine from Rafferty.

Charlotte's face was wan, thumbprint bruises beneath her eyes.

There was a slight blush to both eyes and nose. Maggie wondered if she'd been drinking or crying. Maybe both. She wanted to say something, to try to heal the rift she'd created, but what words could ever be enough to do that?

'What's his address?' Charlotte eventually asked, as she dabbed her lips with a crushed hibiscus petal. Her voice was flat and she wasn't looking at Maggie. 'This Mr O'Lehry.'

Maggie stopped struggling with the fastenings on her costume. 'Why?'

'I want to write to him. Tell him it hasn't been me corresponding with him all this time and that I'm terribly sorry he was deceived.'

Maggie's fingers fumbled as she went back to dressing.

'I don't know where he's staying in Adelaide. I can only give you his Sydney address. He hand-delivered your sister's letter.'

Charlotte didn't reply, but she stiffened, as if she had to brace herself against Maggie's voice.

Despite Charlotte's clear desire to speak no further, Maggie needed to venture something more—she needed to be sure that Charlotte, in all her anger and betrayal, hadn't overlooked the contents of her sister's letter, that she knew her mother was ill.

'Will you ... will you visit your mother?'

'That's my business,' Charlotte snapped. She threw her slippers to the floor and then bent over, sliding one foot in. Out of habit, Maggie reached out to help, but she pulled back before Charlotte noticed. That wasn't her place tonight. Maybe it never would be again.

'And our act?' she asked, her voice barely more than a whisper. The dim light in the dressing tent made the sequins on her costume shimmer as she shifted her weight from one foot to the other. She wondered if it would be the last time she wore those sequins; if, after all that she'd done, she'd be made to go back to her old Lagoon Creature role, feared and despised by all—a role that suited her better.

'I don't see why it should be affected,' Charlotte said.

But she was wrong. It was affected. Charlotte still smiled at the audience when Maggie climbed the ladder to meet her, still tucked her hands firmly under Maggie's thighs to keep her close on her back, but it was not the same. Charlotte's eyes never met hers; there was no secret whispered message, no squeeze of assurance.

For the first time ever, Maggie didn't even notice the tightrope's great height or the dizzying drop beneath her. All she could think about as she pressed her cheek to Charlotte's neck was the warmth of her skin; and then, at the end of their act, the sudden chill as she slipped from Charlotte's back and was alone with her lagoon once again.

***

It was five days since Charlotte had discovered the letters and Maggie had returned to the solitary existence she'd known before. Maggie had buried herself in her work, but it offered little comfort. The crowds had been excited at first by the prospect of a circus that came all the way from Sydney, but without the elephants or any other exotic animals to keep their attention, the audience was starting to dwindle. Rafferty had begun making noise about getting on the road again, trying to figure out a route that would bring them back to the city in time to settle in for the winter.

And then something happened that pushed even this very real problem to the back of all their minds.

'Why, after all this time?' Rafferty bellowed. Behind him Itsuo, his face drawn in the evening campfire's light, was twisting his hands together. Those who were perched around the fire for their tea paused, startled by the ringmaster's sudden outburst.

'Isn't there something you can do?' Maggie, who had been close enough to hear Itsuo's quiet distress, asked. Her thumbnail was between her teeth, and she ripped at it savagely, tearing it to the quick.

Rafferty put a reassuring hand on Itsuo's shoulder, giving it a squeeze that Maggie knew would be of no comfort. 'Of course there is,' he said.

The authorities had announced, via a letter with intimidating crests and references to various governmental acts, that they were going to deport Itsuo.

'They can attempt anything they want, doesn't mean it'll work,' Rafferty said. 'You've been here since you were a kid. They can't just say you don't belong.'

'Don't I, though?' Itsuo asked, his voice bitter. 'All this time and the law still bars me from naturalisation because I'm not white.'

No one had anything to say to that.

'If they've decided on this path, it's a done deal,' Itsuo continued flatly. 'It's not like I can run or hide—the letter made clear the consequences of trying, for myself and anyone who tries to help me. I'm not going to risk six months' imprisonment.'

'Don't give up hope,' Maggie said. Several pairs of eyes swivelled to her, surprised, but all those days she'd spent riding in the wagon next to Itsuo had, if not completely demolished the invisible wall between them, at least crumbled it a little, and she wanted to offer what support she could.

'How can I not?' Itsuo bit back. 'My entire life is about to change. I hardly even remember Japan. What'll I do there? Do they have need for acrobats? And what of my parents—will they be forced to leave with me? Or can they stay here, so that I might never see them again? This is my home. And you—' he gestured to the crowd of circus folk who had gathered around him. 'You are my people.'

A child began to cry, not understanding what was happening but picking up on the tension. Maggie's eyes met Charlotte's, and for once the tightrope walker didn't immediately turn away. Her expression was stricken, and Maggie knew her own face must mirror the look.

'We'll fight it.' Rafferty's lips formed a straight, stubborn line.

'You've lived here all these years without any trouble—I can't see why they'd come after you now. It makes no sense. I can't even understand how their attention fell on you in the first place.'

Two days later, Rafferty had his answer.

A man strolled into the circus just as the performers were drifting into the dressing tent or beginning to prepare their bodies for their acts. He didn't wear the sunburn they'd last seen him in, and his coat and shoes looked new, but Maggie recognised the swagger instantly. She'd been taking the children's freshly scrubbed clothes to hang on a line near the campfire, avoiding the dressing tent until the last possible minute so she wouldn't have to spend too much time facing Charlotte's turned shoulder. Now she changed direction, her arms heavy with the weight of the wet clothes as she marched forward and shouted, 'Rafferty, the pinch artist's here.'

Rafferty, who was stitching a loose button back on to his ruby coat as he walked toward the big top, halted so suddenly that Judge—who'd been following him—collided with his legs. 'What? The one from ...' He paused, as if searching through the names of the many places they'd been to recently. 'Currawarna?'

'The one you threatened to shoot if he ever came back.' Maggie jerked her head back in the direction of the intruder.

Rafferty swore. He took off even faster than Maggie, Judge trotting assertively at his ankles. He shoved his arms through the sleeves of his coat as he went, and Maggie noticed how his shoulders seemed to widen and his chest spread to make him more impressive, more intimidating. The ringmaster really knew how to put on a show.

'You,' he bellowed. The pinch artist was harassing Annie, who'd been twisting and turning to loosen up her joints before the show. He was trying to get his hand under the skirt of her costume; at Rafferty's voice, he turned with a slow, wolfish smile. Annie took the opportunity to wrench herself free, and fled into the shelter of the dressing tent, where she'd no doubt alert those inside to what was happening.

'I told you we're not interested in the likes of you or your stolen acts. Nothing's changed, so get on out of here.' Rafferty flapped his hands, as if shooing away a seagull searching for scraps. The pinch artist slid his hands nonchalantly into his pockets. The muscles either side of Maggie's spine stiffened; was he hiding some sort of weapon in those pockets? She was relieved to see Smith advancing on them, his large hands curled into ready fists, Bastian smaller but no less ready at his side.

'If it isn't the ringmaster who considers himself too good for me. Where's the Chinaman? The wiry little acrobat? Still with you, or has he been booted out of the country already?'

The circus grounds went so still that all Maggie could hear was the steady *drip, drip* of water from the wet clothes hitting the toes of her boots. Before any of them could think how to respond, Itsuo burst from the nearby dressing tent.

'I'm Japanese, you ignorant wombat,' he said, his eyes steely. 'And you're the one who doesn't belong here. You need to leave, right now.'

The pinch artist threw his head back and made a sound like a kookaburra's laugh, only with a sharper edge to it. 'Who's gonna make me? You? You're already in a world of trouble for giving me a beating. Wouldn't want to make it any worse.' He took advantage of the confused silence that came after this to step sharply toward Rafferty. 'Thought you'd won our little skirmish, didn't you? But I don't forget an ill done to me. Followed your ragtag bunch all the way here. You leave a pretty clear trail, you know. Burnt pubs, upset mugs, sunken punts.'

'We didn't sink the punt,' Charlotte said. Maggie hadn't even realised Charlotte had joined the growing group, but there she was, on Rafferty's other side, her arms crossed in front of her. The pinch artist looked her up and down in a way that would have made Maggie shudder if it had been her.

'Going to set Beauty *and* the Beast on me, are you?' he sneered. Rafferty tensed, looking like he was ready to strike the man, but Maggie shook her head at him.

'Not worth it,' she muttered. 'It's just words. And unoriginal ones at that.'

All mirth dropped from the pinch artist's face. He took another step forward. Rafferty refused to let his polished black boots move back even an inch.

The pinch artist's eyebrow twitched. 'I'm the one who went to them,' he snarled. His lips were damp with saliva. 'The government. Told them about your Chinaman—might've embellished a little, told them he bruised me up. Did you know foreigners get deported if they've committed violence against a poor defenceless Australian like me? Add to that how he burned that pub down and caused the whole circus to be run out of town ...'

'That wasn't him, it was me,' Charlotte cried. 'And we weren't run out of town.'

Itsuo's chest was heaving, a flush crawling up his neck and staining his cheeks. Smith stepped close and placed one hand on his shoulder; Maggie couldn't tell if it was to hold him back or encourage him.

'You mongrel,' Rafferty spat. He had one arm out to the side, ready to stop Itsuo from running forward and attacking the man. 'You absolute piece of—'

'Gonna shoot me, ringmaster? Bit hard without your precious rifle, isn't it?'

'I don't need it,' Rafferty roared, his hand snatching the ringmaster's whip that was coiled on his hip. With a resounding crack, it unfurled, catching the pinch artist by the ankles; he went over, landing on his back with a sound that told Maggie the wind had been taken out of him. Rafferty raised the whip again, but Smith grabbed his forearm; aside from the pinch artist, who was rolling breathlessly and trying to grasp his no-doubt throbbing ankles, everyone was still.

'You bruise him up too much and he'll use it as evidence Itsuo hurt him,' Smith growled. 'As it stands, it's just his word.'

Rafferty appeared to be struggling to regain control of himself. He gave a slight nod to the strongman, who cautiously released his boss's arm without letting his own hand fall out of reach.

'You've got what you came for,' Rafferty growled. 'Get out of my grounds unless you want another taste of the whip.'

The pinch artist fumbled his way to his feet, holding his hands up in the surrender position, and started to back away. It wasn't a real surrender; he knew he'd got his revenge. He moved slowly, smirking and when he saw that they weren't coming after him, he turned and limped off, slapping the backside of one of the donkeys on his way past, making it bray. Maggie watched him go, the laundry heavy in her arms.

'It's not even you he's hurting,' she said to Rafferty, her jaw so tight with tension that it ached. Rafferty's eyes were still on the man he'd offended. Maggie didn't think she'd ever seen the ringmaster look so grim: not during the night flitter, not when the town did a freeze on them, not even when Charlotte had frozen on the tightrope in the middle of their act.

'He knows exactly what he's doing,' Rafferty said. 'He understands the best way to hurt me is to hurt one of you.'

Chapter Forty

Charlotte sat on the bed that had once been Maggie's, turning the flask over and over in her hands. There was a single mouthful left in it. She'd downed the rest of the contents only a moment ago, but had left one final gulp for the courage she would need.

The situation with Itsuo itched at her as though she were wearing a dress made of sandpaper. How could he bear it? The uncertainty of the new life waiting for him, the feeling of time passing, unstoppable, bringing him closer and closer to a fate he had no control over?

Rafferty had taken the circus's savings and was looking for the finest barrister he could find. But Charlotte knew barristers were expensive. She remembered Will telling her how much his employers charged their clients; even a good season of performances at small towns, shearing sheds and railway construction camps wouldn't be enough to raise such a sum.

She sighed, running her hand ran over the eiderdown. Seeing Itsuo have the future he'd envisioned for himself snatched away without warning made her reconsider her own life, her own actions. She'd spent that first night after the discovery of the letters furiously scrubbing at the lyrebird tattoo on her thigh until her skin was raw, in the futile hope that it might fade, along with all the memories that went with it. Because she'd felt so foolish, she'd reacted badly and cut Maggie off without thinking. But she missed the woman she'd counted as a friend. She wasn't sure she was ready to forgive her yet, but she had to admit to herself that she did understand what Maggie had done. Was pretending you'd chosen a gift for a friend when you hadn't any worse than stealing a flask which had never been intended for you? Was borrowing a name and life to put on paper worse than trying to steal a taste of your sister's life?

Forgiveness was just so difficult, and she had so little experience with it. She'd never asked for it from her family.

She stood, thumbing the silver lid of her flask open and taking the last mouthful.

***

She found Maggie at the circus grounds, as she'd expected, taking a rare break. She was relaxing on one of the collapsible wooden chairs, her feet propped on a tin tub she'd flipped upside down, a copy of *The Hawklet*, a popular show-business and scandal rag, open on her lap. Charlotte hesitated, watching her for a moment. She wasn't wearing the veiled hat she donned whenever she left the circus grounds, her head instead topped with the plain straw one she'd worn on the road, a thing devoid of any ornamentation. Her face was so familiar to Charlotte by now that it wasn't the tumours she noticed. It was the way her nose was scrunched up and her eyebrows drawn together, an unconscious look Charlotte knew signified she was deep in concentration.

The now-familiar spark of hurt and resentment flickered within her, but it died quickly, replaced by something hollow and yearning. This woman *had* been her friend. Charlotte was almost sure of it. She didn't want to believe that Maggie's lies meant the connection she'd felt was a lie too. After all, her own lies hadn't coloured her feelings toward Maggie. At least, she didn't think they had. They were so bound up in a tangled mess of her own making that it was hard to tell anymore.

Charlotte cleared her throat. 'Maggie?'

Maggie's head shot up. Charlotte had never been nervous to talk to Maggie before, and she squirmed under the unfamiliar feeling.

'I need your help,' she said.

It was the way Maggie instantly dropped her magazine that told Charlotte more than words ever would or could. Despite all that had happened, despite their last, angry words to each other, and the days of silence that followed, Maggie's first instinct was to free her hands so she could reach out to Charlotte and provide whatever help she could. Charlotte had to blink several times.

'Maggie, I think I know someone who can help Itsuo. My sister's ...' It was difficult to say the word, even after all this time. 'My sister's husband. He's a barrister. Last I knew he was working at a very influential firm. I want you to come with me to see him.'

Maggie ran one hand along the side of her neck. 'Why don't you just write to him?' The words were loaded with apprehension, and neither could meet the others' eyes.

'If I wrote to him, he'd only tear my letter up without reading it.'

'I don't understand. Your sister writes to you.'

'She shouldn't.' The words tasted acrid on her tongue. 'Will's right not to forgive me.' Charlotte raised her eyes to see that Maggie was looking directly at her now, her sharp gaze trying to uncover what she was still hiding.

'What do you mean? Your sister stole your life from you. She and Will are the ones who need to ask for your pardon.'

Charlotte's impulse was to lie, habit strengthened by years of resentment and denial. But she pushed the impulse down. It was time to take a leap of faith.

281

'Don't you know that drunks lie, even to themselves?' she asked.

Maggie didn't answer her. But Charlotte didn't expect her to. What could one say to such a thing? That it was the truth? That Charlotte's anger at Maggie's lies was the height of hypocrisy, when she was concealing so many of her own? None of it would change the past. None of it would undo all the hurts.

'Please come with me, Maggie. I can't face them alone.'

Maggie was still staring at her, her eyes seeming to change colour and depth as the clouds above them shifted. Finally, she said, 'Can you tell me why?'

***

Will had moved into Elisabeth and Charlotte's family home after the wedding. His new father-in-law had insisted the newlyweds stay with them until Will had saved enough for a place deserving of Elisabeth. It had been exquisite torture for Charlotte; Will was close to her, and some days—when Elisabeth was instructed by the doctor to rest her slowly expanding body in bed—she even had Will to herself. But she also had to witness him arriving home with a kiss for her sister every evening, his hand caressing the swell of her stomach, as the child they'd created quickened within. Charlotte would watch, able to feel that hand on her own stomach, those lips landing on hers. It was a world in which everything was nearly as it should be, only shifted one place to the left. If she could just take it in her hands and give it a good shake, surely everything would fly up and come back down to land in the correct place.

And then the baby was there. A little girl, who everyone said looked just like Elisabeth. Which meant she looked just like Charlotte. Charlotte could see her own indented upper lip on the baby's mouth, her own expression of distress when the baby wrinkled her face and cried out to be fed. Elisabeth, Will and the baby became their own private little group that could not be penetrated, while others—particularly Charlotte—could only hang on the periphery and look on in pleasure or envy.

Will had made the wrong choice. Nothing had ever been clearer to Charlotte. After four months of observation, she took it upon herself to prove this. Will was at the firm. Elisabeth had taken a stroll, under doctor's orders to get more fresh air and gentle exercise to improve her health, which had continued to flag since the baby's birth. It was quite late in the afternoon, and Charlotte had been drinking. She waited until Alma, who'd been keeping a watchful eye over her granddaughter, left the room on some brief task. She crept forward, then lifted the baby out of her frilled crib. Her body was soft and warm, and surprisingly heavy; Charlotte realised that she had never once held her. She brought her close to her chest now, dipping her head to breathe in the clean scent of her downy hair. A sharp pain ran through her. This baby should have been hers.

Whispering nonsense so the baby wouldn't cry out, Charlotte tiptoed out of the house. She snatched a blanket up on the way, a vague plan forming. They would have a picnic, somewhere that Will would discover them on his way home. Together, she and the baby would look the picture-perfect family, and Will would understand all that he was missing out on, all that should've—and still could—be his.

After a fifteen minute walk, she found them a spot at the base of a jacaranda tree in Wellington Square, where she was sure Will would pass by. The fallen purple flowers made a picturesque carpet for her to spread the blanket on top of, and she bundled the baby carefully in her skirts. She realised she hadn't brought anything to eat, and softly cursed herself. What kind of picnic was this? Still, the baby was settled, and she had Will's flask which she'd filled with rum. It would do.

The next thing she knew, she was being woken by her shouting father. Elisabeth was in hysterical tears, cradling the baby, who had begun to go blue in the cold, and Will had his arms around both of them. Charlotte was disoriented, and in the noise and upset could hardly even remember what her plan had been.

She was dragged back to the house, where Alma turned a pale, disgusted face away from her before disappearing upstairs with Elisabeth. Jakob lectured her, detailing how worried they'd been to discover the baby was missing, how irresponsible and heartless she was, how an opportunistic lowlife could've snatched the baby without her even realising due to her stupor. But she barely heard him; all her attention was focused on Will. He had his back to her, his shoulders high in a straight, quivering line, and his hands were flexing into fists.

Finally Jakob left the room and they were alone. Charlotte took two tentative steps toward Will. Her head was pounding, her mouth dry and sour-tasting. She'd never felt so sober in her life, nor so in need of a drink.

'I'm sorry, Will,' she whispered. Her voice sounded as though she hadn't spoken in days. 'You know I would never hurt her. I only did it because I love you—'

Will whirled around. 'You don't love me,' he snarled, and it wasn't his voice anymore. It was the voice of some creature made from anger and resentment and pure revulsion. A creature Charlotte had created. 'You think you do, but it's not love you feel. When a person loves another, they only want happiness and good things for them. That's how it is between Elisabeth and me. What you feel is–is some kind of possession. You had me first, so you have to have me always.'

Hot tears ran down Charlotte's cheeks and in salty rivulets over her lips. 'No,' she croaked, 'That's not fair.' But Will wouldn't let her say any more.

'You were my first love, Charlotte, but the friend I once knew and treasured is gone, and so is my affection for her. You're not even a sister to me anymore. Somewhere along the line you decided that *this* is more important to you than anything else.' He produced the flask, the engagement gift her father had given that Charlotte had stolen. He must have found it on her when they'd discovered her asleep against the jacaranda trunk, the baby forgotten at her feet. He threw it aside; it skidded along the carpeted floor. 'That's why I turned to Elisabeth; why she turned to me.'

That night Charlotte packed as many of her belongings as she could carry. After some deliberation, she slipped the flask, which she had retrieved from under a chair, into her stocking holder, wanting Will's initials close to her skin. By the time the rest of the family rose to the baby's wails the next morning, she was already gone and on her way back to the circus.

***

As Charlotte trailed off, she had a sense of some part of herself lifting above them, looking down and wondering how on earth the other woman below would respond.

Would she be angry? All this time Charlotte had been pretending to be a wronged sister, yet it was Elisabeth who could have lost everything because of her actions.

Charlotte was about to disrupt the quiet with a painfully unfunny joke about Maggie having offered Mr O'Lehry a better version of her than she could ever be, when Maggie exhaled very slowly.

She reached out a hand, her fingers gently touching Charlotte's.

'Let's go see your family,' she said.

Chapter Forty-One

They disembarked the electric tram on Sir Edwin Smith Avenue in North Adelaide, and began to walk toward Jeffcott Street, where Elisabeth's letters had said she now lived. Charlotte's heart was drumming in such a loud, unsteady rhythm that she could no longer hear her boots on the pavement. It was hard to fathom that her sister had been so near all these weeks. Charlotte was glad she'd never shown up prior to a performance, as she'd apparently done at the Yorke Peninsula circus, where she'd encountered Maggie's Mr O'Lehry. She couldn't imagine how she would have reacted to seeing Elisabeth after so long, right before she was expected to showcase perfect balance.

'This must be it,' Maggie said, coming to a stop a couple of paces ahead of Charlotte. Beneath her net veil Charlotte thought her eyes were questioning: was Charlotte ready for this? She took in a long breath that hurt as it filled every corner of her body.

The house was a freestanding building of grey and brown stone, two storeys tall. The top floor was fronted with a lace-edged balcony that ran the entire width. On the ground floor, a bay window jutted out on the right; Charlotte could imagine the voile curtains twitching at every curious sound out on the street.

The front garden was bordered by a short stone wall topped with white-painted iron fencing. Maggie put her hand to the gate and gave it a push; it swung open silently, the stone path between two small stretches of grass inviting them forward. Charlotte didn't move. She was still staring at the house. Its every detail spoke of luxurious comfort, and it was impossible not to imagine herself mistress of it, in another life, one in which she'd done everything differently.

'Are you all right?' Maggie asked. Charlotte noticed she didn't ask if she wanted to give up and turn away, and she was grateful.

'I think so,' she said. 'It's just strange, being here.' She tilted her head back to take in the full height of the house. 'But there's nothing for it except to square up and get the thing done, I suppose.'

She straightened her skirt and checked her hat was in place. She'd dressed in her best white muslin, as though it were a holiday. Why, she wasn't quite sure. Was she trying to prove at a single glance that she hadn't made poor decision after poor decision? That she was, in fact, doing quite well for herself?

They went down the path, Maggie a little behind this time, so that Charlotte was the one to rap on the door. Charlotte half-expected a housekeeper to answer, but it was Elisabeth herself who opened the door, a near mirror-image of Charlotte's face registering shock as her mouth froze on the pleasantries that had been forming.

'Hello, Elisabeth,' Charlotte said. She took in her sister, eyes raking her from top to toes. Her body had softened, and there were slight signs of age around her eyes and mouth. Her skin was still smooth and clear, though, the freckles a different constellation to Charlotte's yet still similar. Her red hair was parted off-centre and swept down and over her ears and forehead in the modern fashion. The dress she wore was a sumptuous confection of vertical blue and white stripes, with a lace jabot at the throat and excess fabric hanging from the elbows. The toes of white kid leather boots peeked from beneath the wide, embroidered hem. Charlotte was suddenly conscious of the effect several months on the road, and a trip down a river, had had on even her good muslin. She ran her hands self-consciously over her waist, feeling like a dull blot on this pristine world.

'You came,' Elisabeth said. 'I'm so glad. Have you been to see Mother?'

Guilt washed through Charlotte, with irritation quick to follow. Already she had been tested and found wanting. She felt Maggie move behind her, a slight gesture of reassurance. She was not alone in this. She tilted her chin up and worked to keep her tone measured instead of defiant.

'No, not yet. I've come on a different, although rather urgent, errand.'

'Oh. I see. You'd better come in, then.'

Elisabeth beckoned for them to follow her; they stepped into the front hall, then immediately turned right into a sitting room. It was the room with the bay window. It had a black fireplace at the opposite end, although it was far too warm for it to be lit. The ceilings were high, the windowsills deep, the skirting board nearly a foot tall. Every detail evoked a sense of opulent welcome, but as the three women sat down—Charlotte and Maggie side by side on the upholstered walnut settee, Elisabeth facing them on a matching armchair—Charlotte had an overwhelming sense of not belonging.

Elisabeth was casting curious glances at Maggie.

'This is Maggie. She works at the circus, and is a friend,' Charlotte said, hurrying over the final word before she had time to question it. The perplexed line between Elisabeth's brows stayed there. Before Charlotte could say anything more, Maggie said, 'My face is disfigured. You'll understand if I keep my veil lowered. I wouldn't want to frighten the children.'

Charlotte realised then that she could hear the thumping overhead. She turned an enquiring gaze to her sister.

'Helene and Clara,' Elisabeth said softly. 'My daughters.' As if on cue, there was the rolling thunder of feet coming downstairs, then two small figures burst into the room in a cloud of white lace. The littlest raced over to the fireplace, chubby fingers reaching for objects on the mantelpiece that would not be in reach for some time yet. The older girl came to stand by her mother's side, taking her hand and drawing invisible pictures on her palm while she stared silently at the strange guests.

'You remember Leni,' Elisabeth said. Charlotte's breath caught. Could this really be the same baby she'd run off with so long ago? In her memory, her niece was a shadowy, doll-like figure. But here was a real little person, her face framed by the red hair she shared with her mother and aunt, a giant bow tied on one side of her head, giving her a lopsided, quizzical look. Charlotte's hand rose, half-stretched toward the little girl; a strange choking sound, a sob that had years of pressure behind it, tore from her. For the first time, Charlotte realised what she'd done. She could have permanently altered the happy life of this little girl with her irresponsible actions. Could perhaps have ended it, if they hadn't found her when they did.

The shame she'd tried for so long to pretend she didn't feel was so intense it was like drowning right there in that finely decorated room. Charlotte gasped, looking for air. Maggie's hand found its way into hers and squeezed it, offering a lifeline, as tears spilled down Charlotte's face as she stared and stared at her niece.

Helene let go of her mother's hand and tiptoed over to Charlotte, so close their skirts were brushing. She leaned forward, her small palms reaching out.

'Don't cry, it's all right,' she said, patting Charlotte's wet cheeks.

'Leni, this is your Aunt Charlotte,' Elisabeth said.

***

Once she'd got her tears under control, aided by a handkerchief quietly handed over by Elisabeth, Charlotte settled back into the settee.

'Are you all right?' Elisabeth asked. The sympathetic note in her voice did not make Charlotte feel any better.

'I'm sorry for such an outburst. Especially in front of the girls.' The three women looked at them, sitting on the floor where Elisabeth had instructed them to play with their marbles while Charlotte mopped her face and blew her nose. Helene, as if feeling their gaze, looked up. She smiled.

'Sometimes I cry too, Aunt Charlotte,' she said. 'Mama says it's because I'm hungry or tired.'

'Your Mama is right. I was very tired.' Tired of the shame, of the lies, of the weight of her own wrongdoings. Charlotte didn't want to think about it anymore. 'Elisabeth, I'm afraid I got carried away. I was supposed to be telling you about Itsuo, our acrobat.'

This piqued Helene's attention, but as Charlotte explained Itsuo's situation to Elisabeth, the little girl lost interest. She went back to rolling marbles across the floor to her sister.

'Could you, perhaps, ask Will if he might be able to help? He'll be more inclined to listen if a request comes from you. His wife.'

'Of course, but please, won't you stay until he comes home from work?'

'We have a show tonight. I'm afraid we can't stay very late.'

'Then let me send word to Will asking him to return early. Please.'

Charlotte didn't feel able to refuse.

While they waited, Charlotte allowed herself to be fawned over by her nieces. Evidently they weren't afraid of strangers— for Charlotte *was* a stranger to them—because they bustled about bringing her china dolls their mother had made clothes for, beads on strings, and other little toys to admire. Charlotte was glad of the distraction; she could hardly breathe knowing that Will might walk in at any moment.

Elisabeth supplied lamingtons, puftaloonies and peeled apples for them to enjoy with tea that was not drunk out of pannikins but delicate china teacups. Maggie kept them all entertained with stories about their journey from Sydney. She had a showman's quality to her that surprised Charlotte, who was grateful that her friend left out all mention of the fire at the pub, the night flitter, and Balranald doing a freeze on them.

Helene dragged Charlotte outside to show her how, if she rubbed her spinning top with coloured chalk, it left beautiful patterns on the front garden path. Charlotte had to give compliment after compliment before her niece allowed herself to be ushered back inside. Having washed their hands, they returned to the room where Maggie and Elisabeth were still quietly chatting. And then Charlotte heard him.

His voice echoed through the house, calling out to his wife and daughters. Every muscle in Charlotte's body stiffened. She wanted to glance at Maggie for reassurance, but she couldn't drag her eyes away from the sitting room door where he would appear any moment.

Like Elisabeth, he had changed very little. He was thicker around the waist than Charlotte remembered, and grey hairs had begun to thread through the familiar black. He'd also grown a large moustache, the kind that was currently popular. But the smile that lit his face as he opened his arms to receive a running hug from his daughters was the same as it had ever been. It was the smile he used to greet Charlotte with.

'Hello, we have a guest, do we—' His voice broke off. His hat fell from his hands, and the smile that had only a second ago warmed his features disappeared. Charlotte couldn't miss the way his arms protectively moved around his daughters. The sting of it made its mark, but Charlotte kept herself still, composed.

'What are you doing here?' he asked. There was no welcome in his voice.

Elisabeth stood. 'Will, please. Charlotte needs our help. Not for herself, but for someone else,' she hurried to add. 'A man who's about to be deported. All she wants is a little advice to give to him. Won't you help? For this man? For me?'

She had reached Will's side and was gazing at him earnestly. Charlotte could see they had a way of speaking without words. Finally, Will ran a hand over his face; recognising this as capitulation, Elisabeth turned to their daughters and gestured for them to follow her out of the room, saying they were to help her put Daddy's hat away. Maggie rose and quietly announced that she would assist. Will started, as though he hadn't even noticed the other woman's presence until then.

They waited until the others left, Maggie diplomatically closing the door behind her. Then they waited a moment more. Charlotte didn't feel it right to be the first to speak; not after all these years, not in his house, not after what she'd done.

'What is it you really want?' he eventually asked. His eyes would not meet hers, and his arms were crossed, defensive. 'Do you need money? Is that it?'

Charlotte forced herself not to react. She didn't want to ruin Itsuo's chances with her own temper or hasty words.

'I told Elisabeth the truth,' she said slowly. 'There's a man who works with me at the circus—where I earn plenty to keep me going, thank you,' she couldn't resist adding. 'He's Japanese, and the government wants to deport him.'

'People are deported every day. What do you expect me to do?'

'I don't know. But this man's been here for years, living and working. His parents live here. Australia is his home. Sending him to Japan would be sending him to a country he barely remembers.'

'What did he do?'

'Nothing.' At Will's doubtful expression, Charlotte insisted, 'Truly. He's accused of attacking a man, but it's a lie. Our ringmaster offended some lowlife, and he's lying to get Itsuo deported as revenge.'

'What mad kind of revenge is that? If the fella's lying, he has no proof, let alone an actual conviction. Chances are his accusations won't get him very far—he could even get in trouble himself for trying to deceive the government.'

'The accuser is white and Australian-born. Itsuo is not. Does that change those chances? For Itsuo says it will.'

Will sighed. 'Why do you want to help, anyway? It doesn't sound as if this involves you.'

'You don't understand. You should, though. For it's about family. That's what we are in the circus. We have to be; our way of life doesn't offer any other option, even for those who didn't kill their relationship with their real family. You know what family means, Will: you stand up for one another. You defend each other. You do what's right, no matter the cost.'

Finally, Will's eyes came to rest on Charlotte's face. The sensation was almost physical; she felt that familiar pull toward him. It was the lure of nostalgia, though, nothing more. Whatever hold he'd had on her before, whatever desperation had made her do such terrible things, had faded in the hour spent in her nieces' company. Or perhaps it had faded years ago, but she'd clung too stubbornly to the memories to realise it. Charlotte supposed she would never really know. Either way, without it, she almost felt empty.

The fight seemed to leave Will. 'Fair go, Charlotte. You're really putting the acid on. You know that, don't you?'

There was a hint of the old Will in those words, which gave Charlotte the courage to push her luck a little.

'I'll admit I was banking on you being unable to resist defending someone who'd been treated unfairly.'

Will uncrossed his arms. He slumped down into the chair that his wife had occupied only moments ago, indicating that Charlotte should take the one opposite. His fingers drummed on the arms, his eyes flitting all over the room as he considered.

'I'm assuming your circus mate can't pay for my services?'

'A little. Not much. Definitely not what you'd usually charge.'

He gave a single nod. 'I can't promise anything. You need to understand that right now. Going up against the government in a deportation case is almost impossible.'

'Almost?'

'If you have the right connections, you can make anything happen.'

'And do you have the right connections?'

'Maybe. I have a few favours owed me. None big enough to pull your Japanese friend out of the fire. But I might be able to get a meeting to argue for a certificate of exemption, given his work history and the lack of any actual conviction.'

'Promise you'll try?' Charlotte leaned forward, her fingers twisting together. She knew instantly she'd made a mistake. Will shrank back in his chair, trying to escape her nearness. His face, which had been relaxing with every sentence, went hard again.

'I'm still angry with you, Charlotte,' he said. At last, an acknowledgement of all that had happened. It was almost a relief.

'I know. You have every reason to be. You both do.'

'You don't understand. It's been easier for me than Elisabeth. Hating you, being so angry with you, I could dismiss you from my thoughts. But Elisabeth still loved you. She felt such remorse for loving me, for causing you to run away.'

Charlotte pulled at a thread in the upholstery. She'd had no idea that in all the time she'd been running and hiding from her own guilt, her sister had also been grappling with hers.

'She shouldn't have, you know,' Will said. 'Felt guilty, I mean. For what were we supposed to do? Do you know how difficult it was, watching you ruin yourself with drink and being powerless to stop it?'

Charlotte flinched; no matter how fervently she'd tried to convince herself that her drinking had only taken hold after Will and Elisabeth's engagement, it wasn't the truth. Since that first taste, side by side with Will perched in a tree, she'd turned to rum whenever she needed to escape life's unpleasantries: loneliness, resentment, a sense of not belonging, even boredom. She hadn't thought it noticeable, let alone a problem.

'Why didn't you say anything back then?'

'I did. Elisabeth did. Your parents ... well, they didn't want to believe their daughter could have—in their words—such an undignified problem. But Elisabeth and I ...' He sighed. 'Don't you remember? We tried so hard to make you change. Nothing worked. How could you blame us for finding love with each other amid the mess you created? What would you have had us do instead? Deny ourselves comfort or understanding from another soul who knew what it was like to go up against the drink and lose?'

So there it was. Charlotte had been the reason Will and Elisabeth fell in love. She'd destroyed her own future without even noticing it, because she'd fallen so far down into the bottle she held.

'You already had love,' she said. It hardly mattered anymore, but she wanted him to hear it, to acknowledge that he'd caused her pain too. 'You had mine. All of it.'

'Maybe. But the drink always came first.'

Charlotte's lips were still open, poised to give an answer, but none came. She'd heard it said that the truth set people free, but this didn't feel like freedom. It felt sad and wasteful, like a dinner painstakingly crafted over hours and then thrown into the dirt road.

With hands that resisted every part of the movement, she reached for the bag she'd brought with her. Her fingers fumbled inside, closed around familiar crocodile skin. She pulled the flask out and extended it to Will.

'I should never have taken this from you.' Will's fingers reached for the flask, his face etched in a painful combination of remembrance and disbelief. As his fingers brushed hers, Charlotte let her eyelids flutter closed. Was it the warmth of his touch, a whisper of long-ago memories, that she was cementing forever in her mind, in her body, in her heart? Or was it the feel of the flask that had kept her company all these years and soothed her tormented spirit? Charlotte couldn't be sure. Whatever it was, she forced herself to let go.

'Will you help Itsuo?' she asked.

Chapter Forty-Two

Maggie waited until they had reached the tram stop before she said anything. She could see that Charlotte was trying to untangle her thoughts and didn't want to interrupt.

'Your sister is lucky to have two beautiful children,' she finally ventured as they climbed up onto the tram, sweeping their skirts out of the way of other passengers. Charlotte looked at her in surprise, as though that were the last thing she'd expect Maggie to comment on. Maggie pressed her lips together. No one ever considered the Lagoon Creature might want children of her own. Not even Charlotte, who knew her best.

'I suppose so,' Charlotte said. 'Yes. Did they remind you of ... Robin?' She spoke tentatively. Maggie shut her eyes, wanting to take a moment to compose herself before answering. When Charlotte had revealed her lies, Maggie had felt her anger threaten to rise again; but, with Itsuo's future at stake and time being of the essence, she'd pushed back against it. To her surprise, it went easily—as if it had been waiting for a chance to be set free. What she'd been left with was sorrow: sorrow for the wreck Charlotte had made of her own life, sorrow for Elisabeth and Will's loss of one family member just as they'd welcomed a new one, sorrow for the parents who must know their misguided decisions shaped a life of pain and resentment for one of their daughters.

So, when Robin's name brought a pang of wistfulness, Maggie refused to let it spark into an anger that would be pointless and exhausting.

She made her voice kind when she said, 'In a way. Although they'll have an ease in life that Robin will never know.'

'You know what it is to live Robin's life, don't you? That must've made it even harder to leave her behind.'

Maggie shrugged. There was nothing she could say that wouldn't make Charlotte feel worse. She decided to change the subject. 'What did Will say? Can he help Itsuo?'

'He doesn't know if he can, but he's going to try.'

It was probably the best they could have hoped for, Maggie thought, given Charlotte's past with the man. 'How was he?' she asked as they arrived at King William Street and stepped off the tram. 'Toward you, I mean.'

'He's still angry. We both said words, words that I'm not sure helped but were probably long overdue.'

'And now?'

Charlotte's answer was cut off by the shouted greeting of a diminutive man running toward them, waving a bowler hat. Maggie didn't know him and exchanged a quick glance with Charlotte, who didn't seem to know him either. Another forgotten admirer, perhaps?

'Miss Bright, is that you?' he asked as he reached them in a whirl of breathless enthusiasm. He had the type of American accent that made his mouth seem full to the brim with his words; it took Maggie a moment to realise he was talking to her, what with her surname being used so seldom.

'Yes, I'm Maggie Bright,' Maggie said cautiously. 'How did you know?'

Was this man someone from the gaol perhaps, with news

from her father? Her insides tightened, vice-like; a month hadn't passed, so she hadn't been able to see him again yet.

'The gents at the circus told me to keep an eye out for a lady in a veil,' the man said. 'Now would you mind raising it? I can see a little beyond it, but I can't make an offer without getting a proper look.'

Maggie lifted a protective hand to the edge of her veil. What was this man on about?

'Offer? I'm sorry, who are you?'

He laughed. 'Sorry, I've gotten ahead of myself, haven't I? I'm Asa Lithgow, and I work as an agent for Samuel Gumpertz's Congress of Curious People and Living Curiosities.' At their blank looks, Asa Lithgow prompted, 'Coney Island? In New York? It's home to the world's largest collection of freaks.'

Bile rose in Maggie's throat.

'Freaks?' Charlotte's voice turned the word into a high-pitched protest.

'Sure,' Asa Lithgow said. He pulled something from under his arm. It was a large album, and he began flicking through the pictures at so rapid a speed Maggie could barely see them. 'We've got tattooed ladies, armless wonders, human skeletons, immortal couples—you name it.'

'What is this book?' Maggie asked, her fingers reaching out to jab at the pages and stop them flying. Her fingertips came to a rest on an image of an immaculately attired woman in an old-fashioned chequered dress, her hair pulled back in looped plaits, her fingers decorated with rings. One hand rested on what looked to be an ordinary wooden chair, except for the fact that it loomed higher than her head.

'Cartomania's a real fad back home.' Asa Lithgow handed her the album. 'You can make a small fortune selling portraits like these. That tiny lady you're looking at is Lavinia Warren, a stellar example. She and her husband were some of the most successful curiosities ever. I say were; Lavinia's still around, but

Tom—Tom Thumb, her husband, who was just as little as she, if not littler—died quite some time ago. They dined with the likes of the Vanderbilts and Astors.'

'Who?' Charlotte asked. But Maggie didn't care what the man's answer was. She was too busy turning the book's pages, taking in face after face. Although they were all varied, they had one thing in common: all, like Maggie, had the kind of appearance that forever made them different.

'These are f–freaks on display, in America?' she asked when she came to the end of the album.

'If you want to put it that way,' the man said. He finally seemed to register Maggie's reticence and spoke more carefully. 'Another way of saying it is that they've used what God gave them to make a lucrative life for themselves. Very lucrative. That's why we have so many "made" freaks now. Men and women who tattoo every last inch of their skin, or grow the longest beard possible. But that's not where the major money is, and thus not what I'm here for. I'm scouting born freaks. And what I've heard is that the Braun Brothers' circus has a ... a rarity, a wonder, an oddity, like no other. I believe that rarity is you, Miss Bright.'

'That's why you want to see beneath my veil?'

'Indeed. If you are as much a curiosity as your audiences have claimed you to be, I have an offer you won't be able to refuse. An offer to come back to Coney Island with me and make your fortune.'

Maggie was dumbfounded. No one had ever considered her face an asset before. Yes, it meant she could play the part of the Lagoon Creature, but that had been a favour to her father, Rafferty's kindness to a desperate man. Even Gladys, the ringmistress who'd offered her the only other alternative she'd ever had to the Braun Brothers' Royal Circus, had done so out of sympathetic concern—not because of what she thought Maggie might add to her shows.

'You want to take Maggie away to America?' Charlotte said,

incredulous. The man glanced at her, a distracted frown creasing his forehead. It was then that Maggie realised what had been unsettling her. Even though he couldn't yet see her face, the man hadn't taken his eyes off her for a moment—whereas most men would have had eyes only for Charlotte.

'Yes, I do,' he said. 'Provided she fits the bill.' He gestured again at Maggie's veil.

She refused to lift it yet. 'To be stared at? Laughed at? Poked and prodded?'

'No. To be admired. Examined in awe. Never touched. It's not at all like your agricultural shows here—oh yes, I've seen them. At Coney Island you'll be a queen. Or a duchess, or a princess—whatever you like. It'll be up to you. Something regal, though. None of this Lagoon Creature nonsense. American audiences don't like their oddities to be pitiful.'

Maggie stared at the man. Slowly, she raised her hands, taking the filmy edge of her veil. She lifted it high, settling it back on the crown of her hat. Asa Lithgow let out a long whistle of appreciation.

'Marvellous,' he murmured, clasping his hands under his chin. 'All they said is true. Miss Bright, you're truly one of a kind.'

'Thank you.' The words left Maggie's lips without thought. She'd never accepted a compliment before; wasn't even sure if this really was one. But there was a soft glow inside her, something akin to the gently smouldering embers of the campfire once everyone's bellies were full and a contented silence was falling over the circus. Maggie studied the man's face the same way he studied hers. She saw sincerity in him, and perhaps a touch of greed.

'I'll need some time to think it over,' she said. She sensed Charlotte turning to stare at her, startled, perhaps, that she hadn't refused. 'The ringmaster at Braun's has been good to me, and I couldn't just leave without giving the matter proper consideration.'

'Of course. Such consideration does you justice, Miss Bright.'

Asa Lithgow gave Maggie the name and address of the hotel

he was staying at in the city, then said goodbye with a deep and impressive bow.

'You really might leave?' Charlotte asked as they watched him retreat with a confident, arm-swinging walk.

'I don't know,' Maggie said.

It was the first time in her life that she'd been given an option that wasn't borne of pity.

Chapter Forty-Three

Before Maggie could make any decision about Mr Lithgow's offer, they had news from Will. His meeting with the government officials had failed. Even though Rafferty and others in the circus had provided character references, and Will had argued that without conviction of a crime Itsuo's deportation wasn't lawful, the minister in charge would not be moved; he was determined to see Itsuo, and others like him, gone from the country.

Which meant that Itsuo's only chance at staying lay with the dictation examination, a technicality which the deportation hinged on. It was the same fifty-word examination that new migrants faced, and if he passed, the process against him would be cancelled. Itsuo could, of course, easily pass—if it were in English. The trouble was that the test could be administered in any language chosen by the presiding officer. It was a cruel technicality by which the government ensured most applicants failed. Will suggested a well-placed bribe might ensure Itsuo's examiner chose English, but he could go no further in helping them. While he believed the minister was playing outside the law with his interpretation of the *Immigration Restriction Act*, Will could not do the same thing. It would risk his licence to practise law.

The last piece of advice he left them with was how big to make their bribe. One hundred pounds was the penalty given to anyone found to be interfering in the deportation process, so it had to be well beyond this. How much more was up to them, and how desperate they were to ensure success.

'You could always go out bush if it doesn't go your way,' Greta said as they sat around the campfire the night before the test. It was not a performing night, but everyone had gathered behind the tent anyway, a spontaneous coming together to support one of their own.

Itsuo made a despondent noise of disagreement.

'If I fail, they'll take me right then, I'm sure. They won't want to give me a chance to run away.'

'Bah!' Bastian spat on the ground. Maggie saw the way he watched Itsuo; was he thinking of their similarities? Both immigrants, both working for the circus for several years. Only one of them was European and white, and thus able to seek the security of naturalisation.

Maggie turned across the dwindling fire to Rafferty, who sat on a stump. 'You really couldn't tell how the bribe was received?' she asked. He pressed his lips together in a downturned curve. Knowing Itsuo would risk gaol time if he tried to bribe the examiner himself, Rafferty had done it for him earlier that day. The money—pooled from the savings of everyone in the circus—had been accepted, but the official made no promises. They could do nothing more than hope that tomorrow he'd honour his end of the bargain.

'At least I'll know as soon as I sit down for the test,' Itsuo said, his dark eyes trained on the fire. 'If it's in Lithuanian or German, then I'll know it's all over.' He tried to make this last sound light, like a joke, but no one smiled.

'I'm sorry I brought this on you.' The campfire flickered, emphasising Rafferty's hollowed cheeks.

'You couldn't know the pinch artist would do something

like this.' Itsuo's voice was kind, but Maggie could see the way it prickled beneath Rafferty's skin that the one who was most affected was the one trying to be comforting.

'I didn't have to humiliate the miserable bandicoot in front of everyone, though, did I? That's what all this is about.' Rafferty stood abruptly. Muttering something about seeing to the rosin-backs, he strode off. Maggie waited a couple of minutes before saying to anyone who cared to listen that her leg had fallen asleep and she needed to walk it off.

She found him in the dark, not with the horses, but peering at the lettering on the side of one of the wagons, studying it for signs of an unsteady hand. Maggie stopped next to him, resting her arm on the wagon's edge. She knew she was blocking out what little light Rafferty had to see by, but she didn't care; she'd been the one to repaint the lettering, and she knew there were no imperfections to be found.

'You know Itsuo doesn't blame you.'

'I know. But he should. He should blame me, and that pinch artist, and the government, and the whole bloody country.' Rafferty punched the wagon. Then he straightened up, propping his elbows on the wagon's edge and dropping his face into his palms. Maggie could see the skin on his knuckles had split.

She wanted to seek his advice about the American agent's offer—even though he wouldn't want her to leave, she knew he'd have a clear perspective and give her the positives and pitfalls as he saw them. She'd always been able to rely on him for that. But watching him breathe raggedly into his palms, something in her shifted. She thought of all he'd done for her from the moment he'd accepted her father's pleas and taken her in. Now he was the one who needed help, who was doubting his place in the world and the effect he had on others. Maggie wanted to step up and give him all that he had given her.

So even though Asa Lithgow's offer played on her mind, teasing her with tempting notions of money and freedom, she put it aside and instead said, 'You're a brilliant showman, Rafferty. I'm sure after you were done with him, the examiner thought the bribe was his idea all along. He'll give Itsuo the English test, you'll see.'

'We can only hope so, Maggie girl,' he said.

***

On the morning of Itsuo's dictation test, the performers and circus hands gathered outside the Prince Alfred Hotel to see him off. Rafferty tried to find his old showman's voice, declaring with false jocularity that all would be well come evening. No one believed him, least of all the grey-faced Itsuo, who had refused breakfast in the hotel's dining room and now turned down the peppermint Rosemary offered him to settle his stomach. When it was time to go, some could not keep their fearful tears at bay. Maggie saw one slide down Smith's cheek as he embraced the acrobat in his tree-trunk-like arms.

And then Itsuo was gone, walking away with Rafferty by his side until the very end—whatever that end would be.

Maggie couldn't just sit around and wait. She was too unsettled by the unjustness of it all. Even though she wasn't due for another visit, she collected her bag and made the short walk to the gaol.

She gave her name, and her father's name, saying that she'd come to see him; as expected, once the warden checked his books, he tried to turn her away. But Maggie wouldn't go. She dug her heels in and raised her voice until the others in the waiting room turned sympathetic eyes on her. She knew there was no point in arguing; no words in the world could make the warden disregard his rules. But she carried on anyway.

'You know such rules are only ever made and enforced by those who will never know what it's like to live under them,' Maggie snapped. 'You men in power don't understand how difficult it is to be denied your family. How cruel it is to be forced to give up a home when belonging is such a very hard thing to find!' At the warden's baffled look, she realised she'd strayed from making any sense to him. He didn't know about Itsuo; he couldn't understand that it was every corrupt authority she was railing at.

'Fine, then would you at least give him this?' Maggie snarled, rummaging in her bag. She'd brought a book with her, knowing it was likely to come to this. It was the book Smith had given her for Christmas, *New Grub Street* by George Gissing. After reading it herself, she'd thought her father, stuck behind four walls as he was, might enjoy travelling to distant England via the written word to observe the marital escapades of its characters, hack writers all of them, living in the London of the 1880s. She held out the book with one hand, and with the other did something she never usually would: she lifted her veil, exposing her face to the warder.

He gasped, stumbling back. The families of the prisoners perked up, trying to get a look at what had made him react so. Those who could see Maggie's face began whispering, as she knew they would.

Maggie stood there, unwavering, holding the book out to the warder. She didn't know if it was fear or pity that made him comply, but he reached out and accepted it with reluctant hands.

'It can go to the library,' Maggie said. 'Just please let him know it's there, and that it came from his daughter.'

'We'll have to look it over, search between the pages.'

'Of course. You'll want to make sure I'm not smuggling him any words of love.'

This earned her some laughs from their audience; one man even yelled out, 'That's right, love, you tell him.' Maggie's cheeks coloured, both at her own daring rudeness and at the strangeness of being called 'love' by a man she didn't know.

The warder's face darkened. Maggie sensed that the moment was poised to turn against her, and she knew all too well how vicious a man could be when he'd been humiliated in front of others.

'Thank you,' she said with all the earnestness she could muster, clutching her bag close to her body and backing away. She let her shoulders sink inward; her experience in creating characters with nothing but the way she moved allowed her to show the man someone weak, supplicating, spent by the brief exertion of simply trying to give a book to her poor father. 'Your generosity does you credit.' Perhaps it was too much. But the man looked gratified.

There was no guarantee that what she'd set in motion would come to pass, but she'd done what she could. At the end of the day, that was all any of them could do.

Chapter Forty-Four

There was to be no performance that night. Usually they held their breath in anticipation of the show; today they held it in anticipation of learning Itsuo's fate. None of them could settle to any task, their minds on the other side of the city, where Rafferty waited outside a government building, ready to be the first to learn the outcome. Some loitered inside the big top, wandering the stands. Maggie and Charlotte were outside, standing in a loose group near the extinguished campfire with Smith, Adlai and Annie, watching Greta half-heartedly put Judge through his paces.

When a man entered the circus grounds shouting to high heaven, everyone within earshot jumped to their feet, thinking it was Rafferty or Itsuo, hoping it might be both. But it was neither.

It was Mr O'Lehry.

He was marching into the grounds with one fist balled at his side and the other raised in the air, clutching a letter. Maggie's breath caught.

'Miss Charlotte Voigt.' Mr O'Lehry's voice was a summons. Maggie saw heads pop out of the big top. Smith's posture changed to one of readiness, and Gilbert and Bastian appeared as if from nowhere. With a nervous gesture for everyone to stay where they were, Charlotte separated from the pack and went to meet Mr O'Lehry.

'Can I help you?' she asked. Maggie realised she didn't know who the man was. She'd only ever seen him that one time, many months ago in Sydney. Cursing Rafferty's absence, Maggie took an uncertain step forward. She wasn't sure if her presence would make matters better or worse, but she wanted to be close by, just in case she was needed.

'Don't play that game with me, missy,' Mr O'Lehry snapped, waving the letter so close to Charlotte's face that she had to step back.

'Mr O'Lehry,' Maggie called. He glanced her way, and she saw his face twist in distaste. He recognised her from the last time they'd spoken, when she'd taken Elisabeth's letter from him. As he turned away, Maggie scuffed her feet in the dirt, impatient, not knowing what to do.

Charlotte, who now understood who this man was, spoke carefully. 'I thought you would receive my letter when you were back in Sydney. I wrote to you there.'

'I have a colleague forwarding my mail. Luckily, as it gave me the opportunity to come here and find out the meaning of all these lies.' Again, he shook the letter.

Maggie knew the strength of Mr O'Lehry's feelings for Charlotte; she had known he would be hurt, disappointed, perhaps even embarrassed, to learn the truth. But to show up angrily, making accusations in front of so many? Something inside her tensed, telling her to be wary.

'I can assure you I told you no lies,' Charlotte said. Her voice was level, her hands moving up in a supplicating motion. 'I'm sure it was very distressing to find out the truth, but there's nothing more to be said—'

'Like hell there isn't!' His face had gone cherry-red. Smith took a step closer to them, but Mr O'Lehry didn't appear to notice. He was pointing at Charlotte's face with a hand so unsteady the letter tumbled free of it, landing in the dirt. 'You're lying. You wrote those letters, and now you're trying to deceive me. Look, you're even wearing the ribbon I sent you for Christmas!'

Charlotte's hand went to the emerald ribbon tied in a bow around her hair. When had she begun wearing it again? It must have only been that day, for Maggie would've surely noticed it before. Their eyes met. The corners of Charlotte's mouth quirked. She didn't see Mr O'Lehry reaching for her, and her eyes widened in shock as his fingers closed hard around her wrist. Smith jumped forward, but Maggie was faster. She reached them in only a few steps, bringing her arm down so that it broke the man's grip. Without pausing to think, she shoved him hard in the chest. He took several staggering steps backward before landing on his backside, his bowler hat rolling away in the dust, Judge running after it to shake it aggressively between his teeth.

'It was me!' Maggie shouted. All the pressure of the last few days, the last months, the entirety of every year of her life, swelled in her chest, expanding it, cracking open her ribs, until there was nothing for it but to open her mouth and let it out in a scream. 'I'm the one who wrote to you. She didn't lie to you—she just protected me by not telling you it was me. But it *was* me. Me. Me!'

Mr O'Lehry's head jerked from side to side, protestations of, 'No, no!' bubbling from his lips. Maggie was not wearing her veil, and his round eyes were fixated on her face.

'No. I'd never exchange intimate letters with a–a–a *freak*.'

The old, familiar word stung. But the pain felt like habit, as if she were just going through the motions and could barely remember anymore how much it was supposed to hurt. She leaned forward, her breath hot with her rage.

'You should count yourself lucky to have had my friendship. You never earned Charlotte's, and you could never be worthy of it.'

'You devious slut!' Mr O'Lehry scrabbled in the dirt, trying to find his footing. Maggie wasn't sure if his words were directed at her or Charlotte. No matter. She was no longer thinking, no longer wondering what Rafferty would do were he here. She was functioning rather than thinking. She turned, eyes scanning the gathering crowd for the person she wanted.

O'Lehry struggled to his feet. 'You'll pay for this,' he spat. 'I'll see you run out of town. I'll see that your two-bit circus never has an audience again. I'll make sure every decent person knows you're all charlatans and common whores.' He was working himself into a lather, but Maggie, who had spotted Greta, strode up to her, ignoring him.

'Where are your swords?' she asked calmly. Greta's mouth dropped open. In bewilderment, she pointed to the dressing tent, fifteen yards from them. Maggie stalked to the tent, picked up one of the swords and removed it from its protective sheath. She took long, fast strides back to where Mr O'Lehry was swearing and making threats while he tried to claw his hat back from Judge. Maggie whistled, and Judge let the hat drop. Mr O'Lehry was dusting it off when Maggie lunged forward, thrusting the point of the blade at his chest, stopping just short, as Greta would.

'I spent months watching a woman slide this blade just by my ribs, close enough to kill me if she so much as sneezed,' she said through gritted teeth. 'Don't think I don't know how to use it.' She nudged the sword forward a fraction, so that it cut the threads of his brightly coloured tie

'Maggie,' Charlotte gasped, the only one to make a sound. The rest of the circus folk were still, their muscles tensed, ready to respond, as one, to whatever happened next. Even Mr O'Lehry could feel it, as his eyes flicked from the blade, to each of their faces in a desperate, silent plea for help.

'No one threatens my circus,' Maggie said.

'You're mad as a cut snake,' Mr O'Lehry panted.

'Indeed I am. And if you go about flapping your gums, spreading rumours about us, remember this: I have your address. I know where to find you.'

Mr O'Lehry's dusty face went pale. He took a cautious step

back, testing to see if Maggie would pursue him. When she didn't, he jammed the bowler on his head, turned and ran.

The stunned silence that followed was broken by a familiar voice.

'What in the hell was all that about?'

They turned and saw the ringmaster standing next to Itsuo, both their brows high on their foreheads at the scene they'd just witnessed. Itsuo let out an incredulous laugh.

'Don't tell me we're going to have to make more bribes because another man'll be seeking revenge now?' he said. His last words were cut off in a burst of joyous noise as the circus folk rushed at him, asking again and again if the bribe had worked, if the test had been in English, if he had passed—ready to believe it but needing to hear the good news from his own lips. Itsuo's smile widened with every affirmative answer. Maggie stood apart, watching, her sword arm still half-raised, until Charlotte came to meet her and took the weapon from her with a gentle touch. She beckoned Greta over and handed it to her, the swordswoman still wearing a stunned expression, then slid her arm through Maggie's.

'Are you all right?' she asked, her voice low, lips close to her friend's ear. Maggie was shaking a little, but she nodded. She was fine. Better than she'd been in a long time.

'Come on, then,' Charlotte murmured, and urged her forward to join the crowd.

***

Maggie and Rafferty sat side by side on the benches in the big top. How many people had occupied that exact place Maggie now sat in, watching the spot-lit ring before them come alive with spectacles that defied belief? Maggie breathed in deeply, the scent of the sawdust filling her with a comforting mix of nostalgia and something warm but indefinable.

She had finally told Rafferty about everything that had

happened between her, Charlotte and Mr O'Lehry. He deserved an explanation after seeing her threaten the man with a sword. Rafferty, to her surprise, mostly found the tale amusing.

'I'm glad to see you've been living a little, Maggie girl,' he said. They could hear cheers from the impromptu party outside celebrating Itsuo's success. 'I've never liked seeing you hold yourself apart, as though you didn't deserve to partake in everything life has to offer.'

'You think I did that?' Maggie had always thought that life had kept her at bay, not the other way around.

'Didn't you?'

'People were afraid of me. They didn't want me near them. You know that. You saw it yourself.'

Rafferty's face sagged. 'I've let you down in so many ways, haven't I, Maggie girl? I'm sorry. You're right, I did see the way the other children shunned you. And the adults too. I should've done more to discourage it. I just thought that if I pushed things, they would resist even more—you know how stupidly stubborn circus folk can be. I figured with enough time, you would all get to know one another, and it would become a thing of the past. But by the time the others had adjusted, you'd separated yourself so fully from everyone that I didn't think interference from me would be welcome.'

Maggie couldn't answer.

'I'm not saying you did wrong. But I think it's you pushing them away now, Maggie girl, not them pushing you away. I understand why you'd want to keep the world at arm's length. But these are your people—you understand them, and you might discover they understand you too, if you can find it in you to give them another chance. To most of us you're just Maggie— dependable, hardworking, sword-wielding Maggie.'

He smiled at this, crinkles fanning out from the corners of his eyes. Maggie squirmed, somehow both uncomfortable and pleased.

'I'm afraid Mr O'Lehry will try to cause trouble now,' she said, changing the subject. She tilted her head back, training her eyes on the mottled grey canvas ceiling of the tent. It had once been white, but had discoloured with age and constant use. Maggie thought she was probably the only one who had noticed this tiny detail.

'I don't think he will. I saw his face as he ran off—you put the fear of God into the man.'

'Not God, but the Lagoon Creature.' Maggie couldn't help but laugh, despite her concerns.

'Even if he does come back, I know you're capable of handling it,' Rafferty said.

'Let's just hope you're here next time, so you can be the one to handle it. Without a sword.'

Rafferty turned to face her, his head angled to one side so that his eyes were half-shadowed by the spotlights. 'Not likely. I think my time here is done.'

'Done? What do you mean? Is there something wrong with you? Are you ill?'

Rafferty chuckled, patting her hand with a warmth that had become so familiar over the years Maggie hadn't even noticed it. Now her heart constricted with fear that she might suddenly lose it. 'Slow down, Maggie girl,' he said. 'No, nothing is wrong with me. At least not on the outside. But on the inside ...' He paused, and his eyes changed focus, his gaze disappearing somewhere Maggie couldn't follow. 'I think, for me, the circus ended with Ida and Hercules. My heart for the business died with them. I've just been too stubborn to admit it. Not to mention worried about how you'd all survive. But after using the ringmaster's whip for violence instead of spectacle—I can't deny it anymore.'

'I could've sworn back in Sydney you were excited about going on the road again.'

'A showman's trick. One where I was trying to fool myself.'

'I see.' Maggie's pulse was racing. 'And now?' While she had Mr Lithgow's offer, what of everyone else? What of Charlotte, who needed someone to watch over her and stop her from drinking?

Of Itsuo, who had only just found his feet again? Gilbert, Bastian and all the other circus hands? All the children who'd already learned to love this life?

Rafferty rubbed his knuckles along his jawline.

'Seeing what happened to Itsuo, I can finally admit it,' he said. 'To myself, and to you. I don't want this anymore. I don't want to be responsible for anyone else's future, or their happiness. Whatever it was that used to make it all worth it is gone. I no longer have sawdust in my veins. Just ordinary, tired blood.'

Maggie's head drooped. She'd been so enticed by the idea of going to America and leaving the circus behind, but now that the circus was being taken away from her, the loss seemed immense. She couldn't help but think of all the laughter that would be lost, all the notes of music that would never be heard. All the women who, rejoining the regular world, would find that their only role was to run a family—a role that might suit some, but not be enough for everyone, maybe not even Maggie herself. All the country towns that would miss out on the excitement of the circus: sword dancers, strongmen, acrobats, clowns, tightrope walkers, contortionists, equestrians and their show horses. Maggie's eyes were hot, but she couldn't cry.

'Maggie.' Rafferty's hand was on hers again, his voice as soft as his touch. 'I want you to take over the circus.'

'You ... you what?'

'I want to give it to you. To be ringmistress of.' Maggie's mouth dropped open. A second later, it closed again. There were no words. Her head swivelled back to the ring, where night after night they put on a carefully orchestrated performance for audiences who would never understand that the show was only a tiny part of what it meant to be a member of a circus.

'I know you can do it,' Rafferty continued.

'I couldn't even get the animals to listen to me,' Maggie said. 'Remember how we tried when I was young? It's the reason I became a performer. I have no authority.'

'You're not that person anymore. You've been looking after the finances for years now, you know how to budget, set up accounts, balance the books and pay everyone on time. You won't be taken for a fool by suppliers or those who work for you. You have the necessary thick skin for running a business. You know every step in setting up and taking the equipment back down again. You know what it means to perform. And after today's display, I know you'll stand up to any threat made against the circus. Besides,' and here his lips twitched, making Maggie wonder if he was about to tell her he was only joking, and of course the circus wasn't going to be hers to run. 'Crowds will flock from far and wide to see the circus run by its very own Lagoon Creature. Of course, you'll have the power to change that name, if you so wish. As you said, your character could've been sympathetic all along, and I was too blinded by a showman's arrogance to see it. You were right—another example of how you'll make a better boss and leader than me.'

'So you're giving me the circus as an apology?'

'No. I'm giving it to you because you're the best person to run it. But I hope it also goes some way to making up to you the wrongs I've done you, my Maggie girl. Think of it: you won't even have to perform anymore, if you don't want to. The circus is yours to do what you want with.'

It was tempting to cave to her fears: that what Rafferty was offering wasn't possible, that it was too big for someone like her. But then she thought of Gladys, successfully running her own circus. If life was hard for a woman who was a Lagoon Creature, it was even harder for an Aboriginal woman. Gladys—managing a crew, keeping her show on the road, and bringing up her little boy all at the same time—was living proof of what was possible.

Then she thought of the offer Asa Lithgow had made her.

Maggie could run the circus; she could run away to America and become a famous curiosity. Both were within her reach.

The question was which to choose.

Chapter Forty-Five

Charlotte and Maggie sat facing each other on the beds in the hotel room they'd once shared. After their visit to Elisabeth, Charlotte had invited Maggie to return to the room, but she'd turned her down, saying she was more comfortable at the circus grounds, where she could hear the quiet whinnies of the horses and smell the freshness of the earth. Apparently she'd never slept well in the hotel anyway.

'Have you decided what you'll do?' Charlotte asked. Her stomach was knotted, but she tried to keep her voice even. She didn't want Maggie to go so far away, to America and a new life, but she didn't want to influence her decision, either. Not when she'd seen how much it meant to her, to choose what she wanted for herself.

Still, she couldn't help adding, 'For what it's worth, I think you'd make a marvellous ringmistress. The finest in all Australia.'

Maggie had removed her veiled hat, and Charlotte was glad of it. She could see the thoughts that crossed her friend's face, seconds before they left her mouth. Right now she saw pleasure, which made Charlotte smile; then she saw certainty, which made her afraid again. It seemed Maggie had made up her mind.

'I'm glad to hear you say that. Seeing as I'm going to be your boss from now on.'

Charlotte let out a delighted shriek, launching herself forward and throwing her arms around Maggie with such ferocity that she nearly knocked her off the bed. Maggie laughed, trying valiantly to straighten them both up, squashing her discarded hat in the process.

'It turns out I do have sawdust in my veins,' Maggie grinned.

'Oh, I am so glad, Mags,' Charlotte said, breathless with joy. 'I truly think you're making the right decision. It's funny, though, isn't it? Rafferty has always been a bit of a father—not just to you and me, who grew up in the circus, but to everyone who's a part of it. Helping us out of scrapes, soothing our tantrums away, trying to always be fair. And now that'll be you. You'll be the mother of an entire circus.'

Charlotte saw Maggie swallow, trying to keep back a sudden flood of emotion; then her lips formed a smile which looked as though it had been waiting to come forward for a very long time.

'The circus is so lucky to have you,' Charlotte said. 'Only ...' she trailed off. Her insides were performing feats that would impress a trapeze artist.

Maggie narrowed her eyes. 'What?'

'Well, you won't be *my* boss and parent. You see ... Spending that time with my nieces, it ... well, it made me think. Fear wasn't enough to make me give up the drink, nor was loss. But now I feel like I've caught a glimpse of love. True, proper love, the kind you get when you really belong to your family. So—' She took a big breath, reluctant to say the words even though she meant them. 'I'm going to stop drinking. Properly, this time. There's a place you can go where they'll help you, a sanatorium. Henry Lawson went there, so it must be all right. I know how you admire his writing.'

She gave a little laugh, more like a hiccup, uncertain and confused. She knew this decision was the right one, but it was frightening. Who would she be without liquor to bolster her? Could she withstand the hurts and cruelties of life without it? Would she be as sparkling, could she still be fun? Would she even succeed? Or would she sink back into the same Charlotte who had made her family turn from her in shame?

'After that, I thought I might stay with my parents for a while,' she continued, trying to chase the ugly thoughts away. She'd done so much in her life—walked the tightrope, travelled the country by wagon, seen sights so unimaginable they seemed almost magical. She could do this thing, difficult as it might be. 'They're paying for the sanatorium, and Alma—Mother—could use the company, what with being unwell. Plus I'd get to see Elisabeth, Will and the girls. You'll be losing your boom girl, though.'

Maggie smiled, and this time it was a maternal smile that softened every feature of her unusual face. She reached forward, taking the loose ends of Charlotte's hair ribbon. It must have come undone when she'd dived at Maggie. It wasn't the emerald green ribbon, which she still wore sometimes, but a ribbon Elisabeth had given her, a gift from her nieces, who had insisted on sending it because it was pale blue, like the ribbons they wore in their own hair.

As she retied the bow, Maggie said, 'You know, you and I grew up almost as sisters. Side by side, at least for a while, even if we didn't really speak. And I know you have Elisabeth, but I want you to know you also have me. I might not be your boss or some sort of mother, but I am your sister. If you'll have me.'

Charlotte blinked several times. 'Of course I will.' Her voice was thick, nearly as husky as Maggie's.

'There, a perfect bow.' Maggie hesitated a moment, then cupped Charlotte's face.

'You'll always have a place at the circus if you need it,' she said. She leaned forward and planted a soft kiss on Charlotte's cheek.

Epilogue

Maggie sat with her shirtwaist open, a scandalous amount of her chest exposed. The pain of the needle buzzing over her skin was familiar. She would have liked to visit Fred Harris, who'd given her the magpie, but he was in Sydney, and she wanted this done now.

'That's one finished,' the tattooist said, leaning back so Maggie could see his work in the mirror he'd angled in front of her. Next to her magpie was a small lyrebird, its curled tail resting beneath the magpie's feet. Maggie grinned. She couldn't wait to write to Charlotte at the sanatorium to tell her how she'd linked them, irrevocably and eternally, on her skin. If Charlotte one day decided to get a magpie, a sister to Maggie's own, she wouldn't stop her this time.

'Should I get started on the other one now?'

'Please.'

The man's head bent, blocking her view of his work. The buzzing of the needle started up again.

Maggie thought of the circus, and wondered how things were going since she'd parted from them—only a day ago, but it felt much longer. They'd been surprised when Maggie took over from

Rafferty, but no one argued or threatened to leave. It seemed they trusted her, at least enough to stick around and see what happened. Perhaps Rafferty had been right after all; perhaps she had been the one pushing everyone away. She was looking forward to finding out what might happen now she'd accepted that she could, after all, be a part of things. But that would have to wait until another matter was sorted.

Her first move as the new ringmistress was to appoint Itsuo as temporary ringmaster.

'Me? But why?' he'd sputtered.

'Because there's something I have to do, and I'm not sure how long I'll be gone. I need someone I can trust to take care of things. I know you can keep your head when things get rough. And you speak your mind when it's important, even if it's not easy—like when you said it would be cruel to let Hercules fret himself to death. I know you'll always do what's in the best interest of the circus. Even guarding a performer who's threatening to run away.'

Itsuo's cheeks coloured a little at this, and Maggie let him know with a smile that she held no grudge.

'And with Smith as a mate, you've got physical might on your side if your other skills ever fall short.'

Itsuo was uncertain, but Maggie reassured him that he wouldn't have to do it all on his own. She'd hired Nev—who was keen to get back to working for a circus where he was paid actual money instead of just accommodation and food rations—for another stint as their tracker, having seen firsthand how able he was at getting them through any conditions and past any obstacles. He would lead them south of Adelaide, tracing the coast all the way around the Fleurieu Peninsula, across to Lake Alexandrina, then they'd zigzag their way back to Adelaide to spend the winter months. The responsibility of maintaining and balancing the accounts, she gave to Rosemary. The cook knew the demands of feeding a circus on the road, what they needed and where they could buy it, how much hunting and fishing was required to make their rations stretch. Together, they would keep everything running smoothly. It wasn't how Rafferty had done things, but it was a different circus now. What had once been the Braun Brothers' Royal Circus was now the Magpie and Sisters' Royal Travelling Circus. Maggie had bestowed the name with contentment and just a hint of amusement—magpies, if you cared to pay attention, had a sharp eye, an instinct to protect their families, and an intelligence they could turn into a thrilling or moving performance if they so chose. The 'Royal' was kept as a nod to Rafferty.

'I thought your name was Bright?' Greta said when Maggie informed them all of the new name and asked the circus hands to start repainting the lettering on the sides of the wagons. 'Why didn't you call it that?' Maggie was surprised Greta knew her surname. She couldn't remember ever having told her it.

Maggie offered the sword dancer a smile. 'I thought this name more fitting.'

'And what about the men?' Smith muttered. 'Are we supposed to be your sisters too?'

'You can manage, just as we managed being the Braun *Brothers*,' Greta snapped before Maggie had the chance to respond. The new ringmistress stifled a chuckle. Families were not always going to agree.

'It's all about showmanship,' she said to Smith, daring to reach up and clap him on the shoulder. 'We've got to grab attention to sell tickets. There's plenty of circuses already named after brothers and sons. Besides, Rafferty gave it the seal of approval.'

The strongman considered this a moment before giving a conciliatory nod.

Rafferty himself had gone back to Sydney already, the city he felt was most like home. He had hopes that despite his age, he might be able to settle down and create the family he'd dreamed of as a boy. He'd promised to write to Maggie, laughingly extracting a promise from her too: that she would only write back as herself and no one else.

A week after he'd left, Maggie had visited her father, bringing all of her books except for one. He'd slapped his knee when she shared Rafferty's joke, then teared up when she told him she was a ringmistress now. Then he warned her not to dummy the books, saying she didn't want to end up there with him. Maggie shook her head, half-amused, half-exasperated.

'I'm hitting the road again, Pa,' she'd said when the warder called out that it was time to make their goodbyes. When she next saw him—whether it be here at the brass bar separating inmates from their loved ones, or when he was set free and came to join her circus—she would have righted some wrongs. She hoped that he would be even prouder than he was now.

'Finished,' the tattooist said, bringing Maggie's thoughts back to the present. Again, he leaned back, letting her inspect his efforts. Nestled on the other side of the magpie was a robin, smaller than the other birds and delicately outlined. Three songbirds, who by their very nature could entertain, delight or inspire awe; three birds that were born blind and naked, vulnerable until one day they learned to fly.

'What do the birds mean?' the tattooist asked, his head tilting to one side as he admired his work. Maggie began to do up the buttons of her blouse, covering the ink above her heart.

'They're my family,' she said. She stood and grabbed her leather bag. In it were a change of undergarments, a fountain pen with spare ink and nibs, plenty of paper, a good wad of money and a single book: the copy of *Seven Little Australians* that Charlotte had given her. 'Only I've got to bring one of them home.'

She was ready to hit the road now. Not on a wagon, with an entire circus at her heels, but alone—at least for now. The agricultural show would have moved on long ago, but she'd find out where they'd gone next, and she'd go there, and ask again, and again, until finally she caught up with it.

For somewhere out there was a little girl with a face people gasped at. A little girl who was waiting for Maggie to keep her promise.

Maggie walked out onto the street, the city air swirling the scent of horse dung, human sweat, cooking food and factory smoke around her nostrils. She breathed it in, the motion of her rising chest making the new tattoos sting. Maggie gently placed one hand over them.

She would find Robin and tell her a story. A story that began with the death of some elephants and ended with a family. And when Robin saw Maggie's tattoos, she would know.

She would know she was part of that family.

She would know that she belonged.

Author's Note

The phenomenon of travelling circuses, and those that favoured remote, rural and regional areas to perform their shows in, is a very real part of Australian history. The golden age of Australian circus ran from the 1850s until the early 1960s, when circus was the principal form of live entertainment available in non-metropolitan areas. My father, who grew up on a farm in Queensland, shared childhood memories of the excitement of the circus arriving with all the colour, music and exuberance I have tried to convey in the pages of this book. The memory that most gripped my heart, mind and imagination, though, was one that differed from the rest, for it offered a glimpse of the reality behind the fantasy world: a hard, sometimes unforgiving life with demands that went beyond the rigours one might expect of acrobats, tightrope walkers, jugglers and 'warbs'. He told me the sad story of a bull elephant who wouldn't leave the body of his deceased partner, no matter what actions or persuasions his trainers tried. This became the inspiration for, and opening scenes of, *The Magpie's Sister*.

Exotic animals such as elephants were much more uncommon in Australian circuses than their international counterparts. This meant that owning one (or more) did indeed, as Rafferty Braun

331

explains, offer a circus a chance to establish itself in a permanent position in a big city, where the competition for audience numbers would otherwise be too fierce. Rare creatures almost guaranteed return visits from paying customers.

Of the circuses that didn't have such a drawcard, some were lucrative enough to travel via train, but many more relied on horse- and donkey-drawn wagons to cover surprisingly vast distances. Australia's unique and often unwelcoming landscape meant that ingenuity was an everyday requirement of this way of life. The scene in which the characters dismantle their equipment, then float it down a river to be washed ashore and retrieved after swimming the animals across, is drawn from life, and would not have been uncommon. To mitigate risk, experts in navigation and living off the land were hired, which is how some Indigenous men and women made a living as circus trackers.

When it came to nationality, race and gender, Australia's travelling circuses differed from the broader society in which they operated. In a world where Charlotte's flippant line about wives and Aboriginal workers being 'parked' in the stables of a pub alongside the horses was grounded in truth, circus people were comparatively progressive. This is not to say that no prejudices existed within the circus, for they most certainly did, but skill, proficiency and intelligence were the most highly prized attributes and outweighed all else. This meant that women, and people from a wide range of cultural and ethnic backgrounds, could reach even the highest-ranking positions, including ringmaster/ringmistress or manager, as Gladys did (a personal note: Gladys's playing of the blade of grass was inspired by Aboriginal dancer, choreographer and Artistic Director of Bangarra Dance Theatre, Frances Rings, who I was lucky enough to have as a teacher and from whom I learned to play a blade of grass). A particularly famous example is the real-life Aboriginal performer Billy Jones, who was appointed ringmaster of the FitzGerald Brothers Circus in 1900, and whose death in 1906 was reported as far away as New York City.

However, even the most famed circus performers were still at risk of discrimination. The storyline of Itsuo, victim of a sudden and vindictive attempt at deportation, is based on the experience of countless individuals targeted by authorities under the White Australia policy. The *Naturalisation Act* of 1903 precluded people from Asia, Africa or the Pacific Islands from applying for naturalisation. The dictation test for new migrants or those facing deportation, as depicted here, was indeed able to be given in any language that the presiding immigration officer chose, which meant the outcome was usually predetermined—most often not in the test-taker's favour. Bribery was one possible strategy for the few who had the means to attempt it, but passing the text was exceedingly rare. In my research, I came across many records of Australian circus workers lamenting that they never saw their much-valued and loved colleagues again after a hasty deportation. Sometimes they never even heard from them again, although in most cases they never stopped trying to get the government to allow them back.

For those who had the freedom to choose to cross oceans to another country instead of having it forced upon them, the United States held lucrative appeal. Asa Lithgow's offer to help Maggie find fame and fortune in the North American Congress of Curious People and Curiosities (a real attraction at Coney Island) is based on the history of the thriving 'freak' trade there (a term that even then was offensive to many, and could encompass anything from physical disabilities to extreme body modifications, or even outright fakeries). Lavinia Warren and her husband Tom Thumb were among the best-known and most successful examples, but they were also among the luckiest, as abuse and exploitation of intellectually and physically disabled performers was rife. Australia was different, but different doesn't necessarily mean better. While Australian circuses looked down on the notion of 'freakshows', believing circuses should offer learned, practised and perfected skills, audiences still had an appetite for them. The dehumanising circumstances in which Maggie discovers Marley/Robin, the little girl with albinism, on ticketed display at an agricultural fair were sadly true, and it would have been far more likely for someone with Maggie's condition to end up in an agricultural show as the 'property' of someone else, instead of with a circus.

The condition Maggie is diagnosed with, Von Recklinghausen's, is a real genetic disorder that today is known as neurofibromatosis 1. It is quite rare, and in a majority of cases not life-threatening, although the physical and mental symptoms and the effects on quality of life vary from case to case. I did not base Maggie's journey with neurofibromatosis 1 on any one specific person's life, but instead followed the course of how a single person's experience and symptoms might play out over the span of decades.

Thank you to all the people with neurofibromatosis 1 who have so generously and openly shared their experiences in books, articles, podcasts, videos and on social media. In my research, I have drawn extensively on their accounts in order to represent Maggie's symptoms and progression accurately. If any readers would like to learn more from these people in their own words, I recommend the following:

Alexandrea Lee: YouTube @GodsGreatWork; Instagram @locs_nochains

Karina Rodini: YouTube @KaahRodini; Instagram @superandaneurofibromatose; TikTok @kaahrodini

Adam Pearson: Instagram @adam_pearson_tv; *Adam Pearson: Freak Show* (BBC Three); *Beauty and the Beast: the Ugly Face of Prejudice* (Channel 4)

Born Different: Instagram @borndifferentshow; Facebook @Born Different

Penny's Flight Foundation: Instagram @pennysflight, pennysflight.org, TikTok @pennysflightfoundation

Similarly, Charlotte's journey shows only one individual's experience of the course alcohol dependency can take, but it draws on the experiences of many.

I wanted to keep every act depicted in the Braun Brothers' Royal Circus true to real-life acts that have been performed throughout Australian circus history. I imagined the character of the Lagoon Creature for Maggie, but every single movement, skill and trick performed by her and everyone else in the circus was taken from history. Likewise, all the details of life in the circus, such as clothing, equipment, vehicles, slang, food, music, travelling conditions, everyday rituals and the minutiae of arrival, set-up and departure have been kept true to the era. The show in the makeshift ring made of fallen trees, lit by old socks burning in tins of fat, was a composite of many descriptions of circus performances given in remote settlements. Even the titles of the books Maggie reads, and the details of Charlotte's flask, are based on real ones from those years.

The circumstances that led to Charlotte spending part of her childhood in the circus, while fictional, are also based on a real part of circus history. Illegitimate children (including infants) were sometimes given or sold to travelling circuses, to protect both parents and child against the public scandal of illegitimacy. Circuses found that those who grew up in their ranks made for the best and most well-rounded performers, as they began training as early as five years of age. What the children subject to these arrangements thought of them appears to be a somewhat overlooked part of this history, which perhaps tells us a lot in itself.

The locations I have mentioned are real too: the fantastic Wonderland City with its Airem Scarem dirigible, the construction site of the Happy Valley Reservoir, the engineering feat that is the Whispering Wall, and each and every town, city and street visited. I was able to visit nearly all of the sites that still exist today, and much of what I learned on those visits made it into this book (such as the bar separating Maggie from her father when she visits him in the Adelaide Gaol, which a brilliant tour guide described for me). For the few locations I wasn't able to reach, thanks to the Covid-19 pandemic beginning in the middle of the research and writing of this novel, I relied on descriptions, photographs and newspaper articles from 1911 to give as accurate a depiction as possible.

And then there are the little odd moments, which no doubt come across as fun moments of fantasy, such as a kangaroo playfully racing with travelling wagons (one of my favourite anecdotes, which I came across repeatedly throughout research), or an early-twentieth-century man getting a butterfly tattoo on his bald head. I was delighted when I discovered an old photograph of just such a thing—and even more delighted to learn that at this time, tattoos were enjoying a moment of extreme popularity, with the full-coverage clothing of the day meaning one could still keep a 'respectable' exterior while giving free rein to self-expression underneath their sleeves, skirts, hats and trouser legs. Fred Harris, the man who gives Maggie and Charlotte their bird tattoos, was a real tattoo artist who had a significant influence on the development of the art in Australia. He did indeed get his shop on Sussex Street.

The history of Australian circus is fascinating, varied and overlooked, given the impact it had over the span of nearly a century. There are so many people who, even today, remember names like FitzGerald's, St Leon's and Wirth's from their childhood, and I have been privileged to be the recipient of many shared memories. I hope that in my small way, I have been able to do their memories and this part of history—with all its inspiring, ugly, interesting, painful and challenging layers—justice.

Acknowledgements

A finished book is the work of so many. I can not fully convey my gratitude to these people in mere words, but I'm going to try.

Firstly, to everyone at Echo Publishing who had a hand in turning this story into a full-fledged book. Most especially to Juliet Rogers and Diana Hill, for seeing the potential in the story and falling in love with the world and characters as much as I did; for being endlessly supportive of my voice; for valuing my input and allowing me to feel connected to every stage of the process. An added thank you to Diana for tireless patience and communication when things wobbled a bit.

Thank you to Elizabeth Cowell for her editing expertise, most especially with insight into character and motivation. Thank you to Lizzie Hayes and Emily Banyard, for their work in helping the book find its way into the hands of readers, and to Shaun Jury for his typesetting.

Thank you to Christa Moffitt of Christabella Designs for the remarkable way she captured the setting, tone, characters and themes in her stunning cover.

A personal thank you to Nelson, who was still by my side when I wrote the first draft of this book, and to Sully, who took up the mantle while I finished it.

Another personal thank you to my family for their support—particularly to my brother-in-law Sean and sister Elizabeth (who is not at all like the book's Elisabeth, but who I promised I would one day name a villain after—we're not quite there, but consider this a placeholder!). Thank you for your words that kept me going in a difficult moment.

A heartfelt thank you to my husband Ross for always believing in me, even when I stopped believing in myself. Whenever I worry that my dreams are too big, he encourages me to make them even bigger. None of my books would exist without him.

And last on the page, but always first in my mind and heart when I'm writing, thank you to you, the reader. Thank you for allowing me to share my stories with you. It's a privilege I hope to live up to.

Book Club Questions

1. Do you agree with Maggie's father that his decision to give her to the circus as a child was the best choice he could make at the time? Why, or why not?
2. Rafferty, like Maggie's father, believes he had her best interests at heart in the decisions he made for her. Do you think this is true, or are his decisions more self-serving than he is willing to admit?
3. Maggie practises an early form of catfishing by pretending to be Charlotte in her letters to Mr O'Lehry. Is this unethical? If so, is it Mr O'Lehry or Charlotte who is being wronged, or is it both of them?
4. How differently do you think Maggie's life might have played out if she had not sent the letters to Mr O'Lehry?
5. Nev never reveals his birth name to Maggie or the reader. Why do you think this is?
6. Do you think the pinch artist who tried to have Itsuo deported would be likely to come back, not yet satisfied that he has had his revenge?

7. Should Maggie have accepted Asa Lithgow's offer to go to the United States and work in the 'freak show' trade there? Why, or why not?

8. At the end of the book, Maggie sets out to find Robin. Do you think she succeeds?

9. If Maggie succeeds in liberating Robin from the agricultural show circuit, how do you think life will change for both of them?

10. Do you think Charlotte will come back to the circus? If so, will she be able to maintain her new sobriety in that environment?

11. What other changes do you think Maggie will make to the circus now that she is ringmistress?

12. What do you think is the significance of the bird motif throughout the novel?

13. Is the comparison of Maggie to a magpie fitting?

14. What character surprised you the most, and why?

15. If there were to be a sequel or prequel to *The Magpie's Sister*, whose story would you want to read?